VISIONS

THE SECRET WATCHERS
Book One

LAUREN LYNNE

www.LaurenLynneAuthor.com

www.thesecretwatchers.com

ACKNOWLEDGEMENTS:

To my wonderful friends and family who have spent countless hours reading, discussing, brainstorming, encouraging and administering many hugs... THANK YOU! This book is for you!

ONE

A blast of heavy metal rudely jerked me awake, nearly levitating me. I reached out an arm and slapped at the offending noise. A beat of peaceful silence passed and I sighed in contentment.

"Owen! Get up. You have chores before school. Up, up, up," Mom hollered from the foot of the stairs.

"Go away, Mom," I huffed under my breath. More sleep would be good. My dreams and fantasies instead of reality would be even better. I was *so* not loving my life or school. My skateboard, P.E. and cross country were the only bright spots in my otherwise boring day. Ugh, Mondays just plain sucked. Mmmm, about 175 school days a year, times five more years is... 875 days of torture. But wait, less the month of September or about twenty school days. Yay, that leaves only 855 more days until high school graduation, I thought sarcastically.

"Owen Anthony Ryer!"

"I'm coming," I hollered and then under my breath added, "Keep your shirt on, nag." I would never really say that out loud to her. I love my mom but she can be such a pain in the morning with her cheerfulness and positive attitude garbage.

The awful alarm clock started its caterwauling again and I resisted the urge to pick it up and throw it across my room. As I stretched and rubbed my scalp, I wished for about the hundredth time that my hair wasn't nearly a buzz cut. Maybe I could convince Mom it would be cheaper to grow it out and less work for her too. We might save a lot of money by having her cut our hair, but I want a little more style this year.

1

"I don't hear the water. Shower. Come on, times-a-wastin' my boy!"

So much for just getting dressed. How do mothers keep track of all that stuff; like who needs to shower and what we all eat in a given day. It hardly seemed worth it to argue, but man was it tempting. I suppressed a sigh and headed for the bathroom.

I looked at myself in the mirror as I brushed my teeth. Yep, still skinny, still darkly tanned. My eyes are dark brown, deeply set and serious like my dad's. My nose is a little too wide but okay I guess. I see so little of my mom in my reflection but I know she's there.

After my shower, I rolled back to my room leaving damp foot-prints on the well-worn carpet of the upstairs hallway. There are no girls in our house except for Mom which is pretty cool because I can run around in just a towel or my boxers. Hey, I'm a lazy guy.

"Come on Owen, please hurry. It's not like you have to shave or manage your long flowing locks. Get a move on."

"Ok Mom, geez," I huffed as I looked longingly at my computer wishing I could get lost in a game for a bit. I grabbed some boxers, socks and my jeans. I got dressed standing up, hopping from foot to foot. I rummaged for my favorite tee in the basket of clothes that I was still supposed to fold. I snagged my school books and a Tech Deck, or finger skateboard for the uniformed, and headed down the stairs. About then it hit me that I'd forgotten my shoes. I only have two pairs that are school-worthy to choose between so the decision isn't difficult, but it meant a trip back up the stairs. Sigh.

I rounded the corner and slid into the kitchen courtesy of my sock-clad feet. My littlest brother, Lucas the kindergartener, laughed while my middle brother, Alex the fourth grader, rolled his eyes and tried to look superior. Mom hadn't noticed me yet. She was deep in her usual morning frenzy. She had just thrown on some old sweats and had forgotten to comb her hair in her hurry to start the day. She makes me smile. Either she is shrinking or I am getting taller fast. She gives the illusion of a fireball as her compact form zips around. She's Native American and Irish mostly. It's our family joke; an Irish Indian. If you were prejudiced you might think she's

2

a drinker but she's not. Her drugs of choice are obsessive compulsive activity, volunteering and cleanliness. You can't help but love her. She turned and eyeballed me as she scraped her hair into a ponytail, then held it in place with a scrunchie she had on her wrist. "Please clean the cat box and wash your hands. Then unload the dishwasher while I get your brothers on their way. Thanks."

After a few minutes of pandemonium during which Lucas looked for a missing shoe and Alex found his misplaced homework between the sofa cushions, the front door finally slammed shut. The silence was almost deafening. No wonder Dad goes to work early and comes home late. I suppose it could be because he is a chemical engineer for a big Portland firm, works long hours and goes on lots of business trips. Either way, I take after him. He's a tall, dark haired man who's quiet and thoughtful. He's pretty serious so it feels like a real triumph when you make him smile. It's like turning on the sun; a bright flash of white on an otherwise cloudy day. He isn't a morning person either.

My brothers take after my mom. They're not as tall for their age as I was and they're a little bulkier. One has Mom's green eyes; the other has brown eyes like Dad and me. Their hair is more the color of chocolate, not caramel like Mom's and not almost black like mine and Dad's. Their skin is lighter than mine and Dad's, but darker than Mom's fairness. We love to tease her. She burns and freckles while the rest of us tan. Mom and my brothers can hardly wait for a new day to begin. Woohoo, morning and all that. They tackle a new day and new opportunities with lots of energy and lots of talking. Morning people. Gross.

With Mom gone, I decided to run back upstairs and try a little dab of mousse to spike my hair up a bit on top so that it's sorta styled. It's hard to do as short as it is, but seeing as how I was about due for a cut maybe Mom could just take a little off the sides. Looking in the mirror, I decided it was as good as it was gonna get. Yay, no zits today.

Mostly I don't care how I look, but this year I sit next to Lucie Ness in science. She's one of the most popular girls at school. I don't know if she knows it or even cares. She is the most beautiful person I have ever seen. Plenty of other boys watch her too. I doubt she knows I'm alive. I sniffed my pits - yep, deodorant remembered. Thank goodness my favorite Metallica t-shirt is clean. It's black and I figure it makes me look pretty good.

Cat box or breakfast? Nastiness first. Wash my hands. Well duh, Mom. I don't want to catch some weird cat influenza or something. Dishwasher duty again, oh boy. Approaching the cat box with a plastic bag, scoop and an appropriate scowl I was ready to attack, yet filled with trepidation. I hate this particular job mainly because the poof of the scented litter bugs my nose and makes me cough. I suppose it's better than eau de cat dump, though. Well, and any kind of waste is just gross. This is only better than scooping up after the dogs because it takes less time.

As I headed to the garbage can with my bag of used litter I noted that the weather wasn't half bad. Maybe cleaning the cat box would be the worst thing I had to face today. With a half-smile on my lips I returned to the house to wash up and finish my drudgery. I hate chores, but I *get* that I need to do my share.

As I loaded my cereal bowl into the now empty dishwasher, the front door opened and shut. Mom sighed as she slid onto a bar stool and simultaneously picked up her coffee cup in one hand, brushed some breakfast crumbs into a pile with the other and asked, "Dishwasher?"

"Yep."

"Cat box?"

"Yep."

"Try to have a good day and stay out of trouble."

I couldn't help it. I just looked at her. You know... *the look.* Frustration, disgust and outrage warred for a position on my face. I finally settled for disappointed. I know she was pretty once. I have seen the pictures. Now she mostly looks... tired. She peeled off her sweatshirt and tucked a stray bit of hair behind her ear.

Her bright tie-dyed tee about boggled my eyes. I could tell her mind was already jumping to her next project for the day. "Mom, I haven't gotten in trouble since 5th grade," I said, trying to draw her back to the topic at hand.

"Oh honey, I know. You're a great kid. You do what I ask without much complaint. You help with your brothers. You're just so... serious most of the time. I feel like you aren't really happy. I have a feeling that you don't like school and worse yet, you don't really try or care. You're... apathetic."

"You're right. I don't like school. It's stupid," I said, the scent of our old argument thick in the air.

"It's not a choice."

"I know, Mom," I half growled and then my face softened. I know she cares. I wish I could make myself care. I just can't. I often feel like I'm out of sync with the rest of the world.

"Try to have a better attitude about it. Please. You'll need a good job someday."

"I'll work at the skate shop. Then I can get stuff for my board at a discount," I said with the look of pure innocence on my face. Part of me loves to watch her stress out.

"But you could be so much more!"

"I know, I know, settle down."

"Owen!" she replied in warning.

A smile broke out across my face and she smiled back at me. "I'm kidding. Well mostly. I really don't like school that much. We sit, we listen, classes are big and we don't do much fun stuff anymore."

"What do you want to do when you're older? What do you love?"

"Skateboarding," I flipped back at her.

"Besides skating?" she said, sounding a little frustrated.

5

"Animals, I guess. Sometimes I like them better than people. Science is pretty good this year. I have PE this trimester too. That at least makes school tolerable."

"Oh Owen, I know middle school isn't easy for you. Please just try to find some good in it. You're almost done and a good attitude will make it easier for you. High school will be here before you know it and I bet you'll like that better. We'll talk more later. You'll be late for the bus. I love you," she said, hopping up and wrapping me in a quick hug.

"You too," I said as I slung my backpack over my shoulder and headed out the door. I took a breath of the cool, crisp fall air and let my mind go peacefully blank. I made it to the end of the driveway before my *lack of thoughts* were interrupted.

"Owen, hey Owen."

I looked up to see Marlo puffing up the street. "I thought you were gonna miss the bus. I thought I'd check. You look kinda upset. What's up? Let's go, we don't want to be late. Did you eat? Did you finish your essay for social studies? Can you hang out after school?"

All of this was spewed out at me as if he didn't need any air to make his voice work, but then that's Marlo for you. I've known him since kindergarten. I guess I just couldn't help but like him right off. I've never seen anyone who can stay happy *all* the time. I have only ever seen him sad once - his gerbil died. I've seen him mad once too – when a kid named Daniel broke the toy he brought for show-and-tell in first grade. Marlo and I are about as opposite as you can get. He is obsessed with computers, video games and books. His head comes level with my shoulder and he's a little on the fluffy side. I figure more time spent outside and less sitting would be good for him, but then he thinks that more time with books and video games would be good for my brain, so there you go.

I gotta say he has the best smile ever. I know that sounds a little weird coming from a straight guy, but I mean it. He makes me feel lighter and less serious. He can light up a room. You have to see it to believe it. I couldn't help but smile as I shoved at his shoulder. So much for riding my skateboard to the bus stop though. Marlo doesn't ride. I'm not sure what you would call what he does with a skateboard, but it is a sight to behold.

"I'm fine. Mom's just worried because I don't love school like you do. She thinks I need to work on my attitude." At least I could sit with Marlo on the bus. There Mom, *see*, positive attitude.

Each of my classes dragged by that day. I turned in what I had to and said as little as possible, my usual M. O. The bell was starting to peal as I rounded the door jamb for science. One corner of my mouth lifted as I looked over at my lab group and there she was, my lab partner, Lucie. How could one person make me so nervous, speechless, sweaty, and yet I want to be next to her - which is totally crazy. I don't know if she knows I'm alive. Maybe she wishes I wasn't.

Many questions raced through my mind all at once as the bell rang and I moved toward my place at her side. How's my hair? Do I stink after PE? Do I have food in my teeth from lunch? Bad breath? With all the distraction I was not paying attention to my feet, a very bad idea. Somehow my feet found the recycling bin which I, of course, tripped over, dumping the contents. My cheeks burned a bright red as I scooped up the papers and tossed them back in. My teacher is awesome. She just smiled at me and kept on taking attendance. I smiled back and because I wasn't looking again, I almost fell over my stool and landed on top of Lucie.

"Um, hi?"

"Way to make an entrance, Owen."

Wow! She actually knew my name. Then the moment was gone as our teacher called the class to order. Thank goodness today was not a lab day. I would probably spill stuff all over Lucie if it was. I scowled at the thought and she looked at me funny so I shrugged, pressed my lips together and tried to ignore her. I find that's the best policy around her so that I don't do or say anything stupid.

The minute the bell rang at the end of class I scooted out the door so as not to further embarrass myself.

Finally another day had passed and I'd survived. I saved a spot for Marlo on the bus. Everyone was talking as the buses quickly filled with kids. The engines rumbled to life and the aroma – no, stench - of diesel filled the hot afternoon air. Marlo rattled on about his day, his new video game and his plans to meet up with our friend Adrian at his uncle's pawnshop after school today.

I was glad that it took so little to keep him talking as I let my mind slide back to Lucie Ness. The fact that she is a really nice person doesn't go with the fact that she is smart and beautiful. Usually the hot girls know they're hot and act all superior. She has the most amazing blue eyes too. She had a great smile before, but you should see it now that her braces are off. It was only last year that she was taller than me. Seems like I grew all summer and she didn't. Though I suppose when you are already perfect there isn't a need to change anything.

"Well are you?" Marlo asked, frustration in his tone.

Uh oh, I had completely drifted away from the present. All I could see was Lucie and remember her voice – she knew my name. "Sorry?"

"Are you coming with me to Adrian's today?"

"Yeah, sure. Of course."

"Weren't you listening at all?"

"Ummm."

"Never mind. Where do you go when you do that? You had the weirdest look on your face. You actually looked a little less grumpy than you have lately. I really wish you would pay attention though. What were you thinking about? You can tell me you know. It wasn't the math homework. You never worry about school. In case you were thinking about school though, no sweat. I've got it covered. I have a study plan. On math you do evens and I'll do odds. That will cut that time in half. We still have a whole week to work on our social studies project and we have two days to read the next chapter for language arts and three days to get our character analysis turned in. I bet you weren't thinking about school though. Hey, I know - it was a girl I bet. You had a mushy look on your face."

And he wonders why I tune him out. On the other hand, who needs to keep track of homework when one has Marlo? We have all the same teachers, just not all the same classes at the same time and Marlo keeps track of everything. Lucky for me Marlo and Adrian are my study partners for social studies. I do my fair share but they're better at keeping track of due dates, how much we should get done a day and other unimportant junk like that.

"Thanks Marlo!" I meant it. Why he likes me, I couldn't say but he is truly a best friend. Sometimes I wonder if I am some kind of extended science project for him. *The Civilization of Owen*. Or maybe I am a social project. *The Comparison of Life as an Only Child versus Owen the Older Brother*. Regardless, he is the best. Maybe that's all it is in the end. We accept each other for who we are, no questions asked.

The bus coughed to a stop and we lunged up out of our seats for our stop. "See you in about five, Marlo." I jumped off the bus and onto my board in one move and zipped up the street.

As I raced away I swear I heard Marlo breathe, "So extremely not fair." I glanced back over my shoulder and he was shaking his head as he walked off toward his house.

When I got home, Mom was up to her eyeballs in little boys, dishes, dogs, unending laundry and mismatched socks. I pelted up the stairs, threw my stuff in my room, and emptied my pockets of Tech Decks and other miscellaneous garbage I had collected during the day. I then reversed course, flew back down the stairs, jumping the last five or so and reminded Mom that I was headed out with the big boys. Feeling lighter than I had all day, I grabbed my board from where I'd left it in the entry hall and headed out the door. I did the whole 'toss my board and leap onto it all in one motion' thing. I might trip over my own feet and recycling bins in science, but on my board, I could fly!

As I zipped down the hill and glided around the corner, I wondered if that was what was eating Marlo. I needed to remind him that in this outfit of ours, he was the brains and I was the skating ninja. Well, something like that anyway. I pushed up the next hill. My board vibrated with a soothing rhythm. I like to think my board sings to me. I love the sound it makes. It's a great time to think. There is nothing like the swish of the air and the hum of the wheels. Freedom – peace – joy - simplicity. Some day I would have a car, but for now this was the primo mode of transportation.

Marlo and his mom were already in the family minivan as I approached. I popped my board with my toe, caught it and hopped in back. "Thanks for taking us, Mrs. Saggio."

"You're welcome. I'm happy to help. I'll be back to pick you boys up at about 6:00 to have you home by 6:15," she said in a cheerful voice. It's clear to me that Marlo takes after his mom, but then his dad is a pretty happy guy too.

"Sure, fine." Obviously there was some mother action going on if they were both on the same page. I wondered fleetingly if it was a mother mind meld, brainwaves or cell phone towers that kept the world's mothers connected - teachers too. Yeesh, what is with those people? They all have eyes in the backs of their heads and seem to know all kinds of stuff you don't want them knowing. Marlo and his mom held an ongoing easy banter that I admired. I sat quietly in the back. They were used to my quiet. Mrs. Saggio used to worry about me and would try to make me talk. It was painful for both of us. She gave up when Marlo and I were in about fourth grade. We are all much happier now.

We greeted Adrian as we came into the pawnshop. We didn't get to come often but it was pretty great when we did. Both of Adrian's parents work and his dad is on the night shift. We very rarely get to go to his actual house. Adrian has one sister who is younger but thinks she's twenty instead of ten. Hey, don't get me wrong. I like

Amber fine, especially long distance! She usually goes to her aunt's after school but Adrian gets to hang out with his dad's youngest brother: the very cool Uncle Max.

Marlo and Adrian visited with Max. I listened to the banter for a while, then I gradually wandered away, looking in the display cases as I went. I walked the full length of the long, narrow pawnshop, glancing at the baubles on display. Bits of people's lives were here for anyone to see. How had they come to be here? Was it anger, hardship or sadness that drove people to sell their family history? I was reminded of the many museums that my family had visited during the summers of my younger life.

I became aware of a tug at my bellybutton. I had an urge to go to the very back of the store. I couldn't decide if I should fight this weird feeling or not; meanwhile my feet kept moving. It was like one of those dumb books we had to read for school. I heard my *siren song*, so to speak. Going to the back of the store was no longer a choice and I didn't even know what I was looking for - just that I *had* to find it. My focus became complete, my attention unwavering. I no longer knew nor cared what was going on in the front of the shop. I was searching for something... something... something...

There - the center case - top row. I was searching for... My eyes scanned the top row of the case. Still I didn't know what I was looking for amongst all the watches, cufflinks and rings - until I saw it. An old fashioned men's radial watch had called to me. The band was the color of coffee beans, the face was cream, the metal around the face was gold, and the numbers were painted in gold as well. I shook my head to clear it. What was happening to me? My disorientation seemed to be getting worse. I felt for a moment that I would be sucked right into the case...

"See something you like?" I hadn't heard the old guy who worked for Adrian's uncle join me at the case. I sucked in a startled breath.

"Uh, yeah, I guess. I was just looking..." I swear the watch whispered to me. I jerked my head back around to the case. Nothing. I felt a little foolish. Now that was just plain crazy. I turned slowly back around. The older gentleman was waiting calmly like nothing had happened. His eyes were on mine. I'd heard his name before and I knew a little about him from our visits here but I could pull nothing to the tip of my reluctant tongue. My brain felt sluggish. An image of a younger man appeared over his face like a misty mirage and then was gone in the next heartbeat. I blinked several times to clear the image.

My ability to speak surged back. "The... ah, watch, the one with the brown leather band. I've been needing a watch for a while. That one is interesting. Can you tell me about it?" I babbled.

Mr. White Eagle just smiled a smile like he had a secret. Where had his name suddenly come from? "I would be happy to show it to you," he said in a calm, soothing voice.

Big mistake, my inner counselor insisted, but the rest of my mind and body ignored the warning. I held out my wrist and he fastened it on. I almost fell over as images assaulted my brain. I was still in the shop, but somewhere or *some when* else too. I could still see the shop but it was now overlaid with a soft, almost holographic, image of what it must have looked like years ago. Had it not been strapped to my wrist I would have dropped the watch like a hot rock. Instead I staggered slightly into the display case. In a move faster than I could decipher with my eye, Mr. White Eagle caught my arm, his hand over the watch and the images snapped off like a switch was flipped.

"Easy there. You okay?" he asked in that same soft, quiet way.

"I'm... fine. I think I just... saw... something," I stammered.

He released my arm and nothing else weird happened. Maybe I should have grabbed a snack before I left. Hungry, yeah, that's it. I'm hungry. My eyes drifted to the watch. Friend or foe, I wondered. The time seemed to be set about right, the second hand glinting as it swept gracefully around the face. I gazed back at Mr. White Eagle and felt the watch try to communicate with me again. This time it was subtler. *Friend*, it seemed to answer my earlier query. I decided I liked the watch and found myself saying so. I

12

didn't just like it though. I needed to have it. I had to have it. It was meant for me. My desire for the watch was stronger than the cautioning voice in my head.

Mr. White Eagle smiled a knowing smile.

"How much?" I asked, afraid to hear the answer.

He appraised me thoughtfully. "This watch is special. It needs to go to a special person who will take good care of it. It belonged to a friend."

I felt compelled to look him right in the eye. It felt like he was looking right into my heart, my soul and my mind as he measured me against some invisible yardstick. I must have passed because his next words surprised me.

"For you, twenty dollars."

I knew that although one would normally barter or dicker in a pawnshop like this, now was not the time.

"I have about five dollars on me. May I have a payment plan at five dollars a week or could you hold it for me until I collect the money?" I asked, hoping he would agree.

"For you, a payment plan, except you will work here after school two days a week."

"Sir, I have cross country and I'm not sure how I would get here. We are down to one car at my house."

"How about if I work it all out with your mom?"

I was astounded that he would be so bold as to try. I really, in my wildest dreams, could absolutely and in no way see her going for it. He strolled into the back room of the shop as silently as he had arrived. I waited for the next weird thing to happen. I glanced around the shop and back to my friends. No one seemed to have noticed what happened or even notice my absence, though that wasn't all that unusual. Wait a minute, how would Mr. White Eagle call my mom? He had asked me for no information. As if my thought of him had drawn him back, I saw him step out from the back room.

"I had a nice visit with your mom. I have a schedule all worked out. You will work here on Tuesdays and Fridays until the season is over and then we'll see."

"Oh- kay," I said slowly. I was sure he could see the confusion and questions written all over my face.

"You will take your skateboard to school. I will draw you a map of a back way to the shop. I will drive you home when your work here is done. You are to be here no later than 4:30 and I will have you home by 6:15."

"Um, how long..."

"I will hold the five dollars you have on you but you will work off the full amount plus a little interest. When you are done, I will give you your five back."

"My mom actually said ok?" I asked in amazement, not even realizing that he had not really answered my question.

"Yah, you betcha," he said with that same secret smile.

I had a million questions and they all seemed to leap into my mind at once where they sat hopelessly tangled. "Are you going to tell me about the watch?" I finally managed to filter out of my jumbled thoughts. I was almost afraid to hear the answer.

"Tomorrow. That way I know you'll show up for work. Right? Now go see your friends."

I glanced at my buddies, laughing and talking. I turned back to thank Mr. White Eagle but all that was left of him was the swish of the curtain into the back area.

The guys smiled as I rejoined the group. Adrian's uncle asked what I was looking at in the back of the shop. I showed him the watch. "Mr. White Eagle offered me a payment plan or a work-it-off plan.

I guess I'll be here a couple of days a week until it is paid off," I said, realizing that I was a little confused.

"Hey, good. That old watch belonged to a buddy of his. It was part of the lot I bought with the shop. I got White Eagle in the deal too. He's been a fixture here for decades. I'm glad to have him. He's been waiting for as long as I can remember to find the right person to buy that watch. He's had a few offers over the years."

Well now, *that* was interesting. Suddenly I could hardly wait until tomorrow. I wanted to know more.

TWO

The rest of the day, the night and all the next day rolled by and all I could think about was going back to the pawnshop and learning more about my, now silent, watch. I was beginning to believe it had all been my imagination. I only took it off to shower though, just in case. I didn't want to miss anything super cool or amazing. No such luck, not even a wisp of anything.

The minute the final bell rang I surged out of the choir room, raced to my hall locker and hotfooted it out the door. I ran across the back field, jumped the creek and took the foot path over to the road. I was on my board and flying to the shop. I wanna know, I gotta know, repeated over and over again in my mind. In minutes I was zooming up the main drag and the pawnshop was in sight. Yes!

Walking inside I was surprised to see the shop completely empty. It was quiet too. I paused at the front door. Should I call out or call for help. I'd feel like an idiot if I called 911 and nothing was wrong. Maybe I should just sneak up to the back, checking behind the counters as I went and have my cell phone ready. I only made it about five steps before the back curtain fluttered and Mr. White Eagle stepped out. I think in that moment my heart actually stopped. Then it started a crazy galloping rhythm. "You scared me!"

His face split wide with a tremendous grin. I couldn't remember when I'd ever seen him smile like that before. "I like the way you handle yourself. You have passed my first test."

Wow – gee, what an honor, I thought with disgust. I tried to slow my racing heart and keep my face neutral. I thought I was doing a pretty good job, but he started laughing. "You're doing okay on the second test, too. Now let's get down to business. Pull up a stool. May I?" he asked, indicating the watch as I sat.

I held out my wrist. His hand closed over the watch and when he pulled it back the images returned like the ones I had seen yesterday. "Wow," I breathed.

"What are you seeing?" he asked in a calm, patient voice.

"You... wait, you see stuff too?"

"Nope, but I know that you can. I've been waiting for you."

"But I'm early, not late, Mr. White Eagle!"

"You misunderstand me: You are the *one* I have been waiting for. You are like my friend, the previous owner of this watch. He too could see things that others could not. We have been waiting for you for over twenty-five years."

"Are you serious?" I gasped, incredulous.

"You *know* I am. Take a minute and think about it," he said as he looked deep into my eyes. I swear I almost felt an electric arc. Suddenly I knew things and the images changed. I could once again see the old man with a young man's face overlapping each other. More images flashed past, quick as a blink, yet I felt that I would be able to recall them all. Let me tell you, it was WEIRD.

"You're a *spirit watcher*, Owen, a type of guardian. You will be driven to right wrongs. Bad things that have happened or are about to happen will appear to you and you will feel the strong need to fix them. Sometimes bad things happen to good people and they should not. Sometimes a good person contemplates doing a bad thing that will change their true path. It will be your job to help these people. The last *spirit watcher* I trained was the owner of the watch you wear. He died trying to help people and his job was not done. You shall be the next one."

I didn't know what question to ask first or even admit that I believed him just a little bit. It was as good an explanation as any as to why I kept seeing things I shouldn't. I wondered if there were other people like me. He seemed to read my jumbled thoughts.

"If there are others around, I don't know them but you may find them on your life journey. I would not be surprised because there used to be others like you. I believe there would have to be, but for now you are alone. I knew some people like myself years ago but I have lost touch with them." He paused as if sensing my next thought.

"Your power, your gift, comes from within you. It has nothing to do with the watch. The watch just spoke to you louder than anything else you have ever touched because the watch is tuned to a *spirit watcher*. Think of it like trying to find a station on an old radio with broken knobs. Now you are receiving a station, loud and clear - now you are aware. It is similar to waking up. You can see behind the veil that covers other men's eyes now."

"I don't know what to believe," I said in a voice full of wonder.

"We believe that talent like yours can be cosmic chance and not necessarily genetic. That is why it's so difficult to find people with talent, a gift or a power, whatever you want to call it. You can't count on finding talent within a family, it's often random chance. I'm sure you have been doing this for a while and were not even aware of it. I bet you have lost focus sometimes or thought you were daydreaming. Every gift is unique, just like each person's brain or fingerprints. We each think in our own way. That also makes a talent like yours hard to find. It's why I work here. I meet lots of people in a situation like this, but someone like you would be naturally drawn here. Items here have stories to tell and you would sense that. I have been watching you for a while and I was hoping you were the one. You seemed to have the right... *aura*, if you will. I can't think of a better word. Every time you came here you walked the room. The objects were calling to you; you just couldn't quite hear them yet. Owen, it will all become clear to you. It will take time as we work together, but you will see and you will believe one day soon. For now it is our secret. Other people would probably think you were crazy."

I sat on the stool in the back room, wrapped in my own thoughts for several minutes, thinking about what Mr. White Eagle had said and thinking about what the watch had shown me. The man who had owned this watch was happy. He had a purpose. He was doing an important job that few others could do. It almost felt like the watch had respected him. It also felt like it was expecting great things from me.

Mr. White Eagle put his hand on my shoulder and told me it was time to go for today. Where had the time gone? Was I lost in thought for over an hour? Amazing. I hadn't even noticed that he had walked away. Wow, maybe I was losing it after all.

I think I spent the rest of the week in a daze. I seemed to go through each day without really participating in my own life, at least until Friday afternoon came. Suddenly I found myself full of energy again. I could hardly wait to get back to the pawnshop and Mr. White Eagle because I wanted to know more. It had all been so surreal and now it was finally dawning on me. I was cool. I was unique. I was special. I was a super hero. Well, maybe that was a bit much.

Today's training was different. Mr. White Eagle was behind the counter waiting for me. He explained that he had snuffed my powers like he had the day I bought the watch, so that I could get through my daily life until I could control my gift and he would continue to do so for a while. He told me that he had learned how to do that with his friend and the watch was a link between me and his friend Miles. Some of Miles was still in the watch and he would be a help to me also. I guess a better way to explain it is that the watch was such an integral part of Miles that it could show me what it was like to be Miles… so knowing what Miles would have done would be helpful.

We spent the whole hour looking at images from the watch and discussing them to help me get to know Miles. He had been a police officer for a few years and then had become a private investigator when his own gift started getting in the way of his police job. He had died in 1985 while working a case. If ever I had to do a report on the 1970s or 1980s I was all set. I had the fashion of the day down. In a nutshell, today's lessons had been learning that Miles was a good guy with a good heart - trust his instincts. More importantly I should trust Mr. White Eagle. Again he turned off my powers before I left.

Friday night was spent with my family. We had pizza and played board games. I love my little brother Lucas, but it's hard to find a game that a kindergartener can play which appeals to me. We make do, but I can only stand so much Candyland or Chutes and Ladders. We all laughed together and talked about our weekend plans. In other words, an accounting of what was on the family chore list for the weekend. I reminded my mom that in and amongst the fun and frivolity at our own house, Mrs. Lando was expecting me to come mow her lawn if it wasn't raining. Please let it be raining. Chores were a drag. I would get to mow our lawn this weekend too. Oh joy. Mom and the little boys would pull weeds and trim up the yard for fall. Dad would tackle hoses and the gutters. Yippee, not.

Early on Saturday I headed over to Mrs. Lando's to get her lawn out of the way. As always, she was happy to see me. She is a super nice lady. I remember when she used to babysit us sometimes. She always tried really hard to make sure all of us had fun. One of my favorite memories happened around the holidays one year. I must have been about nine because Lucas was so little she was holding him in her arms and Alex was in Kindergarten. I remember she was trying to help us make cookies. She was so patient and always has been with all of us. The sugar cookies came out funny looking and misshapen but Mom almost cried when she saw them. I like to keep to myself and I'd rather goof around than do chores, but for her it's different. She pays me for my work but I'd do it anyway. If she has any family of her own, I've never met them. She's too young for the job, but she reminds me of a grandma. I see a lot more of her than I do my own grandmas and, quite frankly, she treats me better.

I guess I used up all my patience on Mrs. Lando because I wasn't nearly as nice to my dad when he asked me to help him work on the car when I was finished cutting Mrs. Lando's grass. "Sure, I guess. I'll be back when I finish our lawn," I huffed grumpily. The weather was pretty nice for fall and I wanted to skate. I stomped off to mow our grass. I popped in my headphones and blasted my favorite play list. When a really great song came on I would sing along and pretend I was a famous singer instead of a lawn boy.

I put the mower away and slunk back to the dreaded garage. "Owen, I get that you don't want to help me, but the car helps our family. You live here and need to do your share. I don't appreciate the attitude." Guess I should have come in skipping and humming. I knew better than to argue. I didn't want to blow any chance I had of skating later.

"You're right, Dad. I just really wanted to skate and I've been working all day. I guess I just felt frustrated. It's my day off. I know it's your day off too." I saw the look in his eye and decided it wasn't worth complaining about anymore but it just felt so unfair. Maybe he felt that way too. After four hours we still didn't have the dang thing running. When I was on my own I hoped to have the money for a mechanic. I knew my dad thought that all this home improvement and auto repair stuff was good for me but it just wasn't fun. I could hardly wait until Tuesday. I asked my mom if I could escape to Marlo's. I told her I was invited to dinner. I would rather starve than come back early. Knowing Marlo's mom, she'd ask me anyway and I was *so* done with my family for today. I mean really – who asks an eighth grader to work almost eight hours on a Saturday?

Marlo's house is so cool. It's surrounded by big trees and is kinda old and Halloween creepy. Since he's an only child and both his parents work, he has more electronics than you can believe as well as most of the upstairs to himself. His mom's rule up there is, "Keep it clean!" I mean he has his own bedroom, bathroom and

21

even a man cave with a big screen TV. How lucky can you get? I was welcomed like family and invited to dinner! Yes!

"Dude, where have you been all day? I thought you were coming by earlier."

"I had to cut our grass, Mrs. Lando's and help Dad with our dead car. I worked for eight hours. Just like a real job. It sucked. At least Mrs. Lando pays me."

"Are you kidding?"

"Not even a little bit."

"I had to take out the garbage and clean my bathroom. When I keep it clean it only takes me about five minutes to pass Mom's inspection. Today I am glad I'm not you." We smiled at each other. Life was pretty good right now.

Marlo and I settled into some serious gaming that was only interrupted by the best lasagna ever. My mom is a good cook but nobody beats Mrs. Saggio's lasagna! I called my mom and asked to spend the night. I had to ask Marlo's mom to send her a text that it really was fine. Geez, mothers. It was great spending Saturday night at Mar's because that meant waffles on Sunday morning. Yum! Marlo's mom makes amazing waffles and homemade syrup. To be completely fair to my mom, I should admit that Marlo's mom is a chef.

Tuesday finally came! Once again I was out of school like lightening and off to the pawnshop. We spent most of the time clearing up the images I was getting. I would describe what I was seeing and Mr. White Eagle would help me to understand it. Our next several sessions together were spent deciphering the images from various items in the shop that Mr. White Eagle picked out for me. My watch was silent. I figured it just didn't have anything to say. When I was tired mentally I would sweep the floor. It was quieting and strangely therapeutic to do a task that required no thought. Mr. White Eagle had me focus on slow careful strokes. There was probably meaning in the simple task as there seemed to be in everything White Eagle did, but I didn't yet know what the meaning was.

The weeks went by and Halloween was coming up fast. I was spending less time sweeping and more time working on my gift. I was touching all kinds of stuff in the shop and we would decipher the images together. I had started coming in on Saturdays and the occasional Sunday. My mom thought I was crazy but she let me go. I told her I was building work ethic. Mr. White Eagle said that my extra work at the shop could go to help pay for my eighth grade trip at the end of the year. As long as my mom could see that I was turning in my homework and getting decent grades, she was fine with my absence from home. It made my dad a little grumpy but I spent time with him on the car too. We finally got it running the second week in October.

I was expecting something amazing to happen on Halloween. It's a spooky day and I was now a spooky guy. Nadda. Zip. Nothing. Boring! I also should have known better; sometimes you do get your wish but most often not in the way you expected. I was at the shop the day after Halloween and before our last cross country meet. I didn't realize that Mr. White Eagle had not 'turned off' my watch or my gift or whatever. Apparently he thought I was controlling myself pretty well or maybe he just forgot. I thought I was getting pretty good. I was picking out my own objects now. I could tell which ones would show me pictures. Each one would tell me its story, but I had yet to feel that strong pull he had described that would drive me to fix anything wrong. For now I was just an observer.

It was all pretty cool and it was starting to feel relatively normal for me in the shop. I would feel drawn to an object. I would walk over and pick it up or touch it and images would float before my eyes. I could still see what was going on around me. The images had a smoky quality like a hologram floating over reality. Different objects would tell me different things. Usually I could see the previous owner doing something while having the object on their person. The images most often appeared as though I was an invisible

23

interloper. No one in the image would react to me, the images just moved by like events on a movie screen or an old memory.

I had also gotten to where I could almost hear my watch whisper to me about Miles or maybe I was hearing Miles' voice from the past. The watch or Miles and I were better friends now too. I was only getting images when I asked a question or if the watch or Miles thought I needed to know something. It was... well, there aren't words. I was feeling pretty amazing though and people were starting to notice. I guess to kids at school it just seemed like I had more confidence. As my mother always says, "When you get too big for your britches, something will bring you down." Well guess what? She's right, you start feeling cool and better than other people and something will remind you that you are *just* like everybody else.

My days were all going pretty well. I wasn't hating school so much anymore. On my way from the locker room to the bus, that all changed as I felt... something. It was that same strange pull, but something more. I closed my eyes for a moment to understand the feeling. What was it? Where was it coming from? It was a sense of unease and concern. Something was wrong. Most of the boys were loading onto the bus and the girls were just starting to come out. Some kids were in shorts and sweatshirts and others like me were in sweats from head to toe ready for our last official cross country meet. I looked around to get my bearings even though some of my friends were calling me to get on the bus. Kids were swirling around me, but I was the eye of the storm.

Then it happened. Two girls were talking and not paying attention. The tiny brunette bumped into me. Without a thought, I reached out my hand to steady her. I touched her sweatshirt sleeve as I grasped her arm and then I *knew* she was in trouble. My flash of insight showed me that someone was watching her, maybe even profiling her. A man had touched her sweatshirt and it didn't feel good. It felt dirty and creepy. I felt a wave of nausea and fear. I can't imagine the look that crossed my face.

"I'm sorry, it was an accident," she whispered. Her chocolate brown eyes were huge in her pale face. All her freckles stood out in relief against her pale skin. The look on my face had scared her.

"Jerk. Come on Rose," her friend said as she glared at me. She grabbed Rose by the arm and started to drag her toward the waiting bus.

"No wait, Rose. I'm sorry. I was... I mean I was surprised. Are you okay?" Oh help! My powers were on. I had my first job and I wasn't sure what to do. Who was this guy? What did he want? Did she know him? Would she talk to me? What could I ask without creeping her out? Should I call White Eagle?

"I'm okay, thanks. Sorry again for running into you." She smiled a small smile and hopped on the bus.

Adrian was waving me toward the back of the bus but I shook my head and took a seat behind and diagonal from Rose and her friend to watch them and listen. I had plopped down next to a small bespectacled sixth grade boy. Was I ever that small? He looked at me like I was going to eat him for a snack. I gave him kind of a sick half smile. So much for reassuring him, but I had more important things to worry about. I tried to eavesdrop on the girls' conversation but it wasn't easy with all the chatter and bus noise. The bus trip took fifteen long minutes and with all the other talking I learned next to nothing. The face of the guy who had touched her sweatshirt was vivid in my mind at least. I would have to watch for him. Something told me he'd be here today and she had no idea.

We arrived at our meet location and headed off the bus for our team meeting, walk-through and stretch. I tried to focus on the meet, her and the creepy guy all at once. I scoured the surroundings with my eyes. There were too many darn trees and too many places to hide. The already prematurely dark sky was growing darker, the clouds looked more ominous. Rain was clearly in the offing. Great. In the murky dim, it was getting harder to see. There were tons of people milling around from several schools. How was I going to pick this guy out or was he even here?

Adrian came up and bumped my shoulder. "What's up?"

"I ah...," Oh crap, I had not planned on what I would tell him. "I just thought seeing as how this is the last meet I'd really focus and try to get a really good time. Maybe I could run JV next year instead of on the freshman team."

"Oh yeah, good idea. I'll do that too."

That was much too easy. I hated lying to him. Being on JV next year would be pretty cool though. I felt that all my senses were on high alert. We began our walkthrough with the girls in front, as they would run first today. Good. I would watch her until I had to run and then hopefully her mom would take her straight home. Adrian tried to talk to me again but I wasn't good company. I tried to tell him that I was just focused on the race and he left me alone to talk to another friend. I saw Lucie up with the other girls give me a strange look over her shoulder. No time to figure that one out now.

As we entered the curve furthest from the start, I caught a glint of something on the ground near the base of a tree. It was a brass button. I felt the familiar pull in my belly and I knew I should pick it up. It had called to me. The sensation was a tugging and a tingle all in one. It's almost like when adrenaline hits your chest. Images came in a quick flash, the blink of an eye really, as I picked up the button, but again I knew I'd remember. It was Rose's stalker. He was here and he was looking for her. I wanted to throw up when I saw what he wanted to do to her. The worst part was that I knew she wasn't the first victim.

Too soon the whistle blew for the girls to begin their race. I have never taken so much interest in the girls' team. I followed the parent crowd as they quick-walked as much of the field as they could. I tried to watch everything. My eyes were on Rose and the crowd. Again I caught Lucie giving me a weird look. Whatever! The girl ignores me as much as she can in science. I saw no sign of the man.

It was all over before I could find him. I couldn't even tell how well Rose had done.

I kept watching her after the race. She stayed with her friends and was talking with some adults. I hoped her family was there in the group. The whistle blew for us to line up for our race. I would have to trust that she would be okay for the fifteen minutes or so it would take me to run the course. What else could I do? The sky had continued to darken and a light mist began to fall. We were called to attention and the race began. I started off in the middle of the pack at an easy jog. I couldn't see Rose but I could still watch for the man. The first rumble of thunder began in the distance. The runners were starting to spread out and I quickened my pace.

There was now a mix of individual runners and small clots of boys too. The thunder grew ever closer and the rain began. Visibility wasn't good and I was beginning to pant. I could feel sweat beading up on my face, chest and back. I pressed harder. The trees became thicker, the day almost like night, the rain increased and the thunder boomed almost overhead. I saw my first flash of lightening and there he was beside the tree. I almost stumbled. Go after him or continue on? I'd have to find him after the race. What would I do if I confronted him now anyway?

The wind began to pick up and with it the rain came down soaking my already damp body. It did a great job of cooling me off. More lightening, followed immediately by thunder, caused me to put on a burst of speed. I was going to finish this race before they called it. There were no more than about ten kids from various schools in front of me. I pressed for all I was worth. I heard a crash back in the wooded section. Maybe something fell on the stalker. Well, I could hope, right? I dug deep and put on one last burst of speed. Water dripped down my face mixed with sweat. I was completely soaked, even my shoes were soggy and I had kicked up mud all over my back. My breath was coming in gasps and I had a stitch in my heaving side but I could see the finish line. I stumbled across it in third place and passed off my identifier, my time clocked. I bent at the waist for a moment, gasping, with my hands at my sides.

"Wow, Owen, I've never seen you run so hard. Good job. I'm sure you got a personal best." It was Rose, but where was her posse?

"Uh, thanks. You did well too," I panted. Not that I had ever paid attention to how she had done before. I didn't even know her name for sure until today. "Where'd your family go?"

"They're under the covered area. I just wanted to say good job," she added shyly.

"Thanks, be careful on the way home. I'll see ya later." Yes please, get in your car and go home before Mr. Creepy finds you.

"Well, bye. Sorry again for running into you earlier."

"You're fine. Don't worry about it." She smiled a shy smile and jogged off. I had about caught my breath and was ready to look for Mr. Ugly. My eyes darted all around as I hoped to catch sight of him again.

"Got a new girlfriend?" Lucie tried to sound casual but it came out brittle.

"What?" Girls were the last thing on my mind today. Scary men were another story however.

"You know that little Rosy is only in 6th grade, right?"

I should be quicker with this stuff but I was truly dumbfounded. "What are you talking about?" She must have seen the sincerity in my face because she dropped it.

"Well never mind. Good race. I'll see you in science." She took off before I could utter another word. Most folks were racing for their cars by now. I grabbed my gear from the covered area and threw on my sweat shirt. I was cooling quickly from the rain. The crowd was thinning.

"Owen, there you are. Let's get out of here. What an amazing race. I've never seen you run like that. I'd swear you were being chased by the hounds of hell or something."

"Mom!" I knew in an instant she would help me. "Mom, I saw a guy during the run. I didn't like the way he looked at people. He was really watching the girls and it made me feel uncomfortable. He didn't look like anyone's parent, ya know?"

It didn't take long to convince her to help me look for him. We didn't see him anywhere so we went and talked to my coach. I told him that I'd seen the guy watching us warm up, do the walk-through and that he was really watching the girls. We told him we didn't see him now, but I added that I thought I had seen him around school and that I was pretty sure he wasn't a parent. Fortunately he took me seriously. I would remain cautious until this was resolved. How would I wait two whole days to see Mr. White Eagle? I needed to keep his number on me. The rain had saved Rose today but I needed a better plan.

The wait didn't even feel like waiting. I was busy with life. Adrian's feelings were kinda hurt after the meet so I took a little extra time for him. I tried to watch Rose without anyone noticing. I touched the button now and then; to try to get more information out of it. It was silent. Lucie, on the other hand, was not. She talked to me more than ever and even got us in trouble in science. What was with her? Ignore me and then talk my ear off. I don't get it. Not that I minded too much, she is after all… *hot*.

We were having one last practice as next week we would race against the staff. I watched the parent and street traffic as we made our way around the campus for practice. There he was. Yes. Got you, sucker! I broke off from the group amid shouts from my peers and ran straight for our coach. Without turning to look at the guy I described him and told the coach where he was hiding pretending to be a parent waiting to pick up a kid. Coach sent me off to continue the run and went to talk to the guy. As soon as he saw the coach coming his way he took off. Guilty.

Coach got a partial on the plate and would take care of the rest. I touched the button in my pocket and saw the rest of the plate. "Hey Coach, I think I saw part of the plate too." I provided him with the part he was missing and he flipped open his cell and called the police. Hopefully the cops would get him. My secret was safe. Rose would be safe and I had done it. First job complete. Check!

That night I had my first nightmare. I was running through the trees like I had at the meet but no one else was there. I kept running and running, hearing the thunder pound as the lightening flashed and the stalker appeared behind different trees as I ran. Finally I broke through the edge of the woods and ran to a foggy, water soaked meadow. There was Rose kneeling on the wet grass crying, but no matter how hard I ran, I could not reach her. The stalker approached from the other side of the meadow. Although he walked he was getting closer and closer to Rose. I ran harder but only seemed to move further away. "No," I screamed and fell out of bed with a loud thump. I lay there panting and listening to see if I had woken anyone else up. As my pounding heart slowed I could hear my dad's soft snore. I crawled back into my bed but the images wouldn't let me rest.

THREE

Saturday dawned chilly and damp. I quickly downed a bowl of cereal and left a note for my mom. I rushed to the pawnshop as fast as I could and crashed through the front door, panting. Startled, Adrian's uncle looked up from the register where he was helping a customer. "Show a little respect, would ya? He's out back making some repairs. Go back there."

"I'm sorry," I said with chagrin and gently closed the door before making my way to the back room. I set down my board and pack as I listened for White Eagle. At first I could hear nothing, then the soft tink, tink, tink of metal on metal. He had a pair of locking pliers on a nut he was trying to loosen from a bolt attached to an upside down lawn mower. Each stroke of the hammer against the locking pliers made the sound I had heard. I knew he knew I was there but he didn't even look at me. This must be another test. I scanned the shelves around the workshop looking for the rust cutter my dad used. I double checked the work area and saw no can there. I looked over the shelves again and spying what I wanted, moved cautiously to the spray can, removed it from the shelf and carefully set it next to the mower.

White Eagle grunted and applied some spray. He waited a moment and began his tapping again. The nut turned on the third strike. I reached for the can and replaced it on the shelf. White Eagle smiled at me. "Pretty good, my boy. I know you get frustrated sometimes when you have to help out around home. Education is *never* wasted! You never know when one of those tasks your dad has taught you will come in handy. Like just now with the rust cutter. Things you learn from your mom, friends, and teachers are never a waste of time. Now, what weapons do you see around here?"

That was a trick question, right? I knew that the pawnshop sold hand guns and hunting rifles as well as a variety of swords and knives. I looked around the workshop again. I saw tools, paint, lubricant, and tons of other stuff you would expect in a workshop. No obvious weapons though. I tried changing the subject. "I need to talk to you about what happened at the cross country meet."

"I know you do. Indulge me first, please," he said as he removed the blade from the lawnmower and clamped it in a vice.

"Well, I don't see anything obvious here but I know there are weapons in the pawnshop itself. They're all locked up though." He just looked at me. Wrong answer, I guess. I bit my lip and looked around again and went for it. "You could do a lot of damage with the hammer, even more with that sledge over there. I see clippers and cutters, saws and power tools. You have rakes and shovels out here as well as spray cans. You could even hurt someone with a hose." I looked at him hopefully.

"Better. Anything can be a weapon if you know how to use it. Beware though, people can use any weapon against you too. The time has come to teach you self defense." With that he flipped something toward my face which I automatically blocked. "Good, you're quick. You'll need to be. Now tell me your story."

I pulled up a stool and unloaded everything I knew about the creepy guy and Rose. I told him that at first I thought I had solved the problem of Rose's and then about the nightmare.

"The nightmare is telling you that you aren't done. You never are until you know for sure. You are still wondering. Your mind was reminding you to keep watching."

"But the button I picked up is still silent."

"It can only tell you about the things that happened while it was with him. It can't tell you what he's thinking now. It can't read minds. It only knows what it saw."

"Well damn, now what do I do?"

"You keep watching her. I have a friend who works at the police station. She will let us know what's going on. She'll be retiring in a year or so though so we'll need to groom a replacement." He reached into his pocket and pulled out an ancient clamshell type phone. I smiled a little. I eavesdropped shamelessly. I was much too curious to turn away. "Hello Evelyn, it's me... Yes, it's been a long time... Good, good. I find myself in need of your help again... Yes, I finally have a new one. Ah, I see. Well try would you? ... Sure. Here goes. You are looking for a pedophile called in by the middle school cross country coach. They provided a plate. Yeah, let me know. Thanks." He closed his phone and turned to look at me.

I cocked my head to the side. He was waiting for something. "You want me to tell you what she said?" He nodded one slow nod.

"She was glad to hear from you. Maybe she has been waiting to hear from you. She wants to help but it will be difficult because she has changed jobs or something." I looked at him expectantly.

A slow smile spread across his face. "Excellent! You are better than I had hoped. You pretty much got it. She will help us; it will not be as easy as it used to be. We probably won't hear until sometime Monday. You may have nightmares until then. I'm sorry about that."

"May I have your cell number so that I can call you and ask advice?" I asked, unsure what his reply would be.

"I need for you to learn to depend on *you*," he said, tapping my chest. "I will give it to you but save it for emergencies. Make sense?"

I nodded. I would do my best to rely on myself.

"It won't take long before you will know what you are capable of. I have faith and confidence in you." He ruffled my hair. "Now let's get to work. You ever box?" He dug out some old gloves, wrapped my hands and gloved me. He held a padded shield to protect himself and then worked on my form until my arms were shaking and I was dripping with sweat. "Now you sweep."

"What? I can barely lift my arms."

33

"It's calming. It will do you good. Cross country is about to end. I want you to keep running at least three days a week to stay in shape. Lose your board and start running all the places you need to go. Run here. It's fine if you arrive sweaty. When running here gets to be easy, we'll change the route."

Super, I thought sarcastically. I had been right. There was a reason for everything he did. "Ok, I will," I answered weakly. If he was hoping for enthusiasm, he was bent. I would run but I couldn't give up my board.

I called him on Monday after I got home from school. I couldn't stand to wait until Tuesday. I hoped he wouldn't be mad. He wasn't. His buddy at the cop shop let him know that the guy was suspicious and under surveillance. I could relax a little. He warned me to keep watching her just in case. Apparently I was doing enough because my nightmare was not as scary. I seemed to be in better control of it. In my next nightmare Rose was still unaware of me but now I was able to get to her and stand between her and the threat.

On Tuesday I ran to the shop like he asked and we boxed again. He wore gloves this time too. He hit me a lot that first day but he didn't do it hard, just hard enough to get me better at keeping up my guard and blocking. By the time we were done I could barely crawl into his truck to go home. I tried telling my mom that I couldn't do my homework because I couldn't lift my pencil. No joy on that one! She did want to know what I was up to at the shop that was wearing me out. I hated not telling her the whole truth but I settled for a half truth. She thought we were boxing for… fun.

By Friday, White Eagle let me know that Evelyn had called to tell him they had a search warrant and were closing in on him. She let White Eagle know that they might be looking for me to give more information and maybe give me a good citizen award. They both knew that it was a terrible idea to reveal me. Evelyn planned to call the coach herself and let him know that as a youth, I needed to be protected and that my family didn't want any publicity. They would give him the good citizen award and that would be the end of it. I had every confidence that she could persuade him. It had nothing to do with my coach not wanting to acknowledge me but everything to do with Evelyn, who seemed to be a formidable woman. Her age was unclear but I was pretty sure she could wipe the floor with me in a fight. Perversely I was very much looking forward to meeting my new helper and guard dog. Wait, make that guardian angel. If she heard me call her a dog she would turn me into the stuff that comes out the back end of one, which I get to scoop up.

It was a couple of weeks later and after many hard practices with White Eagle that we found the article in the paper showing the arrest of our neighborhood creepy. We boxed every session now as well as worked with my mental abilities. We started a little street fighting the second week in November and would be including some martial arts after Thanksgiving. His martial art of choice was karate. White Eagle's whole focus seemed to be on defense. He also continued training me to recognize all the weapons around me. His favorite was, of course, my trusty broom. I was getting pretty good with it in fact. I could sweep with it *and* swing it around like a mean quarter staff. I could get somebody pretty good and boy would they be taken by surprise. Ha! Once I knew Mr. Creepy was in jail, my nightmares about Rose were completely gone. Maybe I was too quick to think I had solved it the first time around. White Eagle was right again; something really had to be done for me to be in the clear.

The week before Thanksgiving I was drawn to a lone pencil on the floor in the main hall. I knew I had to pick it up. It showed me the boy I had sat next to on the bus, the day of the fateful cross country meet. I saw myself on the bus looking as threatening as I was afraid I looked at the time, yet I could feel hope not fear from the boy. Then I saw another boy, a menacing boy, who brought a wave of fear. I could see the school's bathroom, there was fear there too. I saw the small boy shoved into the urinal and getting pee on his shoe and his pants. I felt a wave of fear and humiliation. There was another similar scene. I also felt briefly the intense need to go to the bathroom and feeling like I could not or should not go. Great, I would be using up my entire collection of bathroom passes for the trimester to help out this poor kid.

I started watching for the bully and the victim. The bully and I had lunch together so he was pretty easy to track. Marlo noticed my fierce attention the first day. I just told him that I was suspicious of the kid and that he seemed mean. Marlo agreed after watching the kid's behavior for about one minute. I still hadn't let him in on my secret but Marlo hates injustice so I was sure that was all it would take to get the ball rolling on his help. I caught Adrian up to speed in social studies. Between us we should have his schedule in about two days. If not I would need to have Adrian try his skills at coercion. He is really good with people and can get stuff out of almost anybody. He's cute, the girls say, and they love him. I would turn all that flirting into a spy network if I had to. Hold on, I would do that now. I needed to know the sixth grade boy's schedule also.

My plan worked better than I could have imagined. I had both schedules by lunch the next day. Marlo and Adrian were all about helping but neither wanted to get into trouble and neither wanted to confront the school bully. Adrian was brave enough to go stand next to the guy at lunch so that I could judge his size. Damn, he was close to my size. Marlo is the shortest and fluffiest of the three of us. Adrian is almost as tall as me but he's even more of a bean pole. I have started putting on a little meat with all the sparring. Maybe I needed to lift some weights too.

I carefully studied the two schedules and found the times I thought I most likely needed to cover the bathroom. I got lucky on Friday. I checked out of science and walked down the hall to the bathroom. No one was in sight so I stepped into the bathroom and looked for the best spot to lurk. The sixth grader came in as expected. I knew his eighth grade friend would be in soon because he would be able to see the sixth grader from his class. It didn't take a rocket scientist to figure out that there were only two times a day when the bully could catch his victim. Too bad the victim was too scared to figure that out. I said nothing, but he sensed my presence anyway and looked at me with a startled expression on his face. I shook my head, put a finger to my lips to warn him to be quiet and then indicated that he should go ahead and take care of himself. He stepped into a stall.

I continued to lean against the wall out of sight of the door. Mr. Bully came in to harass the victim. He went to make his move but caught sight of me and paused. "You're done here," I said with menace in my voice as I frowned at him. He backed right up and out of the bathroom. All the running and fighting was starting to show. I must have looked mean. The boots I had taken to wearing and my dad's old leather jacket added to the aura of danger. Little scares a bully more than another bigger, meaner bully. It probably wasn't a final answer to the smaller boy's problem but I bought him a few days anyway. He would need professional help. I softened my face and my voice so I wouldn't scare the sixth grader.

"Remind your 'friend' that I'm a friend of yours too. Tell him I'm watching. You should also turn him into the counseling office. You don't have to put up with that crap. Go to the counseling office now and turn him in. Please don't mention me." The smaller boy looked at me with huge eyes and nodded once slowly. I turned and left. I kept watching for the bully and making eye contact as often as I could. Marlo and Adrian also watched and recorded his activities.

In less than a week kids all over the school were turning him in for all the things he had done so far this year and was continuing to do. By Friday he had gotten himself suspended. Bye Bye. We won't miss you. My little sixth grade buddy had done his part too. I noticed that he was walking the hall with his head held high. When he saw me he would smile and nod but he never said a word.

I felt good going into Thanksgiving break. Lucie was still talking to me and life in general was looking up. I was starting to feel like I could call Lucie a friend. We were kicking butt in science. It turned out to be her favorite subject too. We had found something in common. I suppose it helped that I had become much less klutzy around her. Then she had to go and spoil it. "Hey Owen, you know that Rose still watches you, right?"

"What?" I hadn't even thought of her in a couple of weeks.

"Well it's not just her. Look at the group in the back corner," she indicated with a flip of her head. I looked away from our microscope and sure enough, all four girls were looking at us. I raised one eyebrow skeptically as I tilted my head to give full impact to my nonverbal, "Really?"

Lucie just giggled. "They're watching you."

"Oh come on, they're probably mad because we've got the highest grades in science right now. They want a piece of our team. Besides, you just laughed. Maybe they think we're making fun of them."

"Are you really that dumb? Geez, Owen, take a look around. All the girls watch you and some of the guys do too. You're different. You're exuding this… presence now. You seem - I don't know, tough and mysterious, like you wouldn't take garbage off of anyone any more."

I just looked at her speechless, my lab sheet completely forgotten.

"Ok, I'll be bold here. Wanna know what I see?" she asked as she leaned onto our lab table, holding my gaze. When I looked into her eyes like that, I lost track of everything around me. I could barely focus on what she was saying.

"Uh, ok, I guess," I muttered. Where was she going with this? Did I want to know what she thought?

"You must be one of the tallest boys in our class by now and you're filling out. You look like you could be a sophomore in high school. With your jacket off, anyone can tell that you've really put on muscle. You've taken to wearing that *hot* leather jacket and boots. Owen, ya' look like a biker or something."

I knew I was changing, I could see it in the mirror. I had patches of beard that I needed to address about once a week and I'd noticed the muscles. Working out six days a week was making me look pretty good but the fact that Lucie had noticed about knocked me off my stool. My mouth was hanging slightly open and my eyes must have been glazed. Ever helpful, Ms. Hodges came over to see if we were in need of help. Lucie saved the day as I recovered myself. I'm not even sure what she said. Our teacher moved on to the next group so Lucie leaned in, putting her hand on my knee. Her face was inches from mine, her breath on my face. "I kinda like the whole stunned silence thing. I feel like I just won something." She leaned back with a 'cat that ate the canary' look on her face. I waited for her to sprout feathers from between her lips. I tried to refocus on the lab but it was a completely lost cause.

When the bell rang Lucie put her hand on my arm to hold me back a minute. Of course I complied, who wouldn't? She got a devilish gleam in her eye.

"What?"

"Look at the group at the back. I have just made them extremely jealous." I chanced a glance in their direction and sure enough the look on their faces was a little scary. "That's awesome. I love it. See you tomorrow," she said, squeezing my arm and then hip bumping me on the way past.

I felt thrilled and used all at once. With Lucie, life was a mixed bag. Knowing my luck, after break she wouldn't be speaking to me again. I have no idea what happened the rest of the day. All I could think about was her. Marlo just shook his head when he saw me on the bus. "Heaven help us," he sighed. "He can take out bullies with one look and melts for a woman. Geez."

"Hold on, how do you know about Lucie?" I asked in surprise.

"Come on. You had Adrian and me set up a social network to bring down a bully. Did you really think it all just went away when you got him? We know everything that happens at this school. Our finger is on the pulse, man!"

Well, some of us had our finger on the pulse. Apparently I was not one of them. Adrian surprised me at the shop when I showed up for practice. He was now planning to work out with me. He had decided that as popular with the women as he was, he wanted to add whatever magic edge I had developed. His uncle was going to let him work at the shop some too to help fund his eighth grade trip. Oh boy, I thought. I love my boys but I don't need them underfoot and interrupting my training. Then Adrian sprung on me that he had a girlfriend and Marlo wished he had one. Yep, my finger was nowhere near the pulse of what was happening at school.

On Tuesday my hair had reached the point of no return. In my attempt to grow it out, it had suddenly become an obnoxious beast with a mind of its own. My attempts at styling it the last two days were completely unsuccessful. I had to admit, growing it out was probably the dumbest idea I'd ever had. We are talking BAD of epic proportions. It was a constant irritation. Every time it touched my eyebrows or the sides of my face I had the urge to attack it with school scissors. My scissor visions led me to wonder how hard it could possibly be to trim it up a little. My dexterity was now pretty good. I hadn't participated in all those sports and done all that training with White Eagle for nothing!

The minute I was off the bus, I sprinted all the way home – I barely said "hi" to my mom and raced for my room. I attacked my desk with a kind of berserker frenzy until I found buried deep in the back of a drawer, my old scissors from elementary school. I leaped in front of my mirror prepared to do battle with my unruly locks.

"STOP! What are you doing?" my mom nearly shouted at me.

"Well, I wanted to grow my hair out and you said I could but all of a sudden I just couldn't take it anymore. It's bugging me something fierce. I can't stand it touching my face so I thought I'd take some off of my bangs and the sides."

Her look was one of appalled astonishment, like someone watching a train wreck. You can't look away but you can't stand to watch either. "Owen, I can make an appointment for you," she threw out as a peace offering.

"I bet they can't get me in today and besides I don't want you wasting money. You've been buzz-cutting all of us for years to save money so we can keep you at home. I'll be okay."

"Oh, Owen, you don't have to do everything yourself. Let me help you," she pleaded. I could see the sense in her words and my grip slackened. Mom gently removed the scissors from my hand and tossed them onto my now cluttered desk. She took me by the hand and led me into her bathroom where she had me sit on the edge of her tub. She rummaged in her drawer and pulled out her professional hair cutting scissors. Mom had never been a hair dresser but she was smart and paid attention. She had also read all the directions and had watched the video that went with the clippers. She now had years of practice behind her. I knew that she had cut some of her friends' hair in college in exchange for work on her car and for other stuff she needed.

"Mom, I know you can do a mean buzz cut but can you do a real haircut?" I asked, a little worried.

"This from the man who was prepared to cut his own hair… with old school scissors? Really?" she said with a disparaging look. "I may not be a professional but I work cheap and if you hate it we can still go with the buzz cut or make an appointment for you, right?"

"Yeah, I guess we can," I said with a smile for her. She smiled back.

"Now tell me what you want."

"Over the ears and across the back - shorter on the sides but maybe two inches long on the top. I definitely don't want it touching my eyebrows."

She handed me her small bathroom garbage can to hold and dampened my hair. Then she combed it carefully and studied me for a moment. She measured out my bangs at two inches and snipped carefully. Then she cut the rest of the top using my bangs as the sample length. She gradually tapered my hair so that my bangs were the longest part on the top of my head. Next she cut over my ears and across the back. Then using the clippers and the comb she finished the sides by holding the comb out at an angle, short on the bottom and longer hair toward the top of my head. She checked several spots and then had me get up and get personal with her

41

mirror to check her work. I ran some water on my hands and then ran damp fingers through my hair to move it away from my face, spiking up the front.

"Wow, Mom, good job. You listened and did what I asked. What do I owe you?"

"Give me a hug and we'll call it good," she said with a laugh.

Adrian was hanging around the pawnshop more now. When he was around we would clean the store, unpack shipments, clean up stuff that came in to be sold and practice our defense skills. It was great to spend time with him but we had to be careful. All the mental practice that I did with White Eagle, to hone my gift, had to be done when Adrian wasn't around and that was getting tricky.

White Eagle's solution was that I would now 'work' for him at his house on Saturdays and at the shop three days a week after school. My parents thought it was great that I was busy running, learning karate, boxing, and working. They didn't know about the street fighting and weapons use. I was now learning about knives. My grades were okay and assignments were getting turned in. I was flying under their radar. Just the way I liked it.

FOUR

The weeks had flown by. It was almost Christmas. The weather in Oregon was rainy of course. The temperature was cold but tolerable. My life was falling into a comfortable pattern. I was ready for something harder, bigger, and more challenging. White Eagle was convinced that the 'big ones' were out there and when I was truly ready I would find them or they would find me. We had begun doing some research to see if we could find others like me so that I could train even more efficiently. We really needed Marlo, my computer genius, but White Eagle and I decided that for his safety we should leave it alone for now. Marlo and Adrian had helped me at school and we still kept watch there but they didn't know my secret. Yeah, I had dropped the mister in White Eagle's name most of the time and just thought of him by his last name. It didn't seem to bother him a bit and it was easier and more comfortable.

I was getting pretty good at deciphering images and figuring out what I was supposed to do with them. White Eagle could not see the images but he had spent so much time with his friend back in the day, that he just knew how to help me. Occasionally Miles' voice would show me things that were helpful. He was really good with showing me images of fighting. I was getting all kinds of ideas to try. It was almost like I had trained before and I was just remastering skills instead of learning them for the first time.

I hardly ever saw Rose at school but when I did she looked at me with an undisguised hero worship that made me feel uncomfortable. If Lucie caught her doing it she would roll her eyes and huff at me in disgust. "What?" I would ask whenever she did this.

"Clearly, she likes you. Why don't you just ask her out and be done with it?" Yet it seemed like the last thing she really wanted.

Women, I don't understand them. As predicted, Lucie was much less friendly in science. She seemed to be serious about school and almost disgusted with me. What did she want?

I made the mistake of nudging her binder in science and was seized by a strong image. I knew I was in her personal business but I couldn't stop what I was seeing. I swear my vision went red. I saw her father standing over her yelling at her. They were toe to toe so she had to bend her neck back at an awkward angle. She was shaking but trying to hold her ground. A tear leaked from her eye. It seemed like she was more angry than sad but both emotions chased through her. I felt strongly protective and worried. The scene shifted focus like a camera changing depth and I became aware of her knee and ankle wrapped in elastic bandages as the shot panned back. I couldn't hear the words, just read the body language. Her father was completely disgusted with her. She had let him down. She was not worthy.

I must have been frozen for a moment because Lucie put her hands on her binder and yanked it away from my touch. "What?" she snarled, anger on her face.

"Are you ok?" I shouldn't have asked. I don't usually approach problems that way. I do research first. She looked at me confused.

"Huh? What do you mean?"

"Your knee, your ankle, what happened." Oh-my-gosh – STOP TALKING YOU DOPE!

Lucie looked completely dumbfounded. "What are you talking about?"

I quickly backpedaled and tried to recover. "I ah, thought I saw you limp," I said lamely. She wasn't buying it. She was silent the rest of class. All I could think was… crap, I've done it again.

On Sunday afternoon I skated down a couple of houses to Mrs. Lando's because she had called my mom. It was time to cut her grass for her and do some of the other heavy yard work that was getting to be too much for her. I don't know how old she really is but it seems like she's a hundred. I'd really rather be skating but since she's so nice and all... well here I was.

Today I saw some tarps on part of her roof and other construction stuff around the corner of her house. That was new. She seemed happy to see me and quickly showed me what was on her mind as far as yard work went for today. A big branch had hit the corner of the house and damaged it. She needed me to cut up the pieces for firewood and stack them. She also wanted me to trim up the damaged shrubs and cut the grass. In addition, there were some leaves that needed to be raked up so my brother would be down soon to help. I sighed in my mind. Her projects would take the whole rest of the day.

I got all the tools I would need out of the shed in the back and got to work. After splitting and stacking all the firewood, I trimmed up the damaged rhododendrons and lilacs. Then I sent my mom a text to let her know I was ready for Alex to come help. While I waited for him to arrive I hauled out the yard debris bins for us to load up the small bits left over from my chopping and pruning.

Alex arrived looking none too joyful but got right to work raking the flowerbeds and filling the bins. I cut the grass, thankful that her mower was the mulching kind so we didn't have to rake the grass too. I even swept her walkways and driveway before we lugged the bins to the street for pickup. I was sweating pretty good by now. Alex helped me put most of the tools away as I glanced at my watch, happy to see that I had only been at it for four hours. I took one last look at the corner of her house and saw something I had missed earlier. A hammer lay on the ground under one of the lilacs I had trimmed up. Alex wasn't quite done with the flowerbeds yet and I wanted Mrs. Lando's yard to be as close to perfect as was possible.

I reached for the tool. The minute my fingers closed around the handle, images assaulted my mind. I saw a man holding this hammer. He wasn't working at the moment but he had been. He was sweaty, disheveled and unhappy. I saw a ghostly image of Mrs. Lando come out of her house and talk to him. She was polite as

45

always but I didn't like the look in his eye. He didn't like her. I could feel it.

The image skipped to another time. The hammer now hung from the man's work belt. He was talking to Mrs. Lando in her kitchen. He seemed overly interested in her checkbook as she wrote him a check. He also kept glancing at her basement stairs.

Oh no, not again. Something bad was going to happen. The man was thinking bad thoughts. He wanted to hurt her. He looked at her like a predator might look at prey. Crap. Now what? I wondered why the hammer had not called to me like other objects do. I had the sense it was hiding or skulking like its owner did.

Mrs. Lando rounded the corner breaking my visions. "Are you done already? You're a hard worker, Owen. I appreciate your help. You were here for four hours and you worked really hard today so I am going to give you fifty dollars to split with your brother." She smiled as she looked at me expectantly but then her look changed. "Owen, are you okay?"

I sucked in a ragged breath. "Yeah, sure... fine. Um, where does the hammer go? It was under the lilac."

She gave me an odd look. "It belongs to that lazy handyman. I got his name from the grocery store community board. My roof needed a little work after the storm. His work is fine. His work ethic... well never mind, he's not your problem. The hammer is his. He has a tool box in the garage. You can put it there."

"When does he come back?"

"Monday, I would guess. He often shows up late. He is almost done so he'll want the rest of his money and good riddance. You on the other hand are a gem. Let's get you boys your money and something to drink."

I helped Alex finish the leaves and then we went inside. Alex was his usual happy self and chatted with her allowing me a chance to think. I still held the hammer but it wasn't giving me anything else so I excused myself to put it away. I found the tool box right away. After touching every tool in the box as well as the box itself, I learned very little in addition to what the hammer had reluctantly shown me. Everything had an almost black and oily feel to it. This was a bad man. He felt different from Rose's stalker and the bully at school. Our school bully was young and inept. The stalker had a creepy feel. This guy had a subtle difference from the stalker. Both were similar but each had his own distinct signature feeling of darkness about him. Someday I wanted to *read* something that had a pure white light instead of this thick, viscous blackness. I *knew* what evil felt like.

I had lost my appetite but agreed to take a plate of cookies home with me. When I got there, I checked in with my mom and gave her the money to split and put in my trip account. I told her that Alex had worked hard and could have half. She looked at me in astonishment. I figured the look was both for the fact that I was willing to split the money in half and also because I claimed that Alex had worked hard. So I added that he had eaten four cookies at Mrs. Lando's. I didn't want her getting suspicious of my generosity. I worried about Mrs. Lando the rest of the day and kept thinking about her as I did my homework. I was so distracted that I let Lucas beat me at checkers after dinner. He hooted and crowed with triumph. Maybe I needed to let him win more often.

I had trouble falling asleep as I keep thinking about my favorite neighbor. I needed to relax and let this go. I couldn't watch her 24/7. I would go by after school - surely she would be fine until then. Please let her be fine until then.

I overslept and had to rush for the bus, granola bar in hand. Marlo looked a little worried as I approached.

"There you are. You look terrible. What's going on with you? It was the weekend. Didn't you rest?"

"I just have a lot on my mind."

"And on your plate. Lucky. How is the job going? I hardly see you anymore now that our social studies project is done. I hope all your running around is worth it. My folks can afford the trip but I would love to come work with you anyway. It's probably the only way I'll see you during Christmas break. Besides my mom is threatening me with the D word, ya know, diet, so I have to do something to keep my mind off food."

I couldn't help it, I smiled. Only Marlo could make *my* life sound good. I was going to have to confide in him soon. My new skills were getting hard to hide from him. He could probably even help me *if* he believed me. Marlo has mad computer skills. The rest of the day slid by without a hitch. Even science was okay. Lucie was friendly and helpful today. Neither one of us mentioned the big doofus she had started dating. I hated that she had gotten a boyfriend but then I hadn't asked her out, so there you go.

When I got off the bus the handyman was working on Mrs. Lando's roof. I couldn't stand around all day watching so I went on home and dressed for a run. I let my mom know I'd be gone awhile and that I had my phone. I popped in my headphones and took off at a slow jog past Mrs. Lando's to check on her again. So far, so good. I sped up to my normal pace and started my loop. I hit as many hills as I could and did some sprints. I had about burned out my frustration and worry. I got Mrs. Lando mostly out of my mind. The air rushing past me was cool and refreshing. It wasn't yet five but the sky was darkening to twilight and black clouds were rolling in adding to the darkness.

As I neared home, I was again feeling really anxious about Mrs. Lando. The guy was still working on her roof as I ran past. I checked my watch – almost five, quitting time. I told my mom that I really needed to see Mrs. Lando to finish a project for her and figured it was a good time since I was already sweaty. She nodded distractedly as she hurried around the kitchen finishing dinner. I rushed out the door. Something told me to grab my skateboard. I trusted the urge even though Mrs. Lando is only three houses away. The sky was now inky dark. Mrs. Lando's lights were out but her car was visible in the open garage and a work van was in her driveway.

I tucked my board under my arm and quietly walked the perimeter of her house peeking in windows as I went. Drawers were popped open with stuff hanging out of them. I had yet to detect any movement. I was reluctant to go in until I had a better grasp of the situation. Then I saw him. The man from my visions was going through her desk in the office. He seemed to see me. His eyes moved right to the window. I froze. My thoughts became a jumble. Get help? Help Mrs. Lando? Where was Mrs. Lando? And worst of all I had a really strong desire to pop this guy in the mouth for taking advantage of sweet little old ladies.

I had waited too long in indecision; he was coming out the front door. I stood motionless in the shadow of a rhododendron by the window. In three strides he would be at his van. I couldn't let him get away. Rage was burning through me, white hot and powerful. I don't know what made me do it but I leaped from the shrubbery like an angry animal - swinging my skateboard around like a club, catching him right across his shoulder blades. The whack made him drop his load. It also cracked my best board clean in half. He growled and came at me. I slipped easily out of his fingers and ran around the corner of the house.

"Mrs. Lando! Are you here? Are you okay? Mrs. Lando?" I screeched, my voice cracking in fear and concern. I ran for the back door and wasted a moment desperately trying to yank it open, only to discover it was locked. It was enough time for him to catch me by the back of my hoodie and throw me off the porch. I landed flat on my back, most of the air leaving my lungs with a whoosh, but I sprang to my feet before he was on me again. I tried to think of all the things that White Eagle had taught me. Too bad I didn't have a broom! On the other hand, I didn't want him to have a weapon either. Too much indecision, too many thoughts racing around in my crazy mind. He threw a punch and I tried to block but he caught the side of my hand instead of my arm. SNAP. It happened in an instant. For a moment my hand felt nothing. It was completely numb. I took a quick breath and flowed into my fighter's stance ready for the next attack. It came from a completely unexpected direction. My finger exploded with pain, burning fire erupted from the break, shot through my hand and up my arm. My knees almost buckled. Son of a ... the rest left unsaid as I took

49

in the smile spreading across my attacker's face. He circled me, looking for a good opening and thinking I would be easy.

"Maybe you should pick on someone your own size, little man," he taunted.

I made no reply. My finger was throbbing in unison with my rapidly beating heart, my breath coming in short hot bursts. I knew I was in trouble even before he began to advance again. It's just a finger. It can be fixed. FOCUS! Focus or you will be in a whole lot more trouble.

"I won't let some... boy ruin things for me." He sneered as he swung at my face.

My arm came up automatically to block. He must not have been expecting it because he was a bit off balance. In less time than it took to think it, my other elbow came up and smacked him in the jaw with a satisfying crunch, sending him stumbling away from me but numbing my funny bone with the impact. He rolled to his feet and growled. Time for attack I decided. I faked right and upper cut with my left hand dealing more damage to his jaw. He stumbled back a step. Before he could rebalance I quickly followed up with a quick kick to his left knee. I rebalanced on the balls of my feet to wait for his next move. Just then Mrs. Lando's back porch light snapped on. I didn't take my eyes off him, but he turned in surprise to look at her. I ripped my eyes from him for an instant. Blood dripped from a cut on her cheek bone, but she looked otherwise unharmed. The baseball bat she held at ready made it look like she meant business. "I have called the police. They are on their way. You will not move or the boy and I will beat you senseless."

I had no doubt she meant it. I have never, in all my years of living next to her, seen her look so vicious. I swung my eyes back and he was almost upon me again. I spun and kicked his knee for the second time taking him to the ground. Unfortunately he caught my leg on the way down. With an explosion of breath, the air was knocked completely out of me this time. I felt a moment of panic before his grip relaxed in unison with a weird thump, like you

50

would hear from an overripe watermelon dropped on the floor. I turned frightened eyes to the fierce figure silhouetted over me, blocking out the porch light. Then the form was slumping next to me. Mrs. Lando fell into a clumsy heap, the bat falling from her numb fingers.

"Dirty rotten nincompoop, push me down my own stairs will he? I think not! He tried to steal my sterling too," she gasped with a dry chuckle. "I'm glad you came when you did. He would have been long gone before I got help otherwise. I don't know why you're here but I can't think of when I've ever been happier to see anyone! Now sit on that bugger while I go find something to tie him up. I'm not as tough as I was when I played softball so he won't be out for long." With that said, she rose unsteadily and limped toward the house. So I did my part and sat on our criminal - hard. I may have been a little rough. He seemed to lose a lot of air when I sat on him because a shaky moan escaped his lips as he expelled a big puff of air. I noticed his jaw didn't look quite right and his knee was at a funny angle. I smiled a small half smile of satisfaction. All that work and training was so worth it. I was so pumped with adrenaline that my hand hardly hurt at all.

I could hear the sirens coming. I knew nothing good would come from this but I couldn't leave her. I knew that as much as possible I needed to keep a low profile or my job would just be that much harder.

The police found us in the backyard. They read the handyman his rights, watched closely as the paramedics put him on a stretcher and cuffed him to it. He wanted to press charges against us! By eavesdropping, I discovered there were several warrants out for his arrest. He had decided that she was easy pickings and had pushed her down her stairs and stolen a bunch of her property which he had stashed in his van. Fortunately for the cops the van was still in her driveway with all the goodies in it and his fingerprints were all over her house and the van.

Had I not picked up his hammer I would never have known what he had planned for her. The police took our statements with quiet efficiency. I was much happier to see the medics who splinted and iced my finger. Mrs. Lando had to go to the hospital for observation and to get a couple of stitches in her cheek. She also has some monster bruises but it looked like she would be okay. Mrs. Lando gave me a long hard look before she left. I knew she would seek me out later but she said nothing in front of the cops that would make them look at me any harder. As far as they knew I was just in the right place at the right time.

The sirens on our street had drawn out all the neighbors including my mom. She handled it all really calmly. I kept watching her, wondering when the explosion was going to come. To put her off a little I decided to take the time for a shower before dinner. My mom noticed my distraction and lack of attention but said little during dinner. I could feel her getting ready to pounce, just like our cat with a piece of dangling string. She asked me to clear the table and clean up the kitchen after dinner. Uh oh, this was it - the grilling.

"Please don't think that I'm not proud of you because I am, but I sincerely hope this is not why you are learning karate and boxing." I could tell that mostly she was just worried about me.

As much as it killed me I had to lie to her. "I really was going down there to make sure she was set for winter. She needed her outdoor faucets capped. When I got there the house was dark but the work van was there and her car was in the open garage. It didn't look right."

"Why didn't you just come home or call for help?" she asked, frustrated that I hadn't made a safer decision.

"I forgot my phone and I didn't want to raise an alarm until I knew what was going on. He kinda took me by surprise. I'm sorry. I'll try to be more careful."

We worked in companionable silence until we were almost done. "I'll break this to your dad. Go on up to your room and do homework or something. Please keep a low profile."

I had just closed the door to my room when I heard Dad's car pull in. My cell phone vibrated in my pocket. Good thing it didn't do that in the kitchen and give me away. I checked caller ID – Marlo. Of course he would have seen the action on our street. I filled him in minimizing my involvement. I'm not sure he bought it.

School was another matter. Somehow the story got out that I had helped a neighbor who was beaten and robbed and I obtained a certain notoriety. It sucked. I hate the limelight. I like to keep a low profile and I know it's easier to do my job if people don't know about me. Lucie did look at me with new respect and that was pretty cool. I was hoping it would all die down over Christmas break which was now just a week away. I guess my taped up fingers lent a note of reality to the stories. I had to have hurt my hand somehow. It didn't get me out of any work for my teachers however.

I threw myself into my workouts with a whole new fervor. I needed to be better both mentally and physically or someone was going to take me out before I could get to them. My hand was a bit of a hindrance but I made do. White Eagle spent hours working on my blocking and hand positions or 'making good fist' as he called it. I had learned my lesson and wouldn't make that particular mistake again.

Mrs. Lando had talked to my mom behind my back and had gone and gotten a gift certificate to my favorite skate shop. Apparently she had found the wreckage of my board in her driveway and recognized it. They had argued about the amount and in the end Mrs. Lando had won; it was for one hundred dollars. When she gave it to me, I too had argued that the wheels, bearings, and trucks were all fine and that there was no need to give me so much or even anything at all. For a moment I thought she was going to cry because her eyes puddled up some. She took a quick swipe at her bespectacled eyes and pulled me into a fierce hug.

"You are a wonderful young man, Owen. I'm so honored to know you. I think you did more for me than you realize. Don't be a stranger over the winter and you know I'll have plenty for you to do come spring. Now go spend your money on a new deck.

Did I call it by the right name?" I nodded as she continued. "You can upgrade your board or get some other gear. I just want you to know how much I appreciate all you do for me. Most kids today wouldn't. Now get outta here." With that she gave me a playful shove out the door and waved a hearty goodbye. I had to admit that I was impressed that she had taken the time to learn the names of the parts of the skateboard.

Winter break flew by. I convinced my parents to let me spend some time almost every day but Sunday with White Eagle. My mom got a weird look in her eye over the holidays and decided to check my height. "Owen, you are going through one crazy growth spurt!" Sure enough, five foot ten inches. Yes! I was now as tall as most men and was broadening too with all my fighting. White Eagle had added weights to my routines, sadist that he was. I guess that to refer to him as someone who delights in cruelty really wasn't fair. He was after all, trying to help me and I had thought of the weights first. Some of his workouts left me sore and aching for days though. I was now much bigger than my mom and gaining on my dad. I figured that at this rate I would be taller and bigger than him by my junior year and he was almost six foot four. Though with my mom only being five foot four and a smidge I might be done growing.

School resumed and Lucie was back on her cold shoulder kick. She had gotten a new boyfriend over the holidays. I probably would have felt jealous but the guy was ridiculous and I was too busy to expend the energy. Their relationship only lasted two weeks. I was so happy that she was getting smarter. She deserved better. The day they broke up was the last day I had to wear my splint so I felt a sense of celebration within that I tried to keep to a dull roar around Lucie who seemed a little sad over the break up. I also noticed that she didn't put her notebook on the desk anymore. It worried me some that she might know more about me than I wanted her to.

Whenever I was at the pawnshop so was Adrian. We were better friends than ever except for my big, heavy secret. It was killing me not to tell my best friends. Marlo and I seemed to have drifted apart. There was little that we had in common from the start but now I had no time for computer games or hanging out. He came to the shop often and worked out with us some but it really wasn't his thing. He had taken to charting our workout routines and progress and then began researching better workouts and stuff. He was reading all kinds of health articles. It was incredibly helpful. He proudly announced in the middle of January that he had lost five pounds and gained two inches since the beginning of the school year. We all celebrated. Of the three of us he was still the shortest and fluffiest but he was looking much fitter. He was also scheduling all of our homework on spreadsheets. What a guy!

I felt like I just wasn't fooling them anymore though. They were both starting to ask a lot questions that I just couldn't answer. They wanted to know what I was so busy with all the time and where my sense of fun was. They would catch me staring off into space more than ever if I was getting a message from an object or just analyzing what I had seen. By the last week in January I couldn't stand it any longer. White Eagle and I were sitting at his kitchen table with several objects between us. "I can't keep this up anymore. I've got to tell my boys. They helped me at school with a bully. They can handle it and I need them. Right now I'm driving them away. It's great to spar with Adrian but he could do so much more. I need a wingman."

"Perhaps you're right. There is safety in numbers but there is danger too. Anyone who knows what you can do could let it slip and put you in danger or worse, they could be exposed."

"I feel I've got to take the chance. Something tells me that being a lone wolf like Miles was, is a mistake." I looked up at White Eagle and he was watching me. We had that strange connection like we did that first day where I almost felt an arc of electrical insight between us. I felt myself once again being measured against an invisible yardstick. White Eagle reared back in surprise. Seemed like he needed a new yardstick.

"Is that your gift I'm feeling? You see things in me, don't you," my words came out almost like an accusation.

"You know what *I'm* doing?" he asked in surprise.

"Sure, why wouldn't I?" Now it was my turn to be surprised.

"Because I have *never* met anyone who felt or even knew what I did. My magic is small. I know your heart and feel your sincerity. What does it mean if you can see that?" He looked completely baffled, leaving me more confused than ever. He shook his head in exasperation and shoved back from the table and began to pace. He stopped as quickly as he had begun and stared at me again. I just looked right back, waiting.

"Owen, you are... Let me try again. I have never seen anyone like you. Back in my younger days I thought Miles was amazing. Miles was nothing compared to you."

"What?" I didn't know what to think and now I was filled with questions. I knew he could see that because he waved me off when I started to open my mouth to ask the first one.

He took a breath and blew it out. "Let me tell you my story, it will help you to understand." He took another breath.

"I was born on a reservation in Montana in 1953. My mother descended from medicine women of our tribe. I was trouble as a young man and got in plenty of scrapes. I was suspended at least once a year for fighting. Much of what I know about fighting is self taught. I never went to college. I worked odd jobs and have done everything from bartending, to serving as a bouncer, to being a mechanic and doing some construction work. I was even a medic in the Army for a time. My dumbest move was being quite a drinker in my youth. That got me into more trouble than anything. I started taking boxing and karate to help control the drinking. My Alcoholics Anonymous sponsor owned the gym where I took the lessons. When I couldn't pay he sponsored me there too. He was a great man and I miss him every day."

White Eagle held my full and complete attention as he continued, "I had felt my gift but I had denied it to myself and to my mother. When I was twenty-five, my grandmother was seventy-five and dying from cancer. She called me to her bedside and with the last of her strength she put my life straight. It was like a vicious slap and a bucket of ice water dumped over me all at once. I still don't know exactly what happened. She reached out and touched my face. She told me she loved me and that I had to fix my life and start helping people instead of hurting them. There was a moment of electrical charge as her cold fingers connected with my temple. My body reacted as if it really had been shocked. When I woke up she was gone and I was slumped across her body, her hand still on my head. An outsider viewing that moment may have thought she was giving me comfort in her final moment and I had fallen asleep waiting for her to die."

White Eagle shook his head and sighed. "I suspect that she transferred her gifts to me and fully awakened mine. Suddenly I knew things I had not known before that moment. I could see her whole life from her perspective as well as my own. I knew exactly what she thought of me and what she hoped I would come to do. I knew all her magic. I have moved forward with her wishes ever since which included going to AA. She had trained twelve *spirit watchers* in her day. I found my first one the week after she died. As soon as I had one trained I would find another. I was having trouble keeping them alive for long though and then I found Miles."

He raised his chin and looked down his long nose at me, "I can sense some people's auras or perhaps the color of their soul. I don't know how to explain it. I can see the good and evil in people in colors or maybe it's the color of their intentions. I don't fully understand it myself. Apparently my grandmother didn't either. Believe me if she understood it, I would. Anyway Miles had the brightest, cleanest most beautiful aura I had ever seen until you. He reminded me of sunrise coming over the Montana Bitterroot Mountains. It almost hurts my inner eye to look at you. You are blinding like the sun reflecting off a clear mountain lake. In all my years I have never met anyone who understood what I did unless they were a mentor like me. I have only ever met two like me. No ordinary man and no *watcher* has ever recognized me 'looking' at them. I feel that I'm not worthy to train you but I'm out

57

of touch now with others like me and like you. After Miles, I just couldn't do it anymore. I shut out that world. I started dreaming of my grandmother after Miles had been gone awhile and I quit feeling so sorry for myself. She let me know that I had to get my act together. She told me you were coming. Now what do I do with you?"

We just looked at each other for a long time. I had never heard him utter so many words in one day let alone at one time. "We need Marlo. You aren't having any luck finding your friends so far, but he might. He is Shazam when it comes to computers. Trust me. I need my friends and so do you."

White Eagle fell into his chair as if all the talking had drained everything out of him. "I guess," he muttered. "I don't have a better idea. Pardon me, did you just say Shazam?"

"Um, yeah, why?"

"What is Shazam, Owen?"

"You know, really good, like the action hero from the... 70s." Now I was perplexed. How did I know that? Who knows, heard it somewhere I suppose.

I pulled out my cell and speed dialed Marlo. White Eagle put his elbows on the table and covered his face with his hands. Marlo answered on the first ring. "Hey buddy, can I talk you into coming over to Mr. White Eagle's house?"

"Wow, really? I'd love to. Let me ask Mom." I could hear his feet thumping down the stairs in the background and then a hurried conversation with his mom. He would be over in ten minutes. I passed the phone to White Eagle so he could give Marlo's mom directions. He looked like he could cry but he pulled himself together to fake good humor on the phone.

White Eagle lived near the pawnshop in a quiet neighborhood. The houses were older with big lots and people kept to themselves. His house was sparse, neat and compact. He had some really cool pen and ink drawings depicting Montana. He kept a picture of his mother and grandmother on the mantle over his fireplace. For a tiny woman, I thought his grandmother looked pretty scary. Maybe I could see her power. If she could haunt his dreams I was afraid she could haunt mine as well.

I heard the car in the driveway and walked to the front door to let Marlo in. I waved to his mom to let her know everything was ok. Marlo bounced in the door full of energy and excitement. He only made it to the kitchen before the mood in the house registered with him. "Wha...?" He turned to look at me.

"We need to talk." I crossed my arms and leaned against the doorjamb.

"Um Owen, don't you know you should never start a conversation like that? It sounds ominous." He was trying for funny but it fell a little flat.

I could tell he was scared so I tried to lighten the atmosphere. "I need to tell you something about me. I hope that no matter what, you'll still be my friend."

"Okay, now I'm kinda scared. Do I want to hear this? Oblivious is good, right?" he asked, backing up a step.

"Mar, we've been friends since kindergarten. You wouldn't be here if I didn't think you could take it. Come in and have a seat." We moved to the kitchen table. White Eagle had vacated his seat and was pretending to look busy in the kitchen. "I've been keeping something from you and I hate it. You've been asking a lot of really good questions about me and my activities. You've even helped me, but you didn't realize how much you were helping. I have reached a place where I just can't do this anymore without you." To his credit Marlo looked both scared and curious.

"Well then, spit it out," he said, showing courage.

"Remember back in September when we were all at the shop - the day I got the watch?" It seemed like as good a start as any. He nodded, saying nothing. "Well, the watch was a little more than I expected. It awakened something in me." I noticed that White

59

Eagle was drilling Marlo in the back of the head with his eyes and nodding his head so I kept going. "I can see things now that I couldn't before."

"What are you saying? Are you psychic or something?" He looked excited for a moment.

"No, but if I touch the right objects they tell me their story. I see images when I touch certain things. I can sense if someone has touched something with evil in their hearts." Marlo just stared so I went on. "Remember when you helped me with the school bully?" He moved his head in a slow nod. "Remember the boy we helped, the sixth grader? I picked up his pencil in the hall. He'd had it in his pocket when he was bullied in the bathroom. I saw it happen, the bullying that is."

"Wow," he said in awe.

"Do you remember the incident with Mrs. Lando? I picked up her handyman's hammer. That's how I knew he was going to steal from her. That's how I came to be there the night he pushed her down the stairs." He was back to the wide-eyed, open-mouthed stare. "Remember the pedophile that our coach got credit for catching? I touched the sweatshirt of the girl he was after and knew he would be at the meet. He had handled her sweatshirt." I swallowed hard at the memory, to keep back my bile. "He had smelled it. It was creepy. Dark thoughts feel like a thick, viscous and oily substance. It makes me sick." White Eagle's eyes popped up from Marlo to spear me. What? Had I said too much?

"You don't just see it? You can feel it now too?" Marlo snapped his head around at White Eagle's words. Apparently he had forgotten White Eagle was even there.

"He really is serious? I want to believe him but come on..." Marlo's body language told me he was as torn as his voice gave away. He wanted to believe but everything he had ever learned told him it couldn't be true.

White Eagle seemed to take pity on me and took up my story. "It's true. I had been waiting for him for a long time. I sensed that there was something special about him the times you boys had come in the shop but he wasn't ready yet. He was ready in September."

"He'd just had his birthday," Marlo blurted.

"Huh, I wonder? He is the youngest I've ever trained. Interesting. I shall have to ponder on this." His eyes lost focus and he looked thoughtful for a moment.

Feeling left out, I jumped back in, "So White Eagle, what do you see when you look at Marlo?"

"He shines with a pure blue light," he said with a smile. I hadn't a clue what he meant but it sure got Marlo's attention.

"What are you talking about? Mr. White Eagle can see things too?" Marlo whispered with wonder.

"He can see your intentions. He can tell that you have a good heart. I don't know what blue means but from the little I have learned pure is good." With that White Eagle actually laughed.

"I'm not sure what blue means either but you are right, my boy, this one is good for the team and just call me White Eagle, no need to be so formal, Marlo."

He stepped up to Marlo and patted him affectionately on the back. Marlo visibly relaxed. We all sat down and talked for over an hour. Marlo gave his word that he would not give any of us away. He was filled with ideas about how he could help and even vowed to work harder during sparring. It was obvious to all of us that his greatest weapon was his brain but he might need to defend himself. He agreed that when I went running he would ride his bike along to build stamina. He was motivated.

For fun I asked if I could touch some of his stuff. I already knew that Marlo's life was good. His jacket and the stuff in his pockets were almost sleepy and peaceful. No wait – blissful. Life was good, simple and pure. "The blue light means you're a good person and you hate injustice, Mar. Your family is good and they love you. I have not looked at such happy belongings before. They have nothing they need to tell me." White Eagle looked a little startled but Marlo just smiled, a happy contented smile.

"I am happy. I was worried about you. Now I know you're ok. I'm your friend and I want to help you. I just hope I don't have to face a robber." I smiled and tilted back in my chair. "You gonna tell Adrian?" he asked hopefully.

"Not yet," White Eagle and I said in unison. Marlo shrugged, then nodded.

Marlo and White Eagle discussed strategy and spreadsheets and internet searches. I tuned them out, lost in my own thoughts. I must have dozed off because next thing I knew I was falling. I landed flat on my back, chair and all, smacking my head on the floor. My friends just laughed at me. "Owen the Invincible," Marlo chortled, "you're my hero." He then laughed so hard he about fell out of his own chair.

White Eagle handed me a bag of frozen peas for my head. He tried and failed to stifle his own laugh. "Next time pay attention."

What could I say? Strategizing and planning was not my thing. I was a man of action. I couldn't stay mad at them though. We went home soon after. Marlo excitedly told his mom all about his new workout schedule so that we could spend more time together. She was still on her health kick so she bought it hook, line and sinker.

FIVE

On Wednesday Lucie was particularly cranky in science. I tried to be mellow and helpful. She exuded irritation. "Luce, what's up? You seem upset. How can I help?" She looked like she wanted to bite my head off and then thought better of it. It was clear that I was not the cause of her distress.

"No one calls me Luce, but I guess you can. You can't help. I have to take care of this." She tried to focus on science but I could tell that her mind was elsewhere.

I stopped her from leaving class when the bell rang by placing a hand on her arm. I caught a couple of images off her shirt that didn't please me. "Luce, whether or not you think I can help, at least talk to me. I promise you I am a good listener. I won't judge you. I care about you."

"Fine, I'll meet you at lunch tomorrow." She walked away with her shoulders hunched. I wondered what she would tell me. I knew her dad was still on her case. It looked like her mom was putting a lot of pressure on her too. Nothing was going right for her. Her shirt showed me that she was sad, anxious, overwhelmed, cranky and frustrated.

Deep in thought about Lucie, I rounded the corner and ran smack into a boy going the other way. I was hit with a mess of images, none of them good. "Hey, I'm sorry. I wasn't looking where I was going. Are you ok?" He looked at me half scared and half defiant. This kid wanted to be part of a group so badly that he was looking in all the wrong places. He looked like he wanted to say something but he ended up shuffling off. I'd put Marlo on this one for now. I hurried to choir, barely making it before the bell.

After school, Marlo grabbed his bike and rode while I jogged to the pawnshop. We had cut a deal to come every day after school. Our parents foolishly thought we were wonderful. I filled him in on his new project. I wanted everything he could get on both Lucie and the new kid whose name I didn't even know. Marlo figured he could hack into the school computer and find out who he was by looking at the record. I described him carefully so that he could set up his 'sort features' on his filtering program. His motto was 'why do something manually what you can have a computer do for you'. Marlo's dad is some kind of computer genius too so I had high hopes for Marlo.

I sparred a little with Marlo but it was mainly for his benefit. I could take him out in one punch. When he went to work on his laptop, I took up punching the heavy bag and worked on my kicks. White Eagle was working on my form. We were trying to add a spinning back kick to my repertoire. He also had me lifting weights and doing cardio. By six I was dragging. I would sleep good tonight. I pulled off my shirt and wiped the sweat off my face. Marlo about dropped his laptop. "Geez, have you looked at yourself lately? Do you have any body fat? I hate you."

"It's not as bad as you think. I just worked out so my muscles are standing out, I'm sweaty and it's the lighting out here." Secretly though, I was pleased with his assessment.

"I hope it's as bad as I think. If I'm the brains that means you're the brawn. You should look tough and you do. I think I found your guy by the way." I pulled on a dry shirt and tried to stand upwind from the brains so as not to offend his nose.

I looked over Marlo's shoulder at the boy's school record which included his picture. "That's him. I need his schedule and everything else you can get on him. Anything on Lucie?" I wasn't sure I wanted to know what was going on with her but she seemed like she needed a friend. A good friend and much more than the acquaintance and lab partner type I had been up until now.

"Other than every one of her grades is an A except for one B? Did you know she does gymnastics? Apparently when she was little she was amazing and they thought she might go as far as the Olympics. She got injured and she has grown too tall. There are some archived articles about her in the local paper." Marlo quickly flipped through the articles as I scanned. It looked like Lucie had been a child prodigy and then something had happened. She was pretty darn amazing as far as I was concerned but she wasn't living up to someone's expectations.

"Hey Mar, have you had any luck on finding more people like me or like White Eagle?" I asked, half hopeful and half scared.

"No Buddy, but don't give up on me. I am the computer genius and guru. I just have lots of stuff to wade through to figure out what is real and what is... well, just plain craziness. I can't let anyone know I'm searching. It's tricky. Have patience."

I got home, showered, ate dinner and started homework at my desk. I fell asleep there with my head on my science vocabulary and dreamed of Lucie. All the bits I had seen when I touched her notebook linked together with the bits that Marlo had dug up from the papers to form my dream. I stood helpless watching, my dream self standing frozen but aware and unobserved. The images of Lucie swirled around me in chronological order.

We were at a gymnastic meet of some kind where Lucie was doing an impressive floor routine. She looked flawless to me and her scores proved it. Was she even five? Her parents were clapping proudly in the stands while her brother sulked in his seat. The scene became foggy and the colors moved like drops of dye in hot water. An older Lucie was now on the balance beam. Her routine scared me with its intensity. I was sure she was going to fall and break her neck. A swirl of color and a slightly older Lucie appeared. She was getting ready to start a routine on the uneven bars. Her father was nodding at her from the sidelines. She chalked her hands and began. It all started off well and looked amazing, graceful and powerful. She was spinning faster around the bars and then looked like she was trying a flip while in a handstand on the upper bar. Her left arm shook and even I could tell she hadn't pushed off right. I couldn't open my mouth to scream or make my legs run to go save her. She crumpled in a heap on the mat like a broken doll. Her father looked angry and then quickly replaced the look with false concern. No one was moving to help her. They were all frozen but in their case it was from shock. Her coach moved first and the scene shifted. Lucie, small and broken, lay in a hospital bed. Her coach kissed her forehead and left the room. Her father walked in and looked at her leg in traction, the bandage on her forehead near the scalp and her splinted arm. Lucie's eyes were closed; she never saw the look on his face but it would haunt me forever.

Again the scene changed. I saw Lucie sweating in physical therapy, killing herself to recover quickly. My perspective shifted and I saw her father arguing with her coach through a glass window, her mother and older brother huddled off to the side looking worried yet bored. My gaze was drawn back to Lucie's father and her coach. Her coach was ripping up a check and throwing it in his face. Good for her, I thought, and again I was sent adrift in a wash of color.

I saw Lucie sitting sad and alone at a football game trying to do her homework while her parents cheered on her brother. Another shift and I saw her at home being ignored at the dinner table while both parents leaned toward the brother and seemed to be engaged in excited conversation. Lucie's father knocked something off the table. When he picked it up I saw a checkbook register. Now his attention was on Lucie. He seemed to be angry with her. Apparently there was an issue about money. No one stood up for her. She seemed small and defenseless but there was a hint of defiance in her.

Another switch and I saw Lucie looking up at the uneven bars and shaking her head. Her coach put an arm around her shoulder in concern. The scene blurred and reformed to show Lucie curled up on a couch looking less sad as she held a mug and talked with her coach. On the T.V., clips of Lucie ran. A look of fear mixed with relief crossed Lucie's face and as they continued to talk I saw a glimpse of joy.

Then one of the images from her notebook returned and I once again saw Lucie toe to toe with her father. Now the elastic bandages on her leg made more sense. She was my Lucie from eighth grade, being blamed for being too tall and having a "B". I realized that her father didn't want her to work with her coach anymore. He didn't want to spend any more money on a hopeless cause. I saw more defiance in Lucie, but she was still fearful. I saw her father raise his hand as if to strike and my body jerked in response, waking me.

Beautiful – I'd been sweating and drooling on my homework and would have to start it again. I tried some of White Eagle's calming techniques but I couldn't get Lucie out of my mind. I couldn't decide if the images of Lucie were a dream or a message. I left everything on my desk, went to brush my teeth in the now quiet house, turned out my lights and slipped into bed. Moonlight streamed softly through my window giving everything a soft silver glow. Lucie was on my mind. I wanted to help her but I didn't know how. I drifted into an uneasy sleep.

The next morning I felt tired, grumpy and unrested. I took a shower to wake up and carefully dressed for my lunchtime 'date' with Lucie. My mom noticed my mood and made sympathetic sounds. I was reminded of the complete and utter difference between her and Lucie's mom. It made me sad. Before she could ask questions I hugged her, grabbed a protein bar and headed for the bus.

On the ride to school I told Marlo about my dream. I felt the need to do it in short bursts so that no one would know what we were talking about. Marlo seemed to understand and was unusually quiet as he carefully listened with a worried look on his face. Marlo told me that he'd had a little luck with the boy at school. He had a name now at least, Jesus, and Marlo had found out that he was getting into trouble. His latest offense was smoking on the school grounds.

I made it through first period okay but by second my eyelids were heavy. My eyes were burning and scratchy. I almost nodded off in class. Thank goodness Marlo and Adrian had my back. Third and fourth periods crept by, but my mind was on Lucie and Jesus. By P.E. my stomach was completely in knots. I had no idea how I would eat.

I was torn between dragging my feet and hurrying to lunch. I looked around but I seemed to have beat Lucie. I bought a bottle of water and settled in to wait. I tried leaning against a wall but I couldn't seem to hold myself still. I tried a calming exercise, but decided I needed to pace. Maybe she wasn't coming.

One of the girls from science that Lucie had pointed out to me approached. You would have thought my scowl would have scared her off. A part of me felt bad for her because she looked both bold and awkward as she approached and I didn't even know her name.

"Hi Owen, I'm Leslie, from science." I nodded and waited. "I, um, wondered if you were going to the Valentine's dance." She said it like a question. Was she asking me to go with her? Thank goodness I wouldn't have to answer that question. I had spied Lucie heading my way.

"I don't know yet. Excuse me," I said, heading for Lucie, answering Leslie's literal question, but not the one I thought she was really asking.

Lucie grabbed my arm and headed to the cooler. She took two yogurts and two apples and dragged me back through the check-out line. She paid for her stuff and handed it all off to me, then again grabbed my arm and headed for an empty table in the corner. "Eat," she said, handing me a spoon.

"I'm not real hungry, Luce." Though, now that she was here and in a pretty good mood I didn't feel so knotted up inside.

She just gave me a look. I was slightly taken aback for a moment because I'd seen my own mom use *that* look many times. We ate in silence and pocketed our apples for later. I took our trash, dumped it and followed her out the door.

"I have to be honest, I almost ditched you. I know you want to help but I don't see how you can. The whole thing is kind of embarrassing, but you really have been awfully nice and understanding all year and I feel bad for being rude to you yesterday. I can see that you want to be my friend and I could use one." She stopped and looked at me, wondering if she had said too much.

I smiled at her to show that there were no hard feelings. "You can talk and I'll just listen. Sometimes if you say something out loud it lessens the weight of it."

"Yeah, I guess." She started to walk again and I stayed by her side. She was silent for a bit. I didn't want to scare her off so I took note of my surroundings. The sky was darkly overcast but it wasn't raining at the moment. It was chilly even with my leather jacket on so I shoved my hands into my pockets. I caught movement out of the corner of my eye. Lucie was rewrapping her royal blue scarf around her neck and pulling on knit gloves. She glanced up at me and I realized that although she looked cute in her denim jacket, the blue of her scarf made her eyes the darkest blue I had ever seen. A few tendrils of hair had escaped her ponytail and blew enticingly around her face. This girl did powerful things to me. I was so distracted that I almost missed it when she began to speak.

"It's like letting a piece of myself go. I know its eating a hole in me but I'm afraid to let it out." She sighed as if she wasn't sure where or how to begin.

"It's okay Luce, I can take it," I said, bumping her shoulder with my arm.

We walked on for a few steps before she began. "I used to be special." I sensed that I should say nothing, although I wanted to let her know that I at least knew she was still special. "I was the favorite or the family pet depending on how you look at it. I was almost like a toy doll… you know, dress her, wind her up and watch her perform. It all got to be too much. I went from school, to online school to home schooling as I had less and less time for school and homework. I had nearly constant practices and the pressure was excruciating. 'Pressure makes diamonds, Lucie Beth, and you are becoming a diamond,' my dad would say. Instead of becoming a diamond, I was crushed by the weight of it. One day it was all too much. I didn't have time to eat, I was short of sleep and I needed to perform perfectly but there was nothing left in me. I was on the uneven bars doing a tricky move and my hand slipped. I lost it on the top bar and fell, hitting the apparatus on the way down. I broke my leg, split open my head and twisted up my wrist, elbow and shoulder. I tweaked my back pretty good too. Instead of sympathy, I heard all about the money that had been invested in me. I was a failed investment. Now my only chance of a really great scholarship is an academic one, so my grades are a huge deal. My grades didn't used to be as good as they are now because I never had time to study. It has been made clear to me that I am the family failure." Seeing the look on my face she stopped and put a hand on my arm.

"But, Luce…" I started.

"You know what? I'm relieved. My brother is the main focus now. He's a junior with an Ivy League future. He does it all: 4.0 GPA, football, basketball and baseball with total focus. He loves the attention. He's already getting looked at by scouts. I have a 'B' in L.A. right now and I could care less, but with my athletic scholarship potential gone… it's all about grades. I'm done being a performing monkey. I don't even know why they had kids. I don't ever want to be like them. I know they love me in their own way but it's not normal love – they just don't know how. My coach loved me. She became like real family to me. Once I completed physical therapy she still tried to work with me. My parents saw that I had lost it but she didn't give up. She even worked without pay after my parents gave up on me. After awhile my coach and I agreed that I didn't want it anymore. I had lost my edge. We parted on good terms. I help her sometimes with the little kids. It's just to see her and have some fun. We do camps in the summer and I love that." She had taken on a happy glow like I had glimpsed in my dream. It reminded me now of the sun breaking through the clouds. "Our last argument was about that. I won't be allowed to work at summer camp this year if I don't keep a 4.0 GPA. His words were, 'You can't play and waste your time at that stupid camp for underachievers if you don't keep a four point.' It's so frustrating." Lucie stopped walking and I took two steps before I realized it. She looked at me, embarrassed.

"Luce, don't. You already look like you're sorry you told me. Close your eyes and take a deep breath." Reluctantly she complied. "Feel better?"

"I don't know, I've never told anyone all that stuff. Now I wonder what you think of me." She had started out looking at me but by the end of the thought she was looking at the ground.

"Luce, I think you're brave and pretty wonderful. You are smart and funny when you want to be. I like being around you and I'll be here any time you want to talk. I'm your friend."

I could tell that she was both pleased and disappointed by what I had said. I just wanted to see her smile again.

"Don't tell anyone about... you know. I don't need any more grief."

"I know what you mean." Did I really just let that slip out? She gave me a speculative look.

"Tell me something about you," she demanded.

"What do you mean? What you see is what you get."

"Come on, you're so quiet most of the time. What goes on in that brain of yours?"

"I guess I just like listening more than talking."

"And?"

"And, I dunno, I don't like the spotlight. I like to fly under the radar."

"And?"

71

"And, I have two younger brothers who do most of the talking at our house so why should I fight to say anything? It's not worth the energy."

"And?"

"I love to skateboard."

"Why?"

"It feels as close to flying as I can get right now. I want a motorcycle but my mom thinks it's too dangerous."

"What do you do after school?"

"I go to the pawnshop that Adrian's uncle owns and do a little work. I also do a little boxing and karate with one of his employees. I guess you could say he's my coach. I run three or more times a week and do homework and chores like everybody else."

"You most certainly are not like everybody else. Did you start the boxing and stuff this school year?"

"Yeah, why?"

"Remember before break I mentioned how you'd changed this year?" I nodded and she continued. "Well, you are different."

"Is that a bad thing?"

"I don't think so but I'll withhold judgment for now," she said with a laugh as the bell rang for us to head to class. We walked all the way to science together. She scooted her stool over and sat right next to me, hip to hip and knee to knee. I admit it. I totally loved it. At the end of class Lucie put her head to my shoulder for a moment and whispered, "Thanks for earlier."

"I'm here for you, Luce," I said as she picked up her stuff and headed for the door. I have no idea what happened in choir or how I got there.

Marlo brought me back to reality on the bus. A girl in math class had asked him to the Valentine's dance and he had said yes. I got to hear *all* about it on the way home.

The next day at the pawnshop the guys let me know that they wanted a little girlfriend time and would not be at the shop every day. It felt like a conspiracy. They both promised to keep watching Jesus and they would activate the social network to spy on him in most of his classes. Marlo had his class schedule and the two of them worked out which of our friends was in a class with him.

White Eagle approved of having the guys around less as it meant more time for us to work on my gifts and fighting one on one. The days when the guys were there, workouts were more fun and light-hearted. We joked, laughed, wrestled, boxed, practiced karate and worked with some padded 'knives' and sticks.

SIX

I found a surprising ally in my brother Alex one evening as we were out throwing balls for our dogs, Buddy our ancient Basset, and Beggar our younger Lhasa Apso. He had been rattling on about school and his friends. I was listening with half an ear until he mentioned, of all people, Jesus. "What?" I turned, startled.

"I was talking about my friend Cory who lives in the apartments by the mall. Mom let me play over there after school. Cory's mom took us to the mall to see their next door neighbor. She works at that clothing store where all the teenagers shop. Anyway she just seemed like a teenager herself and shouldn't be a mom yet but Cory's mom was kinda mad about something her kid had done to Cory." I reached over and touched Alex's shirt as he spoke. I could see the mall, Cory, his mom and a young woman. Cory's mom was worried about him. Looking at the young woman I knew she had to be Jesus' sister and not his mother. They looked so similar. She was worried about Jesus too. "Anyway I just thought it was weird was all," he continued.

"Hey Al, keep me posted on the Jesus thing would you? Big kids shouldn't pick on younger kids. Okay?"

"Yeah, okay. Hey, you think it will snow?" he asked, excited about the weather.

"Maybe, though it only happens about every other year or so around here. We'll see," I said with a smile as I ruffled his hair. "Let's take the dogs in. I've got homework."

February was almost half over. Adrian and Marlo had girlfriends and Valentine plans. They were going on a double date to a movie. They wanted me to find a girl and come along but I wasn't up for it. I thought about Lucie but if she didn't already have a date she would soon enough and I was no good for her. Lucie looked at me like I was the dumbest kid in eighth grade all the way up to the day before the dance. I was pretty sure she was hoping I would ask her yet she never asked me. Between Marlo and Adrian's happiness and Lucie's attitude, I just couldn't stand it all anymore.

I went to the shop on Valentine's Day. I didn't have a girlfriend to impress and I certainly had no plans. I was focusing on some new items that had come in to the pawnshop when I got an interesting hit. I found a mess of items that I could *see* had been stolen and brought into the shop. I was getting all kinds of images off them. I would need Marlo's help to catalog all of them and I needed to figure out who had brought them in. White Eagle could help me with the paperwork. I jumped when Adrian tapped me on the shoulder. "What are you doing?"

"Some inventory stuff for White Eagle," I grumbled, slipping the stuff back into the box and stashing it away for later when I was alone.

"Oh cool. I was thinking I might have Kelly come one of these days so she can watch us spar. Ooh, maybe I will call her right now. You don't mind, right? You like Kelly. Everyone does. Hey, maybe Marlo can come and bring April. We were gonna meet up with them at six to grab a bite at the mall and see the seven o'clock show. I wish you'd ask a girl out."

Adrian just kept rattling on, not realizing that he was stepping on my last nerve. "How about if we just spar now? Then you can get home and shower for your big date."

"Sure, ok. Kelly can come another time."

"Great." He was *so* not getting it. I was dreaming of putting a fist in his face. I was *so* not in the mood to talk about girls and dates today. In addition, he was interrupting my work. We quickly changed our clothes in the bathroom off the shop and got ready. I felt angry so I was looking forward to taking out my aggression fighting. I knew that White Eagle would not be pleased but I had so much building

75

up inside that I had to let it go somewhere. I let the rage fill me and came at Adrian like I never had before. He looked startled and backpedaled quickly. I chased him all over the mat.

"Geez man, what is with you?" he gasped.

I didn't even speak - I just came at him again. He finally started defending himself but he couldn't land any good hits. I don't remember a time when I've fought harder. All that anger and frustration came together in a chemical mix of adrenaline and power. Adrian couldn't touch me. I hammered on him again and again.

"OWEN! Stop it!" I turned my head to look at White Eagle and Adrian popped me a good one. Blood spurted from my nose and splashed on my shirt. "We're done here for today. Get cleaned up and go home, Adrian. I want to talk to the avenger here." He threw me a rag for my nose and jerked his head toward Adrian whose back was turned.

"Sorry Adrian, I was mad and I took it out on you." I knew better but it had sure felt good at the time. He could have a normal life. I never would again. He could have a girlfriend and he didn't understand why I didn't. I didn't even feel like I could go on a simple date. I looked down at my feet knowing it wasn't his fault, it was mine. I was glad that he had been wearing full protective gear today.

I felt ashamed. White Eagle put an ice pack on the back of my neck. "Put some pressure above your upper lip under your nose. You can't lose focus like that, Owen. I take that back, you were quite 'focused' in a very bad way. I know you have a lot going on inside. Next time let's talk. It would be terrible if you let this happen at home or at school."

I nodded once, feeling worse, but I met his eyes. He still held the ice pack to the back of my neck. "Now let's look at that nose. Move your hand away from your face. You'll be fine. You just popped a blood vessel. Be careful for a day or two until it heals all the way. Today's lesson will be about calming yourself. Go get cleaned up and put your watch back on. I think Miles has a story to tell you." He took the ice pack, placed it back in the freezer and found something to tinker with on one of the workshop's bordering tables.

I took a long look around. The workshop had changed much since I had first stepped behind the curtain to see it. It really was a couple of bays and a half. They could have pulled a large truck in here and still had room to work on it with the tail gate down and all the doors open. The edges were completely ringed with workbenches, stools, shelves and drawers. The middle was currently taken up with all our workout gear salvaged from the pawnshop itself. Adrian's uncle and White Eagle had been very generous. We had thick mats on the floor, a heavy bag hanging near the corner, gloves and other fight gear and pads. We even had a weight bench now. A new addition was a rack of wooden practice blades wrapped in special foam. White Eagle caught my eye again and did the head jerk thing toward Adrian who was just walking out of the bathroom. "I wanted to apologize again, Adrian. Your family has done a lot for me and so have you. I... I was wrong. If I was going to snap, I'm really glad it was you. Imagine if I would have snapped at Marlo or a kid at school."

"It's ok, Dude. You're getting kinda mean though. Tough, I mean. Nobody better mess with you, right? I don't know why you worried about Marlo though; he'd just chuck his computer at your head!" We both laughed and it felt good.

After I had showered in the small bathroom off the workshop and Adrian was off, White Eagle put some instrumental music on the stereo that had also come from the pawnshop. His choice was soft jazz and it was quieting. He had me sit on the mat and close my eyes. I invited Miles to talk to me. The images that filled my mind were vivid like my own recent memories. He had a much bigger anger problem than I did. His outlet of choice was a boxing ring somewhere. Sometimes when a guy was down, he had trouble stopping, which created a bad reputation for him.

The image changed and I could see him dancing with a beautiful woman. The scene was almost painful to watch but my eyes were already closed so I couldn't shut it out. The power of their love was humbling and it made me feel all the more like an intruder. It was different with my parents. They were more like a team, their love was soft and warm like a well-loved quilt or an old teddy bear. Instead of soft and warm this love burned with an intensity that almost bordered on obsession. The feelings crashed into me like being blasted with a fire hose, almost physically knocking me back.

The scene changed again. Miles was holding her limp body in his arms. Guilt and anguish were so strong that tears leaked from my own eyes. The view changed to a cemetery and then I saw Miles standing in front of her grave marker. The scene changed again to show Miles standing side by side with White Eagle on a cliff overlooking the ocean. The grief had mellowed some but the guilt was still strong. I wished I could hear the words that were spoken. White Eagle put an arm around Miles' shoulders and Miles turned to hug his friend and sob. White Eagle was all that kept him from jumping off the cliff I was sure. That and the need for... revenge. Miles wanted revenge and justice. The last scene I saw was White Eagle holding the watch and looking down at two gravestones: thirty four year old Miles almost to the day and... hold on... Miles' wife Melissa and an unborn son. A sob escaped, ripped from my throat.

The image broke as White Eagle put his arms around me much as he had Miles. I sucked in a ragged breath and scrubbed the tears from my face. "He showed you the end." It was a statement not a question. "Miles would want you to know that he would not change a thing. Melissa was the best thing that ever happened to him. She was his light in the darkness. He didn't have a lot of friends besides Mel and me. He let his rage and desire for revenge ruin him. Don't you do that to yourself. Love others and accept what happens." He waited for me to regain my composure. "Now we practice peace. I don't want the anger to own you."

He had me get up and slowly stretch with him. It was almost like yoga. He asked me to quiet my mind. I was to picture a glass of water and pour it out. The water was to represent my problems, worries and thoughts. He told me I could pick my own image if something else came to mind that worked better. Then we moved into a type of Tai Chi, a slow martial art meant for concentration. The skill to focus on was slow movement with perfect form. "Peace needs to become a well within you. Picture a vessel to hold peace within you if you need to. Then when you need it you can draw some out. Use calming moments to refill your vessel. They can be small moments, even one breath. I like to look at nature. When the weather improves we will go dry camping away from people and I will show you."

Now that my head was clear the box under the counter came back to me. "Hey, I was going through a box before you got here. The stuff was stolen. I got a ton of hits. Can you help me with it? There was so much that I think it would be best if Marlo catalogs it all for me."

"Ya, sure." We walked up front. The shop was dark and the sign was flipped. Adrian's Uncle Max must have left. I walked to where I was sitting when Adrian had come in. I searched frantically not believing my eyes. The box was gone.

"It's gone. What does this mean?" I asked concerned.

"I don't know, but I will look into it. Let's get you home," he replied stiffly.

When I got to the shop the next day the atmosphere was tense. Neither Max nor White Eagle seemed to be speaking to each other. White Eagle shoved a broom into my hands and told me gruffly to sweep and dust and then come work out. Neither Adrian nor Marlo showed up. I'd put money on the women in their lives keeping them busy. Max said nothing to me while I worked and then hotfooted it out the door right at five pm flipping the sign to 'closed'. He looked like he couldn't wait to leave.

White Eagle gave me the workout of my life. I was drenched with sweat when we finished. He seemed disappointed with my performance and told me I needed to eat better and put on some weight. He had said nothing about the box and I was almost afraid to ask. Finally on the way home he loosened up enough to tell me that

Max had resold it without inventorying it, a big no no, and an argument had ensued. Something was up.

I got out of the car thanking White Eagle. He still seemed worried and uptight. The sky was the gray-black of evening, a few flashes of sunset peeking through the heavy clouds. Lightening came darting in from the west. The soft yellow flashes behind the clouds brought the image of angels snapping flash pictures. It brought a smile to my lips. The thunder was still so far away that it was muted. Occasionally a brighter flash would throw the fir trees into relief like silhouettes cut from black felt. It was such a beautiful scene that I couldn't tear my eyes away. Mother Nature was putting on a free show; it seemed like a disservice not to stay and enjoy it. The night touched my skin softly in a feather-light caress. It made me think of Lucie but then many things do. I was stealing a Zen moment like White Eagle had just taught me. I had to balance the bad moments with these moments so that I could call upon the good memories when I needed to calm myself. Lucie wasn't always the best focus because sometimes I found her extremely frustrating but this moment would be a good one. I took a deep cleansing breath and then another. Peace, calm and inner strength.

I walked up to the house lost in thought yet aware of my surroundings as I had come to be most of the time. Sometimes images were strong enough that I would get distracted, but I tried to always be aware of what was happening around me. The family SUV was not in the driveway.

The front door was unlocked so I moved in stealth mode. I noticed right away that the house was unusually silent. I paused in the entryway and listened. I heard the soft rustle of paper coming from the living room. My mom was curled up in her favorite chair with a book. She was wrapped in a sweatshirt and hugged a pillow from the couch. She looked up, startled, sensing my presence. Her whole face lit up when she saw me, like I was the best present she had ever received for Christmas. "How was your day?" she asked with genuine interest.

"Not bad, I just had the workout of my life though. Where is everybody and can I grab a bite before we chat?"

She flashed me another smile and sprang from her chair. She quickly marked her spot and dragged me into the kitchen. "The horde has gone to an Imax movie. I don't expect them until nine. I went to the store today and bought you some protein bars to keep in your backpack and I bought fresh hamburger. You aren't eating enough. You look like there isn't any fat left on you." I wondered fleetingly if she had been talking to White Eagle or if he had sent her a mental note. Who knew with these two?

My mom threw two burgers on the electric grill and got out all the stuff to go with them. "How are your classes? Your grades are looking really good. Did you know you have 99% in science? I am so proud of you. I was so worried at the beginning of the year and now look at you. I think Mr. White Eagle has been good for you."

"You have no idea," I said with a smile. "How come you didn't go to the movie?"

"For one, I wanted to spend a little time with you. We don't have much time for each other these days and..." she lowered her voice like she was sharing a secret, "Imax makes me motion sick." She smiled and winked and we both laughed. It was true. She could be on a floating bridge and feel the motion. "You know, Owen, it's so good to see you laugh. You've seemed even more serious than usual lately. I feel like you're worrying about things. How can I help?"

I struggled with what I could tell her. What should I tell her? "Well, I had a... productive conversation with Lucie at lunchtime."

"*The Lucie*, Lucie Ness from sixth grade? Or should I call her Lucie, the fallen angel?"

"Fallen angel? What do you mean?"

"That's what the papers called her when her gymnastics dream died. It about broke my heart. She seems like a really sweet kid. I'm sure it's for the best though, that kind of life has so much pressure."

81

"She talked about the pressure. She's glad to be done but her folks are real disappointed. They think she let them down. Now it's all about her grades. She doesn't want me to talk about it though."

"She wouldn't. She was never in it for the spotlight. She just seemed to really love it. Then she fell and it all ended. It's too bad about the pressure from her folks. I'm sure she will be successful with whatever she chooses to do. That fire in her belly wouldn't have died just because her gymnastic dream is over. So what's up? Are you going to ask her out?"

"I really like her but I guess I'm not ready to do that. I wish she would just wait for me. I'm afraid that if she's my girlfriend now we might not even be able to be friends later and I don't want to lose that. It has taken me almost two years to even get up the nerve to talk to her."

"Just go for it. Remember to be friends first though. Exit gracefully and you could still be friends in the end or ask someone else you like and see if you still feel the same about Lucie. This will sound way off topic but bear with me. When you were little you loved sticks. You always wanted to pick them up and swing them around. Maybe you were part pirate. Anyway, one day you weren't careful and you walloped me a good one. I was angry and took the stick away. We forgave each other in about five minutes and you found another one. You had to keep trying sticks until you found the right one I guess. Either that or little boys just have a great affinity for sticks! Your brother Lucas got me today with one on the way home from Kindergarten. It reminded me of you. You've come a long way. Keep looking for the right stick or girl as the case may be. Don't settle. While you are finding the right stick, swing it around a bit and have some fun. That sounded a little wrong somehow but you know what I mean and don't wallop your mother!" With that she rolled up her pant leg to show me a beautifully blue bruise. "Yours was bigger!" We laughed again. "You know, Owen, you shouldn't be afraid to get hurt. As humans we hurt each other on purpose and by mistake. It's all part of life and helps us learn and grow."

"I guess it just made me feel really sad and helpless to hear Lucie's story from her perspective. I felt such a contrast between her family and ours. I want to help her but I don't know how."

"For now, be her friend and a good listener. I bet all this will work itself out. I know that whatever you choose to do will be right. When you do something you do it with your whole heart. You have a strong sense of right and wrong. You want things to be fair and equal. You have always fought for the underdog. It's just one of the many things I love about you." I felt surprised by her words. It was true that she had a reputation for walking into a room and knowing who was guilty but did she know about me and my secret?

"What? You have the strangest look on your face."

"I guess I just haven't thought of myself that way." She looked at me like she was pretty sure that wasn't what I was really thinking. Could she read my mind?

"You need to work on your poker face. No, I can't read your mind. I just know how your mind works; I am your mother after all. I've been dealing with you for over fourteen years now. Besides, your body language says... guilty. What are you guilty of?"

"Nothing important. Can we talk about it later? Please? I have homework and I'm tired." Did I really just play the homework card? I didn't even have any.

"Tell me when you're ready. Just stay out of trouble. I'm here for you."

I avoided her as much as I could over the next few days. My mom could just see way too much. I even managed another overnight at Marlo's. While I was there we compiled our information on Jesus. The old social network was working decently to track his movements. Kids don't like bullies or bad guys. Marlo's family seemed to be oblivious to his new activities with me so we talked about how to outsmart my mom. Good luck on that, we decided. We even discussed her advice on love. Should I ask Lucie out or the girl who asked me to the dance? What was her name? Lana, Lilly, Lori... no, Leslie.

After thinking about Leslie from science for about thirty seconds and listening to Marlo talk about his girlfriend, April, I decided that I was no longer objective when it came to Lucie. I had thought of her as beautiful for so long that all others paled by comparison or perhaps I was just comparing all others to her. I had liked her since sixth grade but now I was afraid to get close.

Lucie kept trying to be nice but she seemed almost frustrated by me. She didn't ask me out and I couldn't bring myself to ask her. So we stayed in our odd 'friends but wanting to be more' limbo. As much as I wanted to be near her it was a relief to go to the pawn-shop and work out. Sweat seemed to remove Lucie from my mind like nothing else could. Running gave me unwanted thinking time but sparring kept my mind busy.

I was sitting at the counter in the pawnshop holding down the fort for White Eagle as he finishing a repair on a chain saw. If anyone came in and needed help, I was to call him. Max had left to run some errands. I enjoyed the quiet and used the time to sweep, dust and organize the items in the shop. The jingle of the bell snapped my head up.

A short heavyset man was coming through the door of the shop. His beer gut drooped over his belt and hung out below his t-shirt. He wore mirrored sunglasses. His hair had a greasy, messy look to it. His beard and sideburns were in need of a trim. His skin was pockmarked. There was something about him that felt... wrong. He looked around the shop completely overlooking me. It wasn't that he didn't see me, just that he completely discounted my existence. He grunted and finally looked at me. "Max here?"

I did not like this guy. Something distasteful was rolling off him in waves and I don't mean his smell which wasn't good either. "He's out. I can take a message or have Mr. White Eagle come up front."

"Huh," he grunted and turned and started for the door. As an afterthought he turned back. "Remind him Clive doesn't like to wait." If he could have slammed the door he would have, I was sure.

I stood there for a moment processing what I had just witnessed. He was familiar somehow. As I pondered, White Eagle stepped out from behind the curtain. "What's up? I thought I heard the bell."

"You did but he left. A guy named Clive was looking for Max," I said, still trying to figure out how I knew the guy.

"Clive? You sure that's the name?" I nodded. "Huh, never heard of him. That's odd." White Eagle disappeared behind the curtain and I went back to work.

Uncle Max showed up with Adrian at five. The guys had slacked off coming to the shop because it was more fun to hang with their girlfriends. They only came in a couple of times a week now. Adrian was having a blast stalking Jesus though. We were still gathering data and figuring out what to do about him. It was scary how often he would escape us. Adrian was now a man on a mission; he had to know where Jesus went when he disappeared. Apparently that was one of tonight's missions. Adrian had had his uncle pick him up at school and they followed Jesus' bus home to see exactly where he lived even though we had his address from his school records.

I gave Max his message. His facial expressions changed rapidly from irritation to fear and back to irritation. He stepped outside and got right on his cell phone. I watched him through the glass of the shop's front door. His body language was both fearful and angry.

Jesus definitely lived at the address that Marlo had gotten from his school record. His guardian seemed to be his sister though that fact could not be confirmed or denied at this point since school records aren't always perfect or up-to-date. Adrian and Max had watched the apartment but saw nothing and did not want to look suspicious. Marlo was tracking down the sister's work phone number to see for sure where she worked. Adrian was just finishing his report when he was interrupted by his uncle's raised voice. Neither of us could make out the words but the body language was clear. He was upset. He jabbed his finger at his phone shutting it off and stomped back into the shop, nearly cracking the glass in the front door.

"Adrian, we gotta go. Now." Adrian looked at me, shrugged and walked out behind his uncle.

I finished up my chores at the shop and White Eagle and I headed for home. I was slumped down in the passenger seat gazing at the rain beading on the window when it hit me. "Ugh. That's it. White Eagle, the guy that came in the shop today looked familiar. I couldn't figure out where I'd seen him before. It's the guy I *saw* when I had that strange box of stuff. It was him in the images. The box felt terrible, the blackest, thickest, oiliest stuff I have touched yet and that guy Clive has something to do with it! You know I was touching that awful stuff right before Adrian came in. What does Uncle Max have to do with this? It's that same box that disappeared."

"Other than suddenly taking in things that he can't prove the origin of and reselling some of them before they are put in our inventory? I don't know. Something doesn't feel right to me either. Max has always been friendly and open with me. He has always been honest. We've been a great team up to now but he won't talk about this. I'm really worried. Be at the shop as much as you can. I've never seen Clive. I bet he knows to avoid me but *you* he will not know he needs to worry about."

White Eagle was right again. Clive was back on Saturday. White Eagle had left to run some errands. All I had to do was find a way to touch Clive and if I got really lucky, get my hands on his stuff. I played dumb and hoped that Clive and Max would treat me like lots of folks treat wait staff and cleaning crews, invisible. I swept the floor and eavesdropped shamelessly. They were arguing, it was clear, but they were keeping their voices low and being cryptic. It was clear to me that this was not the last load. What did he have on Max? Max really didn't want to do this but he had to. Why?

Clive kept half an eye on me every time I got within about ten feet of him with the broom so I switched to dusting. I tried to get really close but he seemed to sense me behind him and turned to give me a foul look when I was about five feet away. I dropped my eyes quickly so that he couldn't read my anger until I could get it and the other emotions pounding at me under control. This was not Max's idea at all I was sure. This guy had something on him. He was making him launder loot, but how and why? It was all there in the body language and the flow of power between them.

Damn. My next ploy was to start moving stuff around the shop. Max didn't seem to mind my presence at all. Clive, looking disgusted, shoved a box at Max, took a wad of bills off the counter and turned to walk away. I purposely dumped what I was holding right in front of him. I couldn't have even told you what was in my hands until the glass shattered all over the floor. I reached out to touch his arm as I squeaked, "I'm so sorry, let me get that." I tried to sound and look as weak and inconsequential as I could.

Success. I touched his jacket for a brief moment. I got one visually loud and ugly image. His jacket had more to tell me but I was out of time. Clive smacked my hand away and shoved me into a display case. My elbow smacked the corner and a strange mix of tingles, pain and numbness shot up my arm. I didn't resist his shove as now was not the time. "Hey!" Max yelped, appalled. "What are you doing? Leave the kid alone."

"I'd be careful if I were you." Clive smiled a sickening smile as he pointed his finger at Max and made a shooting motion. He laughed a slightly unhinged laugh and sauntered out the door.

Max was white-faced and rigid, though from anger or fear I wasn't sure. Where was White Eagle when I needed him? "Do you want to talk about it?" I asked Max.

"Absolutely not. Stay away from him, you hear me? Clean this up and watch the register for a moment," Max said somewhat unsteadily as he grabbed the box and headed for the back area.

I gave him a brief head start and then followed him to the curtain. It wasn't quite closed. I peeked through. Max was headed out the back door. I zipped through the workshop and peeked out the window. He was putting the box in his trunk. I zipped back to work as he shut the lid. By the time he returned I had most of the glass bowl that I had dropped cleaned up. I worked silently as Max pulled out the ledger and began writing like mad. I straightened the display case that I had crashed into. I spied a slip of paper under the edge and quickly pocketed it. Then I began straightening the contents as I glanced at Max who was still deep in the ledger.

"If there's nothing else I can do for you here, I'll be out in the workshop."

"Yeah, sure," he said without enthusiasm.

I fingered the paper in my pocket. Yep, it was Clive's all right. It didn't have much to tell me but then this was turning out to be my most difficult puzzle yet. I needed to be patient. I also needed Marlo to do some recording of information. He would be in on Tuesday or better yet maybe I'd see if he could squeeze me in tonight or tomorrow.

I put on my workout gear and lifted some weights, jumped rope and hit the speed bag. White Eagle still wasn't back so I punched and kicked at the heavy bag and then moved onto our Wing Chung dummy. I needed Lucie to teach me gymnastics. My front kicks and side kicks were pretty good. My back kicks needed some work and my spinning kicks and tumbling sucked. I finished with some Tai Chi. I had been at it for two hours. I was starving and White Eagle still wasn't back. I was taking a protein shake from the fridge we kept out back when White Eagle finally made his appearance through the back door.

He took one look at me slurping my shake as I leaning against the fridge and stopped in his tracks, cocking his head to the side. "Hmmm," he whispered. "I thought so."

"I need you to pick a lock. You haven't taught me how to do that yet," I mouthed at him. He nodded once. "Max's trunk," I mouthed again. One more nod and he was gone.

I wandered up front to keep Max busy. There was no need. He was still playing with the ledger and looking at the computer screen. I picked up my trusty broom and started sweeping again. "I think the floor has had more than enough attention today, but you could clean the glass on the front door and the windows," Max said without looking up.

Okey dokey then. I put the broom away and got out the glass cleaning stuff. I cleaned the inside and pushed the handle to go out and got another hit on Mr. Creepy Clive. What an idiot. He had touched the door. Most surfaces had nothing to say to me but Clive had to be about the purest evil I had yet encountered and that would leave a mark. The man was clearly insane and needed medication. He was mean, selfish and an emotional deviant. He held no remorse and had no empathy. The door only held clues to his personality and character, nothing else.

I was just finishing the last window when White Eagle pushed through the curtain. "Owen, go eat. I bought you a burger."

I gave him an odd look but nodded and put away my cleaning supplies. White Eagle began bustling around the shop as I headed to the back. The box was on the workbench with a digital camera next to it. A quickly scribbled note read, "Hurry, get the job done then put this back. I bet you have fifteen minutes tops."

I snatched up the camera, suppressed the flash and took a shot of the box. I opened the lid and took out each item and laid them out in order of removal. I quickly snapped a picture of each item and then replaced each one in reverse order taking a moment to get an image or two off of each one. I hid the camera behind some cans of paint and took the box to the car. The trunk looked closed but was slightly ajar. I put the box back the way I remembered Max setting it and gently closed the lid.

I had a lot to process. Yikes. I took the memory chip out of the camera, took a quick look around to make sure everything was back where it belonged and told White Eagle and Max good bye. Still in my workout gear I ran home, my duffel slung over my back. The run did me good and cleared my head.

The minute I got home I was hit up to do some chores with the family. I had a really hard time holding it together. Didn't they know I had more important things to do? Nope, they didn't, so I would have to suck it up and help out. We cleaned the garage so my Dad could pull the car in to take the snow tires off and then helped to put the regular tires back on our small sedan. Thank goodness the SUV had four-wheel drive and he hadn't put the snow tires on it this year. Poor Alex, no snow for him.

I gratefully crawled into the shower. I stood under the hot blast for quite awhile trying to get the ache out of my muscles. I barely dried myself, wrapped the towel around my waist and headed for my room. I looked around and realized that I was never home enough anymore to even make a mess in here except for my overflowing laundry hamper. I tossed the damp towel on top, quickly dressed, slipped my cell into my pocket, took the hamper and headed for the laundry room.

I checked my pockets and threw in a load. All I found was the scrap of paper from earlier and a few gum wrappers. The gum wrappers went into the trash, the scrap of paper turned out to be times and dates followed by initials. I could see Clive holding the scrap and gesturing to another man. These were upcoming robberies I suspected, but where? What were the letters for? I texted Marlo, "Need 2 C U ASAP." Then I wandered into the kitchen and opened the fridge.

"What are you doing?" my mom asked, like she already knew the answer.

I peered over the fridge door at her. "Rummaging for food." Did she really want that question answered?

"Well stop. Your dad went to get chicken. He should be back soon. He's getting a whole bucket so you won't starve." She moved toward me as I closed the door to the fridge and gave me a hard look. She reached out and grabbed ahold of the hem of my shirt and lifted it up. "I take it back, you are starving. I'm a bad parent," she said with remorse.

She was serious. "Wait Mom, no, I'm fine. I have actually put on five pounds and I'm still about as tall as I was last time you measured me. It's okay. Besides, my other mother, Marlo, is tracking what I eat and the calories I'm burning. I want to play football in the fall so I'm just getting in shape."

She still looked a little worried but let it go. "You ready to talk yet?"

"Mom, I'm fine, I'm a teenager. I don't tell you everything anymore. It's normal." I tried to look all grown up and serious but she laughed.

"Okay, Bud. Go round up your brothers and pick a game. It's time to hang with the family." Great, I needed to see Marlo, but these guys were important too.

My phone vibrated as I headed for the sounds of thumping and bumping coming from upstairs. Marlo had a date tonight with April but could see me tomorrow. Super, I thought with sarcasm. Family game night here I come. Whoopee! My brothers' room was a total disaster. I looked at it with new eyes; old eyes. I now saw it with new wisdom. I had become old. Making a mess meant that you had more to clean up and it was harder to find what you needed.

"Hey guys. It's almost time for dinner. Dad's getting chicken. Let's clean this up before you give Mom a heart attack." Their cheers over the chicken quickly disintegrated into groans over cleaning. I tried to make a game out of it, but I just wasn't as good at this stuff as Mom was. She hadn't been a kindergarten teacher for nothing. We got the worst of it before I heard the car door slam announcing Dad's arrival. "Come on guys, let's go. At least Mom won't cry when she sees your room." They laughed and hooted happily as they ran for the stairs. I shook my head and smiled.

Amid the happy conversation at the dinner table, I had eaten the equivalent of a whole chicken and a ton of sides. My mom looked relieved. Alex's mouth hung open when he caught sight of my chicken bone pile. His mouth was half full of partially chewed chicken, the leg bone dangling from his nerveless fingers. Dad looked at Alex and then at me with a mix of disgust and envy.

"What?" I asked, bewildered.

Lucas giggled, "You're a pig!" He snorted and laughed harder. I just smiled at him indulgently.

"I was hungry and besides I need to bulk up to play football in the fall," I winked at him.

"Yes! Finally!" My dad looked happier than I had seen him look in a long time. "I love football," he exclaimed. As if that was news to any of us. "Football's good for you, builds character. I played football." He had a happy glow about him. I sensed a rare story was about to break loose out of his usual quiet reserve. "I'll never forget my senior year. It was the homecoming game. I tackled twelve guys. It's the perfect way to hit guys without really hurting them, most of the time anyway. It's a great way to burn out your aggression." He paused with a dreamy look on his face. "At least you have hair to pad your helmet." I had let the top grow some but still kept it pretty short because it was less to deal with. "I started losing my hair about then," he said, running a hand over his receding hairline. "Do you think my head is growing or is my hair shrinking?"

"No, Dad, it's your mind that's going," I said with a laugh and we all joined in. I slept without the dreams that frequently plagued my sleep. Maybe a little family time really *was* good for me.

SEVEN

Sunday dawned bright and clear with a layer of frost on the ground and a hint of snow. Please Dad, don't put the snow tires back on! By the time Marlo called it had all melted. Marlo brought over his laptop and we hid in my room most of the day uploading pictures and entering information on each item for a spread sheet. It was helpful but boring to compile all the information. He was really worried and felt we needed to bring in Adrian. Not yet, I insisted, even though I was pretty sure that Clive was not working alone. I thought I could handle two; besides the goal was to do this stuff without fighting.

Marlo suggested that we watch for Clive to show up at the shop again so that we could get a plate. His next mission was to hack the DMV. Oh boy. I hoped he was as good as I thought he was at this stuff. What would we do if he ever got caught?

On Monday Lucie was sitting hip to hip with me again. She said little during science; she just seemed to need my presence. It was almost like she was trying to absorb some warmth and quiet friendship from my body. She seemed melancholy today. I wished that I could put my arm around her. I settled for doing most of the work in science and talking to her quietly. Many other kids had been reassigned seats but we made such a good team our teacher left us alone. We still had the highest scores in class and we rarely interrupted. Whoever sat at our lab group did well too.

"Are you okay?" I whispered when we were turned loose to work on our lab.

Lucie scooted slightly closer so I rested my hand on the back of her stool, almost but not quiet touching her. "It's nothing. I'm feeling a little down and cold today. You seem so warm inside and out. I guess I just couldn't help myself. I needed a little sunshine today."

"Lucie, I'm here for you, whatever you need."

She smiled a soft smile, pretended to work and curled into my side. She looked disappointed when the bell rang. I felt nearly devastated. Why couldn't science last the rest of the day? She gave me a hug and left the room without a backward glance.

Jesus was proving to be wily and elusive as a fox. He frequently missed school and since none of us did, he was hard to keep track of. He was being more careful about getting into trouble at school except for his truancy. It seemed that he was spending an unusual amount of time at the high school. Marlo had confirmed his home address and the sister's, definitely not his mother's, work location. Their parents had returned to Mexico to tie up some loose ends, something about a sick relative. In their absence Jesus had picked up a possible gang connection. This one would take a light touch. I needed to talk to the sister.

That afternoon White Eagle took Marlo and me over to the mall. Lucky for us Adrian's uncle had been keeping him away from the shop, or more likely away from Clive. Marlo lead us right to the shop where Jesus' sister worked. White Eagle found a bench outside so that we could call him if we needed him but otherwise he would stay out of it. He didn't want to scare her and thought we could do a better job by expressing our concern as her brother's friends.

The conversation went better than I thought. She totally believed that we were concerned friends; of course Marlo's puppy dog eyes were a big selling point. She didn't even question how well we knew her brother or how we had found her. She was so distressed that she would grab any port in the vicious storm her life had become. She was trying to go to school to become a nurse's aide or something, work and take care of her brother. An old boyfriend of hers from a toxic high school relationship was trying to start a gang at the high school. She hoped that Marlo and I could turn Jesus around by being the right kind of friends. I thought maybe she had the answer to this one. We could put our social network to a new use.

The first Saturday in March, Clive came to the shop to see Max. This time Max clearly did not want me around. I thought it was a perfect time to head into the back area where White Eagle was working on refinishing a cabinet that had recently come into the shop. I whispered to him that Clive was back and I wanted to check his plates. He dropped what he was doing and followed me outside.

We crept around the side of the building, looking for cover. We moved to the dumpster to scope out the cars and trucks in the lot. There were only three we didn't recognize. Our heads flipped around in unison as we heard raised voices from the pawnshop. Clive came bursting out the door still screaming at Max. He hopped in a small rusty piece of junk and revved the engine. He didn't pay any attention to us as he roared out of the parking lot. While my attention was on the plate that was partially obscured by mud, I heard another engine catch and White Eagle was after him.

I ran back to the shop to write down what I had gotten from the car. I snatched up a pen and some paper and started to write before I realized that Max was gone. A moan came from the floor. Not gone – on the floor behind the counter with a bloody nose and a rapidly swelling eye. I could smell the rusty hot odor of the blood as it dripped onto his shirt.

"Max!" I vaulted over the counter instead of going around. I tried to check him out but he waved me off.

"Ice and a towel?" he pleaded. I ran for the workshop where we kept first aid supplies. I rushed back as he was sitting up. I helped him get the worst of the bleeding under control and held the ice to his face. "Help me into the back. I don't want anyone to see me." I helped him get unsteadily to his feet and stagger into the back room. "I just can't have you boys here anymore. It's not safe."

"Max, no! Let us help you. What is going on? Why don't you call the police?" I cried in outrage.

"I can't. He'll hurt my family," he said, sounding defeated. "He said he'd shoot my nieces and nephews... at school... all of them. He showed me pictures of them at recess and coming to and leaving school. I can't...."

"You have to - it's the only way to protect them."

He looked at me in despair. "I'm afraid I'm in too deep now. I've already cooked the books." He seemed to realize that we were alone in the shop. "Where's White Eagle?"

"Following Clive."

"Oh no!"

"Don't worry. He won't confront him. He's just after information." I prayed I was telling the truth.

The bell rang and I went up front to see what was up. I tried to pretend that everything was normal as I helped three customers. The strain was killing me because legally I wasn't allowed to run the cash register. I about vaulted the counter again to hug White Eagle when he came in the front door looking weary. He looked at my face and said only, "Max?" I hooked my thumb toward the back curtain, saying nothing. He looked even more tired as he dragged himself into the back.

I could hear their soft voices but not make out the words as I continued to stay up front managing the customers and cleaning up the front of the pawnshop. White Eagle finally came up front and told me we were closing early so that we could take Max home and clean him up.

I called Marlo with the information I had and added what White Eagle had been able to find. He'd given me the address of where he had lost Clive. The rat zipped into an alley and vanished. Mr. Creepy had to have something going on nearby if he had a place to stash his car that fast. Marlo looked up the area and gave me a list of businesses and an apartment for rent at the intersection where Clive had disappeared. I would go back and check it out.

White Eagle stayed with Max. I told him I needed to get home but not that I was going to check out Clive. At home I checked the bus schedule from the mall to the area Marlo had narrowed down. I asked if I could meet some friends at the mall. Mom offered me a ride but I talked her out of it and took my skateboard. It wasn't raining. I got to the transit center at the mall and confirmed the route and hopped my bus. After two transfers I was only three blocks from where I hoped to find Clive.

I knew where I was supposed to be; I was just having trouble finding it. The address that Marlo had given me was confusing or maybe it didn't even exist. Where did this guy live? Or what business was he involved in here? The streetlights came on and the change in lighting made me realize what I was looking at. Above the old storefronts were apartments. He had to be in one of those. I crossed the busy street to get a better view and sure enough there he was in the second window and he looked like he was fixing to leave. I saw the small, beat up, rusty piece of, well you know, car he was driving earlier race out of the alley and nearly cream another car. I took off after it as fast as I could on my board. There was no way I could keep up for long; I was just hoping to get a better look at the plates. I prayed for a light to change and make him stop. He blew through the first yellow light but got stopped at the second. I only got part of the information I was hoping for as he was fast and quickly left me behind. I rode back to the apartment to see if there was any other information I could get from there. Nothing. I couldn't find a way into the building and I sure didn't want to be seen. I caught a bus and headed back to the mall.

I hopped on my board and made my way home. My skin still felt hot, my clothing damp as I stepped off my board and onto our front steps. A cool breeze kissed my overheated skin and feathered around my body ruffling and drying my still damp hair. I could not help but lift my arms and turn my face to the sky as the moisture and heat lifted away from my body. I felt good, powerful and peaceful, like for a moment I was one with this place, this moment.

Moments like this helped ease the bad waking dreams that haunted me. I fought to sort out images of Lucie, the kid from school and Clive. I was struggling to keep them at bay. Fortunately they didn't happen much at school where I seemed to have a built-in filter that held out all but the petty middle school drama. I was getting better at figuring out which images were giving me real problems to solve. My nightmares and waking dreams helped some too. I guess my brain just had to work some things out and the dreams were how that happened. Still it seemed like there was lots of weeding out to do as problems of equal or greater importance wanted to intrude on whatever I was currently working on. It was like being interrupted by someone else's arguments frequently. It was frustrating.

I was thankful for Marlo. He had started a spreadsheet of my exploits so we could keep them straight. He also sat down with me and White Eagle to catalog the items I had touched and a brief account of the images I received. We also tried to prioritize my tasks. All this organization stuff sucked but to be honest it was a big help. It kept me from running around like a crazy person and spinning my wheels. It also helped to have him do some research for me now and then. It felt wrong to include too many people. Yet I could feel Adrian's pain at being left out, just as I had felt Marlo's pain as Adrian and I practiced sparring. Surely he could help too; he could help with some of the smaller problems or maybe even the big ones I was reluctant to tackle on my own. He could really be my wingman. Besides he would never forgive me if I didn't let him help with his uncle.

I knew Max was doing something he shouldn't. I was afraid to look too close. I didn't want to see the bad side - I really liked Adrian's uncle Max. I was dreading touching every item in the shop until I found the rest of the story. I didn't know exactly what I was looking for. Marlo would have to follow me with his laptop and catalog it all. What a pain in the ass and so NOT fun. Now I just had to convince White Eagle and figure out how to tell Adrian.

Adrian was kept busy helping his uncle at home for a couple of days while the rest of us ran the shop. Max had yet to contact the police but I prayed he would cave in soon. It took us the whole time Adrian was gone to catalog the shop. There were only two Clive-related items left. They had both been stolen from the mall. It was a place to start at least, as the car seemed to be a dead-end. It was stolen and I didn't have the skills or bravado to break into Clive's apartment. Yet.

I was making another trip to the mall today to do some scouting. I could check in with Jesus' sister at the same time. The friendship angle was going painfully slow but we were trying. It was the perfect day to go. I had overheard Lucie and a couple of her friends at lunch discussing a shopping trip after school. I could watch her and watch for my newest bad guy.

I strolled around and pretended to browse the shops. I wandered in to see Selena, Jesus' sister. I decided to ask for her help with Clive. I told her that he was a guy rumored to be hanging at the mall and ripping people off and I knew about him because we had been warned at the pawnshop. I gave her a description and she said she'd keep an eye out. Jesus had actually mentioned us to his sister. They had seen one of the school counselors together and were looking at after school programs to keep him busy and on track. There was nothing I could do about the high school angle for now. While I was leaning up against the counter chatting with Selena, Lucie and her chick friends came in. Lucie looked at me and Selena and immediately got the wrong idea. I could see it in her face. I excused myself and approached her.

"Hey Luce, can I talk to you?" I said with my most winning smile. I was afraid she would say no.

"I guess," she said to me. "I'll meet you guys at the food court in a little while, okay?"

The girls smiled and giggled and said, "Sure."

Lucie and I walked out into the mall and strolled down toward the bookstore. We simply walked side by side without talking. It was nice.

"Are you going on the Washington D.C. trip this summer?" I asked to get the conversational ball rolling.

She looked up at me from the corner of her eye. "I'd like to. I signed up, but babysitting isn't bringing in the money fast enough and my parents are reluctant to cough up much. How about you?"

"I'm definitely going, so are Marlo and Adrian. It should be lots of fun."

"Yeah, my brother went so I think they owe me the chance too. It also gets me out of the house. I have a better question for you."

"Oh?"

"Who was the girl at the shop? Isn't she a little old for you?"

"Who, Selena? Yeah, way too old for me. She's a sophomore in college. You know my friend Jesus? She's his sister."

"Oh. I guess I was just surprised to see you hanging out at the mall. It doesn't seem like your style. I thought you hung with the boys at Adrian's uncle's pawnshop or maybe at a skate park."

We reached the bookstore and by mutual decision turned to lean on the railing overlooking the lower level.

"We do. We help out in the shop doing odd jobs to fund our trip and we learn boxing and karate from Mr. White Eagle. I haven't been to a skate park in a while. I've been too busy."

"Does Mr. White Eagle take other students?"

"Nah, just us for now. He's not professional and it's not a licensed studio or anything. What about you? Besides babysitting, what are you doing to keep busy?"

"I'm working with my gymnastics coach a couple of days a week to help with the younger kids. She pays me a little bit and I get to use the equipment to stay in shape. It makes me happy."

"Luce, I'm glad. I hate to see you sad. The other day in science about broke my heart. I wished we weren't in class and that I could just hold you. You seemed like you needed a hug."

We leaned our forearms on the railing shoulder to shoulder looking down at the crowd below us. It felt comfortable and thrilling at the same time. Lucie leaned over and rested her head on my shoulder. "This is nice," she sighed.

"Yeah, like the eye of a storm, the quiet amid the bustle."

Lucie pulled back and looked up at me. I loved having her this close to me. She smelled pretty good too.

"You come up with the deepest, most intriguing comments. You hardly ever talk and then you pour out this wisdom stuff. You almost sound old. It's kinda weird, you know?"

I rolled my lips in and held them together with my teeth in an effort to say nothing.

"Don't get mad. I meant it as a compliment. You just keep surprising me is all."

I turned to face her, leaning my hip against the railing instead. She rested one elbow on the railing to face me. She was so close I could feel her breath on my neck past the open collar of my shirt. I felt myself losing all focus except for her beautiful eyes. They sparkled in this light like fine gems under a jeweler's lamp. My gaze and thoughts drifted down to her perfect pink lips. I moved in slightly, drawn into her. She must have read my intention because she turned back to the railing. Too much too soon for her I guess. I sighed. "I'm not mad at you Lucie." Let her take that however she wanted. I changed my position so I was once again leaning my arms on the railing, my hands clasped so that I wouldn't touch her like I was burning to.

She threw one arm over my back and squeezed. "I gotta go; the girls are meeting me at the food court. I'll see you in science on Monday."

Here I was again with mixed feelings, watching her walk away. I was bad news for her but I couldn't resist her either. She was my own personal drug, my own private hell. Things were better when she kept me at arm's length - like the times she had a boyfriend. I would think, "Fantastic, she is off the market," and be consumed with jealousy at the same time. I needed to get a life or at least a different girl. Maybe one I didn't like so much, but I just couldn't hurt anybody like that. I'd rather keep hurting myself. I supposed it was better to hurt than to feel nothing. I didn't want to be numb but some days a little Lucie anesthetic would be nice. What a mess.

My head was so full of Lucie that I almost missed the guy. It had to be him. I would have to get closer and maybe even touch him or something of his to be sure. Something was a little different about him today. One thing was for sure. He was not going to threaten Max any more and make him take stuff he knew he shouldn't sell in the shop.

I followed at a distance. He didn't seem to be doing anything except for casing the mall and watching people. He almost seemed to see me or to be aware so after awhile I gave up and headed home.

I was able to track him again the next week and White Eagle also found him once. Each time, Marlo was able to find a blurb in the paper from the same day and either a customer's car had been broken into or a shop would report a theft. At least he had not been back to the pawnshop. Sadly, Max still had not called the cops.

With Max unwilling to talk to the police we tried to get as much on Clive as we could but we couldn't prove anything yet. We'd see him at the mall and people would get robbed but we never actually saw him do it. It was so frustrating.

I was following him for the third time hoping to catch him in the act. As careful as I tried to be, I was not careful enough. I was well and goodly sick of the mall by now so I'm sure I no longer looked like a shopper. He caught me watching. When our eyes met I saw recognition. He smiled that sickening smile of his and made the shooting motion with his hand. Damn it.

I turned and quickly walked away. He was across an open section of railing so I didn't think he could catch me. I wove my way through a big store, hiding and checking over my shoulder to see if he followed. I could see him scanning the store for me so I headed outside, then I moved quickly back into another store, through it and finally back into the mall. I looked around and made my way through the home store and back outside once more. I took the long way home, checking over my shoulder frequently but I seemed to have lost him.

The rest of the week I kept my guard up constantly. It was wearing and made me tired. I missed having Adrian around the shop which was kinda funny considering it wasn't long ago I had wished him away. I still didn't know how to break the stories of his uncle and myself to him. I tried and failed a couple of times. His girlfriend broke up with him and that kept him busy for a while. He was distracted and she was all he talked about at school.

EIGHT

On Wednesday I came home from the shop tired from our training. I felt at loose ends and didn't know what to do with myself. I killed some time texting my friends, seeing what was up on Facebook and doing a little homework. Mom was riding herd on my brothers and the dogs. I tried to help out but seemed to be more of a hindrance. I tried taking the dogs for a walk while Mom settled in my brothers for bed but it seemed like it was too much for Buddy. He looked at me with his Basset-sad eyes as if to say, "You're kidding, right? I'm old and arthritic. Leave me to nap, but take the young stupid one with you." I took pity on him and turned back around.

I thought I saw movement near the neighbor's house but could make nothing out when I turned to stare into the gathering darkness. I tried to stay alert but it was a challenge with the two dogs. We plodded on home, Beggar pulling at her leash and Buddy, practically dragging behind me.

I still felt restless at bedtime but couldn't put my finger on my unease. I could hear my parents talking softly in their room, their door shut for the night. I looked in on my brothers and just listened to them sleep for a while. The house was quiet except for the click of Buddy's nails on the wood floor. He had trouble sleeping these days and had been banished from my parents' room. Sometimes he slept with my brothers but often it was just too much work to haul himself upstairs so he slept on his doggy bed in the living room.

I decided to see if he needed to go out one more time before I called it a night. He went out willingly enough and did his business, but then he seemed to feel it necessary to patrol the yard so

I rolled back into the kitchen to grab a snack. He woofed softly at the back door so I let him in. I finished my snack, cleaned up after myself and went to bed.

It seemed to take forever before I fell asleep and then I was haunted by horrible nightmares. Clive was after us. My family, Lucie and all my friends were running from him. He chased us mercilessly through the field near my house. Lucas was falling behind so I ran back to scoop him up and began to run again. I could hear Alex crying. How could I carry them both? I would have to try. I was struggling under my burden. I could tell that I wouldn't make it. I couldn't decide who to save. I knew I needed to sacrifice myself. My mother screamed as I fell to my knees and the dog yelped.

The dog yelped again and I realized I was no longer dreaming. I practically levitated out of my bed and promptly fell to the floor, my legs hopelessly tangled in the sheets. I ripped myself free and flew halfway down the stairs before vaulting the stair rail and landing on the balls of my feet on the main level. The thump of my feet had alerted someone. I could hear my parents getting up and a simultaneous crash from near the back door. I heard a strange scrambling sound coming from the kitchen that was in time with my own feet slapping toward the kitchen. I slid around the corner and into the kitchen feeling a stab of pain in my foot. Lights began to come on upstairs; my mother was soothing my frightened brothers while my dad's feet pounded down the stairs. I leaped over the rest of the broken glass and out the open back door. A figure jumped our fence and was off. There was no way to catch him without shoes.

"What in the world?" my dad shouted as he flipped on the kitchen light. I stood on the back deck shivering in my boxers and t-shirt, looking through our destroyed back door, my foot dripping blood.

"Call the cops Dad, he got away. I can't chase him without shoes."

"Where's your cell?"

"Hopelessly lost in the many folds of my bedding," I sighed, frustrated.

My dad growled something unintelligible and got on our landline. "Do something for the dog," he said to me, then turned his attention to the 911 operator.

I limped back into the house and saw Buddy lying amid the glass. I could tell he was gone. There was nothing I could do for him now. I sat and stroked his elderly head anyway, tears forming in my eyes as I said my good-byes. My mom rounded the corner holding Lucas in her arm and Alex by the hand. Seeing me with Buddy she quickly took my brothers to the living room. Dad left me in the kitchen and ran to get some pants and a sweatshirt so he could meet the cops. He slipped on his shoes without socks and went out front to wait, tight-lipped and stoic. I gave Buddy one last pat then limped to the first aid cupboard to address my foot, leaving bloody spots and smears all across the floor.

My mom came in as I was pulling out the glass. She shoved my hands away and proceeded to clean and bandage it herself. "I'm so sorry," she whispered. "Are you okay?"

We looked at each other as the sirens came to a stop out front. "I'll survive," I told her. I walked to the living room to sit with my silently weeping brothers. "Where's Beggar?" I asked, concerned.

"I left her locked in our bathroom," she said as Lucas climbed into my lap and hugged my neck tightly. Alex moved up tight to my side and spread the quilt that he had taken from the back of couch over all of us.

The police politely interviewed me and my parents. They remembered me from Mrs. Lando's robbery. A crew came in to dust the kitchen for prints. It seemed to be the only room that was touched. Buddy had given his life to warn us. They had to take him as evidence since they weren't sure if he had been poisoned or had a heart attack. Personally I thought the green fluid in his vomit was pretty telling. We were always careful at our house and he never left the yard without us. A tech swabbed my cheek to compare to all the blood in the kitchen if necessary.

Lucas only relinquished his hold on my neck to let my mom hold him during my interview and then he came right back to me. He finally fell asleep in my arms around five in the morning as the folks in the kitchen were finishing up. Alex was dozing against one side of me, my mother on the other. My dad hovered near the kitchen watching everything, broken only by the concerned looks he threw over his shoulder.

By six, everyone had left our family alone. Dad picked up Alex and took him back upstairs. He quietly asked me to bring Lucas. We left my mom asleep on the couch and secured our back door. He then left me in charge so he could go shower and get to work. He had an important project going and felt we were plenty safe. The police had convinced him the guy would not be back. I knew better but I didn't let on.

I tried sleeping and had just dozed off when I felt a small warm body crawl in next to me and snuggle close to my back. I cracked one eye open and whispered, "What's up Luke? You usually climb in with Mom. Is she up already?"

"I'm scared and she wasn't in her room."

"It's okay, Luke, he won't be back." He sat up.

"Really? Promise?"

I sat up too. "Luke, I won't let anyone hurt you."

"Okay." He looked at me with his big brown eyes and I felt my heart melt. Nobody would hurt my brother, not ever. "Owen, am I a baby?"

"Why would you say that? Because you were scared? No way. It's okay to feel scared."

"No, I had an accident. Babies have accidents." He looked down at his chubby hands clenched in his lap.

"No, Lucas, you are not a baby. You had a rough night," I said sympathetically.

"Don't tell Mommy," he pleaded.

"Okay. Shall we go wash your sheets?"

"I think Alex is still sleeping."

"Okay, we'll do it in a little bit."

"When I grow up like you, will I be gone all the time? Is that what it's like to be a man? Daddy is gone all the time. If I was gone, I would miss Mommy." His lower lip stuck out and quivered slightly.

I pulled Lucas onto my lap to hug him. Such big worries for such a little man. I suddenly felt old. I vowed in that moment that I would be around more for him, Alex and for my own kids when I had them. "Dad is an important man at his company. His job makes good money so we can have a good life and have Mom at home, but it means he has to be gone a lot. It doesn't mean he loves us any less than Mom. It just looks and feels different. I've been hanging out with my friends and working to earn money for my eighth grade trip. I'll try to be around more. Okay?"

I realized that Alex was standing in the doorway and waved him in. He took stock of the scene and said nothing. He shuffled forward and crawled up on the bed right next to us and put his head on my arm, much as he did last night. I slipped my arm around him and squeezed him in a half hug.

Now I was victim to Alex's big green eyes. Sounding much like an adult himself, Alex mumbled, "Sometimes you're more of a dad than he is." Then he quickly changed the subject to ask, "What's going to happen to us? What will we do without Buddy? Won't Beggar miss him?"

I sensed Mom had come up and was lurking outside my room. She just leaned in the shadows outside the door listening. I said nothing else about our dad. I knew he meant well and that my brothers were scared and feeling the loss of him and Buddy. "Buddy has gone to dog heaven. He's in a better place. He was trying to protect us. He scared the bad man away. The bad man won't be back. Beggar will miss Buddy and be sad for a while like all of us but she will heal and so will we. We'll all be okay. We're a team and we stick together." Mom peeked in, a sad smile on her lips, then turned and walked away. "Let's go see about some breakfast," I said, trying to force some cheer into my tone.

I found her in the kitchen with her back to us getting out the makings for pancakes and trying to act normally. I could tell she was crying. She kept up a good front the whole time my brothers were in the room. After breakfast they trotted upstairs to play and get ready for school. I watched them take off and turned to my mom. A sob escaped her throat that she had been holding back.

She stepped forward hugging me and weeping, "Where has my baby gone? He's all grown up and taking care of all of us. I hate it but I'm so proud of you at the same time. Where did your childhood go? Worse yet, what's going on? We aren't safe in our own home? And why do you have that guilty look again?" she asked, pulling back to look at me.

"Mom, I think I've seen the guy before at the pawnshop. He may have followed me." Seeing the look in her eye I quickly went on, "It's not the pawnshop that's the problem. The guy was trying to sell stolen goods to Adrian's Uncle Max. I'll call him and White Eagle. We'll call the cops and let them know."

"I don't even know what to say. Take care of them and the police and I will take you to school later. I'm going to clean up and take your brothers to school while you do your phoning. When I get back I am finding martial arts lessons for me and for your brothers and I'm calling a security system company."

I made my call to the pawnshop and talked to both men. Max finally agreed to call the police. I felt relieved and worried. I hugged my brothers goodbye, whispered to Lucas that I would change his sheets and went to take a shower myself. I shaved and fixed my hair, then dressed carefully in black jeans, black boots and a deep blue button up shirt. I was expecting the police would want to talk to me again and I sure didn't want to do another interview in my boxers. I stripped Lucas' bed and threw his stuff in the washer, washed up and gathered my gear for school.

My mom was nothing less than scary when she came home. Apparently she had been thinking. She talked about what she had heard earlier of the conversation with my brothers. She apologized for crying and being hysterical; her words, not mine. She would try to do better, but she wanted me to confide in her. I just couldn't yet. I knew she was worried but I couldn't bring myself to add to it.

I was pulled out of science at almost the end of the period. As soon as I saw the slip was for the counseling office I knew it was either really bad news or the police were here. Lucie eyed me curiously. I said nothing about our break-in. I walked slowly into the counseling office. Sure enough, two detectives wanted to re-interview me. This time my mom instead of my dad was by my side. Max was in trouble, but if my story checked out and he helped the cops they would do what they could for him.

I thought carefully before I answered each question. My watch that had been silent for weeks seemed to wake up and I almost felt that Miles was standing with me too. I tried to paint Max and White Eagle in the best light possible. I told them it was dark and that I was not positive it was the same guy but that he had the same build which was a total lie. I knew that it was not Clive, but his buddy that had broken into our house. How could I tell them that I had touched something Clive had stolen and saw his buddy in an image that flashed in my mind and *that* was how I recognized him?

I had not gotten heads up from White Eagle so I did my best and prayed that he had been on the same page I was now. I mentioned seeing the guy at the mall the day I had talked to Lucie there and that I thought I had seen him the day I felt that I was followed. I talked about the confrontation I had had with Clive at the shop the day he pushed me into the display case. I talked about him beating up Max, gave his make, model and license plate number, even though I knew it was stolen, and let on that we thought we knew where he lived. They nodded, looked back at their notes and re-asked questions over and over checking my story and comparing it to the others they had gotten. I felt Miles' approval. The detectives seemed satisfied and let me go.

School was out by the time we were done. Mrs. Lando had stayed with my brothers and had even cooked dinner for us. She gave us each a hug when we walked in the door. Something told me to check my phone. I realized I had missed calls from Marlo, Adrian, Max, White Eagle and Lucie.

I excused myself and stepped out back to return my calls while the ladies chatted and finished dinner. Each one wanted the whole story and was worried about me. I was the most pleased to talk to Lucie. She told me how nice she thought I had looked today. Well she actually said 'hot' which made me smile. She had grilled Marlo and decided that I was a hero. I told him that I appreciated his help, but to please butt out when it came to Lucie.

My mom called me in to eat as I was finishing with Marlo. I looked across our yard as I went to put my cell in my pocket and saw something fluttering from our back fence. I approached cautiously. It was a piece of the guy's jeans the police had missed. I put out a tentative finger and touched the fabric.

It was definitely Clive's 'friend'. They were working together and they would be at the mall tonight. I also knew he had come to our house to scare me away. I wasn't scared. I was furious. Nobody threatens my mom, my brothers or my family! Nobody kills my dog! He had poisoned Buddy. He was waiting for him when I had let Buddy out. How long had he been waiting for us to make that mistake? Was it only last night? It felt like such a long time ago. Now I just had to fake my way through dinner.

I ate a few bites while texting Marlo under the table to bring him up to date. Then I texted White Eagle and hoped he knew how to open his texts on his antiquated phone. I begged Mom to let me go to the movies with Marlo and she agreed that I could probably use some time away from the house. Marlo's mom picked us up for the seven o'clock show. She too told me how nice I looked. She said

I looked grown up. She was sorry about the break-in and Buddy. She's a sweet lady. Marlo takes after her. I'm lucky to have him as a friend. I hated lying to her and putting her son in danger.

When we got to the mall Marlo and I walked in the theater entrance to be sure we had fooled his mom. Then we kept on walking across the food court and into the mall itself. We cut across the mall and walked out the outside door. I hoped that White Eagle would get here soon. Just then my cell vibrated in my pocket. My caller I.D. said it was White Eagle. "What's up?" he groused. "I can't open your damn text."

"I got a hit off a piece of fabric Clive's friend left on my back fence. They are going to be at the mall tonight. Marlo and I are here now."

"What!!!" he screeched so loudly I had to pull the phone away from my ear.

"I didn't know you couldn't read my text. I thought you'd be here. They are doing something tonight and right now the light is about right so it's gonna be soon. Can you get here? We're on the south side by the restaurants."

"You boys go home NOW!"

Too late. There they were, across the parking lot breaking into a car. As Clive popped opened the trunk of a dark sedan with some small tool he held, he seemed to sense me and our eyes met. "He's here now and he sees us."

"Ff....." I closed my phone and put it back in my pocket. No doubt he was on his way now. It should take him about ten minutes if the signals and traffic are in his favor. Marlo stood at my side not knowing what to do. I didn't suffer so much from indecision any more. I turned toward him without taking my eyes off Clive.

"Marlo, go find the mall cops. I'll keep these guys busy." He stalled for a moment then made a break for the mall at a fast walk. Marlo is a smart guy. I had complete confidence that he would get the job done.

Clive said something to his buddy and they started to walk away. I ran toward them. "I will always dog you. I know what you're doing. You may not get another chance like this," I taunted bravely... or foolishly. "I'm right here. Last night didn't scare me."

His buddy ran on but Clive stopped. I was close now. "I know what you've been doing. It's over. The cops have the last of the stuff you stole. It was still at the pawnshop. You are done hurting people and stealing stuff. Max has turned you in and they fingerprinted my whole house. They even know your friend poisoned my dog. See that rip in his jeans? The rest of it was on my fence at home."

"They won't catch me and they'll never find you." He came at me then but I was ready. He had thought I would be easy to catch. My bravado probably took him by surprise. I was, after all, the kid he had pushed around at the pawnshop. I just had to hold them off until White Eagle or the mall cops made it here. He swung a big meaty fist at my head. I dodged easily and gave him a quick jab in the side. He tried swinging with the other arm but I ducked and scooted under his reach, turning quickly to kick him in the lower back.

He howled with rage. Now I had placed myself between the two men. I needed to move. I ran between two cars to put space between us. They moved in on me again but at least I could see both of them. Clive's friend still held back, like they were doing tag team fighting. What was he waiting for?

Clive came at me again and tried to tackle me. I was too fast for him. Instead of running away I ran toward him. As he bent to lunge and tackle me I jumped over him using him as a springboard and knocking him to the ground. I spun to keep both men in my sight.

Apparently he was done playing around because he pulled out a knife. I stepped forward and pushed it up with both hands and kneed him in the gut. He dropped the blade as he bent over. His buddy had snuck around behind me in that moment and tried grabbing me around my chest and arms. As he lifted me up I used the momentum to kick Clive in the chin hard - laying him out. The momentum shoved the guy holding me backward. I struggled with him and finally slammed my head backward crushing his nose. He dropped me and grabbed his face. I didn't hesitate. I quickly spun, kicking him as hard as I could in the gut, knocking the air out of him. He fell back onto a car and slumped to the ground, vomiting.

I turned back to Clive. He was up and had recovered his blade. He took another swipe at me and missed but it brought him closer to his own man. "Worthless," he screamed in a rage and kicked the downed man. The man on the ground made a horrible gurgling sound. I thought he was drowning. Clive turned back to me with death in his eyes and I thought I'd make a run for it. I made it three whole steps before a car slammed into me from behind. I flipped up onto the hood, my shoulders and head smacking into the windshield. I was momentarily stunned before I was lifted off the hood and hammered once more onto its surface by Clive.

I rolled off and away from Clive, landing hard on my hands and knees, my left leg collapsing from the damage the car gave me when it hit. Before I could rise I was kicked in quick succession in the gut and the ribs by two sets of boots. My ribs failed at the third kick. The sound of the rib cracking echoed in my ears. I struggled to breathe as I collapsed on the ground. I was not ready for three attackers. I had not seen three. I turned my head to look under the car and across at the second man. He was still out, flat on his back, likely dying. They paid no attention to him.

Get up, I told myself. The third man picked me up by the back of my jacket. How thoughtful. I tried to kick backwards but I barely brushed his legs. He held me away from his body so I could not head butt or elbow him. Clive looked at me for a moment, smiling like he sensed victory. He flipped the knife from hand to hand and then lunged at me. I had nowhere to go. I threw up my arm in a desperate attempt to protect myself and twisted as much as I was able. The knife missed the intended target and skimmed across my side, my jacket taking most of the damage. The knife tangled in the fabric and fell to the ground. Clive snarled and went after it again.

I tried to kick at him and slip out of my jacket simultaneously as he recovered the knife. I did little damage and only managed to get twisted in the material. Where was my help? I was almost done. The man I could only smell shook me and changed his grip holding me against his stink while he choked me with an arm across my neck, both restraining and squeezing. Spots danced before my eyes, my hands clawed at his arm. At least I would have skin evidence under my nails.

Clive came at me again so I raised my free arm in a feeble attempt to protect my face. The knife bit deep into my forearm causing me to suck in a breath. Warm blood washed over my arm, its distinctive scent filling the air and mingling with the blood odor of the man down on the other side of the car. A woman screamed from over near the mall entrance and the third man threw me to the ground, further damaging my hands and knees.

I tried to crawl under the car but I was too big and having nowhere to go I rolled into the fetal position. Clive stomped on my already damaged leg near my ankle before I could move it and it snapped under the pressure. The sound echoed across the mall as I let out a scream of agony and collapsed back on the ground. "Get him in the car. We've gotta get out of here." I tried to resist but Clive smacked me in the side of the head with the hilt of his knife, dimming my vision. I guess he was pretty tough against downed men. I knew if I got in the car I was dead but I couldn't get away on this leg and my head wound made it hard to focus.

I struggled for all I was worth, which wasn't much at this point, but the two of them managed to throw me in the trunk anyway amid much cussing. I clawed and bit any body part I could reach. Before I could extract my damaged body from the trunk, they tossed the man who had killed my dog in on top of me, further damaging my body as there really wasn't room for both us in there. When they slammed the trunk lid the air was forced from my lungs in a whoosh. I fought to remain conscious.

There was no room to move and I could barely breathe. I tried to save my energy to fight back when they opened the trunk. I attempted to get to the taillight to break it out and remembered my cell. It had GPS. PLEASE! I begged to God or anyone who could help. I tried 911. The operator could barely hear me. I tried telling her where I was using my GPS. We were headed south on I 205. I let her know when we turned onto 224 and guessed we were headed toward Carver. I told her what I could about the car and its occupants and listed my injuries. I was using her to stay conscious.

I worked at stopping my bleeding. It was incredibly difficult to untuck my shirt but I managed to rip a strip of it off and tie it over my arm as best I could. There was nothing I could do for my leg. The back and side of my head seemed to be bleeding. The guy smashed in the trunk with me was a lost cause. They had let him die. He was still warm. I was too scared to be horrified.

I tried to leave as much evidence as I could in the trunk by smearing our blood everywhere. When the car slowed I tried to tell the operator what was happening but I was fighting for consciousness and losing. I gave her one last location and hid the phone. "PLEASE help me," I begged with a choked sob, praying she could still hear from my inside coat pocket. I left my phone on hoping that they could use the GPS to track me in reverse.

I held very still watching through slitted eyes as they heaved their 'friend' out of the trunk and threw him unceremoniously out of the way. I heard the thud and sound of him tumbling down a steep bank and wondered what would become of me. I played dead and waited. They hauled me out and tossed me before I could do anything but whimper with pain. Then even more pain exploded all over my body as I tumbled down the thickly brambled bank unable to save myself. I lay still for a moment when I slammed into a tree and heard the car drive off.

I tried to evaluate my injuries. They felt like they were many and serious. I struggled to get my cell out of my pocket. It must have taken me nearly twenty minutes just to do that one task. I cried in despair when I found it smashed and useless. I wanted to scream but couldn't get a deep enough breath. I attempted to crawl but I could barely move. My leg was badly broken and bleeding. I had lost a lot of blood from my arm and head. I was pretty sure I had a concussion and at least two ribs were cracked. I dragged myself as far back up the bank as I could. When I stopped to rest I passed out.

I woke up groggy and confused. I tried to drag myself again, but didn't even manage to go half my body length before I collapsed again. I looked at my watch in the moonlight that broke through the clouds. Eight forty-five p.m. Surely Marlo or White Eagle...? I couldn't even finish the thought. I dragged myself four more feet and passed out again. I tried not to cry but the tears would not stop. I worked my way further up the steep bank and slid back some. I closed my eyes to rest a moment and fell again into unconsciousness.

I woke up to a bright, nearly full moon. I took the pain and misery in stoic silence. The moaning had ceased some time ago and what passed for screaming with cracked ribs before that. Tears still trickled from my eyes, my jaws clenched. The agony had been going on unabated for so long that I finally was able to grasp a thought other than, 'Stop! Please God, make it STOP'. All the pain had created its own kind of numbness. I will die now and it'll be okay, I thought. Death would be better than this. I won't hurt anymore and people will go on without me. I can go now and the pain will end. Please.... let it just... end.

I thought of Lucie, my mom, Lucas, Alex, my dad, White Eagle, Marlo, Adrian, Sarah Lando, my other friends and even Max. I said goodbye to each one as I visualized their face. Just as my first thought had been, my final thought was of Lucie. I saw her beautiful face and thought I heard her voice as I drifted off trying to reach out and touch her.

I saw a light from behind my closed eyelids. This is it. The end is here. I'm ready; just stop the pain, the aching unending pain. Please...! Pain exploded anew in a fierce assault as I was jostled. Death is horrible. Please God, end it now. A wretched half sob, half moan escaped my lips in a broken, ruined way.

"Young man, can you hear me?" I didn't know who it was but all I could think was go away and leave me in peace. Snatches of conversation fragments brushed over me. So I was aware of some things and some not so much as I drifted in and out of consciousness.

"Did all this blood come from this kid?"

"What happened here?"

"He's alive, his pulse is weak. His breathing is shallow but good. Get the medics."

"Geez, look at this kid. Somebody sure did a number on him. Put a collar on him and get him on a backboard, then we'll splint the leg."

"Does he have any I.D.?"

"Yeah, here."

"Well Mr. Ryer, good thing you carry your school I.D. Your family is looking for you."

"This poor kid is lucky to be alive. There is so much damage. Cut his shirt and jacket off and let's see where this blood is coming from so we can get him outta here."

"Look at the bruises on his side and chest. Somebody kicked him good."

"It's just the arm and his head. Looks like he tried to bandage his own arm. He tied part of his shirt right over the jacket sleeve. Smart kid."

"My God, he dragged himself almost forty feet."

"Hey Frank, there's another one over here. He doesn't look so good. Never mind, he's gone."

"You don't suppose the kid took him out?"

"If he did this to the kid, I sure hope so! On the downside it's a whole lot more paperwork."

"I hope the kid can tell us what happened here."

"The leg is bleeding too. Cut the pants so I can see what we've got."

"I told you something didn't look right. I heard on my police scanner you were looking for a kid in Carver. I saw the tire tracks and the beat down blackberry bushes. I found him. I'm a hero. Do I get a reward?"

"Yeah Buddy, you're a hero. Now go with the nice police officer and answer her questions, would ya?"

The hands all over me, hurting me, were more than I could stand and I began to shake. I thought I was going to fragment into a million pieces. The ambulance ride was even worse. I passed out for most of it, in self defense I'm sure. I couldn't decide whether or not I was glad to be found and be alive. I was going to have to think really carefully about my story on this one. Maybe I would just sleep for a while and worry about it later.

I woke to beeping and the distinctive smell of a hospital. My dad was crashed on a really uncomfortable looking roll away bed. "Dad," I croaked. Was that my voice? He leaped off the bed like he'd been shot. He looked terrible. He had aged ten years. I could see the shine of his scalp through the thinning hair on his head. He had bags and dark circles under his bloodshot eyes. His eyes looked like he had been terrorized.

"Owen," he said and began to weep. I had never seen him cry.

"Dad," I rasped, "I'm okay." When my words registered he began to laugh with a slightly hysterical edge.

"I love you son, please don't ever do this to me again." I nodded and went back to sleep.

The next time I came to I was aware of a cool hand holding mine. My mom was now next to me sitting awkwardly in a chair as she reached to touch me. She was in better shape than my Dad had been. "Hi, Mom," I croaked. She smiled and smoothed my hair. I tried to look around but I hurt everywhere. I was hooked to machines and fluids. My arm was bandaged and my leg was in a weird looking cast. I felt a little warm and tried to remove some blankets only to discover my ribs were wrapped up too.

"What is it, Owen? Let me help you," she said, concerned.

"I guess I'm just evaluating my situation. Water please?" She opened a swab, dipped it in water and swabbed my mouth. "Ice chips?" I croaked. She kissed my forehead and scurried from the room. I reached up with my bandaged arm since it wasn't hooked to an I.V. I had a bandage on the back of my head and special tape near my hairline on the side of my head. Moving my arm made my ribs hurt.

Mom returned with a nurse who tortured me and then rewarded me with more pain meds and ice chips. She was only doing her job I guess. She took my temperature, blood pressure and pulse. I told my Mom I loved her and passed back out.

The next time I woke up I was a little more lucid. White Eagle was sitting in the visitor's chair trying to read. He sighed a heavy sigh when he caught me watching him. "You scared me to death. It was Miles all over again. Never, ever do that again. Marlo is probably going to need counseling. He blames himself. But then I do too. I'd ask what you were thinking, but I think I know. You have got to be more careful!"

"Water," I begged, trying to change the subject.

"Rotten, no good kid, you're lucky I love you!" He helped me to sit up. That's when I discovered the catheter. I was completely humiliated and blushed to the roots of my hair. He saw my discomfort. "Take it easy kid, they'll probably take it out tomorrow if you ask. They want to watch your leg for swelling. They had to put a pin in there to fix it. Rolling down a hill after it was broken really wasn't the best thing for it. It will be better than new after some physical therapy. I know you're tough and will work hard."

I took a sip of water and asked the question now burning in my mind. "Where's my watch?" His reference to Miles had gotten my brain working again.

"Your mom has it." I must have had a worried look on my face. "I doubt that the watch will communicate with her. Even if she had the ability to interact with it, I doubt it would talk to her. Don't worry. Just get well."

"What happened after they found us?" I croaked.

"Ah, so you know about the dead guy. The cops have made an I.D. and they are watching Clive's apartment. As soon as they get a warrant I'm sure they'll search it. Marlo was right, the car was stolen. They found it abandoned with your blood all over it. I'm sure the cops will be in any time for your statement."

The next day went by in a blur. The good news, I got my catheter out and I'll have some awesome scars to share. The bad news, my ribs were cracked in three places. They hurt like hell and I'll kill anyone who makes me laugh. Sneezing was the worst! My leg was broken in two places but the breaks were pretty clean. I'm mostly bruised inside and out. They put in close to fifty stitches. The pain meds suck. They make me feel weird. At least I haven't had to give much of a report to the police. The good guys didn't win this one. I've still got to find Clive and the third man if the police don't. I can't do this anymore by myself. I need Adrian. I need someone who can watch my back.

My mom was there first thing the next morning even before official visiting hours. I could tell that she was worried about our family's safety. The police confirmed that the dead guy was the one who broke into our house. They said they were making progress and wanted to talk to me again today. I was at war with myself: To tell her how I got into this mess or keep her safe. Mom misunderstood my mood and thought I was worried about the police. To distract her, I asked her to ask about cutting back the pain meds and to beg them to let me come home. She worked her magic and they agreed to let me out today if I could use the crutches to get to the bathroom by myself. Yikes.

The police came when I was trying to eat some lunch. It was just as well. The food was *not* to my liking. I retold the story of the mall: How I saw a guy in the parking lot breaking into a car and I thought he was the same guy who broke into my house. But either way he had to be stopped. I said I had sent Marlo to call for help and I was keeping an eye on them but they saw me and came after me. I said that a third man had tried to run me over with the car and all three had tried to beat me. They found some of my blood and hair on the windshield and on the grill they found some blood and fabric from my jeans as well as my blood in the trunk. The bad guys had tried to wipe the car down but had missed some prints in their hurry.

I repeated what I knew about Clive from the pawnshop. How they could think I had mistaken short chubby Clive for his taller druggy "friend" I don't know but they didn't catch that one. Clive is balding and the other guy had a scraggly pony tail so maybe. Both dressed the same. It was basically what I had said before and they had my 911 tape and my wrecked phone from which they had retrieved some data. They said that I had done a good job trying to save myself. Maybe they blamed any confusion on the concussion and pain medication.

Mom brought my brothers to see me in the afternoon. She said that Dad would have come again but the alarm company had arrived for our installation. My brothers were initially afraid of my appearance but warmed up when they realized that I would be okay. Mom kept their visit short. Lucas wanted to crawl in the bed with me and try it out. He was so cute but the fourth time his exuberance made me wince, she said it was time to go. Alex was quiet most of the visit. He had a worried expression on his face the whole time. He did not try to hug me; he just laid his head next to mine for a moment.

Marlo and Adrian came to see me after school. I still hadn't made it all the way to the bathroom completely alone but I was very determined. I was chalky white and sweaty from my latest attempt when they arrived and I think it scared them some. It only took me an hour to convince Marlo it wasn't his fault and that I thought he was very brave. "Mar, you can't blame yourself. You did exactly what I asked. Blame me."

Marlo told his tale. He had rushed into the mall and right up to a sales counter demanding attention. He had told the saleslady that he needed security because a car was being broken into and his friend needed help. He argued with her briefly because she wanted him to wait in line, but then she finally relented to his agitation, at last believing him and calling security. By the time the mall cops showed up all that was left of me was my blood on the pavement and White Eagle looking at the scene. There was a tense moment while all parties tried to determine who was on whose side and work out what had happened. When Marlo saw the blood he admitted that he had broken down on White Eagle as the mall cops were calling the police. Poor Marlo was so scared and worried that he had puked on White Eagle's shoes. He was afraid all the blood was mine. Ironically I had called the police so one unit was already headed to Carver and after their call a second one was sent to the mall. Marlo pointed out the car with the popped trunk. Someone had left prints behind. We hoped it was Clive.

I told my story to their horror. Fighting might seem cool; taking a beating was not. Adrian had received some information from his uncle and was a little mad about being kept out of the loop but was so happy to have me alive that he quickly forgave me my part in it. As far as Adrian knew, the bad guys had followed me from the pawnshop just to have another place to rob and Marlo and I had come across them by accident. Both of them hugged me shamelessly and left.

I finally made it to the bathroom completely by myself around dinnertime and the doctors decided to let me go at eight. Dad brought me sweats to wear home since my old clothes had been cut from my unconscious body. He drove carefully so that he would jostle me as little as possible. Mom had made a bed for me on the couch. Dad took the first shift in the chair that night in case I needed help getting to the bathroom. Once I was up on my crutches it wasn't so bad. It was getting up off the couch that was murder. Mom stayed with me the second night and by the third they had gotten me a new cell phone and stayed in their own room. Lucas and Alex wanted to stay with me but my mom talked them out of it. Alex would have been fine but Luke would have wanted to crawl in with me at some point and I was still too fragile.

On Monday after Mom dropped my brothers at school, I got to go see my doctor to have my stitches out and check my progress. He was amazed that I was healing so well but he encouraged me to take it easy. They x-rayed my ribs and leg to check the healing. I was looking good for the shape I was in. I was a little over a week post injury and he said that I could expect about five more weeks of misery while my bones healed. He said my ribs could take up to six months if I wasn't careful. I knew I didn't have that long. He asked about pain meds but I refused everything but over the counter medication.

My teachers, bless them, put work together for my Mom to pick up. They decided to keep me out of school one more week since the following week was spring break. The grading period would end just before spring break but they would save my grades until after break so I could catch up. For most of my classes I would take my finals after school the first week back. Many teachers excused a bunch of work for me. They earned my eternal gratitude.

By the time spring break rolled around I was desperate to get back to a normal life. I begged my mom to take my brothers out for a movie or something so that I could hang with my boys. Marlo finally convinced her that he would call her if anything was beyond their control, but that they would take *very* good care of me. I hugged my brothers goodbye and told them they had been good nurses while shaking my head "no" at my mom to help get her out of the house. They did their best but I can only watch so many cartoons and play so many board games while they try to entertain me.

Marlo and I finally broke my big secret to Adrian. He didn't believe it until I tried my gift on him. I had to touch his tennis shoe before I finally got a hit. "You were at the pawnshop today and had to do a little work for Max," I said, looking him right in the eye.

"Marlo could have told you that. What do you take me for?"

"That's true, but does Marlo know that while you were there you broke an antique revolver while spinning it around like a cowboy in a western? We both know we're not allowed to touch the firearms. You dropped it and the pearl handle grip broke. You hung it back up on the rack backwards to hide the damage." My well placed bomb had landed a direct hit. He about fell out of his chair in shock.

We called White Eagle and had Adrian talk to him. He gave himself up and they talked about me. Adrian was on board to help. He'd be spending a bunch more time at the shop again anyway, working off the revolver. He would start tomorrow and spend the rest of spring break there working every day, all day. Bummer for him but he knew better.

After my mom came back with my brothers, I begged her to let me go to the pawnshop at least a couple of days during spring break. "Absolutely not!" she said emphatically. "What if Clive comes back?"

"I'm sure the police are watching the shop, just like they are our house and Clive's apartment. Please."

"It's not safe Owen. Until you can defend yourself you are stuck with me." I gave her a look. "Owen Anthony, nobody messes with my boys!" I swear I heard her growl. It was mother bear. In that mood she would kick Clive's ass. I desperately wished, and not for the first time, that I could identify the third man. He had pale skin and some kind of tattoos. He was grease-stained and was perhaps a mechanic. I knew he was taller than me and strong. The smell of his unwashed body, mingling with a sickly sweet odor I could not identify at this time, would be unmistakable if I was near it again.

Lucie came by the last Saturday of spring break. I had warning so I was able to clean myself up pretty good in the laundry room and wash my hair in the utility sink. I hid as much damage as I could so I wouldn't scare her. Her visit was a little uncomfortable at first. We just didn't know what to say to each other after almost three weeks. I had missed her.

She wanted to hear the tale but I was afraid to tell her the whole truth. I told her it was more than a mugging and that I had tried to stop car thieves who in turn hit me with their car. As I told my story she worked her way closer to me. It was almost funny to watch as she moved off the chair to sit on the floor and lean her back against it, then lean forward, and finally scoot forward until she was right in front of me, her neck at an awkward angle as she looked up at me. I patted the couch next to me and she moved there gingerly so as not to hurt me.

"I won't break," I laughed, careful of my ribs. She looked at me skeptically and then gently put her arm around me. My mom started to walk in about then to check to see if we wanted anything but quickly did an about face before Lucie saw her. She had been great today doing extra work so that I could see Lucie looking as well as possible. There was no sign that I was *living* in the living room. I figured my ribs and leg were ready to make the trip upstairs to my room tonight.

"I don't think I have ever seen you wear sweatpants," she commented.

"They are lots easier with the cast."

"I remember," she said with a fierce look. "The physical therapy will suck, but I'll help you." She held my arm and looked at the pink scar left from Clive's knife. Then she reached up to push the hair back from the scar on the side of my head.

"Wow, they really got you." Her fingers were gentle and cool. I resisted the urge to purr like our cat. She had me turn my head so she could look at the scar on the back of my head. Her fingers played with the stubble of my re-growing hair. "Maybe you should think about a hair cut right before you go back to school to hide the damage?"

"Hey Luce?"

"Yeah?"

"The public version is that I was attacked by muggers and not that I had an incident with car thieves who also broke into our house. Please don't say anything. As far as I know they haven't caught them yet. I'm trying to keep a low profile."

"Sure Owen, no problem. I suppose we better get some science done. It was, after all, my excuse for coming over here."

"Ugh, homework."

"Come on, it will be easy. I have already done it once and I know what's on the test!"

Lucie helped me with my homework for almost two hours. She went over everything I had already done and helped me finish up some things I hadn't gotten to. I was feeling like I would do okay on the tests that I would have to finish this next week.

"Did they mail you your schedule for the new trimester? Mine came with my grades."

I called my mom who brought it in off the fridge when I asked. We would have three classes together now: science, choir and health. Oh boy, that wouldn't be awkward. Nope, not a little bit - a whole big bunch of awkward.

Lucie's phone chirped in her pocket and she looked at the readout frowning. "I gotta go. I'm really glad you're okay. I'll see you at school and don't forget the haircut."

"No problem, I live with my barber." I winked at my Mom who was coming from the kitchen to say goodbye to Lucie.

"Yeah, and I don't come cheap," she said with a laugh as she saw Lucie out the door and to the waiting car. She waved politely at Lucie's driver.

She left much too soon for my liking. But now I had something to look forward to come Monday, three classes with Lucie. Monday dawned cool and rainy. My nightmares had returned. Clive and a faceless man were in most of them. Mom drove me to school. The day was a drag and wore me out. I was determined to make it to science. I now had health in place of PE so I had no good excuse to go home early - besides Lucie would be there.

I was quite the novelty that day. Many kids wanted to be helpful but I stuck to Marlo and Adrian as much as possible. I tried to remain polite but distant to other people. My boys and I had more classes together this trimester too and I was very thankful. I now had choir with Lucie but all the second sopranos sat on the other side of the altos. As a second tenor and sometimes baritone it placed her far from me. Everyone in science had new seats except for us. Our teacher figured I needed Lucie to get my science groove back on. Lucie was a little distant both physically and emotionally which I found really disappointing as well as surprising after our visit on Saturday.

I wished so many times that I could tell the real story. I kicked some ass. I got my butt handed to me, but that's the way it goes sometimes when it's three on one, especially when one of them is wielding a car. Cheater. Marlo and Adrian both knew about me now which I realized had released some pressure in my chest. We would be the dynamic trio with some training and recovery on my part. Looking back I didn't see how I could have changed a thing. If it took me getting beaten up to catch Clive and his crew it was worth it.

My mom was scarier yet, if possible, when she picked me up from school. She said little because my brothers were in the backseat but I'm sure she suspected something more was going on than what it looked like on the surface. Even White Eagle seemed to be a little afraid of her. I had only gotten a few emails, phone calls and texts, yes texts, from him. Marlo was teaching him how to use his phone and was trying to talk him into an upgrade. I bet Marlo was having a blast watching the old *technophobe* squirm. At least he was trying, I thought fondly.

I can't tell her in front of my brothers, I thought. I want to tell her and yet I don't. Maybe it would be good if she knew. Then I wouldn't have to sneak out on crutches if the need arises. On the other hand I think she said I was grounded forever anyway. She has said a lot of crazy stuff lately. She seemed to know there was something wrong with the story I had been telling which had me really worried. My thoughts seemed to chase endlessly around and around without gaining any ground like a hamster in a wheel.

NINE

Tuesday I got to miss some school to get my first walking cast. As soon as we had taken my brothers to the elementary school we were off to the doctor. Folks were amazed that I was doing so well and we set up my physical therapy. Today I got to use a cane. What a deal. It makes me feel ninety. Getting around school was much easier though. One good thing about being disabled is they let you carry your backpack around instead of making you go to your locker. I had two tests to take after school to clear out last trimester. People were still more interested in me than I would have liked and Lucie was *less* interested. Go figure.

On Wednesday I was still using the cane but was getting around a little better. I was trying to decide if fate was with or against me in health. Lucie and I sat right next to each other in a strange alphabetical phenomenon. Who would have guessed that there would be no names between Ness and Ryer? For the nutrition unit it was fine. When we did the sex education unit I knew I would die of embarrassment. Any other girl I could ignore.

As I sat at lunch with Adrian and Marlo we discussed my last three tests that I would get to endure today. They gave me all the tips they could think of. They also told me that in my absence they had been working hard at befriending Jesus and that it was going pretty well. He had been missing less school. What was going on at the high school was still worrisome but we couldn't fix everything, right?

I had taken to sitting with my back to the wall at lunch. It felt safer. I couldn't put my finger on what was eating me. Jesus wandered over and asked to sit with us. He was still shy and didn't often seek us out but we always tried to make him feel welcome. He said his sister had heard about me and asked how I was. She was happy to have one less bad guy at the mall. We finished our lunches, chatting and laughing. Suddenly something felt really wrong. I quickly scanned the room. I could feel angry eyes on me. Clive? No... I closed my eyes for a moment and let my *other* sense take over. Right side, near the exit – I opened my eyes and saw... Lucie. Hold on, what? Not Lucie – with Lucie, an angry boy I did not know. I didn't even stop to analyze how I knew how to feel for the danger.

Marlo looked at me and then followed my gaze. "Calvin," he said in a sad, disgusted tone. "We didn't want to tell you but Lucie has a boyfriend. He doesn't know you and he already hates you. He started school the first Monday you were out. The story is that he was the biggest fish in the pond where he came from. He thinks you're a huge threat to his reign here. I told you, Adrian and I get gossip from *everywhere*."

"I have him in my math class," Jesus sighed. "He's a real a-hole but he seems macho so the chicks dig him. Most guys don't. He brags all the time. I guess he does some martial arts and year-round sports. He's totally full of himself. I'd love to turn him over to the guys at the high school."

Adrian jumped in, "Jesus is right. I have him in PE. He thinks he's a gift to women. I have no idea why he would pick someone as nice as Lucie. Sure she's cute and all, but she doesn't have that edge that some of the so called popular crowd has. She doesn't buy into that garbage."

"Worse yet, what on earth does she see in him?" Marlo asked. "I'm sorry," he said, putting a hand on my shoulder.

I wasn't happy to spend the last three periods of the day with Lucie now. Why hadn't she told me? Wasn't I her friend? Wasn't I more than her friend? No. I was her friend, but I was still hurt. She would not meet my eyes in choir but I wasn't worried. I held her captive in science.

I beat her to class. I didn't even want to think about what held her up but I was afraid I knew; five foot eleven inches or so, blond hair,

131

blue eyes, good build and a bad attitude. When she came in the room she took one look at me and sighed heavily. She slumped over to her stool and dropped her books on the desk. "When were you going to tell me?" I asked in an angry voice that I held to just above a whisper.

"I didn't want to tell you. I still want you to be my friend," she spoke in a soft, hurt voice. "I just wanted both, a boyfriend and a friend. I'm sorry. I was afraid this would happen, but you made it clear that you just wanted to be friends and besides, you promised you would always be there for me." She turned as far from me as she could. My heart was aching but she was right, I had promised and I had pushed her away. It was hard to be mad at her; this one was on me.

The bell rang and class began. I tried to focus on science but neither one of us was up to our usual standard. Lucie had nearly always been the best part of my day. Today was not one of those days. I let her stew for most of class and finally turned toward her at the end. "You're right, Lucie. I did promise. I am your friend. I was hurt you didn't tell me. I'm still here for you." Even if it kills me, I added in my mind. Lucie gave me a somewhat watery smile and offered to carry my books to our next class. Too bad Calvin was waiting for her as we exited.

"Oh... hi, Calvin," Lucie said, surprised. "I was just walking Owen to health."

"Owen looks like a big boy," Calvin sneered, sizing me up. All I could think was *seriously*? Dude, I'm in a cast. I can't run and I'm not doing anything to you. He couldn't seriously be jealous because his girlfriend was my lab partner. By then I thought that beating him with my cane was sounding pretty good.

"It's fine, Lucie. I'll see you later." The last thing I wanted to do was make trouble for her.

"Not if I can help it," Calvin said. He had my back up and calm breathing wasn't going to do it. I bit my tongue hard so as not to reply. I tasted the iron of blood. Now was not the time. Why he was goading me right now was a mystery. I had done nothing that would make any normal guy jealous. Maybe I just existed. Lucie reluctantly handed my books to me and I nearly dropped them.

I covered my mistake quickly as if the books were just slippery and moved off toward class. She had handed me her day planner by mistake. Visions of Calvin and Lucie came to me unwanted. I felt like a voyeur. He had been charming in the beginning. He picked Lucie from a selection of many, it seemed to her. He had started out new and interesting and I was gone. She was lonely. Her father was on another mean kick and she had been grounded for staying too late at a friend's house on the same weekend I was beaten. She had needed to talk to me, the one friend who understood, and I wasn't there for her. She wondered why I didn't answer my phone and was hurt by my rejection. It was days later before she learned of my accident.

Calvin was more than happy to oblige by filling in for me. He spent every moment he could with her. She liked the attention at first but now it seemed a little obsessive. It seemed like he was using her to gain status.

I tried to pull myself together for health. Lucie sat as far from me as she could at our double desk, but as soon as Calvin's dark shadow had left the doorway she scooted right up next to me like she often did in science. Part of me wanted to push her away but most of me wanted to pull her close and away from Calvin.

"I'm so sorry," she said quietly, resting her head on my shoulder like she used to.

"Lucie, you don't ever have to apologize for someone else's behavior," I said firmly. "He is a little uptight though."

"He's just new and he doesn't know you," she said in his defense.

I turned my lips in and compressed them as I did sometimes when I was afraid the wrong thing would come out of my mouth. Now was not the time to harangue her about Calvin. Without a word I slipped her day planner over to her. She gave me a weak smile and stayed where she was. I thought she was pretty brave for staying so close to me. After spying us sitting together in science I figured the boyfriend would take a bathroom break to check on us during health. Sure enough, there he was halfway through class. If looks could kill I would be a dead man. I settled for brief eye contact with a blank expression on my face and then turned back to our teacher. I gave Lucie a small bump and pointed a finger to the door.

She surprised me when she turned to the door, glared, crossed her arms over her chest and just stared at him without moving away from me. He glared back at me. Because… I was doing what? Letting her sit by me? I wasn't forcing her. Our teacher noticed our inattention but glanced out the door before punishing us. Smart lady! She chased him right off.

"You know you're going to pay for that small act of defiance, right?" I asked with a smile when our teacher turned to write on the board, lecturing once more.

"Don't start," she grumbled, but she didn't move away. She seemed to need to suck up more of my warmth and friendship than ever.

I wanted to be sure she made it to the bus okay but I was in a hurry to get to my finals. I settled for telling her to be safe. My tests went okay and I was glad to be done with them. My mom was waiting by the office when I finished. "How'd it go?"

"Pretty good, I think. We'll know by the end of the week. Where are the little people?" I asked.

"Mrs. Lando has them. She's been dying to see you. She's fixing dinner again too. I don't know why she has adopted us but I think it's pretty great. Why her family ignores her I don't know, but I for one want to keep her," she said with conviction.

She took my backpack from me and waved to the school secretary before putting her arm around me. "Looks like you're about done with the cane. You're recovery has been much better than I had hoped. You seem a little down though. What's up?"

I hadn't been good at talking to her lately so I decided it was time to share... something. Lucie was what was weighing most heavily on me so I talked about her. I told her how I had liked her for so long and was trying to be her friend. I told her how I had promised that I would always be there, not realizing that it would feel like this. I explained how I felt that I had let her down even though I couldn't help it. I told her about what Lucie had said about wanting both a friend and a boyfriend.

My mom, the family diplomat, mediator and counselor, had an answer for this one too, no surprise. "Often the first thing a person says is the truth - before they have a chance to remove the sting. Sometimes that truth is painful, but it is nearly always better than a lie. I'm sure she wanted more from you, but you weren't ready to give it. She still values your friendship. Take heart, this Calvin thing won't last forever." She kissed my forehead as she helped me into the car.

I was stuck. The words she had said to me about truth and lies had a double meaning. My own hatred of lies drove me to meddle when maybe I should take a step back. I sure should have taken a different route on the whole Clive fiasco. I was most certainly lying to her both by omission and with the *small white lies* I had to frequently use. It was killing me.

"Mom?" I had to tell her about me.

"Yeah?" She glanced at me as she drove. It was the perfect opportunity and... I couldn't do it so I settled for a weak half truth.

"I'm sorry about the trouble I've been in lately. I just feel driven to help people. Maybe I need to become a cop or something. I feel the need to protect the innocent. You know, like Mrs. Lando, the cross country kids and my brothers. I don't understand people who hurt other people on purpose." I had settled. I wasn't proud of myself but I needed for her to understand me some at least.

"I understand how you feel Owen, but I know what you're doing isn't safe." What she said was a major understatement but she didn't know that... yet.

"I feel that same kind of need to protect the innocent, but I have obligations too. It is a tricky balancing act. I don't know what I'd do if I could only save one of my boys. What a horrible choice to be forced to make. I would kill myself trying to save you all and perhaps in doing that fail you all. I understand you better than you think. I love you and I need for you to be careful. Don't be so quick to throw your body in front of danger. I don't want to lose you. You are, after all, one of my three favorite children." Leave it to my mom to try to end a serious conversation on an upbeat note. I smiled at her.

"You're my favorite mom." She giggled like a girl. It was one of my favorite sounds in the whole world.

I was so tired I just wanted to eat and go to bed, but I had promised more family time. Mrs. Lando had cooked a turkey breast and made mashed potatoes and gravy. *Nice.* I got out of cleaning the kitchen. Alex and Lucas were recruited to help Mom while Mrs. Lando took me into the living room to put my leg up. It was my overprotective mom all over again.

"You seem to have become the neighborhood watch dog. You want to tell me about that?" she asked, her keen intelligence showing.

"To be honest, not really," I hedged.

"You know I didn't just used to play softball. I have lived a full, busy life. Do you know where I worked before I retired here?" Where on earth was she going with this?

"No ma'am," I answered, feeling the situation called for formality.

"Would you believe that I worked for none other than the FBI?" I think my eyes must have popped out of my head because she threw her head back and laughed. "It's true. In my line of work I have seen a lot of interesting things. *You* are becoming interesting. I have my eye on you," she said, patting my good leg. "I know something is up. I'm here for you, dear. I might be able to provide more than a baseball bat next time you get yourself in trouble, as I'm sure you will," she said with a twinkle in her eye. She stood and then bent down and kissed my forehead. "Be careful," she whispered.

"Well Lila," she said with greater volume to be heard in the kitchen, "thank you so much for having me over. I do so enjoy your boys. You keep the leftovers because I have the urge to do some other cooking. Oh and Owen, you get well soon. As much as I enjoy Marlo, you do a much better job on my lawn." With that she scurried out the door and was gone. Mom and I were both staring after her openmouthed. I know because I turned and looked at my mom who was standing in the doorway at the same time she turned to look at me.

"Marlo?" we said in unison. I had not given her lawn a single thought since my 'accident' and I'm betting my mom hadn't either. Marlo had said absolutely nothing. Wow, Marlo, what would I do without him?

The phone rang as I was working my way up the stairs to bed. Hopping had killed my ribs before the walking cast. I was so glad I was past scooting up backwards. It just took me forever. I fondly remembered running up the stairs.

My mom caught the phone but quickly came after me and signaled frantically. Dad would be home really late, she relayed to me. A note had been left on his windshield at work. Our 'friend' Clive wanted him to know that he didn't appreciate us making his life difficult. He had included a picture of my mom picking Lucas up from school. It was dated Monday. The police would be calling in the big guns. A patrol car would be on our street tonight. She kept her voice quiet so as not to scare my brothers, but she needed me.

To her credit Mom was incredibly calm. I know that inside she was fracturing. She had me stay put on the stairs. She called Mrs. Lando to be sure she got home safe and to thank her again for dinner. She sounded only slightly strained on the phone. Then she sent Lucas upstairs and had Alex wait by the door while she went out on the deck to potty Beggar. I started working my way back down the stairs. When they were back inside she told Alex to gather Luke and to pick a movie for us to watch in her room. She would make popcorn and we would have a pajama party. Alex gave me a hard look on the way past. He sensed that something was really wrong. I wasn't a bit surprised. "Do as Mom says. We're a team remember. We'll be okay." For the first time in my life I wished that my dad kept a gun in the house.

I limped into the kitchen as she was getting out the popcorn popper. She was shaking, but her eyes were dry. I put my arms around her and we just held each other. A dry sob racked her body. She took a couple of gulps of air, patted me on the back and stepped away. She nodded at me and made the popcorn without a word.

My leg was starting to really ache after my long day but I wasn't done yet. I pulled out my cell and called White Eagle as I started around the perimeter of our main level making sure windows and doors were locked and that all the outside lights were on. I knew they could still get in, but I just hoped to slow them down. White Eagle answered on the fourth ring. "We need you." It was all I had to say.

"I'll be right there," he said and hung up before I could say anymore.

Alex must have been doing a stellar job with Lucas because there was a minimum of thumping and bumping from upstairs. My mom went to check on them once to make sure all was well and to lock the upstairs up tight. Then she returned to wait with me for White Eagle. Although I recognized the sound of his truck, I still carefully checked to be sure it was him before I opened the door. A patrol car drove by just then so I waved.

We quietly told him everything we knew. He and my mother reassessed each other carefully. I could see them weigh and measure the worth of each other as their strange staring contest continued. I looked back and forth between them like a tennis spectator waiting for the final point to be scored.

"I'm glad you are here, but I feel like you are part of the reason my boy is getting into so much trouble. It's why I've been keeping him away," she said raising her chin and giving him a hard look. I opened my mouth to speak but White Eagle waved me off. I was proud of my mom. She was tougher than I had given her credit for. I knew she hated confrontations. She just didn't realize that she was picking the wrong battle.

"I know it looks bad, but I have nothing to do with Clive and his crew. I've been teaching Owen some skills to help him on his life's journey. He's an exceptional young man. He will do great things but he has a lot to learn yet. Please let me help guide him." There was an interesting power behind his words. I could almost feel it wash over me, gentle and sure. It must be something his grandmother had taught him. His body language and voice were asking her to trust him.

She cocked her head to the side, considering. My mom was such a great reader of people that I wondered if she would feel his power even more than I did. She seemed to soften and said, "I know he's driven to help other people but he's got to be careful. He can't keep sacrificing himself. This thing with Clive... Look, he's only fourteen. I wouldn't want my twenty-four-year-old son involved in anything like this. It has now come home to threaten my six and ten-year-old boys. I won't have it!"

"Owen is special. Have faith in him, in me and in you," he said with the same magic in his tone. My mom seemed to relax a bit. "Please let him come back and work with me. I can help him."

My mom looked at me. I could see so many different emotions travelling over her face.

"Please, Mom," I added.

"Go watch your movie. I will keep watch down here but I'd like to talk to Owen first if that is okay," White Eagle said gently as if sensing how hard won his victory had been.

My mom gave us a long look and walked slowly to the stairs. The wear and strain showed in the stiffness of her shoulders and the rigidity of her spine. She was trying to be ready to fight yet hide it from my brothers at the same time. I again marveled at the strength and courage she showed.

I turned back to White Eagle and saw similar things in him. I was betting they showed in me as well. I guess you collapse under pressure or you keep fighting back. I indicated the chair my mom often read in with a flip of my hand and hobbled over to the couch to sit and put up my leg. "Well? Now what?" I asked, not sure I wanted to know the answers but feeling the necessity.

"Now we wait, but we've got to get you back into training. Even the little things could make a big difference at this point. Clive has become a much bigger problem than I anticipated. I wonder if he senses something in you or if he is just plain crazy. Why would a young man such as you be so interesting to him?"

I shrugged, then asked, "You were doing something with your body and your voice when you talked to my mom. What was that?"

He gave me that startled look again. "Owen, you have more going on than I expected. You're more than a *spirit watcher*. Maybe your link to Miles through the watch is to blame?"

"The watch has been really quiet lately, but what do you mean exactly?"

"Miles had quite developed senses. You could say he had a gift for it. He could sense the mood in a room and could almost smell danger coming at him. He had some training in it, but it was almost like he had been through an extensive military program or spy training or something. He had not. I wonder if the watch doesn't talk to you any more because you have completely absorbed all that it had to offer and it's now a part of you. You seem to be developing something else too. You can almost look into people like I can, but you *feel* it, you don't just see it like I do. I still can't get over the fact that you can sense what I do. You may become the most powerful *watcher* ever. That really worries me. You know I believe in balance. If you are becoming this powerful, what is out there to balance you?" His eyes lost focus as he continued to gaze at me. I said nothing and let him finish his evaluation. I tried evaluating him. I could only sense that he was good and pure but not innocent; he had seen too much. He had not always been good but his grandmother had turned him around. I didn't see it in colors; I just knew or *felt* what people were. I also knew that we were linked somehow and maybe that was why I understood him as well as I did. I genuinely liked and respected him. We'd built trust.

"You still have that almost blindingly white light around you. It is so glorious that it fragments into rainbows at the edges like a prism. I have never seen anything like it. It is beautiful to look upon. I have been thinking about Marlo and what I saw. He has no talent like you do but he is loyal, intelligent and true. I don't usually look at normal people so intensely. I guess I was surprised. I, too, am still on my learning journey."

"I have to admit I find it almost strange that you admit you don't know everything. So many adults act so superior, like they know it all. They look at me like I'm just a kid. You have never done that. You treat me like an equal. My mom has started to do that more and more too. It's almost weird. I'm in eighth grade and I feel... like an adult."

"You are fast becoming one. When do you start physical therapy?"

"Next week."

"I wonder if your mom would let your 'Grandpa' go along," he said, making air quotes around the word grandpa. "I want to know what they say and recommend so that we can push you as hard as possible without pushing you over the edge. We want to get you back in top physical shape as soon as possible. We can start working on your mental abilities right now." Oh boy.

We worked for over an hour. It may have been all mental but I was exhausted and sweaty by the time he called it quits. We had practiced breathing, focusing, body language, tone of voice, listening and tuning out. I was also learning how to scan a room to see if any objects had an important story to tell me. I could almost see them glow or sense a hum of energy from them. I had gotten to where I could manage about a twenty foot radius without having to expend too much energy and focus. It was *way* cool! It sucked to walk into a room and get bombed with every object around me vying for my attention. You couldn't hurt an object's feelings so it was fine to ignore the lesser problems and just plain old normal stories. Objects that were associated with bad energy had a different hum than happy stories so I was getting to where I could pick them out easily. Instead of a glow, dark objects almost seemed to have a blackness about them, like they had sucked up all the light. Not that there was much to *see* at our house but we had practiced this skill at the shop too.

Tonight he also worked with my hands. He worked on all the ways I could hold my hands for offense and defense. Tomorrow after school we would work with my cane. I didn't really need it anymore but White Eagle thought I should keep it around as long as possible for defense since I was slowed down by my ribs and walking cast.

My dad was escorted in the door at a quarter after ten looking weary and exhausted. They had interviewed him extensively, searched his whole office building, looked at the surveillance tapes from the company parking lot and had taken his car in as evidence. The officers would wait outside in the extra patrol car assigned to our street. As White Eagle said, we would all wait.

My dad said little to White Eagle beyond what courtesy demanded. He went upstairs to check in with my mom. I offered to get White Eagle some bedding but he turned me down. I dozed on the couch. If he slept I was unaware of it. We left the lights on.

School was a real drag. I tried to be my best self for Lucie but I was so tired I could barely make it through the day. I hardly gave Calvin a thought and he settled for glaring at me whenever the opportunity arose. Our schools had been alerted that only our parents were to pick us up. Mom picked me up after school tight-lipped, and took me to the pawnshop. She made sure that I was inside and that White Eagle was there before she left. White Eagle would bring me home. The routine went on for the rest of the week. At least Adrian and Marlo were at the shop with me. We spent most of our time bringing Adrian up to speed, practicing our stances and practicing 'Good Fist', as White Eagle had come to call our hand practices. I would never have to give my hand position a thought again.

Nothing happened at home all weekend. We were beginning to let our guard down. My mom gave in to the pressure and went on a cleaning frenzy. All of us worked to eradicate every speck of dirt from the house. We attacked the windows and woodwork along with all the usual fun housework chores that go on regularly at our house. Dad got to do the grocery shopping... alone. He thought that was safest for all of us.

TEN

I was thrilled to go back to school on Monday. My room and the rest of the house were so clean they looked like they belonged in a home magazine. Things felt a little more normal. I had more energy for school. I had no need for the cane but I kept it anyway as White Eagle had suggested. I still had the urge to beat Calvin with it but I resisted.

At lunch Marlo and Adrian brought over some girls to sit with us. These were not the girls they had dated earlier in the year. I was feeling selfish, like I had been way too focused on myself and my own problems and had not paid enough attention to them. They brought over three girls. Super. Introductions were made all around. Again I had that feeling that I was a local celebrity. Not my favorite role but I played nice.

It was obvious that a cute girl named Melissa thought Marlo was the best ever and held his hand during much of lunch; looked to me like it was hard to eat that way. Adrian had hooked up with Jill. I didn't have either of them in any of my classes. The girls seemed plenty nice. They had brought their friend Katie with them. She was tiny and made me feel like a giant.

Katie had a soft voice that almost sounded like she was singing as she spoke. She was a first soprano in choir I discovered. Apparently she had noticed me, but I never noticed anyone. She was also in algebra class with Marlo and me. She sat by Marlo and I had never paid any attention. She wasn't Lucie but I really did enjoy her company. She seemed to be sweet and easygoing. I saw Lucie across the way with Calvin. She didn't seem happy.

Lucie flounced into science. She sat up very straight and tall on her stool and was really focused on our teacher for most of class. Toward the end of class she finally decided to talk to me. "What's up with the girl at lunch?"

"I don't know. I don't really know any of them. They're friends of Marlo and Adrian's. I just met them today."

"I'm sure they'll know you soon enough. You are mysterious, interesting and tough. Most girls around here want to be seen with you."

She seemed serious but I couldn't help it. I snorted.

"If you think I'm kidding you really are dumb."

I just gave her a look. I wasn't buying. She was full of it. I was no more interesting than any other guy at school. I guess I got points for being tall, points for having decent skin, points for not being a jerk and points for being in shape. Now take off five points for the cast and for looking stupid for getting beat up at the mall. Yeah, I was a real prize. I sat shaking my head, a half smile on my lips.

Lucie was in a better mood in health. We quickly finished the assignment we were teamed up on and spent the rest of the time talking quietly. Today was my first day of physical therapy. She told me what to expect. It sounded like today would be mainly an evaluation of where I was at and where I needed to go. I bid Lucie farewell and thanked her for her tips.

Mom was waiting at the office to pick me up and White Eagle was behind the wheel of his truck waiting for us at the curb. "Hey, great, you decided to let him come," I said, pleased.

"He is our security detail," she sniffed. "Why didn't you tell me about Sarah Lando? She is retired FBI! She is staying with your brothers while we do physical therapy. I may love her like family but I want my life back; they have to catch Clive and his partner! All this being on alert all the time is… frustrating."

Sounded like she had spent too much time alone and thinking today. She looked straight ahead out the windshield so I decided her question was rhetorical and did not require an answer. She was just venting. White Eagle seemed a little tight-lipped himself so I guessed their peace was an uneasy one.

Physical therapy was just as Lucie had said. They showed me around the facility and wanted to get me swimming as soon as my bones could handle it. We would also do some stretching and rebuilding of the muscle I had lost due to inactivity. They too were impressed with my healing and thought I was in pretty good shape considering. White Eagle and my mom asked all kinds of questions. I was glad that they were so interested. It left me to think about other things. They tested me to see how far and how long they could push me. I was glad when we were done. They left me with a few exercises that White Eagle vowed he would make sure I performed perfectly.

On Tuesday I was tired. One would think that I would be used to my cast by now but it still kept me awake. If it wasn't the cast then I would turn wrong in my sleep and my ribs would protest. When it wasn't physical it was mental. I continued to have nightmares. I guess it is no surprise. Clive and the third man kept coming after me. I would run through a field of cars with no end in sight and on they would come. I would grow weary but they never seemed to. I could smell the stink of the man I could not identify and see Clive's evil grin and the glint of his blade. I needed a vacation from me. A family vacation would be great but Dad was already at work more than he was home. Putting together money for a family vacation wouldn't happen right away. Besides, I would be going to Washington D.C. with my boys in just over two months. I needed to find that well of peace that White Eagle talked about.

When I reached the kitchen that morning, no one was their usual happy self. Even Lucas was grim. Breakfast was cold cereal. My mom took pity on me and handed me a protein bar with caffeine in it and the lunch she had packed for me. I could ride the bus today because mom was going to volunteer at the grade school. The extra complications in our lives were wearing on everyone. I told my mom I was done with the cane and left it hanging on the coat rack in the entryway.

Marlo tried to perk me up on the bus. He thought a little romance would brighten my world. According to his girlfriend Melissa, Katie had liked me for months. She just wasn't sure how to approach me. Now she thought she had an in and had begged Melissa to help her. Oh boy.

"Fine Marlo, I give up. What do you want me to do?" I asked in resignation.

"Come with us on Friday to the movies," he said, excited by the prospect. "When the movie is done we can walk around the mall, eat, hangout or whatever." He seemed so happy, how could I say no?

"Ok Marlo, you win. You plan the logistics and I'll show up," I sighed.

"Geez man, show a little enthusiasm would ya? Oh and sit with all of us at lunch. Be nice to Katie," Marlo said as if I needed help in the social etiquette department.

I smiled a little. Maybe I did need a little help in that department. I had been working with so many adults lately or much younger kids that I was forgetting how to be one with my peers. Besides, I needed a little fun. All the fun had leaked right out of my life lately.

"Thanks Mar. I don't say it much, but I truly appreciate you. You're a great guy to have around. I heard you've even taken over my job with Mrs. Lando. What would I do without you?" I asked seriously.

Marlo had the good grace to snort. "Why so serious? Without you I would have no social status. I am the friend of 'Owen the Mysterious' whom every girl at school from sixth to eighth grade wants to date. I even hear there are freshman who have heard about you and can hardly wait until you get to high school. You 'da man. You're a phenomenon. Besides, you bring adventure to my boring, humble life." The last was said with one hand on his chest and the other held aloft like a dramatic actor on stage.

I laughed and realized that I only got a small twinge from my ribs. Hooray. Today was looking up. "You're so full of crap."

"I'm only partially joking. The women do find you appealing. You grew and worked out. Do you even know how good you look to the women now? You look like a man. If that's not bad enough, as much as we try to keep it quiet, word gets around. People know you had something to do with the guy during cross county. People know you helped a neighbor who was being robbed. They know you helped get rid of the school bully and now the mall thing. We have a police officer assigned to the middle school just like the high school does. Rumors spread. If something perceived as cool happens around here, your finger is in that pie. Lots of guys think Lucie is *hot* but she only really talks to her girl friends and the two of us. All these pieces add up in some people's minds, making you a minor celebrity. This is part of the reason Calvin hates you, that and the fact that Lucie is still so tight with you. That guy is weird. He is all possessive of Lucie but the rumor mill says that he talks to other girls all the time. Him, we have our eye on." Marlo seemed to run out of steam and turned to look out the window.

I had a lot to think about. I had to find a way to keep a lower profile. Maybe hanging out with Katie and acting normal would make me seem more normal. I was thankful that Marlo had warned me on the bus, otherwise I would have been stunned to find Katie waiting to mug me when I got off the bus. I saw her leaning up against the wall near the entrance scanning every bus as the students hopped off. She was trying to look casual but to me she just looked a little overeager. When she saw me her whole face lit up.

I smiled at her and began to limp in her direction. She took off at a gallop toward me, narrowly missing other students in her mad dash to my side. I could tell she had taken special care of her appearance today. Her long dark hair had some kind of fancy braid running through it, she had on lots of mascara, sparkly lip gloss and the most uncomfortable looking shoes I had yet to witness. The look was... dazzling. The shoes made her blue tights-clad legs look like they went on forever. She wore a denim miniskirt and a blue lightweight sweater that looked like it was soft as down. She had big gold hoops in her ears. She wouldn't last ten seconds in a fight and she'd never be able to run. This girl needed to work on practicality. Lucie always exuded a subtle elegance. She often wore skirts or slacks with button up shirts. Her shoes were somewhat fashionable but always looked comfortable. Her makeup and hair were always simple and neat.

Before she even reached me, I smelled her. She smelled good, just strong. I prayed it would wear off by lunchtime or she would have my eyes watering. "Hi Katie," I said, plastering on my best smile and trying to hold my breath.

"Hi Owen, I hoped I'd see you this morning," she said breathlessly as she did an about-face to walk into the building with me. She seemed to spend a lot of time looking to see who was watching us. Plenty of people it turned out. Too bad for her I was only dressed in a skate shoe, a pair of jeans ripped out at the side to accommodate my cast and then pinned over it and a plain blue tee. At least I had showered and had done something with my hair. I had grown it out a bit and had taken to moussing it to stay in the latest fashion. She seemed pleased with all the attention and slid her books to the arm away from me and took ahold of my arm with her free hand.

With her heels on she still barely cleared my shoulder. She was pretty cute; I had to give her that. She reminded me of an elf or a pixie. The thought made me grin. I think she mistook my smile because she wrapped her arm more tightly around my bicep putting her even closer to my side. Nice, but pungent. I had to tell her.

"Katie, you look really nice today." I realized that her sweater was as soft as it looked. "Your sweater is really soft too."

"Thank you. I just got this sweater. I like it a lot. I just love blue, don't you?" She looked up at me with her big brown eyes. Eyeliner too. Ugh, too much!

"Um, blue's fine I guess. Hey by the way, your perfume smells nice but it's a little... strong." She looked hurt. Great. "Look, I'm sorry, I'm not trying to be mean in any way, you're just kinda... giving me a headache," I said with a pained look. *Give me a break*, I thought.

I'm trying to play nice and hang out with you but I can't hold my breath forever.

"Oh, I'm so sorry. It will wear off," she said with a weak smile.

We had reached my locker. I grabbed what I needed for class and dumped the rest. I snuck a peek at my watch. I had five minutes to get to class. "So, I guess I'll see you in math, right?" I really didn't want to hurt her feelings.

"Yeah, I'll see you in math." She turned and bounced off.

Oh boy. What had I gotten myself into? I wandered off to Spanish and made it just as the bell was ringing. The teacher looked at me but decided to give me a break. At least the cast was good for something.

Class ended and I gathered up my stuff. I looked up to find Katie hovering in the doorway. I plastered a smile on my face and sighed inside. Day one: Is this really what life was like with a girlfriend or at least a girlfriend wanna be?

"Hi, my class is right next door to your Language Arts class so I thought I'd walk you over if that's okay," she said, smiling and hopeful.

"Sure, why not?" I liked her fine, but I would need to dig lots deeper to find some enthusiasm. Now, if Lucie were here I would feel different. I felt a happy lightness in my chest when I saw Lucie. Maybe Katie sort of felt about me that same kind of way. Maybe I could give her a chance.

Again she grabbed my bicep and stayed close by my side as I limped along at a slow pace. She was right, her perfume was starting to dim. It was still strong but not migraine inducing. I found I couldn't resist asking, "Don't those shoes hurt your feet?"

"Don't you like them?" She seemed disappointed.

"They look fine, Katie, they just look painful to me. I, for one, am not into pain for fashion," I said, smiling at her to take the sting out of my words.

"Oh, they're not so bad."

"I was just worried about you. I think some of those ballerina flat type shoes would look just as cute and you wouldn't risk breaking an ankle," I said with concern.

"You were worried about me? That's nice."

Oh Geez, this was hard. She took everything the wrong way. No... more like she read too much into what I said. It was nice that she liked me but it felt a little overwhelming. I wondered if this was how Lucie felt about Calvin and then felt guilty because I shouldn't be thinking about Lucie.

"So tell me about yourself." I looked at my watch. "Well, the condensed version for now, we only have three minutes," I said with a smile so she wouldn't take offense.

She beamed at me, glad I was interested, as we walked toward class. She rattled on about being the youngest of four girls. One was married last summer in the most beautiful ceremony ever. So romantic, too bad I didn't see it, she lamented. Yeah, right. No thanks. I got to hear about dresses, flowers and hair styles. Awesome – not.

I was happy for once to reach L.A. "Well, I'll see you in math," I said, extracting myself from her grip and making my way to my seat.

Adrian and Marlo gave me pleased looks. I was behaving myself. They quickly interrogated me before class officially started. Yeah, Katie was nice but a little over the top. Sure, I was still on for Friday. I just had to convince my jailor mother. Being out with Katie would be a whole lot better than staying at home right now, no matter how much perfume she wore.

L.A. was as awful as ever. Our teacher was a little odd and granola for my taste. Today she was starting a poetry unit. Oh joy!

151

So *not* my favorite. I could write song lyrics all day but poetry was just so very boring. I felt a big eye roll coming on as she intoned, "You can't just read the poetry to understand it, you have to feel it, experience it, and live it. It is spring, the time of love and unions. We shall be experiencing the poetry of spring and love today. Ah, spring, when a young man's fancy turns to... young women."

Had my fancy turned to young women? I was willing to give Katie a try, so maybe. Did I want a girlfriend? Not really. Did I want to do love poetry? Big negatory. On the other hand, maybe I could write some good lyrics to keep my teacher happy and disguise it as poetry. I had plenty of fodder. The love you want is not within your reach and the love you don't really want is reaching for you. *Hey, I might have something.*

Marlo and I headed for math. Katie caught up with us in the hallway and this time pushed herself in to walk between us. She took my arm as had become her habit. I smiled at her but kept quiet and let Marlo do all the talking. He was much better at it than I was anyway. Katie actually thanked Marlo for introducing us as if I wasn't even there. It was kinda weird. Marlo took it in stride and started talking to her about Friday.

I walked her to her seat by Marlo and heaved a big sigh of relief as I slouched into my own spot as the bell rang. Katie could be Marlo's problem for the next hour. We had some time at the end of the period to work on some problems. I slid my seat over by Marlo as usual and we started to work. Katie slid over by us but had trouble focusing.

"Don't you guys do your homework at home?" she asked hopefully.

"Sorry, we get as much done at school as we can. We have stuff to do after school so there isn't always time for homework," I said quietly, getting right back to work. Marlo and I were whipping right through the math problems in our usual fashion; do the problem, see if the other was done and check our work. If the other person wasn't done, go on and then check back later. If we disagreed we would stop and discuss it. To her credit Katie tried to keep up with us and not interfere. Her stock had just gone up in my mind. We had mastered this plan of attack earlier in the year and we were good at it now. Katie had it figured out by the end of the period. I was impressed.

"Wow, you guys are good at this. I had no idea you were so good at math, Owen. I knew about Marlo because he sits next to me. I actually like the way you do homework. I usually just visit with my friends but now I only have five problems left. Cool!" she said with real enthusiasm.

I liked her much better like this. She was a real person, participating and not just trying to impress. Nice. We all headed out the door together. The atmosphere was much more relaxed.

"I need to hit my locker. I'll see you guys at lunch," I said, heading in that direction. I could see someone leaning against my locker as I approached. Calvin. Well swell, and my day had been looking good so far too. He straightened when he saw me approach. I wasn't surprised he had found my locker – nothing is a secret in middle school. I hoped high school would be better. I blew out a sigh as I looked at Calvin. Like my mother – confrontation was not my favorite.

"Ryer," he said with disdain.

"What do you want?" I asked in a tired voice not wanting to deal with him.

"I don't like you sitting so close to my girl. It isn't right," he said with a shadow of threat in his voice.

I opened my locker and threw in my stuff, snagging the lunch my mom had packed for me. Marlo had been providing her with nutritional menu items that were supposed to help me heal faster. I could be harsh about my healthy diet but Marlo was looking pretty genius as far as Mom was concerned. He was on a health kick himself and who was I to interfere.

I turned my attention back to Calvin's scowling face. He and I were close to the same size. He was a little taller and was trying to use that to his advantage. His feet were spread and he had crossed his arms over his puffed out chest. His head was tilted slightly down so that he could look at me from under his brows. Who was he trying to kid? I knew all about intimidation and body language. I wasn't having it.

"Yeah, whatever," I mumbled and turned to walk away. He stopped me with a hand on my shoulder. "Get. Your hand. Off. Me." I snarled through gritted teeth, slapping his hand away. I turned and used all my intimidation training against him. I did not touch him or say a verbal word. I gave him my best stink eye and held myself rigid then relaxed into a quasi fighter stance, legs apart, arms slightly out from my sides, hands ready to form fists. I must have been doing my job because he blinked and took a step back.

"Walk away Calvin," Adrian snarled from behind me. Like magic he was there. Guess I wasn't so scary after all. Adrian was looking pretty fierce. Jill and Katie stood behind him looking worried.

"I'm just saying is all," he said a little more quietly.

Katie came up and put her hand in mine. "What's up Calvin?" she asked, trying to diffuse the tension. He looked at our joined hands and a slow smile spread over his lips, though it never reached his eyes.

"Well then, never mind," he said as he headed for lunch.

"What was that about?" Katie asked.

Adrian and I looked at each other before I turned back to her to answer. "Calvin has decided he doesn't like me. He doesn't know me, but he doesn't like me. He also hates it that I have three classes with his girlfriend and she's my friend. We even have assigned seats next to each other in two classes." I thought it was better that she know. I would still be Lucie's friend. Katie was new to my galaxy and Lucie had lived in it for a long time.

"I know Lucie, she's nice. I thought you were dating her but then she went out with Calvin. Jill told me that Adrian told her that you were available. Shall we go to lunch?" she asked softly.

154

I realized that I was still holding her hand. It seemed like it would take too much effort to change that so I let it slide and we walked to lunch.

"You know you were pretty brave to talk to Calvin like that," I said quietly. "He seems pretty antagonistic to me."

"It's fine. His bark is worse than his bite. He just likes to act tough. He thinks it makes him look cool. Personally, I think it makes him look like an idiot," she said with conviction and I had to smile. Seemed like I had been smiling a lot today, thanks to Adrian, Marlo and Katie. It felt good and normal.

Lunch was actually fun and the conversation flowed much more smoothly. It was nice to put all the bad stuff out of my head and just hang out with friends. I again caught sight of Lucie. She was sitting a bit away from Calvin and he was deep in conversation with another girl. There seemed to be mostly girls at his table. I watched as he reached out an arm and dragged Lucie across the bench next to him. She seemed to lean a little away but he kept steady pressure on her shoulder. He might know how to use body language but he sure didn't know how to read it.

Speaking of body language: Katie had released my hand to eat her lunch but was as close to me as she could get without actually sitting in my lap. Her perfume was down to a dull roar that I could actually appreciate, if not enjoy. She was using every strategy she had to tell me how much she liked me without using words. I wished she would relax and just be herself. I figured the rumor mill would be in full swing by the end of the day and, like it or not, Katie's name would be linked with mine.

Lucie seemed a little down in science but put up a good front. We worked hard and were able to finish our packet so that we wouldn't have homework. Lucie's planner was between us on the table open to this week.

"Hey," I said pointing at the planner, "I see you are meeting with your gymnastics coach. Good for you." I didn't even hear her response as my finger connected with her planner and several quick images came to me. All revolved around Calvin and none looked very good. He was giving her a bad time about me. He hated that we were friends and he didn't want her to have anything to do with me. Luckily we had classes together and he couldn't change that. *We* couldn't be friends but he was trying to be 'friends' with every girl at school. He sucked up attention wherever he could get it. I couldn't figure out why he didn't just let Lucie go. She seemed to be some kind of challenge. She was... status. He would leave her when he was done with her but she wouldn't be leaving him. No one left him. He had even rubbed in my supposed defection from Lucie at lunch. He was telling the whole table that I had a girlfriend. Super.

Lucie was giving me a strange look and began to slide her planner from under my limp fingers. "You do that sometimes. Space out. What are you thinking?" she asked curiously.

"Luce, I'm glad you're seeing your coach. I know you like her. I'm glad someone makes you happy. I worry about you and Calvin. I don't like the way he treats you."

"I don't know what you are talking about," she said firmly to let me know the conversation was closed.

Fine Luce, I thought, deny it. I patted the hand that was on her planner and started gathering my books. Calvin did us the honor of not showing up between classes and we made it to health in peace. I kept up my best behavior and tried to be a good friend to Lucie.

Katie was waiting in the lobby to tell me goodbye. I told her it had been nice to hang out with her today and that I would see her tomorrow. She seemed happy as she boarded her bus. Marlo, Adrian and I all gathered together to be picked up by White Eagle. I had the ugly feeling that we would soon be running to the pawn-shop after school. I dreaded getting back in shape. Staying in shape was much easier.

A new shipment had come into the pawnshop. It was such a relief to be able to 'look' at it in front of Adrian. Marlo set up his laptop and began to catalog the items that I received information from.

There was nothing very exciting or dark in this batch. I explained to Adrian how I find the *dark* things. These were pretty normal objects but the dark stuff drew me to them.

White Eagle came into the back to check on us and my gaze rocketed to him. "Hey, I haven't felt anything *dark* in some time. Why is that?" I asked, suddenly curious.

"You hadn't said anything to me and I wondered that myself. Maybe your gift understands that you can't fix anything right now or maybe it's just quiet out there. Sometimes life is just like that though. It will give you time-out. We all deserve a break once in awhile to heal our wounds," he said calmly, exuding wisdom as he so often did.

"Hey, White Eagle, can you run us by the library on the way home?" Marlo asked. "We need to find some books on poetry for Language Arts." Adrian and I just smiled and nodded. That's our boy, we said to each other without words, just the look.

The rest of our time at the shop passed quickly. Marlo and Adrian worked out and I did what I could. We all did my physical therapy. Hey, why not, they had said when White Eagle asked them to join us. For him, everything was a learning opportunity.

Thanks to Marlo, the super genius, we were quickly able to pick out some books for class. He knew which section to go to without looking it up. He had done a preemptive strike and had looked up the books before we left the pawnshop.

White Eagle had sat in his truck and watched the ducks that hung around the library. For all I knew they were part of his spy network and were communicating with him. Adrian wanted to know what I found so funny. So I told them. Marlo rolled his eyes and handed the books to me so he could climb in the back seat of the truck. "Get used to it. He does that all the time. He goes off in his own little world and analyzes everything."

We all laughed until I tried to load myself in the truck. I put the books in the center of the front bench seat and pulled myself in.

I pushed at the books to move them over and my hand came in contact with a smallish one I had not noticed earlier. I froze and my eyes lost focus. Everyone in the truck froze with me waiting for what I had seen.

"There is an old man, not dying of the cancer that riddles his frail body, but of regret. He is dying alone and mentally wounded. He blames himself for killing a little girl." My voice caught on a half sob, I was so overcome by his hurt and grief. The grief was just rolling off the poetry book and I wondered why I hadn't seen it sooner. They all just stared at me and then they all began talking at once.

"Marlo, please hack the library's database and figure out who he is from the book's checkout record. We need to find his address and his story. I stared warily at the book almost afraid to touch it again but knowing I needed to do so to help this poor man. The message it gave me was clearer this time.

White Eagle dropped us all off at our respective homes and was on his way. I was unusually quiet at dinner. My mom picked up on my mood and assumed that it was the captivity wearing on me. "You should be happy. You got to ride the bus this morning. It has been quiet. Our protection detail is pulling back from us. They think Clive's gone," she said, sounding both scared and relieved.

Marlo called just after dinner and said he had found what I needed. He had sent it to my email and I could print off all his attachments. If I had any questions I was to call him back. Looking over the stuff I felt even worse that I had earlier. I stuffed all Marlo had sent me into my backpack and wished I could tell my mom everything. For the first time I wanted her with me on a mission. Her worried face came to mind and I couldn't remove it. I had lied to her. True they were lies of omission but they still cut me deeply. I wanted to cry. I walked downstairs and past the living room where she was reading to my brothers.

"I need to go to Marlo's. We mixed up our poetry books. I swear I will be careful and observant. I have my cell phone," I said in

158

my most grown up voice while I tried to look trustworthy and dependable.

She looked at me, her heart in her eyes. I could see the struggle going on in her mind. It was written all over her face. Protect me or let me grow up and be a man. "I guess," she finally said reluctantly.

I waved to my brothers and closed the door gently behind me. I couldn't get Mom's face out of my mind. The worry, the fear and the courage she showed. She also was showing strong faith in me. I limped down the driveway and turned back to look at the house, my mind on my mom. Thoughts are dangerous I've determined. About the time the idea of actually telling my mom crossed my mind again, there she was. I'd thought that I was alone looking up at our house before I left to fight evil.

"Can I talk to you for a moment?" She spoke in a library-like voice so as not to disturb anything around us. A hush had crept over the night, soft and comfortable, like a favorite blanket.

"Yeah, sure Mom." I noticed that she had that mother bear look on her face now that she was close enough to see clearly in the gathering darkness. Obviously she was in overprotective mode.

"Why are you drawn to these bad situations? Worse yet, why are these awful people drawn to you? For example, your mugger, Sarah Lando's burglar, the creepy guy from cross country and other weird and unexplained events. I want you to tell me about them. This all has something to do with Mr. White Eagle, doesn't it?"

I sighed and caved. Apparently all the thoughts of her were telling me it was time. I watched her carefully as I began to speak. "Yes, but don't be mad at him. He's helping me. I have a gift. It's almost like being psychic but I'm no psychic. Objects tell me their stories in pictures. I have to help the victims like Mrs. Lando. Sometimes the bad guys know that I *know* things I shouldn't and that gets me into trouble. I'm still learning."

"What?" she asked alarmed.

"I see the images like a memory of my own. Sometimes it's like a hologram that overlays what I'm seeing in the real or present world. I see either bad things that people have done or their intention to do bad things. It's almost like I can read their guilt. I'm driven to fix these things that I'm shown. It's as if it's my job to correct the flow of too much bad energy and bring it back to neutral. This is not a choice. The gift is in me. It's what I am meant for," I said softly, my whole body trying to convey my entire story.

I reached toward her and touched the collar of her blouse and looked down into her eyes. "You were at the elementary school today. Lucas had a substitute teacher. You look worried. I think you are worried that this teacher doesn't know to watch Lucas carefully. You're filing papers for the teacher. They're going to recess. You look... torn. You are trying to decide if you should stay inside or go with them. You're trying to be brave yet cautious. You're deep in thought as the kids leave with an aide. The teacher came up behind you, startled you and you dropped all the papers you had in your hand."

She sucked in air in a gasp. "You can see that and you know how I felt?" she said like a sigh. "I knew something was going on. Owen, you have to stop. Look at yourself. You're still in a walking cast. Your scars from your stitches are still pink. Your bruises are gone but I know your ribs still hurt you sometimes. What if this happens again? Your body can't take this. I can't stand to have you beat up like this. Next time could be worse," she gasped, in a voice choked with emotion. "Owen, I love you, I have to protect you. I want you to have a normal life. Just choose *not* to do this."

I jammed my fingers through my hair in frustration. How to make her understand? "I have no choice. It would eat me alive if I didn't do my job. I am driven, like the need for food or the need to breathe. This is a part of me, a part of who I am! This is who I'm meant to be. Until my heart stops beating I will be obligated, no – it's more than that. I can't *not* help people," I told her in a choked voice, needing for her to understand. It had been easy to tell Marlo and Adrian. This was the hardest thing I'd ever had to do.

160

My story came out in a rush. I told her about all the people I had helped and where I was really going tonight. I watched her face as I poured out my story. I could tell she was reading the raw emotions travelling across my face, just as I read them on hers. Silently she reached up and smoothed my frown away with cool fingers. I saw tears begin to pool in her eyes. She seemed to hold tight to them, like she seemed to be holding herself tightly together. I felt that she didn't want me to see any more of her fear and grief.

"It's killing me to watch this bad stuff happen to you. It's changed you. You aren't the boy you were just months ago. You have a hard edge to you now. I hate it. I miss my Owen." A lone tear escaped her tight hold.

"I'm okay, Mom," I said even though I really wasn't. It was a small lie. She was right, I had changed. I couldn't lie to her anymore, even though I now realized, it's what you do when you love someone. You lie to protect them. Now, because I loved her, I had to tell her the truth so that I could keep doing what I was destined to do. I felt like the grownup I was becoming. My childhood was done. "I'm actually not okay but I will be. You have to trust me," I said softly.

I knew my face had reverted to the protective mask I often wore because she reached up to touch my face again. "I do understand," she whispered. "I've always known. From the first moment I held you in my arms I knew there was something special about you. You will do great and amazing things that most people will never know about or understand. Just don't push us away. Let us have as much of you as we can. Don't keep secrets from us, let us help you. Don't push your friends away either. I've seen the way you look at Lucie. Don't be afraid to love. People will come and go from your life. You will touch them all. Don't let your fear of the danger to any of us make you push people away. You don't have to be alone." She sighed and stepped away as she wiped another escaped tear. "I sort of have a... gift too. Well it's not really a gift, I think I'm just more observant than most people but I know things about people that others don't notice. I read their body language more so than anyone else I know of. I don't have a Mr. White Eagle. I've never even been trained, but I realize I see things in you now. Let me know if I can help you, otherwise I'll stay out of your way. I love you and I will always be here for you." She smiled a watery smile, turned and slipped back toward the front of the house.

"I love you too, Mom." She turned slightly at my voice and then was gone. I looked longingly one last time at my favorite structure, the place that held my family. The windows glowed with a soft yellow light. A gentle breeze ruffled my hair. It reminded me of how my mom used to ruffle my hair with a feather-light touch and then I knew - she was there with me even when she wasn't and she always would be. My mom, my guardian angel, my personal nag, would always be with me. For the moment she had other charges to tend to back in the house.

I wasn't surprised by her announcement that she too had a special ability. I think, like her, I had always known she was different; no, not different just more than most people. I could really use her but she had my brothers to care for. I knew that was her most important job at the moment. At least I could talk to her now. I felt lighter, as if my heart wasn't working so hard to beat.

I started to limp down the street but paused when I heard an engine around the corner. I caught the flash of lights. I melted into the shadows and changed direction. I would rather get a little muddy in the field than face my dad right now. Maybe I was a coward but I thought this was one battle that was better left to my mother. He would try to stop me and I had work to do.

Thank goodness tonight's job was an easy one. If I had to fight I was at one serious disadvantage. This job was perfect for someone messed up physically like me. I was counting the days until I was off restrictions and outta my cast.

In my backpack was all the proof that Marlo had collected for me. I headed up the main drag and cut through the convenience store parking lot past the coffee shop and deli. A few blocks down and across the street was the retirement home. I was feeling tired. When had I last walked this much?

I paused in the shadow of the trees across the street from the retirement home. The moon hung weightless in the sky, huge and full with a soft halo around it. I watched the place to see how much activity there was going in and out, not much this time of night. Apparently old people go to bed early. An older model station wagon turned into the parking lot. I paused for traffic and crossed the road following the wagon. The people in the car didn't seem to see me at all.

A man and a woman getting out of their car, took a sleeping toddler from a car seat in the back and made their way to the main entrance. I slid silently behind them. Not so close as to draw attention but close enough to catch the door before it clicked closed. The nice people stopped to speak to someone at the desk and I walked right by as if I belonged. If there was a camera to be caught on, I did not see it. If there was one I had missed then it should look like I came in with the young couple but chose not to say 'hi' at the desk. I walked down the long hall keeping my eyes peeled for room numbers and the stairs. I figured that the numbers upstairs would be the same as they were on the lower level.

Halfway down the hall I found the stairs. Behind me I heard the young couple coming. I slipped inside the stairwell before they rounded the corner and listened at the not quite closed door. They seemed to be coming my way but stopped at the elevator. I waited until I heard the ding signaling its arrival. I could hear their soft whispery voices but I couldn't make out what they were saying. I heard the elevator doors whoosh shut and silently moved up the stairs as fast as my cast would allow. At the top I again listened at the cracked door. The couple walked the other way. YES! The numbering was exactly like the lower level. I figured I had to be looking for a room at the end of the hall.

When I reached the door I could hear the soft sounds of a television going inside. I knocked and waited. I could hear his labored breathing and shuffling footsteps through the door. Of course he would be expecting a neighbor. He opened his door and gazed at me with surprise. Before he could recover I stepped in and shut the door. Startled, he backed into the wall beside him. "Who are you? What do you want?"

"I'm here to help you, Mr. Johnson."

"What? I didn't ask for any help."

"I'm here to tell you about Emily Wilson. You were misinformed." My words seemed to take all the strength from him as he slid right down the wall and sat hard on his backside. He put his hands over his face and began to weep. "Mr. Johnson, she's not dead. Give me a chance and I can prove it."

He looked up at me with watery blue eyes; his whole face had a crumpled look. I grasped him under his arm and hauled him to his feet. "Come on, let's go sit and I'll show you." I led him to a small kitchen table just off the short entry hall. He flopped unceremoniously into one of the chairs. He propped his elbows on the table and gave me a long look. "Can I get you something?"

"Water," he rasped and flipped an unsteady hand toward the cupboard by the sink. On the counter under the glass cupboard were more pill bottles than a pharmacy. It was depressing. I quickly fixed him a glass of water and sat opposite him.

"Mr. Johnson, my name is Owen Ryer. I know you are hurting over Emily's death but I'm here to show you that there has been a mistake in identity." I slid off my backpack and opened it, pulling out the contents. I handed him the April of last year article showing his car accident when he hit a little girl on a bike. It also indicated that both he and the girl were taken to the hospital to treat their injuries. I pulled out and handed him the next article showing that one night later a woman by the same name as the little girl had consumed too much alcohol and had crashed her car into a pole down near the river. She was taken to the same hospital. Then I pulled out and handed him the little girl's school picture from this year. There was her smiling face with her classmates, the date clearly marked. He just shook his head. Then I uncovered the last bit; this year's registration for school. That last bit gave him pause.

He looked at all the pieces for several minutes. I kept thanking Marlo and his hacking skills over and over in my mind.

"How could this happen? I had asked and they said she was gone."

"It was an honest mistake. If the person who told you realized what they had done, I'm sure they would have let you know. The Emily who rode her bike in front of your car is fine. She broke her arm and was released the day she arrived. The people at the hospital were confused. You had to stay overnight. The only Emily they had record of at the hospital was the one they had admitted to the morgue. Your Emily was only ever in the emergency room and not the main hospital. It was a mistake. You can let it go now." He took a deep steadying breath.

"Thank you," he breathed. "Please leave these. I'd like to be alone now."

I stood quietly, grabbed my backpack but left the papers behind and slipped out his door. I looked both ways and made for the closest exit. I slipped into the cool arms of the night. It felt good after the too warm apartment.

"Go in peace," I whispered up toward his window and limped off down the street toward home. At the corner as I waited for the crossing signal, I pulled out my phone and called Marlo. It went right to voicemail. "I'm done. You were a great success. Call me when you can." I was wondering how much hell there would be to pay when I got home. Whatever it was it would be worth it.

I had never felt so happy and so sad all at once. He could go peacefully. I had helped but he had suffered. No one should have to endure a long painful death like he was.

When I got home the house was quiet. They had left a light on for me. I carefully locked up and dragged myself upstairs. My parent's door was closed and I could hear them talking quietly. I gave the door a soft tap.

"Come in," Dad said in a harsh voice. Great. They were fighting and about me it seemed. The waves of emotion rolling through the room were almost more than I could stand after what I had been through tonight. I glanced at my mom and then held my head up high and looked at my dad, ready for whatever he was going to do or say.

"You are grounded. You are to go nowhere except to school," he said, his voice shaking with anger.

"No," Mom and I said in unison.

"Believe me if I could ground you too I would. How can you do this to me, Lila? I thought we were a team and now you have sided with... *him*, against me and my wishes. What were you thinking?" he asked, flipping an angry hand in my direction. "I can't believe you let him out unsupervised and at night too! It is dangerous for him to be out."

I opened my mouth to speak but Mom beat me to it. "You don't understand, Brad."

"You're right, I don't and I don't want to," he said interrupting her.

I couldn't decide if I should speak or not. Should I stay or go. This argument was about me yet I felt like I was invading their privacy. I knew that I was seeing something I should not see. They had always showed us the team face. They had always seemed to get along and to work together. This was something I had never seen before. She had pressed her lips together and stood rigidly staring at him. He was staring her down just as intently, neither one giving an inch. He ripped his eyes away from her and turned back to me.

"You are grounded until we move. I have been offered a job in Atlanta. We move next month. I am leaving on business tomorrow to get things all set up," he said firmly.

My mouth hung open for a moment in shock. "Dad, No! I'm not going. I can't. I'll stay with someone and finish school."

"You most certainly will not. I decided today. It is too dangerous here and the job in Atlanta is a better job. WE ARE MOVING AND THAT'S FINAL!" he ended on a roar.

"No," Mom and I spoke in unison again. I had never seen him like this. I didn't understand. "Brad," she continued in a strong soft voice, "you may go if you wish. I wish you well, but the boys and I are staying here."

Alex edged into the doorway. I stepped toward him to save him from this terrible moment. I saw the look on his face... he had been listening. He knew. He threw his arms around my waist and leaned his head against my side.

"This is getting out of hand. We need to discuss this calmly," my mom said softly. She held her hand out to my dad but then let it drop as he looked from Alex and me to my mother's outstretched hand, then up to her face.

"I have made my decision. If you aren't packed up when I get back, I am going without you. I see how it is here. You have pushed me out. Fine." He looked at me. "I am very disappointed in *you*." With that he snapped his suitcase shut, picked it up and brushed past us to the door. "I'll be back in two weeks."

The front door slamming was followed by the revving of an engine and the squeal of tires.

Alex was the first one to break the heavy silence, "Oh well, he's never here anyway."

Mom looked stunned. She slowly regained her composure. "Oh boys, I'm so sorry. When he calms down he'll be sorry too. He was speaking out of anger. He'll do some thinking while he's in Atlanta and we'll work this out."

Part of me knew it was not the moment but the words she had spoken to me earlier floated up to my consciousness. "Mom, you once said, 'that often the first thing a person says is the truth - before they have a chance to remove the sting. Sometimes the truth is painful, but it's nearly always better than a lie.' I think that applies here. We'll see. You know I'm always here for you."

"I deserve to know what is going on," Alex pleaded.

"Alex, you're right, but we need to give Mom some time to figure out what that is. All we know right now is that Dad was offered a job in Atlanta and we need to decide if we are going to move there. If we are moving then we need to decide when. We will figure this out. Dad is trying to do what he thinks is best and so is Mom. We need to give them time to work it all out."

"I don't want to move. I like it here. I have friends here. This is my home," he pleaded.

"I know, Buddy, I don't want to move either. I'm sure Mom is taking that into consideration. Let's try not to worry about it tonight. Let's give it some time to settle out. Come on, let's go get you ready for bed." I dropped my backpack on the floor and picked him up. My mom cringed. I could feel the strain in my body but he needed me and she needed a minute to gather her thoughts.

I took Alex to his room and he slid down my body and into his bed so that I wouldn't have to bend over with him. I pulled the covers over him and eased down next to his bed. I looked over at Lucas who miraculously had slept through all the drama. "See Lucas over there?" I whispered.

"Yeah," he whispered back.

"Listen to him breathe."

"Okay."

We listened to several quiet sleepy breaths. "Lucas isn't worried. He's dreaming some happy dreams. Pretend you are like Lucas and don't have any worries. Just focus on breathing like him. Tomorrow we will talk about this. For right now we can't fix it so we'll let it go. Just breathe," I instructed in a soft soothing voice. Alex reached for my hand and closed his eyes. I sat beside him until my arm fell asleep and my backside was numb. I looked up and saw my mom watching from the doorway. Her body was still and her eyes were dry. Her feet were crossed at the ankle and her arms were crossed over her stomach. I gently pried Alex's fingers from my hand, stood and walked toward her. Alex snuffled in his sleep and rolled over.

I walked back into my mom's room and picked up my backpack. She walked past me and sat on the side of her bed patting the spot next to her. I walked slowly over to sit.

"So, were you a success? Did you meet with the man you told me about?"

"Yes, but that hardly seems important right now," I sighed.

"I thought about what you said. Please understand your dad doesn't know the whole story. It's your secret to share or not. I didn't do a good job explaining. He feels left out of the loop. He and I have made a mess. I'm so sorry you saw that. He is often gone for work while I take care of things here. I don't keep him out on purpose; I just keep doing what I have to do. He can separate work and home. He wants to come home and fit seamlessly back in like nothing has changed since he left but life here is dynamic and changing all the time. He'll realize that. He's also scared. He doesn't like to see us in danger and he still thinks you brought it here."

I put my arm around her. "The man I saw in this room tonight I've never seen before. It's not like Dad to give ultimatums. I have to be honest though. I won't be moving. I can't."

"I know Owen, I won't make you move. I won't be going either, I don't think. He can take the job if he wants. It nearly doubles his pay. He's hardly ever here like your brother said. He could afford to come see us and he could afford to fly us out on your school breaks. Maybe he won't take the job or they could make some other arrangement. He thought he was solving all our problems by taking this new job. He has been making so many decisions alone, like I have, that he forgot to ask us what we thought. He didn't mean to do it. He thought he was protecting us and was shocked that I didn't, we didn't, agree. The three of us should talk when he is himself."

"I'm not ready to tell him, Mom. I just feel like it's not the time. He's not ready to hear it. I knew somehow that the time had come to tell you. I think you knew that too and that is why you met me outside tonight."

She nodded her head. "I don't know what's going to happen. We just have to keep doing the next right thing, whatever that is, and then we will have to live with the choices we make."

We sat there side by side, my arm around her until almost eleven, our heads resting against each other. Finally she broke the moment by saying, "You should take your own sleeping advice. I'll see you in the morning. I love you."

"I love you too, Mom. I feel like I should say it's going to be okay but I promised myself I wouldn't lie to you anymore," I said softly.

"It will be okay – I just don't know what *okay* is going to look like yet."

I brushed my teeth and went to bed. I fell quickly into a dreamless sleep.

ELEVEN

I couldn't believe it when Marlo was at my house the next morning before my brothers had even left for school. He beat me into the kitchen where he was eating my mom's pancakes with his favorite topping, peanut butter. Mom must have talked a little to Lucas because he was telling Marlo about Dad going to Atlanta for two weeks and that we might be moving but we didn't know yet and not to worry. It was almost comical to watch the emotions travel his face at warp speed to keep up with Lucas' banter.

Alex was quiet but serious this morning. He added little to the conversation, just repeating that he didn't want to move. My mom moved over by Marlo and patted him on the back and told him not to worry. Marlo gave her a strange long look as she was rounding up my brothers for school. "Clean the kitchen please, would you? Oh, and don't forget your cast comes off today. I'll meet you at school after lunch some time. Your lunch is in the fridge." She was gone in a swirl of little boys and dog.

I ate breakfast and Marlo started cleaning up the kitchen. There wasn't a lot to do because my mom always cleans as she goes. I was guessing that Marlo got his efficiency from his mom. He had the dishwasher loaded and was starting to wipe down the counters before I had even finished eating. He looked at me periodically but said nothing. He rinsed the kitchen cloth and then brought it to the table as he sat across from me. "Are you ready to tell me yet?"

"How did you know to be here today?" I asked suspiciously.

"I called you like twelve times last night and you never called me back. I bet your phone was on *silent*. I was worried. When I got here your mom was talking to Lucas. I think she was trying to get to him before Alex did. Sounds like your dad got a great new job that will take him to Atlanta and you all are trying to decide what to do."

"Well that's the polite version, but yeah," I sighed, feeling discouraged. "Actually there was a big argument and some ultimatums made. It's my fault. My dad thinks I am this horrible person and now my mom knows about me and he doesn't get why she is siding with me instead of him. What a mess."

"I'm so very sorry," Marlo said, looking down at the dish cloth. "You can always live with us. We have lots of room. If your family moves, I mean."

"Marlo, you're the best but I was thinking White Eagle might take me in. He doesn't have anyone and I don't want to disrupt your family," I said as I reached out to shove affectionately at his shoulder. I grabbed the dish cloth and wiped down the table, threw my plate in the dishwasher and started it. Marlo was still staring at the table.

"Mar, I'm not going anywhere. We have a job to do. Now let's get to school."

"Speaking of jobs, how did it go with Mr. Johnson?"

"He took the news okay but he is in terrible shape. I could feel the waves of sickness rolling off of him. I almost felt nauseous and weak when I was there just being around him."

"I don't know what to say. That's a lot to deal with in one day."

"It is but we do what we have to do. Come on and remember, I've got you."

Katie met us at the bus again. She seemed to sense my mood and was a little calmer. I noticed that her dress and perfume were also calmer. She still wore a skirt but had given up the *torture shoes* for more practical flats. She seemed incredibly tiny next to me. Today she didn't try to hold on to me but settled for walking by my side.

Marlo was still unusually quiet. Seeing his girlfriend get off her bus seemed to lighten his mood significantly.

Marlo and I broke the news to Adrian about my life's possible change in Language Arts. He looked a little worried but took the news better than Marlo had. I told them that I would try to get to the pawnshop after my cast was off but that I wasn't sure what my afternoon held. The rest of the morning slipped by - I was quiet and reserved. When Katie showed up I played nice but didn't make any special effort today. She worked with us again in math but we didn't talk much and stayed focused. I paid little attention to what was going on around me.

Lunch was more subdued today but the conversation flowed fine. I learned more about Katie. She sat as close to me again as she could but otherwise did not try to hold my hand. I welcomed her presence. Today she was the kind of friend I needed – a quiet, supportive presence.

I was focusing most of my attention on her and she seemed pleased. She was telling me about a trip she had taken with her family last summer when I saw a sudden movement out of the corner of my eye. I tore my eyes away from Katie in time to see Lucie jerk to a standing position from where she was eating lunch with Calvin. As she made to walk away he reached out and grabbed her arm forcing her to lurch to a stop. She yanked her arm away from him, storm clouds on her face. I had never seen Lucie look so angry. Calvin made to reach for her again and I stood up. I needn't have bothered: the scathing look Lucie gave Calvin had him holding his hands up in defeat as Lucie stormed off. He then proceeded to lean over and flirt with the girl next to him. Katie's story had stuttered to a stop and she stared open-mouthed from me to Lucie and back.

I noticed her distress. "Lucie is still my friend. It bugs me to see him treat her badly," I spit out through gritted teeth.

"I understand," she answered softly. "I hope you would do the same for me if I needed it."

I slowly lowered myself back to my former spot. I picked up Katie's hand and looked her in the eye. "I wouldn't want anyone to treat you badly," I said seriously.

I realized that all conversation at our table had stopped and everyone was looking at us. Katie, bless her, was quick to explain that Calvin was being a jerk and had made Lucie mad. She also said that I was afraid he would hurt her and was only trying to help. She unfortunately had a look in her eye close to hero worship. Uh oh, what have I done now?

I walked slowly to science wondering what I would say to Lucie. I couldn't decide if I wanted my mom to be late so that I could talk to her or be early so I wouldn't have to. Poor Lucie. Why didn't she listen to me about Calvin?

When I reached class, Lucie was nowhere in sight. She nearly always beat me into the room. It gave me extra unwanted think time. She rounded the corner just as the bell rang. Her eyes were slightly red but mostly she just looked mad. Maybe she broke up with the idiot. As she sat down I leaned toward her and asked, "You want to talk about it?"

"Not even a little bit," she said through stiff lips. She then scowled at me. "You don't look so good yourself. In fact you looked almost tragic this morning."

"I don't want to talk about me."

"Well there you go – I don't want to talk about me either."

Our teacher had just started to lecture when a student I didn't know came in the room to hand her a pink dismissal slip. I would have bet my sack lunch it was for me except I had already eaten it. Yep, I was right. I leaned over to Lucie as I picked up my books. "Take good notes for me, Buddy – the cast comes off today."

"Good luck Owen," she whispered with a sweet smile that I never saw when she looked at Calvin, the pig.

The whole cast removal thing was a little less exciting than I would have thought. The smell was pretty amazing in a *really* bad way. Forget the pawnshop until I can get a shower and get this stink off of me. They fitted me with a special brace that I would wear for a couple of more weeks. Then we were off to an extra visit with the physical therapist to check on my progress and for new exercises.

My mom put her arm around me as we walked out of the clinic. "You know, I'm proud of you. I'll always worry about you but I know that what you are doing is important. I'm glad that not all your adventures are as exciting as Clive. I'm hoping he is far away by now. We haven't heard anything in awhile. I hope no news is good news. I even talked to Max today. I called just to say hi and check in with him and see if he'd heard anything. The agents assigned to the case are pulling back to follow other leads. They think Clive and his buddy have moved on to California. There has been some similar activity down there. Max's attorneys and the police are trying to help him. He should have come forward sooner but I understand his fear. He loves his family. He may well owe some fines but he shouldn't have any jail time."

"He *is* a good guy. It seems so unfair that Clive and his gang could use him like that yet it's Max who's in trouble. The system is messed up somehow."

"You aren't wrong about that. Hey, I hate to tell you this but I made another call today," she said, her tone serious.

Uh oh, I thought. Do I even want to hear this?

"I only know of one retirement home that you could have walked to from our house. I called to check on Mr. Johnson. I hope you're not mad but I wanted to help."

I shook my head at her to let her know I wasn't mad.

"He's gone, Owen. He didn't come to breakfast so they went to check on him. He died in his sleep. I'm so sorry for your loss."

I didn't know the man well but his story had touched my heart. It brought on a choking tightness in my throat. I tried to fight it off. I felt like I had swallowed a baseball. I had too much pain and sadness going on in my life right now. I looked up at the sky and tried to breathe. I watched the branches of the nearest tree quiver in the soft breeze. Tiny green leaves swiped at the sky like an artist's brush on canvas. Cottony clouds were pressed against the soft blue of the sky. "I hope he's happy, Mom. Maybe he'll throw a ball for Buddy for us."

"Oh Owen, I hope so. He owed you that much."

By the time I got home and took the first real shower I'd had since my accident it was too late for the pawnshop anyway. I texted my boys and White Eagle to tell them I was fine but spending the evening with the family. Mom ordered pizza and we played board games. She even let us have soda pop with our dinner which was a rare treat for us. We all seemed to hold tight to each other, all of us feeling how our family had shrunk and not knowing how long it would stay that way. I helped my mom put my brothers to bed and then spent a half hour on the little homework I had before I tried to go to bed myself.

My dreams were a strange mix of Clive and the unknown man chasing Lucie and Katie through endless fields. Buddy, our dog, barked incessantly at them. Lucie and Katie ran and stood behind my mom who was holding a sword, my brothers behind her dressed like Halloween ninjas. Clive and the unknown man turned into bats and flew away. About the time they were specks in the sky there was a bright flash and Mr. Johnson floated down to collect Buddy. He turned into a dove and also flew away. Next, Calvin was standing in the field having a temper tantrum. Marlo, Adrian and I stood shoulder to shoulder, our arms crossed, staring him down.

The peal of my alarm clock woke me up. I felt like I hadn't slept at all. I dragged myself through the day again paying little attention to what was going on around me. I only spoke when spoken to and most people left me alone.

I guess my sadness showed. There is a side of life that fourteen year olds just shouldn't have to see. I could see the dark side now in vivid detail. I could see great goodness out there too but it seemed like the dark was smothering out the light. I felt the weight of being the one standing guard against the dark tide. My weariness must have shown on my face. Lucie had been watching me closely since yesterday but had said nothing to me. I was taken by surprise when she sat down right next to me at lunch. I smelled her first but I had assumed she'd walk on by like she usually did. Not today.

"That's it Owen, I can't stand it anymore. What is it?" She slapped her tray down next to mine and picked my hand right up off the table. I was too surprised to do anything but look at her for a moment. Her hand was warm and soft. Her fantastic eyes were gentle and kind. I could see worry in the wrinkle of her brow.

"What do you mean, Lucie?" I saw Marlo out of the corner of my eye head my way and then abruptly change direction as he grabbed Adrian by the arm and dragged him off to an empty table where they could watch the proceedings from a safe distance.

"I'm worried about you. You started the year like usual; quiet. Then you actually became a little more fun and outgoing. I got it when you were quiet after your accident but that was weeks ago. Now you seem almost sadder than you did right after it happened. Did your other dog die?"

"What? No." She was still holding my hand and people were starting to notice. I could sense the rumor mill starting to grind but there was no way I was letting go of her hand. Instead I twined my fingers with hers. Both of us seemed to have forgotten our lunches and the other people in our lives. No one came and sat by us, not even Lucie's friends. The sixth grader I had rescued from the bathroom bully looked in our direction longingly for a moment but then he too changed direction. Good. "I just have a lot on my mind right now and a lot going on. It'll be fine. Thanks though, I appreciate your asking."

"I understand if you don't want to talk to me but please talk to someone. You look like you have a ton of stuff bottled up and I know what that feels like." She seemed to realize she still had my hand because she awkwardly disengaged our fingers.

"What's with you, Lucie? What do you have bottled up?"

"You don't want to hear it."

"Sure I do." I tried to smile winningly at her but it came out a little limp.

"How about another day when you don't look like... Well, like your dog died." She seemed to notice that we were drawing some attention. She turned back to her lunch and quickly took a few bites. "Want to go for a walk?"

"Best offer I've had all day." I took both our trays, dumped our trash and turned the trays back in to the kitchen. We walked next to each other out of the cafeteria and then outside. We were almost to the tennis courts before she spoke again.

"So how did getting the cast off go?"

"Pretty good. I start more intensive physical therapy next week. I'm actually kind of looking forward to it. I miss my skateboard." She gave a delicate snort and smiled at me. I reached out my hand and took ahold of Lucie's. She looked at our entwined fingers and another small smile touched her lips. She gave my hand a small squeeze. For a moment I thought she would release it but she didn't. She held on as we strolled along saying nothing. It was nice, peaceful and comfortable. For now it was enough. It was great not to be arguing with her and it was a relief to have her back by me and away from Calvin the terrible. I wished that we could just stay like this forever, good friends, maybe more than friends, not hating each other, maybe loving each other a bit. I also wished, not for the first time, that I could put her on a shelf and save her for my older self. Other girls had pretty much lost their appeal for me. Sure I looked, but nobody compared to Lucie. Katie was nice but she would never be Lucie. High school was coming; maybe I would meet *the* girl. Right now I couldn't see past this, past Lucie Elizabeth Ness.

"I remember having a cast. I remember the pain and I remember the joy of getting the darned thing off. I still hoped that I'd recover back then. I'm in a healthier place now overall. I also remember looking in the mirror and discovering that my leg had shrunk. I was scared to death it would stay that way for life. Want to show me your leg?" she asked with a twinkle in her eye.

"Not on your life. Not to bring up a bad subject but where is Calvin today?"

"He really made me mad yesterday at lunch with his flirting so we're taking a break."

"Mmmmm. His idea or yours?" I wondered aloud.

"Mine. I have avoided him all day and you know what? It's been kinda nice. He hates it when I hang out with you but I've missed you. I've been at war with myself – be *true to myself* or avoid you like Calvin wants. You've been my friend for two and a half years. Why should I let him wreck that? He, on the other hand, thinks he can do whatever he wants even when he is sitting right next to me. So I thought, well, just do what you want and I will do what I want. I miss my friend. Now, tell me, why so glum?"

"A friend of the family died of cancer. It was a long tough battle. I didn't know him well but it still makes me sad. Also, my parents are having a pretty big misunderstanding and I feel partly to blame. There's some other stuff going on too. I guess I just feel like I have too much negativity. It's weighing me down."

"Hang in there. I'm here for you and surely things will get better."

"Thanks, Luce."

My progress was still a little slow with the brace but we were near the school when the bell rang to head back to class. Today would go in the record books for the greatest change, in my opinion, of a day's value. This day had gone from tolerable to amazing and then, quick as a blink, went back to terrible. As we came into the building I caught sight of Katie. I had hurt her. I hadn't meant to but I had.

I both loved and hated myself in that moment. She did that to me, made me feel all the best and worst parts of me at once. That was Lucie and that was what kept drawing me back to her. She had me so confused, I didn't know what to think, but what I felt was magnetic and so big it ached like nothing I had ever experienced. I just couldn't pull myself completely away from her no matter how much I wanted to and now I had hurt Katie because I couldn't seem to get Lucie out of my heart and mind. I had to admire my own tenacity when it came to Lucie though; here I was setting myself up for my own heartache again.

I felt I owed Katie something. I looked for her between classes and after school. I finally found her looking hurt and angry as she headed for the bus.

"Hey Katie," I said softly, stepping up next to her.

"What do you want?" she replied in a hurt tone.

"I know I hurt you. I wanted to say that I was sorry. I never wanted to do that."

She sighed heavily as she started to board the bus but turned back. "I'll see you tomorrow."

I started to walk away but I turned back to look at the bus. Katie was watching me from the window. She gave me a sad smile and then turned her head away. I sighed and walked over to the parent pick up area, my thoughts in a jumble.

Having had physical therapy yesterday I was free today. Adrian's Uncle Max picked all of us up to take us to the pawnshop. Now that I had a smaller and lighter brace on I could do some gentle fighting stances. It was wonderful. I had a long road to walk to full recovery but I knew I could do it. White Eagle moved all of us through some Tai Chi moves and then we actually did some... wait for it... yoga. We couldn't believe it but he insisted that we needed flexibility to go with our strength. My ribs and leg only complained a little.

We did some work too. Adrian was left to do any heavy lifting. I swept and dusted. Marlo was starting to work on inventory and an accounting program that Max had purchased for him.

About ten minutes before it was time to go, White Eagle called me into the back and asked me to bring my broom. He wanted me to go over all my defensive moves with the broom while taking careful note of my ribs. It went better than either of us expected. He was ready for me to start walking further. It would take me awhile to get back into running shape. Too bad he didn't have a magic wand that would allow me to get right back into fighting shape. I hated feeling weak and vulnerable.

The evening at our house was quiet. My brothers entertained themselves and played with the cat and dog. My mom read a book and I did some homework before I settled in with a book myself. I was pretty fidgety.

"What is it? Something's coming isn't it?" my mom asked in a hushed voice.

I gave her a surprised look. I was feeling something but I didn't know what exactly. I knew she had nailed the matter on the head.

"I can't describe it. Something just feels... wrong, or off, maybe. It's almost like watching a movie you've seen before and knowing the scary part is coming so you're preparing yourself for it."

"Exactly. I feel it too, or at least I know you can. I wonder if I just think I can feel it because you feel it. I think my own gift is waking up or something. I have always been able to tell more about people than most folks can but this is... something more. Maybe I always ignored it before but now I'm *listening*.

"I don't know, Mom, but you know who we need to talk to. Right now though, let's double check the whole house inside and then out."

We walked the entire house checking every window and door. We took the dog with us as we walked around our house and found... Nothing. Nothing called to me. I stopped for a moment when we got back to our kitchen door. I closed my eyes and just felt for a moment.

"Mom, the problem isn't here. Something bad is going to happen though, I'm sure of it. I think this is a gift that Miles gave to me. White Eagle and I talked about it some. That was really his *watcher* gift. He could sense the bad things that were coming and could measure the degree of evil in any room he entered."

"Let's get back inside and try to get some sleep so we can face whatever is coming."

"Hey, Mom?" I asked as we made our way back in. She looked at me to show she was listening. "How much trouble are you going to be in with Dad when he gets home and finds out that I am not grounded?"

She ducked her head, not wanting to meet my eyes. I could feel her guilt. "I'm hoping he won't ask and I can play the game of omission. I agree that he isn't ready to listen to you yet. I don't know what to do. It's not in his nature to believe in magic of any kind. He's too much of a scientist. He won't buy that you have a gift. I think that even if you showed him what you can do he won't believe it. He doesn't believe in psychics either. I know you aren't one but what you do is similar. I have thought about it, I just have no answers yet."

We relocked the door, set the alarm and went upstairs to put my brothers to bed.

I woke up with a little of my mom's enthusiasm. It was Friday. I didn't know if I still had a date but at least it was almost the weekend. When I got downstairs my mom was sitting at the table making a list while my brothers ate.

"Oh hey Owen, if Alex poop scoops, do you think you can handle mowing our lawn, if it doesn't rain that is?"

Alex and I both looked at her. Oh joy. Family chores. Well, I needed to get back in shape so why not cut the grass.

"I guess. Alex?"

"I guess," he answered, sounding about as enthusiastic as I felt.

"Hey, Mom, I hope I already asked you this but can I go to a movie at the mall with the guys and some other... friends?"

"Owen has a *day-ate*," Lucas said in a sing-song voice.

"Is Lucie one of the friends?"

"Mom!" I said giving her a dirty look. I felt my cheeks growing warm and my brothers giggled. I cleared my throat. "It's actually a triple date. I'm not taking Lucie though because she is still kind of dating Calvin. I'm taking a girl named Katie. She's in my math class. Marlo set it all up.

"Sure. How will you be getting there and home?"

"I asked Marlo to set up all the details since it was his idea. Can I let you know?"

"Okay honey. I'd like to know what time you will be home and keep your cell phone on you, please."

Marlo was up and at 'em bright and early. He arrived at my door again before my brothers had even left for school. "Good morning, Mrs. Ryer, Owen, Alex and Luke!"

Another morning person. Today I didn't mind so much.

"Did Owen talk to you about tonight? My mom can pick everyone up in our van around six and she'll pick us up at the mall at half past nine. Our movie starts around seven," Marlo quickly explained with a huge grin.

My mom laughed, "Okay Mr. Matchmaker, but take good care of my baby. He is not fully mended yet." This caused much hooting and laughter from my brothers. They howled even louder when Mom added it was my turn to clean the cat box again and as if on cue our orange cat jumped into my lap and reached up a paw to pat my face.

"Yeah, yeah, okay I get it. You're neglected," I said, scratching him under his chin. Being a cat, he mostly ignored us all, thinking he was a higher being I'm sure. When he wanted attention he let you know loud and clear.

Alex interrupted, "I'm just glad you're better Owen. I didn't like doing most of my chores and most of yours. The only good thing was that Mom made Lucas do some of mine. Of course she helped him." The last was said with an eye roll followed by a grumpy scowl from Lucas.

"Okay, okay, let's get to school, boys." That's my mom for you; the keeper of the peace.

When the herd, including the Beggar, had left, Marlo started rummaging in the fridge. "How about an omelet? Eggs are really good for you."

"I don't know, my friend. Are you cooking or am I?"

"Oh no, I'll cook. You clean the cat box. I know how much you are looking forward to it. Besides, you have cat hair on you now and there's no way I want that in my omelet."

"Yeah right, I live to serve the cat. He was so much cooler when I was in preschool and my mom did all the work. Oh, and no peppers in the omelet."

"I know, I know, it gives you heartburn. Do I take care of my boy or what???"

"Um, Marlo?"

"Yeah?"

"About yesterday... I appreciate you running interference with Katie. I'm sure you did even though my mind was completely on Lucie. I did try to apologize to Katie. It's so confusing and difficult. I don't actually owe Katie anything but I don't want to hurt her either. Lucie is technically taken but whatever I feel for her is still there and I did promise to be her friend. I feel like I'm making a big mess. I really want to go tonight but I don't want to lead Katie on either. I want to give her a chance and see if I could like her but what if I don't?"

"Geez, relax will ya? Katie's feelings were a little hurt. I reminded her that you and Lucie were friends and added that she needed you. I'm sure it meant a lot to her that you said you were sorry. She knows, or at least claims to understand, that she's not your actual girlfriend... yet. She's still coming tonight and she's still hopeful. Catching you is just turning out to be more difficult than she thought. I think she hangs on for two reasons: one, she really likes you and two, there are about four hundred other girls who would love to be in her shoes for even one day."

"Yeah, I'm a real prize."

"You are - you just don't see it. You're still in decent shape, you're tall, and you're good looking. Life is so unfair.".

"What? Women love you."

"Yeah, usually because I'm smart and outgoing. I don't have the whole tall, dark and handsome thing going, but at least I know I look okay, I have a great personality and I'm modest. Now get on that cat box. I'm about ready to pour the eggs in the pan."

"Yes, Mother."

Katie was waiting when we got off the bus. She was the most dressed down I had ever seen her. She wore jeans, a designer tee and colorful cloth tennis shoes. She even had her hair in a pony tail. She somehow reminded me of a small dark Lucie. She had lessened her makeup and only smelled of shampoo. Wonderful. Now this was a girl I could really like.

"Morning, Katie."

"Can I talk to you for a minute?" she asked hesitantly.

"Sure, what can I do for you?"

"Look, I know you're friends with Lucie and I know you don't really owe me anything but... well, if you were going to talk to her I wish you would have let me know and... seeing you holding her hand and talking to her like that... well I just wished it was me I guess. I know that no one can take what isn't mine. I just..."

Without waiting for her to finish I reached out and pulled her into a gentle hug and whispered into her hair, "I'm really sorry for hurting you. I like you. If nothing else, I would really like to be your friend. Maybe we can be more, I just don't know. If you're done waiting for me to figure it out, I understand and no hard feelings. If you would like to give me a chance, then I'm still up for the movie with the gang tonight."

She held onto me loosely at first but her grip tightened as I spoke.

"Hey, no PDAs," some kid yelled.

We broke apart and smiled at each other. Katie took my hand and we walked to our first period classes.

Math went well with Katie teaming with me and Marlo as had become her custom. Now that she was being more herself she was a good contributor to our group and seemed to be really good at math. We finished all of our work before the period even ended so Marlo could catch Katie up on all the finalized plans for tonight.

We headed for the cafeteria. It was a bit awkward as Lucie and two of her girlfriends joined us. I ended up with Lucie on one side and Katie on the other. I barely ate lunch while trying to keep up the equal attention thing. I tried to listen to all the conversations and reply as fairly as I could. By the end of it I was exhausted.

Lucie, Katie and I headed for choir and Marlo, Adrian and the rest set off for their fifth period classes. We walked down the hall three across. I continued to flip my head back and forth as each of the ladies spoke. Both seemed to be making a supreme effort to be on their best behavior. The only good thing out of all this was that Calvin was nowhere in sight.

Katie and Lucie would both have solos for the end of the year concert. Our teacher was having trouble getting the guys to participate in a solo or even a duet. He pulled me aside after class. Lucie and Katie both hovered just outside the door, both clearly waiting for me and neither saying anything to the other. I suddenly realized they were dressed almost identically and both had pony tails; Lucie tall and blond, Katie petite and dark. Bookends. It made me smile. It was the most casual I had ever seen Lucie dress.

"Owen, I know how talented you are. I also know that you hate the spotlight. I want you to put aside your hatred of that and sing for just one person - *you*. Shut the rest of it out. Here's a list of the music I have or you can go buy your own. Let me know on Monday which you choose. You really need to do this. It will also count toward your grade and guarantee you an 'A' in my class."

"Okay," I sighed, taking the list from him. I looked up to see both girls smiling. Great. Maybe science would go better.

The three of us headed through the gym and into the main hall. The ladies seemed excited about their pieces and both thought it was a fantastic idea for me to sing. I would kill Adrian. He got me into choir in sixth grade when I didn't know what I wanted to do for music. He had dropped out this spring because of scheduling conflicts. Maybe I could get him to sing a duet with me anyway. Either way he was in big trouble with me. Katie gave me a quick hug at the door to science and told me she'd see me later. She probably wanted to leave Lucie with a certain impression.

"So, you're going out with Katie now," Lucie stated.

"Um, not exactly. Marlo and Adrian set up a movie thing tonight and Katie and I are going. I like her fine. She's nice, but she's just my friend right now."

"Uh, huh." I wondered how someone could put so much meaning into two words that weren't really words at all. "Well, good luck with that. I think you have bitten off more than you can chew. We'll see," she ended cryptically.

Lucie smiled all through science and health like she had a private joke. By the end of health I couldn't stand it anymore. "What?" I groused at her.

"Owen, whether or not you want to admit it to yourself, you have a girlfriend. People have thought many times that we were dating. Now they see you with Katie. We're lucky Calvin was absent today. By Monday he'll have cooled off. Yesterday he was sizzling mad at you. It's kinda funny because he flirts all the time, but he says it's different for him. It doesn't mean anything. You're my friend but he knows there's a little something more between us that we keep pressed down for the sake of friendship. He hates it. Now Katie sees *me* as her big competition. I hope you're ready for the tug of war that you'll soon feel. Welcome to my world."

Lucie picked up her stuff and hot-footed it out of the room before I could process all that she had said or even try for a reply. No doubt about it. I had complicated my already complicated life. Oh boy.

Marlo, Adrian and I were all going to try to walk to the shop and hang there for a little while before our big night out. I was feeling out of shape by the time we arrived. We had walked slowly and I had made it but my leg and ribs were aching. White Eagle ran me through my physical therapy and we all did more Tai Chi together followed once more by yoga. White Eagle was anxious to get me into a pool for some swimming. He drove Marlo and me home and Max took Adrian.

I hurried through the shower and dressed in black jeans, shoes and a button up shirt hoping the look was luckier tonight than it had been the last time Marlo and I had gone to the mall. I cringed at the thought. Tonight, at least, we were really going to a movie. I prayed that Clive really was in California. All protection details had now been pulled off of us. We just got an extra patrol from the police. I shook off my paranoia and headed downstairs to say goodbye to my mom and wait for Marlo.

The movie bus, or Mrs. Saggio's van, was a tight squeeze with six of us plus the driver but the trip to the mall was a short one. The atmosphere was happy and expectant. Mrs. Saggio dropped us off outside the theater and told us that was where she would pick us up at 9:30. We all coupled up and headed for the food court and theater entrance.

Katie took hold of my hand and practically bounced all the way inside. I had not yet witnessed this level of enthusiasm. It was kind of fun. She had changed from her school outfit and was back to her over the top look from Monday. Tonight she was in hot pink tights, a miniskirt, and a low cut hot pink top I knew my mom would not let her daughter out of the house in. Melissa and Jill were dressed similarly, right down to the eye makeup and big dangly earrings. The high heels were killing me. I guessed if we got into trouble the spikes would be great as a weapon but these girls weren't running anywhere. I hoped their feet lasted the evening.

Marlo and Melissa were a little ahead of us and I almost laughed out loud when I realized with her heels on she was taller than Marlo. It didn't seem to bother him a bit. Adrian was all decked out so he and Jill looked like they could step off the pages of a teen fashion magazine or stand as a display in a window.

Marlo led us over to buy our movie tickets first and then we discussed our food options. Did you know that women travel to the bathroom in packs? Did you know that women don't seem to care about food when they are on a date? I was having the best time ever analyzing and laughing at young American dating rituals. I bought the food that sounded good to me. The others all seemed to evaluate what to eat based on the potential spillage, mess and bad breath factors.

I couldn't decide who was more fun to watch - the girls or Marlo and Adrian. I guessed I was pretty funny my own self. Katie stayed right by me when we each bought our food. She was in such a good mood that I found it infectious. She laughed often and I found I did too. It was nice.

When all the food was ordered, we met back up in the middle of the food court and slid two tables together and then crowded around them. We talked about the movie we were going to see as well as other movies we had seen with the lead actors. The girls picked at their food. Marlo and Adrian didn't do much better. Having chosen a burger, fries and a milkshake I did fine! Katie seemed more interested in me, my milkshake and fries than in her salad. Chicks! She was practically plastered to my side. It gave her good access to my food but made eating challenging.

I liked the way she asked if she could have some of my fries and then would snatch them like I would take away the privilege at any moment. I hadn't smiled this much in ages. She asked for a snitch of my milkshake. As slender as she was I figured it was a good idea to get some calories in so I encouraged her to have all she wanted. She offered me some salad but I told her I had plenty of rabbit food on my burger.

We decided to walk around before the movie. Katie slipped her arm around my waist like the other girls had done to Marlo and Adrian. Oh well, I thought, at least her perfume was tolerable. I loosely draped my arm across her back and held onto her opposite shoulder. She chatted and I made appropriate noises in return. She had begun to slide her hand lightly up and down my side from my lowest rib to my hip bone. It made me a little uncomfortable but it was okay. It just seemed a little bit much for having only known each other a week. Eventually she settled for grasping my belt loop with her fingers and the tip of her thumb hooked in the waistband of my jeans. Her thumb was cool against my warm skin. It was all I could do not to spin away from her. It felt wrong, too intimate, too soon. I settled for gently taking her hand and placing it around my bicep like we had walked the first day I got to know her. Everyone was turning to head back to the theater so I thought I had it made.

I wish I could tell you about the movie but I really didn't get to see it. I spent most of the show gently extracting myself from my date turned octopus. It was fine when she started out with her arms wrapped around one of mine and her head on my shoulder. I was just getting into the movie when I realized Adrian was kissing Jill. Weren't they here to see the movie? Was there something wrong with me? Clearly I had a cute, willing girl with me. It just didn't seem right.

I was so thankful that Marlo and his date were sitting between Adrian, his date and us. I could have kissed him! Not really, but you know what I mean. I felt like he was my buffer and I *really* appreciated it.

In hindsight I think Katie must have noticed Adrian too. She changed position to tuck her feet under her which raised her up more on level with me. She put her arm around me and leaned in even closer. I would not have imagined that it was possible as she was already glued to my side. Sadly we were sitting in the seats with the arm rests that rise. She had flipped it up when we first sat down. This wasn't like science when Lucie sat close.

When Katie kissed my neck I about levitated out of my seat and so it went for most of the movie. She would attack and I would retreat. I guess I just didn't like her like that. Now, if Lucie had been kissing my neck... nah, don't even go there.

Finally towards the end of the movie, and I know because I surreptitiously checked my watch many times, Katie leaned in and whispered, "Why don't you just kiss me?"

Geez, where to begin? "I'm not sure that's a good idea. I don't know where we stand yet and I don't want to lead you on."

"You can lead me anywhere," she said leaning in and touching her lips to mine. I felt... well, freaked out hardly begins to cover it. I felt guilty. I didn't want to take advantage of Katie and I felt like I was cheating on Lucie. Lucie wasn't mine to cheat on, but still. It also felt... too soon or rushed. It was nice to be kissed yet...

"Um, Katie?"

"Yeah?"

"Can we step out and talk a minute?"

"Okay."

I took her hand and lead her out of the theater. So many thoughts were racing around in my mind I didn't know where to start. I tried three times to get the words out as she stood there holding my hand and facing me.

"You like me, right?" she asked in a soft voice.

"Yeah, I like you, but right now you are... freaking me out a little bit," no, *a lot* my mind screamed. "I have really only known you for a week. I'm not ready for... Look, I like the girl from math class who was a team player and held comfortable conversations. I find the girl who came to the movies with me tonight to be a little... um..."

I watched the emotions streak across her face. Finally she settled on jealous. "It's Lucie isn't it?" She would have to be that perceptive!

"I'm not dating Lucie. She has Calvin. She's my friend but yeah, to be honest, I do like her some too."

"Well, when you get it figured out, you let me know," she said as she whirled and headed for the bathroom almost stomping her feet. You could stomp in heels? Who knew? What had I done now? Nothing that I could see. She had to know how I felt. I really didn't want to lead her on. I was here to have fun. I hadn't come to the movie to make out. Yikes, how had things gone so terribly wrong? I was still deep in thought when the movie disgorged its patrons. The girls took one look at me and headed right for the bathroom. Adrian wanted to know how I could ruin everything. I kind of wondered that myself.

We waited for them outside the women's restroom. Marlo asked me what happened. I guess he *had* actually watched the movie.

"Well," I started in a low voice so others couldn't overhear, "I've only known her for a week. She isn't even really my girlfriend and she had her hands... well let's just say that I'm not ready to have her wrapped around me like a monkey in a tree. She kissed me too. If this is where we are in a week, I don't even want to ponder where we go next. It kinda freaked me out."

Marlo just stared but Adrian busted up laughing.

"Geez, Owen, you prude, you should be happy that a girl wants to make out with you. Are you nuts?" Adrian choked out through his laughter.

"No Owen, you're right. Be true to yourself and listen to your heart. If it's not right, don't force it," Marlo sagely advised.

"I tried to tell her nicely," I almost whined.

Adrian tried to pull himself together and Marlo smiled. The ladies rolled out of the bathroom arm in arm, Katie in the middle, not meeting my gaze. Oh, well. I said nothing and just fell into line behind them as we made our way to the exit. Marlo's mom was right where she said she'd be. The girls all piled in the back of the van and I got to ride shotgun. Due to location, I got the *dis*pleasure of filling her in on the movie and dinner.

"Well," I began in a small voice, "it was, ah... okay I guess. Dinner was good. I had a burger, fries and a shake. I think Marlo had some kind of chicken teriyaki thing. We walked around and then went to the movie."

"Wasn't that new actor from Australia in it?"

I wracked my brain trying to remember as much as I could from the movie and the previews. "Yeah, he was in it. He did a good job."

She finally let the subject die so she could clarify where the girls were getting dropped off. I was so thankful that she let them off first I wanted to jump up and down in my seat. I rolled down my window to bid Katie an awkward goodbye and told her I'd see her Monday. She just waved and gave me a half smile. Oh boy.

We dropped Adrian off next and then finally got to my house. Was it my imagination or was that the longest date ever? I was not looking forward to Monday *at all*. "I'll see you tomorrow at the pawnshop, right? I'm going to try to walk over."

"Are you sure?" Marlo asked, worried. "It's a long way!"

"Yeah, I need to build myself back up. You can come if you want. I could come by a little after eight. We'd have plenty of time to get there then."

"Mom, is that okay?"

"I guess, but call me when you get there so I know you made it safely. I have a breakfast group I'm catering so I'll be gone anyway."

"Great. Thanks Mrs. Saggio, for the rides and the loan of Marlo. See you both later."

I walked slowly up the front walk. Tomorrow would be a good day. I hoped it would make up for tonight. What a mess.

The house was quiet. My brothers were likely in bed. My mom was reading in her favorite chair. When she heard the door open she put the book down. "How'd it go?" she asked with a big smile.

I watched her smile slip away as she took in my mood. "Not as you expected, I take it."

"It started out great and I was really having a good time. Katie just wants more from me than I am ready to give. I do like her and I don't want to hurt her feelings, but I like Lucie too. I guess I like Lucie more, but she is dating Calvin."

"Ah... well remember, you can always take a relationship forward but you can't take it back. If you kiss a girl it is hard to go back to just holding hands. Take it all slowly. You won't be sorry you did. You might regret it if you go too fast. Most importantly, always remember that Lucas is the youngest child who will live in this house. All others are welcome to visit. Be careful and be responsible. Be thoughtful about how much of yourself you share. Think about the kind of person you want to be."

"Ugh... nothing bad happened and don't start in with *the talk*. I'm not ready to do *that* with anyone. I would have just been happy to hold her hand. She just moved a little fast for me. I didn't expect her to put her arm around me or hold my belt loop. She kissed me too even after I indicated I wasn't ready to do that, but... I talked to her and told her that I had really only known her for a week and I just wasn't ready. I hurt her feelings but I just... had to," I ended on a shrug.

"Nobody ever said being a teenager was easy. When, if ever, the time is right to kiss her, or anyone else, you'll know."

I quickly changed the subject to save us both further embarrassment. "I'm tired. I'm off to bed. I want to leave early for the pawnshop. I am going to try to walk it."

"Wow, are you sure?" she asked, surprised.

"I'd like to try. Marlo said he'd go with me."

"Well, good. Don't forget you have physical therapy tomorrow to make up for last week. Then next week you'll be back on the two days a week schedule."

"Okay. Love you. See you in the morning."

"I love you too, sweetie. Happy dreams."

I thought for a long time about what I could have done differently with Katie but I couldn't come up with anything. I had tried my best and was honest with her. I needed to let it go. I visualized the glass of water that White Eagle had taught me about. I filled it with my problems and poured them out to quiet my mind. Breathe, I told myself. Just breathe.

TWELVE

I was startled awake by Lucas. He hopped onto the foot of my bed all happy and ready to start the day. I tried to groan and roll over but I caught sight of my alarm clock. "Oh jeez, is it really almost eight? I'm supposed to meet Marlo to go to the shop," I cried as I leaped out of bed.

"I thought we were doing family chores today," Lucas said with a mix of joy and sadness.

"I will later today and tomorrow. I have to go work for a while."

"Okay. You just said you'd be here more and I was hoping 'more' would happen now." I could hear the sadness in his voice as he slumped out of my room.

"Hey Luke, I'll make some time for checkers, okay?"

"Okay," he said, happy once again. If only I could fix all my relationship problems with checkers.

I skipped the shower, dressed in shorts, a tee, a sweatshirt and my running shoes. I threw some clean clothes in my duffle and hurried downstairs to grab some breakfast on the go.

"You be careful about overdoing it. Call me if your leg is aching," my mom nagged.

"Okay, *Na hag*," I said with a laugh.

"What? I'm not a nag!"

"N.A.H.G. not N.A.G. Not Always Helpful Grownups! I crack myself up."

"Wow, awake and joking around. Did you have a good night's sleep or are you becoming a *morning person?*" She smiled to lessen the sting.

I left for Marlo's with a spring in my step. It felt good to laugh and be lighthearted. It had been awhile. Marlo was up and ready to go when I got there. Since he was a much better planner than me, he had remembered to set his alarm.

We headed out on our long walk to the pawnshop. I figured it might take us around forty minutes to get there. I wasn't far off. Marlo and I were both puffing when we arrived. We made sure to call our moms to let them know we were safely at the shop.

White Eagle was surprised to see us. We told him we had walked for exercise and were sorry we were a little early but we weren't sure how long it would take.

"No, you misunderstand. I thought you were Max. He's late. Maybe I'll call him. I hate to bother him but he usually calls me if he won't be here to open the shop. Today he didn't call."

We left White Eagle to his chores and headed to the back to stretch after our walk and start some Tai Chi.

"You know what? I think if you're willing, I may actually try to run with you. You were so far ahead of me because of cross country that I thought I could never catch up. With you starting out walking again I think I might have a chance."

"That's great, Marlo. I would love to run with you when they clear me to do that. I have to start swimming. Maybe you could do that too."

"I don't think I will ever look like you but I think I could give Adrian a run for his money."

We both laughed and my cell phone chirped. It was Adrian.

"Hey, are you at the shop? Is my uncle there? He was supposed to get me and he isn't answering his cell." Adrian sounded worried.

"He's not here but White Eagle was trying to call him. Let me go check," I said, walking toward the main shop.

I found White Eagle up front looking concerned. I raised my eyebrows at him. "Any luck? Adrian's on the phone. Max didn't pick him up."

"Is he still on the line?"

"Yes."

"Let me talk to him."

I handed him the phone and he began to speak rapidly. "When did you last talk to Max? ... When was he supposed to pick you up? ... Do you have a key to his place? ... Bring it... We'll be there in five to ten minutes."

He turned to me with worry clearly etched on his features. "Get Marlo. We have work to do."

I hurried to the back, filled Marlo in and took hold of his bag while he brought his backpack quickly up front. White Eagle had flipped the *open* sign to *closed* and we hustled out, locking the door behind us. We jumped in his truck and he revved the engine.

I was fully expecting a speeding ticket but we got lucky. We were at Adrian's house in five minutes flat. He was already on the front porch. He joined us in the truck and we were off again.

When we reached Max's house, his car was in the driveway but the house looked... dead. We all piled out and cautiously approached the front door.

"Something's wrong. I can feel it." My gut was clenched in that particular way that let me know something dark had touched the house.

"Give me the key, Adrian. Marlo, stay with me. You two, around back. Be alert," White Eagle said in a tight voice.

I jerked my head to the left to get Adrian moving and I went right. I looked in as many windows as I could on my way to the back. I was reminded of the time I had walked around Mrs. Lando's house. This time I didn't see any destruction like I had there, past what you would normally expect from a bachelor's house. Adrian and I met at the back door. I raised an eyebrow at Adrian. "See or hear anything?" I asked in a hushed tone.

Adrian shook his head. I indicated that he should try the back door. His fingerprints would be expected because he was family. I had only been here a couple of times and it had been awhile. As Adrian reached for the door it swung slowly open. The lock had been broken. The kitchen was in decent shape with only one chair looking *off*. I touched it gingerly with the back of my hand.

The image of Max with a black pillowcase over his head and his hands tied behind his back slammed into me, knocking me back in synchronization with Max being pushed to the back door and tripping over the chair. "Wow, what just happened, Owen?" Adrian asked, alarmed, forgetting to lower his voice.

White Eagle and Marlo burst into the room from the other side. I shook my head at them and reached for the chair again. I closed my eyes this time to focus. The image replayed. I looked for *who* was pushing Max and the lighting in the room. I let go of the chair, rolled my head on my neck and reached out again all with my eyes closed. Then I began to speak, "The image starts with Max near this chair. He has a black pillowcase or hood or something over his head. There's blood on his shirt and his hands are tied behind his back. It must be late Friday night. Max is in a t-shirt and boxers with bare feet. He looks wrinkled so they must have woken him up. He is being pushed by the guy I couldn't see well the night they got me. He is tallish as I thought and I recognize his tattoos. He has muddy brown dreads. He looks *off* somehow, like there's something wrong with him. I wish I could see his eyes but he's wearing shades. His jeans are ripped and dirty." I gagged and my eyes flew open. I took two deep breaths as everyone converged on me.

"S... s... sorry. I'm so sorry. I remembered his smell and then I felt Max's fear and remembered my own," I stuttered, in a rush.

"Did you see Clive?" White Eagle asked.

"Not in that image," I said, coming back to myself.

"Okay, here is what we need to do. Marlo, Adrian, you stay here and touch nothing. Owen, walk through the house, touch as little as possible but get as many readings as you can. I'll call the police, which means *you* have maybe ten minutes to read the house. Hurry. We will honestly tell them everything that happened right up until we hit the front porch. Then our story is that we all came in the front door with the key to look for him because he was late for work and didn't answer his phone or the door. Clear?"

We all nodded and I was off. I closed my eyes and felt the essence of the eat-in kitchen area. There was nothing else here. No wait, the doorway that lead to the hall by the bedroom. I walked quickly in that direction as White Eagle began to speak into his phone. I touched the doorjamb. Max's shoulder had hit here but the rest of the image was similar to the *hit* off the chair. I closed my eyes again and focused on the hall, waiting to see what would call me.

The door to the bedroom *spoke* to me next. I touched it. Max had purposefully been slammed into this one. I took a deep breath and stepped into the room. Only my need to hurry and stay focused kept me from collapsing right onto the floor. I froze for a moment in indecision as waves of dark energy rolled into me. I looked for my inner well of peace like White Eagle had taught me. When I was calm and centered I tried again. The strongest images were coming from the bed.

I moved forward like a sleepwalker and touched it. I could see Max sleeping and then he seemed to sense something because he was waking up. Before he was fully awake he was bludgeoned on the head causing him to fall into semi-consciousness. The room was dark but I knew there were two people besides Max. A flashlight blinked on and was shown on Max, blood trickling from his damaged temple. A tall figure grabbed Max by his t-shirt and dragged him from his bed and dumped him on the floor. Black biker boots from my own personal nightmares attached to the same dirty ripped up jeans kicked Max repeatedly. The figure bent over and flipped Max onto his belly. I could see his dreads in the flashlight. He pulled a plastic restraint from his back pocket and quickly zipped Max's wrists together making Max bleed again. He touched a finger to the blood and put it in his mouth. Gack! Clive? Yes, Clive must have said something to him because Dreadlocks Dude lunged at him, knocking the flashlight from his hand and the room went dark.

I reached out for the rug on the floor by Max's bed. The images here started from when Max hit the floor. I got more impressions of Dreadlocks Dude. He was the darkest, thickest, oiliest, nastiest entity I had ever encountered. Was he the polar opposite to my light? Fear seized me, bile rose in my throat, and I collapsed completely onto the floor. A sob was ripped from my throat. I tried not to vomit on the floor and destroy the crime scene.

White Eagle came in the room and helped me to my unsteady feet. "I'm so sorry, Owen. I wish I didn't have to put you through this."

He began to lead me out of the room. Another object was tugging at me insistently. "Wait!" I barked, my voice tight. I shook off White Eagle's helping hand and went to the dresser. The flashlight had rolled underneath when Dreadlocks had knocked it from Clive's hand. I reached toward it and touched the edge of its base with the side of my index finger. Even I could see the blood and bits of hair stuck between the glass of the lens and the body of the flashlight. I collected the burst of images and pushed the flashlight to the edge of the dresser where it would be more visible.

White Eagle made impatient noises behind me. He hustled me out of the room and to the entryway. I took a quick glance at the living room and *asked* it if it had anything to share. Nope. "Pull yourself together. They are on their way," White Eagle forced through tight lips as he shoved me out the front door and into the driveway.

"Everyone breathe, relax and be calm." He took us through two breathing exercises. "They should be turning the corner. It's showtime."

I leaned up against the fender of White Eagle's truck and practiced my breathing. In... out... in... out... re...lax. I rolled my shoulders and shook out my hands. I looked at Adrian and Marlo. They were both staring at me like I had sprouted another head.

"What?" I grumbled.

Adrian spoke up first. "I'm totally freaked out about Uncle Max, but I've never seen you work before. That freaks me out in a whole other way. I hope the cops are done with us quickly. I have so many questions, I'm about to burst."

"Owen, buddy, I'm so sorry. This one's really getting to you, huh? I'll do everything I can to help, but I'm so glad right now that I can't *see* it. You look awful." Marlo spoke in a hushed, awed tone.

An unmarked police car pulled into the driveway before Marlo had even finished speaking. White Eagle approached the driver and started to give his story. The lady detective approached us. She cocked her head and looked us up and down.

"You with the leg brace, you must be Owen. I'm Detective Marybeth Listner. I haven't seen you since we hauled you up the bank at the river. You look awful. You think it's the same guys, don't you."

I simply nodded.

"Tell me what happened," she said crisply, as she took a tablet and stylus from her bag. She touched some icons on her tablet and asked me to speak. I told her our agreed upon version... Max was not at the pawnshop when we got there. He didn't answer his land-line or cell for either Adrian or White Eagle so we came by to see if he was okay. We used Adrian's key to open the front door.

"Did you touch anything inside?"

"I don't think so. We stepped in and took a quick look. I think the back door was ajar."

"What makes you think it was the same guys?"

"You're kidding, right?" Nope, clearly she wasn't and I couldn't tell her the truth. "If you were at the river, then you know the rest about Clive's forcing Max to take stolen property. How could I *not* think they're related? Our safety details were just pulled off of our families this last week," I said, defensively.

"Point taken."

Detective Listner interviewed Marlo and Adrian, taking all their information. Her partner, who turned out to be the *Frank* from my shattered memories of the riverbank, had gone into the house. She then had each of us read our electronic statements to check for accuracy.

We waited to be dismissed. Doing nothing was killing me - I needed action. I looked at my watch and realized that my physical therapy was about to put a big monkey wrench in our next move. I reminded White Eagle that my appointment was soon. He called to the detectives to let them know we needed to go. They waved us off, saying they knew how to reach us. A crime scene unit was just pulling in. At least we wouldn't have to wait the normal wait time on this as it was an ongoing case. I thanked God for favors like this one. Max needed to be found right away.

When we were all back in the truck and safely down the street I let them know what I had seen. I warned Adrian that it would be tough to hear but I knew I had to tell all of it so that we were prepared and so that they could process it. Adrian was crying by the time we reached the shop. Marlo had his arm around him. "There is good news though, Adrian." He looked up at me with bloodshot eyes. "I haven't told you about the flashlight - It's one of those big metal jobbies that takes four D batteries. I moved it a bit so that the police will see it. It's out of place and should attract their attention. I hope they get Clive's prints *AND* Dreadlock's. The flashlight belongs to Dreadlocks. He frequently uses it to hit people and dogs. He calls it *my big black friend."*

"He hits dogs? Who would do that?" Marlo said, appalled. His expression clearly showed his distaste.

"Someone who does not value life of any kind," White Eagle answered.

We shuffled into the shop but left the *closed* sign up. I went right to the back room and sat on our practice mat. I looked at my watch again. We had about thirty minutes until my mom would be by to pick me up for physical therapy.

"What are you doing?" Marlo asked curiously.

"I need to focus on the flashlight and sort through the images. Would you catalog them for me? Let's see if I can pick out anything useful."

"Of course." Marlo got out his laptop and powered it up.

I closed my eyes and turned my inner eye to the flashlight. It repeated the first image it had given me. *Yes, I know you hit Max while Clive was holding you and then your owner hit Clive, lost his grip and you fell to the floor,* I almost felt like telling the flashlight. I visualized touching it and then pushing it from under the dresser with the side of my finger, trying hard to smudge where I touched it in the process. I pulled up all the dark stuff that I could out of the images and feelings coming from the flashlight. I *saw* it hitting people and hitting dogs, especially a huge Bullmastiff I could see cowering in a corner. I tried to turn my focus from the dog to concentrate on that location. It was the corner of a filthy kitchen. Judging by the flooring and appliances, circa 1950's, the house must be old. I could almost see the house in a heavily wooded area. I saw dog runs and a shed. Clearly it was a rural area. There were no visible neighbors and the house was partially obscured from the road by the trees. No wait - not a road - it was a highway. I could tell by the way the lines were painted. I tried to pull my vision to the mailbox but I couldn't quite do it. The number on it was five digits long and the name was McFadden or something like that.

I opened my eyes and looked at Marlo who was waiting patiently for me. I gave him all the important bits. He began opening multiple windows on his computer. He stared at the screen and typed, paused, read, switched screens, and repeated the process. He flipped so fast through the screens that I couldn't tell how he knew what he was looking at. I was so busy watching Marlo that I didn't notice when my mom poked her head through the back curtain.

"Owen honey, it's time to go," my mom stated quietly.

I turned to look at her, startled, still lost in my own thoughts. Marlo nodded at me. "This will take awhile. Catch up with me when you are done with physical therapy."

As I walked out through the front of the store, I saw that White Eagle was trying to make Adrian feel better and must have let her in. Mom paused, then walked around the front counter to give Adrian a hug. "Hang in there," she said, looking at White Eagle. "We'll all do everything we can."

Physical therapy was arduous. I was so distracted. All I could think about was Max. I pushed myself as hard as I could. My mom stood quietly off to the side and took notes about exercises as another therapist talked to her and handed her printouts. I was sweating and aching. They finally had me shower and change and try the pool. It felt great to be without the brace. I found the water soothing and calming. I was so tired by the time I got out of the pool that I found my body was quivering and my hands were shaking.

I headed for the dressing room, showered again and dressed in the clean clothes from my duffle bag. I wandered back out and found my mom still talking to a physical therapist. I sat down to wait and made the mistake of closing my eyes. My mom's gentle hand on my shoulder brought me back around. I must have dozed off. She put her arm around me as we walked out. I noticed that she seemed to be on heightened security. I had never noticed her being this aware of her surroundings before. She said nothing until we got to our SUV.

"White Eagle didn't tell me much. I know Max is in trouble. Clive and the other man who beat you have him. He said it really hurt you to *see* Max get beaten too. I'm so sorry. I wish I could *see* it for you."

"Where are the boys, Mom? You've been away from them for what, almost two hours now?" I asked rapidly, suddenly panicked.

"It's okay Owen, they are with Mrs. Lando. As of today she is out of retirement and assigned to us. She stopped by about a half hour before I came to get you. She already knew that Max was taken last night. They had him under some kind of video surveillance but they weren't quick enough. Apparently the cameras operate when there is motion. They have only one guy who monitors the feed. We all had become a low priority. A black jeep came in and two guys got out. It was hard to see in the dark. Then the camera shut off. The next shot, when the camera reactivated showed Max being dragged out by the two men. They must have noticed the camera as they left because it was found destroyed at the scene. They also found out yesterday that the lead to California was a false one. Mrs. Lando told me that I wasn't supposed to know any of that. She asked me sarcastically if I thought they'd fire her for telling me. She told me a little about Clive too. It sounds like he is completely crazy. He's wanted in at least four states. He should be locked away."

"Does Dad know?"

"I haven't talked to him since he left. He hasn't called and I just couldn't pick up the phone. I don't have anything to say. He won't believe us anyway. The Clive part alone would make him want to put us in witness protection. I can't do that to any of us, especially you. White Eagle needs you and you need him. We need each other and Sarah Lando. I think you and White Eagle would agree that this is something we need to solve and not run away from."

I pulled my cell from my pocket saying, "Let's see if they're still at the shop. Marlo was working on some stuff I *saw* and I want to know how Adrian is doing."

"If no one's home maybe Adrian could come to our house," she said, throwing out a mental lifeline to my friend.

"Hey," I said when White Eagle picked up, "you still at the shop?"

"Yeah."

"Can y'all wait there until we get there? We're on our way now."

"Yeah, you betcha."

"They'll wait," I said to my mom.

Mom drove like a crazy person all the way to the pawnshop. She took risks she didn't normally take and was consistently at least five miles an hour over the speed limit. I said nothing. Her driving was better than White Eagle's but I was ready for my own license. I couldn't wait to get my permit in five months and eleven days.

Marlo let us into the shop. "I got something."

We all waited while Mom relocked the door. All eyes turned to Marlo before the lock even clicked into its final position.

"Come to the back," Marlo said, leading the way. He sat at his laptop and we all took up various positions around him. "I have narrowed the search areas. There are only so many rural highways with five digit addresses and trees. I cross referenced McFadden and all other names I could think of that looked similar. There is a piece of property south of here that belongs to a Margaret McFarlder. It was purchased in 1954. There are other close matches but that one has the most things in common with what you told me."

Mom, White Eagle and I all reached for Marlo at the same time. When our hands met, the strongest static shock I had ever experienced shot up my arm causing my hair to stand on end and me to jump back along with Mom and White Eagle.

"What in the world?" Mom asked confused.

White Eagle pulled his head back on his neck and stared at my mom. "Wow, Lila, you look like a shaft of sunlight coming through the pine trees back home."

"What?" she asked, still confused.

I laughed. "You had never *looked* at her? She reads body language. She's like a super charged body language reader. She sees more than a normally trained person would. We kind of figured out together that she might have a gift. She felt she had something going on, but just recently she became sure. I think I got my gift from her."

We all looked at each other at a loss for words. Adrian came around first. "Hold on, I knew about Owen. Are you saying White Eagle has a gift AND your mom has one? What about Marlo? What about me? Does this help us save Uncle Max?"

"Yeah, I have a gift alright. I have an amazing sense of smell. I can smell evil!" Marlo laughed.

"I know you have a mess of questions but hold on a minute, would you?" White Eagle took ahold of Adrian's shoulders and stared into his eyes for a long moment. "Sorry Adrian, just as I thought, you are a good person but not magical."

White Eagle turned to us. "Put out your hands," he asked of me and my mother. We did so and all touched hands. A milder electric shock ran up my arm. We released hands. He cocked his head to the side, deep in thought. "Lila, focus on your ability, think of it as something you could put in a box and then mentally give it to Owen. Owen, think about Max and what you saw at his house."

White Eagle closed his eyes and put out his hand. My mother looked at him, then laid her hand on his and closed her eyes. I followed suit. The shock shot up my arm but dulled as I closed my eyes and focused. The images replayed but this time I had a stronger sense of what the three people were *saying* with their bodies. The ability to sense the people seemed to flicker and waver and then it was snuffed as my mother gasped.

"Amazing!" White Eagle shouted. "Wahoo!!!" He actually danced in a circle. We all looked at him like he had lost his mind.

"Owen," my mother said concerned, "I could see some foggy images from Max's house. What I saw was terrifying, but it looked like I was watching through a thick veil and I couldn't hear anything at all except what was going on in this room.

"Yes, yes, isn't it wonderful?" White Eagle crowed.

Again we just looked at him. He seemed to catch on that we weren't *with* him.

"Oh, sorry. I have heard of this ability, but I've never seen it. It must be because you are mother and son, but I could be wrong. Anyway when we put you together we get MORE."

"But I touch Owen all the time. I have never experienced that!" my mother yelped.

"Me either," I added helpfully.

"I think I am acting as a bridge or a conduit or something. I don't know. Marlo, we have got to renew our research into others like me and Owen. I know they've been difficult for you to track. We stay deep underground as a rule because we need to be secret to do our job, but there has got to be a way to make contact." White Eagle was so excited he was barely making sense.

"So, great! It's cool, but what about Uncle Max?" Adrian whined.

"Indeed. Let's see if we can bring you boys into this," White Eagle said.

Marlo and Adrian stepped up and we all tried to link hands and... nothing. "Okay, Marlo step out," White Eagle suggested. Nothing. "Okay, Adrian out, Marlo in." A faint flicker. "Well," White Eagle said disappointed, "it was worth a try."

White Eagle shook himself like a bird resetting feathers. "Now, what to do?" he wondered aloud. "Do we go check out the address

Marlo found or do we try an anonymous tip to my friend at the police station?"

"Adrian?" I asked, since he was staring at his feet.

"I don't know what to say. I want to rush out and save my uncle, but I'm scared. I had all these questions about what you had *seen* and I wanted to *do* something, but then when you started telling us what you *saw* and felt, I just... I just want it to all go away. How did you ever have the courage to face those guys at the mall, Owen? I thought I was brave and tough, but I have been sitting up in the front of the shop crying for my uncle and crying about feeling helpless and scared. Why am I even here?" Adrian asked, his voice cracking.

"Adrian, do you remember when I was still in the cast and Calvin faced off with me in the hallway? Who had my back? You did. Calvin didn't back down because he was afraid of me. He was afraid of *you*."

My mom moved closer to Adrian and wrapped her arms around him. Then she nodded at me as if I should continue. Adrian looked uncertain, so Marlo patted him awkwardly on the shoulder in a show of support.

"Adrian, White Eagle has taught us many things. He's taught us how to fight when we have to, but he has also taught us that when there is another option, we should take it. Never once did he say it wasn't okay to be scared. We just can't let the fear control us. Some fear is good because it makes us cautious. We're a team, Adrian. All of us don't have to be strong all the time." I spoke with a soothing voice that I put all my training behind. I used everything I had learned about tone of voice and body language and I hit him with all I had. I tried to tell him without words that he *could* do this. I wanted him to know that it was possible to be both scared and brave at the same time.

My mom looked at all of us. "Do you realize how much you all look alike now? You still have different eye color, but with your dark hair cut so much the same and all of you working out with

White Eagle... my goodness. It's just amazing and it's an honor to know such courageous young men."

I swung my gaze between Marlo and Adrian. I was still the tallest and Marlo was the shortest, but she was right. The differences between us were shrinking and becoming more subtle. "Well, there you go, Adrian, we even look like a team. Now we just need Mom and White Eagle to cut off their hair and dye it dark."

Marlo sported a huge grin and Adrian seemed to be loosening up a bit.

"I think we need to go scope the property out and then call the cops, but I'm much more interested in what Adrian thinks," I said, looking right at him.

"Well... yeah, that sounds best," Adrian said as he straightened away from my mom.

"Okay, let's saddle up then boys. Mom, I'll see you at home."

"Forget it, Batman. Batgirl is coming with you on this one. I'll call Sarah and have her stay longer. If I suck up, she may have dinner for us in a little bit," she said, whipping out her cell phone like she meant business. "Hello, Sarah? It's Lila. I need about two more hours at most with Owen. Can you stay that long? How about dinner? Can we make a deal? ... Super! See you around 6:30."

We were all gaping at her, open mouthed as she snapped her cell shut. She just smiled at us. "Well, Marlo the navigator, do you have the GPS fired up and ready to go?"

Who was this woman and what had she done with my mom?

White Eagle hopped in the backseat with Adrian and me while Marlo rode shotgun with his laptop fired up. He pulled up a satellite view of where we were going and Mom was off. We took the main drag south to the freeway and then Marlo had Mom exit and keep heading south and east on the rural highway. We were on the road for close to thirty minutes. The trees were becoming denser. Marlo closely watched the GPS on his laptop. The three of us waited tensely in the backseat. Finally, Marlo had Mom pull over and let some cars behind us go past.

"There is a road coming up on the right in less than five hundred feet. It looks heavily treed and may take you by surprise so go slow. I'll have you turn there and then we can hike in," Marlo said with all the seriousness of a Navy SEAL team leader.

All I could think, as we turned onto the road Marlo indicated, was *heaven help us*. My mom is on a mission. She rolled to a stop at a wide spot in the road, then asked us to wait as she popped the back open on our SUV and sat on the tailgate to change her shoes. Next she opened the safety kit back there and handed out a flashlight and the tire iron. She rummaged around some more and came up with some duct tape. "Always be prepared?" she asked with a shrug.

Geez, I guess, I thought and we were off. White Eagle led the way with Marlo and his laptop next. The going was slow to accommodate Marlo and his equipment. The house was just coming into view through the trees when Marlo's cell chirped. Faster than I could believe possible, he had slid his laptop to my mom and whipped out his phone.

"Hi Mom... Yeah, I'm fine... No, no, we're not at the shop. We had to… run an errand... Um actually, Owen's mom is here. Would you like to talk to her?" You should have seen the look my mom gave Marlo. I thought Marlo's hair would catch fire. Adrian and I had to cover our mouths so we wouldn't make a sound as we shook with laughter. My mom passed the laptop to White Eagle as she took Marlo's phone with all the dignity she could muster while standing in the bug infested woods up to her ankles in mud. She had fir needles in her hair and a smudge on her cheek.

"Hi Marla... Oh, we should be back in about an hour... Oh dear, I'm sorry. It's completely my fault. I took the boys on an errand to Mulino.... I should have asked first. I apologize... Well, could I just keep him overnight then? Great. We'll see you tomorrow... Okay.

Good bye." She turned a murderous gaze on Marlo. "You are in *so* much trouble right now."

Marlo actually looked scared. I was trying so hard not to laugh that my eyes were watering. Tears were running down my face, in the woods, where I was standing in the mud with my mom, White Eagle and my friends, swatting bugs AND we were hunting bad guys. I couldn't help it; a snort escaped.

"SHHHHHH!" everyone hissed at once. Sadly it only made me laugh harder.

"Perhaps we should all silence our cell phones to avoid any further mishaps?" White Eagle intoned piously.

Another snort escaped but was quickly silenced when there was movement near the house. We all froze and watched as Dreadlocks took out the garbage. White Eagle whispered that we should spread out and circle the house. We should keep to cover as much as we were able and look in windows if we could. In fifteen minutes we were to be back here. We were to avoid the dog kennels which looked empty but might not be. If anyone got into any trouble they were to make a run for the road. White Eagle took the driveway to defend anyone who needed it. Marlo and Mom got the right side of the house, Adrian the left and I took the back.

We all kept low and moved toward our objective. I watched everyone as much as I could. Hiding behind trees and shrubs was pretty easy as they were dense. I moved forward reaching the back door and tried to peek through the glass. The room was lived in, but no one was present. I was sure that I recognized the corner of the kitchen. I could hear a TV in the front room. I could also hear another faint noise. Was it a moan? A whimper? I ducked down and looked from side to side. To my left was an old fashioned window well that no human could actually be expected to climb out of. A pane of glass was broken leaving a small hole from where the sound had escaped. It was dark down there. "Max?" I called softly. To my surprise I was answered by a soft woof. "Max?" I tried again. Another woof was layered over by a human groan.

I was startled by movement in the house. An internal door banged open and I froze by the basement window. The light popped on and I got a quick glimpse inside to my horror. "Shut the hell up!" screamed Dreadlocks. At least I thought it was him. Clive was nowhere in sight and it didn't sound like him.

I crept around the corner of the house and headed behind a tree to wait. Sure enough, the back door banged open and Dreadlocks looked around. When he slammed the door, I released the breath I didn't even realize I was holding.

I looked at my watch and saw that I still had five minutes so I made my way cautiously over to where I thought my mom and Marlo would be. I caught sight of them headed back to our rendezvous point so I went to check on Adrian. He was crouched behind a tree, shaking, his eyes covered with his dirty hands. He jumped and let out a small squeak when I touched him. "He's here," he moaned softly, "and he looks bad."

"I know Buddy, come on. Let's get out of here so we can help him." I slowly dragged Adrian back to the rendezvous point where White Eagle was pacing. We quickly shared our reconnaissance information. White Eagle opened his cell and speed dialed his police contact.

"Hello Evelyn, it's me... I really need your help... I know something that I should not know. I need you to enter an anonymous tip... It has to do with our missing man... Yep, I know the FBI is in on it, but I can't very well call them now, can I? ... Has anything been released about Max? Watch for this guy kind of stuff? ... No? How about Clive? ... Perfect. Say he's been spotted at this address." He rattled it off quickly and then listened some more.

"We couldn't get an answer out of Max so I have to assume he is either in bad shape or unconscious. Please get someone here soon... I have to go; I can't be seen here... Keep me posted." He hung up the phone looking serious. "We're about out of time. We have to go, but she'll keep us in the loop. Adrian, I know this is nearly unbearable for you but you can't be found here. Come on."

White Eagle wrapped an arm around Adrian's shaking form and walked him back to our SUV. Mom and Marlo turned serious eyes on me. I shrugged and we followed White Eagle. What else could we do? Mom and Marlo had seen drug paraphernalia, White Eagle had seen multiple weapons including firearms and Adrian and I had seen a flash of a bloody beaten Max chained to a support beam with the Bullmastiff I had seen from the images, tied up with him. This was more than we were ready to handle.

We scraped off as much mud as we could and piled back in the SUV. White Eagle's phone was vibrating before Mom even reached the highway. Marlo was busy plotting the quickest route home. Adrian seemed dazed as he stared straight ahead from the center of the back seat where he was wedged between me and White Eagle.

"Yep?... Evelyn, thanks for calling back so fast. What have you got?... Super. Let me know what happens next would you?... Thanks. I owe you." He snapped his cell closed and smiled a quirky smile. "They are on their way with reinforcements. She'll call as she has more intelligence for us. Adrian, it's going to be okay. You did everything you could. I know your uncle will be proud of you!" Adrian turned to look at White Eagle but gave no further reply.

The trip back to the pawnshop seemed to go faster. White Eagle secured everything and was headed for his truck when it hit me. "Hey, where do you suppose Clive is? Maybe you should stay with us until we know something. We need to watch each other's backs."

"I think you're right. Lila?"

"Come stay with us for at least tonight. I think everyone would feel better. Adrian, how about if you stay too?"

White Eagle put an arm around him. "Whatever you want to do, we are all here for you."

"I'd like to stay, but I don't know what my folks will say," he said sadly.

My mom took matters into her own hands again and made the call. Adrian's parents were willing to turn him over to her. They thought he could stand some time away from the worry about Max. Little did they know.

True to her word, Sarah Lando had a great dinner ready for us when we all arrived. She had made enchiladas that smelled fantastic. She took in our muddy appearances without a word. "We'll clean up later. Let's eat!"

We introduced Mrs. Lando to Adrian and White Eagle. Marlo, she knew from mowing her lawn. We joked about the lawn and agreed that I would take it back over next week. She decided she would try to find work for all three of us. Then the conversation turned serious as Mrs. Lando learned that Adrian was Max's nephew. She and White Eagle shared information while the rest of us listened. Both were careful about what they said around my brothers.

We all helped clean the kitchen and then Marlo, Adrian and I took my brothers in the living room to play board games, including the promised checkers match. Right in the middle of my match against Lucas I heard White Eagle's cell phone ring. Finally some news; please let it be good. I was so busy listening to White Eagle's side of the conversation that Lucas beat me. You have never seen such a happy little man. He proudly challenged Adrian next. Marlo headed off for his turn in the shower and I moved closer to White Eagle so I could figure out what was going on.

He turned and looked at me, then indicated a chair by Mrs. Lando. She reached out and took ahold of my hand. "See, I knew there was something about you! There is something about *him* too," she said, pointing to White Eagle. "Where has your father gone this time?"

"He is off looking at a new job in Atlanta. He'll be back Tuesday after next or so."

I thought that I had given nothing away, but then maybe she was just really perceptive.

"I smell trouble. You and your mom don't want to move, do you." she stated like she knew what was going on.

"No, not really," I answered resigned. "Do I even want to know how you know?"

"I have been living on this street since the development went in. Due to my line of work I guess you could say I'm a natural neighborhood watch captain. Not that we have a neighborhood watch going. My point is this: I have observed your family for a long time. I'm someone who knows about character. Your father's a good man but he has come to love his work and his science more than what is happening around him. You and your mother tend to go less for the cerebral and more for gut instinct I think. You're both plenty smart; I think you use more than just that part of your arsenal, however."

I did nothing but stare at her. I was at a total loss for words. Thankfully I was relieved of the necessity to answer by White Eagle.

"That was my contact at the police station. They have smoked the house and are closing in."

"Why is it taking so long?" I asked, worried.

"He or they are fighting back. It shouldn't be much longer."

Mrs. Lando was patting my hand as Mom came in the kitchen with a towel wrapped around her wet hair. She had on her oldest jeans, fuzzy socks and a tee. She looked younger than she had in years. "Any word?" she asked.

We filled her in as Marlo came down the stairs. He and Adrian joined us in the kitchen. We brought them up to speed too. Adrian was reluctant to go take his shower but Mom finally talked him into it. Marlo had borrowed some clothes and had to roll the pants up, though it wasn't as bad as I would have thought. Mom was right. We were all starting to look the same.

I really looked at Marlo for a moment standing there in my borrowed clothes. He came up to my ear in height now. The jeans that were loose on me fit him a little snugger. The tee that fit my shoulders was a little loose on him. If he got rid of his glasses he could almost *be* me from a distance. I turned my attention to Adrian's retreating form. He went for skinny jeans and fitted tees for more of a *hipster* look. He too would look like me if dressed right and no one knew us well. It could be a good strategy for another time; to make us all look alike.

In only fifteen minutes, Adrian was back and we still hadn't heard anything so I took my turn in the shower, glad that we had one of those endless hot water, water heaters. The bathroom was steamy and damp. I looked at my foggy image in the mirror. Here my mom looked younger and I had aged. No one in high school would pick on me. I looked like I was sixteen, easy, maybe more. I threw on jeans in the bathroom since we had so much company in the house and made my way to my room to find socks and a shirt. Mom had laid out sets of clothes for all three of us and had even thrown some sleeping bags in my room for later.

When I got downstairs, I found out the call had finally come. Max was going to be okay. He was on his way to the hospital. They had captured Dreadlocks Dude and had plenty on him to keep him locked up for a long time. There was no sight or word on Clive which, needless to say, had us all concerned. Max would not let the dog go. Evidently they had helped each other in the dark basement and Max wanted to keep the big dog, who, it turned out, was a big pussycat. It sounded like Dreadlocks Dude was hoping the dog would eat Max or something equally grim. The dog was clearly much smarter than Dreadlocks.

We split up into teams and played a few more board games. Mom and Sarah, as we were now to call her, cleaned up! White Eagle and Adrian were pretty tough but the ladies could not be beaten at anything we tried. Adrian looked so much better by the time my brothers had to go to bed. I think the end of the evening was a big success. Adrian perked up even more when his dad called from the hospital with a report on Max. He was cranky, hungry and beat up.

He would have no permanent damage and he very much wanted to press charges! He would be released tomorrow. Then the tricky part came... could we come get the dog for the night.

After much negotiation amongst those of us who were still up, we finally settled on White Eagle, Adrian and me going to get the dog out of Adrian's dad's car. All the way over to the hospital parking lot I kept praying that White Eagle had some really good doggie juju.

Adrian's dad met us at the hospital entrance with his car keys. He would be staying with Max for the night. He was hoping the dog had not eaten his car. "Little brothers, what we wouldn't do for them, right, Owen?" he said with a smile.

We approached the car cautiously. All was still and quiet. White Eagle peered in the nearest window causing a huge head to fill the rear passenger window. The dog tilted its massive head to the side. There was a pause and then a huge tongue flopped out the side of its mouth in a big doggie grin. "Woof," it said happily and began thumping its tail with such enthusiasm that it rocked the little sub compact car. Was this dog for real or was it playing with us?

Adrian's dad unlocked the car and White Eagle cautiously opened the back door. The beast tried to make a break for it but White Eagle quickly snapped on a lead borrowed from our house. The big dog made it as far as the end of the leash but that was far enough for it to tackle Adrian, knocking him flat on his back. The big dog's paws held down Adrian's shoulders while it licked him thoroughly like a tasty lollypop.

After a brief moment of stunned silence we all busted up laughing! The dog leaped off Adrian and bounced in an enthusiastic circle. Adrian slowly got to his feet while trying to wipe off the dog drool. "Yeech," he spit.

"Adrian, man, what's with your dog?"

"What do ya mean? He isn't my dog."

"Looks like he picked you," White Eagle said smiling as the dog sat on Adrian's foot and looked up at him like he was the greatest ever. It was quite a feat to mix that sappy look with the whole tough dog image.

"Max said his name is... Thor," Adrian's dad supplied.

"I guess I do have a dog. Good thing I spend so much time with Uncle Max. Maybe when he gets used to us he won't be such a sissy. He totally needs a new name."

We hugged Adrian's dad goodnight and took Adrian's new beast home. I rode shotgun and Adrian rode in the back under a layer of dog. Both would need a bath when we got home. Mom would be so pleased. Ha! Maybe we could slip her a glass of wine.

Mom, Marlo and Sarah met us in the front yard with Beggar on a leash. Beggar woofed happily, all ready to play. Thor tried to hide behind Adrian. After much coaxing we finally got them to sniff each other. Thor must not have known that he was ten times Beggar's size because he rolled right over in a submissive position.

"Well, a Bullmastiff named Thor! He should be the toughest dog on the planet. Instead you have the biggest girly dog ever! I mean really, he's afraid of everything!" I said laughing all over again.

We all laughed. I was glad that we could have these moments of happiness. Most of the time we spent together these days was tracking down bad guys. It was exhilarating and scarier than anything I had ever done. I wanted it to end and for my life to go back to normal and at the same time I didn't. I knew we were all growing, changing and becoming the grownups we would one day be. The three of us, Marlo, Adrian and I, would always have a bond. I knew in an instant of insight that we would be friends forever, no matter what. I wondered what stories we would tell when we were old men.

It was midnight before we had the dog washed and mostly dry and Adrian rewashed. Mom handled the whole thing much better than expected and even gave us an old blanket for Thor who would not leave Adrian. She agreed to let him spend the night with us, seeing that he was no threat.

White Eagle walked Sarah home so he could make sure that her house was safe and so she could get a good night's rest. They had decided that White Eagle would stay with us at night and Sarah would be on the day shift until we knew about Clive.

My boys, Thor and I all settled into my room. Mom and Beggar went to her room and White Eagle took the couch. I swear I felt my house heave a sigh of relief as we all quieted down. We were too tired to visit much. We did laugh with Adrian about Thor though; the dog was not happy unless he was right next to Adrian. Thor finally heaved the biggest sigh ever heard as he curled up back to back with Adrian. I think they both sucked up a bunch of comfort from each other.

THIRTEEN

Sunday turned out to be a perfect kind of day. We all had pancakes and eggs that were cooked up by my mom and Marlo. Then the men took off for the pawnshop for some exercise and training. After sweating it out for close to two hours, we all showered and cleaned up at the pawnshop. We returned to my house and I started my laundry. Marlo, Adrian and I were in shorts, having burned through every pair of jeans I own. We also finished all the chores on Mom's list and even got our homework done. We spent the rest of our time together just lazing around.

Max was released from the hospital in the late afternoon to go home with Adrian's dad. Max's house was still off limits. Marlo had to go home about the same time, but we would get to keep Adrian and Thor for another day until things with Max were settled. I felt Marlo's absence; it just wasn't the same without him. Adrian and I had never spent so much time together, just the two of us.

Evelyn called White Eagle around dinner time to let him know that they had recovered the flashlight and had put a rush on the processing. It did have both Clive's and Dreadlock's fingerprints on it, as well as hair and blood evidence from Max. Dreadlocks, otherwise known as Darren, had tried to burn his house down or at least burn a bunch of evidence. He was not successful so they had plenty to keep him. They had even found evidence of his involvement with dog fighting. He would be off the streets for a long, long time even though he refused to talk.

When my brothers were upstairs getting ready for bed and we had the TV to ourselves, I felt like I could finally talk to Adrian.

"How are you feeling now?" I asked, a little worried about him.

"Okay, I guess, it's just a lot to take in. You know? I realize Clive is still out there but I feel like half our problem is gone. I'm sorry to impose on your family but they gave Uncle Max my room. I'll go home tomorrow and help take care of him. We'll clean up his house and move him back when the cops let us. I just hope they find Clive soon," he concluded, sounding worried.

"We've had quite a year, huh? And speaking of that and the end of the year... I was wondering... would you sing with me for eighth grade graduation?"

"What? Really? You mean it? I'd love to. What do you have in mind?" Adrian asked excitedly.

"I'm thinking that we could go for some '90s Boy Band type stuff. Mom has some CDs and our choir teacher gave me a list of music he had. You know Marlo can sing pretty well even though he went the orchestra route and maybe Jesus. He's in choir with me. What do you think?"

"Sounds good. Let's pick something out! We could practice now and then we'll be ready to add our background singers!" Adrian crowed.

We settled on music and then sang with the CD about twenty times. My mom came down to see what we were up to. She loved our plan. She even helped us get the karaoke machine out of the garage and found a karaoke CD with our song on it. We practiced it a bunch more and I thought we were sounding pretty good. There were few times I remember having this much fun with Adrian.

It was weird to share my room on a school night. I'd not had a bad dream in awhile but tonight was an exception. I dreamed of Clive. He was menacing all the people I care about. He had my dad tied to some lab equipment and stood between the rest of us and dad. Every time I would try to protect someone he would go after someone else in a strange version of keep away and tag combined. Finally he'd had enough of me and tackled me. The air left my lungs in a whoosh, my ribs complaining loudly. I opened my eyes to find Thor pinning me down. He gave me a friendly slurp and returned to snuggle with Adrian. Geez, had I wakened up the dog? I'd be glad when they went home. Love ya, but go away would ya?

Morning came early. Lucas bounced in before my alarm even went off. He was so excited to have company on a school night. He happily told a sleepy Adrian that if he couldn't keep Thor then *he* wanted him. I laughed when I visualized Lucas being walked by Thor. I figured my brother could just about ride him. My laugh brought Alex in. Thor slurped my brothers and ran for the door. I heard him pound down the stairs and my mom squeal. I rushed downstairs as the back door banged open.

I noticed White Eagle was just waking up on the couch as I rushed toward the kitchen. Mom stood with her arms crossed over a graphic tee, her hair a jumble. She turned on her slippered feet and scowled at me. "That dog," she growled. She was wearing some plaid sleep pants in florescent pink and bright orange. It was quite the look.

"Did those jammie pants keep you awake last night?" I asked with a straight face.

"What? Wait, you're joking? In the morning? You?" she asked, her mood lightening.

I smiled at her as I crossed to the window to watch the dogs run, chase and cavort in the backyard. "So, you really like having a big dog in the house, huh?"

"Not even a little bit," she said with a smile. "One more day. I miss my quiet life."

"Sure you do," I said with sarcastic good humor. "Besides, your life was already *so* quiet."

"Owen, I'm going to find a way to go back to work. I think you and I need to prepare for your dad not coming back. He still hasn't called."

"Have you called him?"

"No," she said somewhat sheepishly.

"Do you love him?"

"Not in the way I used to. He loves his job more than us, I think. If his job was here I wouldn't give up on our relationship. I would keep trying to make it work but you can't move right now and I don't want to. I hardly ever talk to my mom now that she is remarried and busy with her own life in Arizona. I never talk to your dad's parents. I haven't been to my dad's grave in awhile but I like knowing it's close if I ever want to go. I guess I'm saying I love my life here more than I love your dad. I'm sorry. Please don't let it affect your relationship with him. I probably shouldn't even say anything but our relationship, yours and mine, feels so different now. You seem like a grown-up and we have this weird connection..." She faded out and then shrugged.

I walked toward her and gave her a hug. "Somehow this will all be okay. Don't give up yet. You're right about one thing though, I can't leave White Eagle. I'm not ready yet."

The dogs barked at the back door. We let them in and got on with the morning. Adrian was still excited about singing and was even more excited when Marlo met us at my house instead of at the bus stop. We talked him into singing with us for graduation and practiced a little. A laughing White Eagle told us he couldn't take it anymore and left for the pawnshop. I had physical therapy today, but the other two were to head to the shop right after school. Marlo's mom would take them today just to be safe.

Mom sent a note with Adrian so that he could ride our bus without difficulty. We had fun on the bus. I had mixed feelings when we got off and Katie was not there to meet me. Jill and Melissa found my boys right away, so I walked to class alone. I didn't see Lucie or Katie all morning. When it was time for math, Katie was the last one in the door and didn't make eye contact. She only talked to Marlo until the very end of class. Without looking at me directly she whispered that she was sorry for our misunderstanding and turned and fled before I could say anything. I didn't know what to do about Katie. I liked her as a friend but I felt bad for both of us and the whole situation. Who knows why we fall for the people we do?

I went to my locker, swapped out my books and grabbed my lunch. I closed my locker to find Calvin standing right behind the door. I was so done with this guy. "What do you want, Calvin?" I asked with a weary voice.

"I'm just here to say me and Lucie are back together. If you know what's good for you, you'll leave her alone." He was trying to sound so tough. When was this idiot going to learn?

I expelled a puff of air that wasn't either a laugh or a sigh, but a little of both. "Okay," I said calmly. This time I said the "whatever" part of the sentence in my mind.

"So you don't talk to her, sit by her or even look at her."

"You're kidding, right? You do understand that we have assigned seats in our classes and that she is my lab partner? How exactly am I supposed to do what you ask under those conditions?" You big *doofus*, I said in my mind but I'm pretty sure my facial expression showed my true feelings about him.

"You distract her," huffed Calvin.

"Are you serious?"

"Her parents like me - so you're done." With that he turned on his heel and walked away.

Well that was interesting. I walked slowly to lunch deep in thought. Lucie was sitting by a gloating Calvin. What on earth she was thinking, I couldn't guess. She seemed to sense my gaze and turned to look at me. She looked more resigned than happy. Calvin threw an arm over her shoulder, snatching her attention from me. I couldn't put my finger on it, but something was all wrong with whatever was going on with them.

I made my way over to my boys. Jill and Melissa were already sitting there with them and Katie, who had an empty spot next to her. She looked both hopeful and scared. Everyone had their full attention on Adrian who was regaling them with our exploits over the weekend. I hoped that in his exuberance he had not let it slip about our spying on bad guys. Marlo looked completely calm so all must be okay, I thought as I slid in next to Katie. "Hey, Katie," I said softly.

"Hey Owen," she answered, still not looking at me.

I decided I better try to fix things with her the best I could. "Katie, I'm really sorry that I hurt your feelings. I just need to be your friend before I can be anything more than that. Can we try to be friends, please?"

She nodded, still looking at her mostly uneaten lunch. I sighed a little and started in on my own. She peeked up at me and smiled. Then she slowly scooted over and very deliberately laid her head on my shoulder. I set down my, Marlo-approved, healthy sandwich and put my arm around her shoulders in a side hug. She briefly hugged me back, her arm around my waist, and then went back to her lunch and the group conversation.

The three of us tossed our garbage and hurried to the choir room so we could present our idea for eighth grade promotion. My choir teacher was thrilled. Marlo and Adrian rushed off to their own class and Katie beamed at me. As she entered the room, Lucie sent me a sad smile and quickly found her seat.

When the bell rang signaling the end of class, Lucie, Katie and I walked toward science chatting about our end of the year promotion stuff and choir. I kept expecting Calvin to pop out and threaten us. Katie headed for her class and Lucie and I took our seats. I looked up to find Calvin scowling in the doorway. I stared back for a moment and then focused on getting ready for class. As the tardy bell rang, I saw movement in the doorway and figured it was him darting away.

Once we were going on our lab work, I turned to Lucie. "So, I got a message from Calvin before lunch, but I don't think you got the memo or you wouldn't have walked with me to class."

Lucie gave me a hard look and then relented. "He came by on Saturday to say 'hi'. My parents just love him and wanted me to give him another chance. 'He's such a wonderful boy and just right for you.' Can you believe that hooey? Anyway, I thought - what the heck. I am going to do my thing and if he doesn't like it, he can lump it. You're my friend. I'm sorry that he gave you a bad time. Just ignore him. I do when he's stupid," she said and turned her full attention on our lab work once more.

The rest of the day passed in much the same fashion. Calvin scowled at me and Lucie and I ignored him and did our assigned tasks. Working with Lucie was as good as working with Marlo. She was just as focused and we were able to get enough done that we wouldn't have any homework today. YES!

Katie met me in the lobby on her way to the bus. "Thank you, Owen, for accepting my apology and for being such a nice guy. I'm lucky to have you as a friend. I just have to remember that I have liked you for longer than you realized and well, I just wanted you to know how much I like you. I guess I was kind of trying to *buy* my way in. It just didn't have the effect I expected. See you."

"See you tomorrow, Katie," I said, not knowing what to say to the rest of her statement. She saved me the discomfort by heading to the bus. I waved to Marlo and Adrian as they loaded up with Mrs. Saggio and then my own mom pulled in.

She asked how my day had gone. I filled her in on the promotion song idea that was approved. Then I told her about Lucie and Katie. "I don't understand chicks," I stated at the end of my explanation.

My mom gave me such a big grin that I was afraid she would hurt herself. "Well, my dear - that is half the fun isn't it?" My mother, the philosopher; gotta love her.

I was happy when physical therapy was over and we could head to the shop. Mom dropped me off so she could go home and start dinner. White Eagle would take Adrian to his house, then he would drop off Marlo and finally we would go to my house where he would take over for Sarah. Life had become complicated again.

The three of us quickly cleaned and organized the shop while White Eagle served some customers. Marlo broke off a little early to finish some bookwork for the pawnshop. With the short time we had left, Adrian and I tried a little sparring. I wasn't as good as I had been, but I was better than when I first started.

White Eagle parted the curtain and watched for a few minutes before he spoke. "Adrian, you're looking pretty good. Owen, you're trying to protect your side and your leg. I understand and I don't blame you, but I hate to have you practice like that. Your leg is getting stronger and it's protected by the brace. Have a little more faith. If I give you something to protect those ribs, do you think you could take a hit?"

"I could try," I said with more bravado than I felt.

White Eagle had me strip off my tee and put on a specially padded practice shirt. Adrian helpfully commented that I didn't look as muscular as I did before my accident. I just looked at him. If he was trying to rev me up to really hit him, he was doing a good job. The practice shirt felt a little heavy and awkward. It was almost like wearing football pants with pads. I shrugged and stretched until it felt about right and we started again.

"He's still protecting his side, Adrian. Go get him!" White Eagle bellowed.

Adrian came at me full force, throwing punches, kicks and jabs. He quickly dodged all my counter attacks. Neither one of us would give an inch. Finally Adrian got his moment. I punched and he quickly came in under my guard and smacked me good in the ribs. We both froze for a moment and looked at each other. It only hurt a little bit more than any other hit I had taken from Adrian. A slow smile spread over my face.

"So, what? I wear the practice shirt all the time now?" I asked almost hopefully.

White Eagle had the good grace to laugh a little. "How about just to practice and on any missions? Now, go again, would you?"

Adrian and I circled each other again. He came at me as if to tackle me and I neatly stepped out of the way and spun to use his momentum against him. He was expecting it and turned what would have been a fall into a neat bounce and roll. He flipped to his feet and came at me again. I used his momentum to move him away from me, this time following it with a jab to his kidney. Marlo must have come in the back room because he hooted and clapped from the sidelines for both of us.

White Eagle called us off and told us to get ready to go. Tomorrow we were to get to the shop on our own. He told us to call from school before we left for the hike to the shop. We locked up, and then loaded in the truck. We dropped Adrian off and promised to bring Thor over soon. Next we dropped off Marlo and then headed to my house.

We all had dinner that Mom and Sarah had cooked together. The ladies had gone grocery shopping while my brothers were at school. After they picked up Lucas they had cleaned out most of Sarah's pantry to supplement our dwindling supplies. Then they had picked up Alex and the four of them had done some strategic meal planning with the new influx of foodstuffs. Mom had me load a forty pound bag of dog kibble for Thor into White Eagle's truck, gave Thor a hug and sent us on our way to Adrian's house.

I have never seen a happier dog. He joyfully knocked Adrian to his knees in happy greeting. He was gentler with Max who was ensconced on the sofa, but Max still groaned at impact. Adrian's dad just rolled his eyes. Adrian's sister, Amber, tried to act all superior but when Thor came over to greet her she melted like chocolate on a hot day. Adrian's mom smiled from the kitchen doorway. I knew this was a special time of day for their family. It was their magic twilight time. Adrian's dad had not yet left for work but was up to see his family and Adrian's mom had just come home.

White Eagle and I both gave Max a gentle hug and wished him well. We also promised to take good care of the pawnshop for him and then left him in his family's loving care.

"He's bruised and he'll have a couple of good scars, but he came out of his little adventure with those monsters better than I did," I said, sounding disgusted even to my own ears. I guessed I was a little jealous.

"Don't be hard on yourself," he said, seeming to sense my mood. "Be proud. They surprised Max, so they subdued him quicker. You fought back so they beat you more. In both cases, I think they were trying to scare you and both times things went wrong. We're lucky they are either not too bright or have killed brain cells with drugs and hard living. I'll be much happier when Clive shows up. I hate having this worry constantly hanging over all of us. Let's head to my place so I can pick up a few things and clean my own perishables out of my fridge. Your mom and Sarah were pretty smart to clean out Sarah's stuff. With us all eating at your house the least we can do is help contribute. Besides, I kind of like having two lovely ladies cook for me," he said with a big smile.

I didn't know if he had just come to love my family that much or if it was Sarah Lando that he was finding interesting or even a little of both and I didn't care. I knew that I was very glad to have him around. He was a little old to be an uncle and too young to be my grandfather, but I was much closer to him than the one I had left. My Cuban born grandfather was always serious, even more so than my own father. I had never felt a bond with him. White Eagle was becoming very important to me.

We quickly checked White Eagle's house and gathered anything that wouldn't keep. He planned to stay until my dad returned for which I was very thankful. He tossed some clean clothes into a small duffle and we were back on the road.

Mom, Sarah and my brothers were making caramel corn when we got home. It was a rare treat that we usually only indulged in around the holidays. I could tell that Mom was trying really hard to keep things normal and happy for my brothers. She poured the caramel and Sarah stirred. Lucas was practically jumping up and down in anticipation. We all sat around the table, talked and ate too much of the sweet, gooey goodness. Our evening together was short but wonderful. White Eagle again walked Sarah home and Mom sent me up to supervise tooth brushing and jammies while she cleaned the kitchen. I was just finishing the first book Lucas picked out when she poked her head around the corner.

"Do you have homework you need to finish?" she asked in her mother voice.

"Nah, I'm good. We got it done in class today."

"Good for you. Lucas, want me to take over?"

"Nah, I'm good," he said imitating me.

"Oh brother, Brother, you really need to come up with some original lines," guffawed Alex. Then he howled at his own humor.

Mom went over to tickle him making him laugh even more than he already had with his pun. She gave him a big hug, a kiss and then handed him back the book he was reading to himself. "I love you, middle boy. You're my favorite. Now, don't tell the others I said so."

Then she came over and hugged and kissed Lucas. "Good night little man. Love you. You're really my favorite. Now, don't tell the others."

Finally she hugged and kissed me. "Good night my biggest boy, you know the drill, you're the favorite so don't tell."

"You're my favorite Mom," I said seriously.

"Me too," my brothers chorused.

She smiled, waved at us and was gone. I read one more book to Lucas, hugged my brothers, tucked them in and turned out their light. I went looking for my mom. I found her in her favorite chair, book in hand, staring into space. "What's up?"

"I feel like I should apologize to you. I do everything I can to make life normal for your brothers but I don't do that for you. You're fourteen and I have been treating you like a grownup ever since... I don't know when I started. Anyway, at the beginning of the school year you and I were two different people. Part of me wishes I could take it all back and have a do-over and part of me knows this is the road that you and I are meant to walk. You just seem like you have it so together. It's weird. I think I'm a bigger emotional wreck than you are," she said in an awed voice, like she couldn't quite believe what she was saying.

"Mom, I'll never be the same. Did we ever tell you about the watch?"

"Not really. Why?"

"Well, the watch was the trigger that activated my gift. Partly I had to be old enough and partly the watch called to me strongly because it had belonged to a strong *watcher*. The man, whose memories were in this watch, was a police officer and then a private investigator. He had just celebrated his thirty-fourth birthday when he died. He had a wife who was pregnant. He died trying to avenge her. I now have his memories that I have come to see just as strongly as I do my own. He had the watch for about twelve years or so. In other words I remember my life and then I remember his life from about age twenty one or so on. You think I'm an adult? Well I remember being one. It is so strange, you really have no idea."

"You're serious? I don't know what to say. I'm sorry doesn't seem to cover it," she babbled away. Clearly I had completely stumped her this time.

White Eagle found us in the living room still staring at each other when he came in. "What did I miss?"

"The lipstick on your cheek for one thing," I answered, deadpan.

He flushed bright red and Mom giggled as he scrubbed at his cheek with the back of his hand.

Mom quickly changed the subject. "Owen was finally getting around to telling me how big a part of his life that watch really is. Apparently he remembers being Miles as strongly as he remembers being Owen."

"Really? Well, isn't that something? It explains a lot. Do you remember this?" he said, coming up behind me where I sat on the couch and putting me into a headlock, which I quickly removed myself from by dumping him unceremoniously across the back of the couch and onto the floor. My mom sharply inhaled in time to White Eagle's body thumping the floor.

"Yep, that's Miles all right," he wheezed. "I didn't teach Owen that." He wheezed again. "Having Miles in there could be useful."

"I'm so sorry! Are you okay? It was like a reflex or something," I breathed out in a rush.

"Ahhrgh," he moaned and started pulling himself to a sitting position. "I'll be all right, just give me a minute."

My mom looked from one to the other of us then went over to White Eagle to help him up.

"Well, I'm way too young to have a thirty four year old son. Now what do I do with you?" she asked, half kidding and half serious. "I would have been four when you were born. Gross." Her giggle was slightly hysterical.

"Lila, he's still Owen. He's just a really mature Owen," White Eagle said, trying to sooth her.

"And to think I was giving you advice on your love life. Miles can probably give you plenty," she continued as if she really hadn't heard White Eagle. "Maybe I should be asking your advice..." She finally stumbled to a stop and stared at me for a moment. "How is reliving middle school? Oh, wait you don't remember that part." Again she laughed a slightly hysterical giggle.

"Well Mom, I can tell you this. I will not be getting plowed on my next twenty first birthday. It is so not worth it. I never want to be that sick again!"

We all laughed, breaking the strange atmosphere my admission had created. "I'm off to bed. I'll see you tomorrow. Love you, Mom," I said giving her another hug.

"Love you too," she replied as she hugged me fiercely.

"Night, Owen," White Eagle added.

I smiled at him and left. They started talking before I was even up the stairs. The topic? Me of course. I didn't even care to listen. They could work it out between them. Heck, they were two of my best advocates anyway.

The rest of the week fell into a pattern: school, pawnshop, physical therapy, dinner with Sarah and White Eagle, being nice to Katie and Lucie. I noticed that as the week went by Lucie seemed to get more and more blue. By science on Friday she looked like she wasn't sleeping well. I reached out to touch her sleeve to get her attention – instead the image I got, got my attention.

"Lucie, what are you doing?" I asked angrily.

"What are you talking about?" she asked surprised, looking over her lab notes like that was the problem.

"I'm talking about Calvin. I don't understand you at all. I thought I knew you. I thought you were stronger than this. You're putting up with his verbal abuse because your parents like him. Do they know how he talks to you?" My tone was still angry.

"How do you know how he talks to me? What's it to you anyway?" she asked, sounding a little angry herself.

"Let's just say, I'm observant and I care about you. I wouldn't want any of my friends to be treated badly."

"Mmm," was her only response. She turned back to our lab and tried to ignore me.

The image, though I could not hear the words, held ugly body language. Whatever he said to her made him feel superior, and in turn, pounded on her self esteem. It seemed clear to me that she didn't want to be with him but was *afraid* to leave. Oh Lucie, WHY? Not long ago she would've scooted close and put her head on my shoulder, but today she seemed to shrink down into herself. I tried to talk to her again at the end of class. "Lucie, I hate to see you sad. You're one of my favorite people. How can I help?"

"Just leave me alone, Owen. I'm not worth your energy," she said wearily.

"Lucie Ness, you are most certainly *worth* my energy," I said, angry once more.

"I'm not one of the problems that you and your buddies need to fix, okay?" I was so stunned that I just let her walk away. Did she know? How much did she know? I was afraid to ask.

Calvin, the big dope, tried to stare me down in the hallway again. I wasn't having it. If I couldn't fix her, maybe I could fix him. I walked right up to within six inches of him. It forced me to look up slightly but I didn't care. "If you're going to stay with Lucie, then you be nice to her. Don't cheat on her and don't talk down to her."

"Or what, Ryer? I'm not afraid of you, Gimpy."

"I feel that if you are going to make fun of someone, you should use some valid arguments," I said with menace in my voice.

"You're so weird; I don't even know what you're talking about. I can do whatever I want anyway. If she didn't like it – she'd leave. I could have any girl I want, but she suits my purposes now. Every guy in this school thinks she's *hot*. Since she's done with the gymnastics thing her dad thought she could model, but she's gotta lose her fat ass. I'm helping, I don't let her eat lunch," he gloated like he was doing her a favor.

"You'll leave her completely alone. Don't speak to her and don't touch her," I seethed.

"Owen, what are you doing?" Lucie asked, sounding appalled.

I turned to look at her and saw movement. I flipped my head back to Calvin, ready for the blow, but he was almost running away from me, probably because a teacher was coming.

"Nothing," I said as I took Lucie's arm to walk her to health. She yanked her arm away from me with a frown.

"Leave it alone. I can take care of myself. Mind your own business."

I looked back over my shoulder and the teacher was gone. I went into health relieved only about not getting in trouble with the teacher but more worried than ever about Lucie. Lucie didn't speak to me the rest of the day.

Katie met me in the lobby after school as she often did. The way she was switching from foot to foot told me something was up.

"What's up, Katie?" I asked, taking the bull by the horns.

"Um, well, there is a... um... dance next Friday," she ended in a rush.

I sighed inside, but I had promised to play nicely with others. "I didn't know. Did you want to go?"

Her face initially looked sad as I said that I didn't know about it, but immediately brightened when I asked if she wanted to go.

"Yes please, it starts at seven. I'll meet you there. Thank you," she said, giving me a quick hug and running for her bus. Oh boy.

The guys showed up before I could worry much about next Friday. They were in sweats and running shoes so that we could walk with a little jogging on our way to the shop.

"Why aren't you changed?" Adrian asked.

"Busy day," I said wearily. "Hey, is there a dance next Friday?"

They both looked at me like I was nuts and then in unison pointed to the poster on the wall right near me. Two things were immediately apparent: One, I needed to pay better attention to what was going on around me and two, we were spending way too much time together.

"Well then, I suppose we're going?" I asked.

"We are. We didn't know about you and after last time..." Adrian answered.

"Katie kind of asked me to ask her. So I did. I guess then we're all going. I'll go change and then we can head to the pawnshop."

We headed out, dressed for the walk and jog to the shop. Each of us was loaded down with our backpack full of school books and binders and a small duffle with our school clothes. It was a pain to run that way but the extra weight was good for us. White Eagle said it built both character and muscle.

We were all sweaty and tired when we reached the shop so White Eagle took pity on us and let us have a break by organizing the clutter that had accumulated in the shop and the back room. He tossed each of us a banana and a protein shake. Bananas are fine but protein shakes are not in my top 1000 favorite foods.

I asked about Max and Thor and was informed that they were at the shop part time. Max came in for the busiest hours and would pick up more hours as he felt better. He would be in all day Saturday when they were busiest. He had promised White Eagle some vacation time to make up for all his extra work.

Today was my first day back to lifting weights. Can you say so *not* fun? White Eagle set up a circuit for us to run through so that we didn't get in each other's way. As I did my crunches I watched Marlo lift with White Eagle. I had to say that his fitness had really snuck up on me. Adrian and I had always had similar builds. All of us were much better muscled now than when we started the year. But Marlo, wow, I noticed for the first time that nearly all of his fluffiness was gone and he actually had muscles in his arms. All this time I always thought his biggest muscle was his brain. I had done him a disservice.

"Marlo, Dude, you're looking like an athlete instead of a geek!" I shouted to him when he finished his set.

I guess he could have taken offense but he took it good naturedly. "Yep, you can't just work out one muscle. Isn't that what you used to try to tell me when I wouldn't leave my computer?"

"Well men, I really don't want you in my truck smelling like you do but we ran over. There's no time for showers here. Let's get y'all home, shall we?"

"Way to spoil the mood, White Eagle," Adrian said.

"Yeah, you're a downer, Dude!" Marlo added.

White Eagle just rolled his eyes as we ran from the shop yelling "Shotgun!"

FOURTEEN

Our weekend was busy but uneventful. There was no word on Clive. He seemed to have dropped completely off the face of the earth. Darren of the dreadlocks still wasn't talking or at least if he was, there was nothing that White Eagle's friend or Sarah's contacts thought was worth sharing with us. I texted Lucie and she ignored me. Katie texted me twenty times and IM'd me on Facebook. Sigh.

Monday went by slowly. I tried to be extra nice to both the young women in my life. Lucie was really worrying me. She looked like she had lost weight, not that I thought she needed to lose any to start with, and she still had circles under her eyes. Physical therapy would have been a complete waste of time, except that I was out of my brace. Hooray! Today I was back in the pool. One of the good things about swimming is that even when you work hard you don't get all sweaty. After I worked with the physical therapist I got to swim some laps.

My mom seemed edgy on the way home. Looking back I guess it had started over the weekend. She was the mad cleaning woman the entire time and was really quiet this morning. My therapy ran over so it was pointless to go to the pawnshop. I texted White Eagle to let him know and then turned to my mom. "You're worried about Dad, aren't you?"

She looked over at me. Her jaw was clenched and her knuckles were pale on the steering wheel. She purposely loosened her grip. "Yes," was her one word reply.

When she said nothing further, I asked, "Do you want to talk about it?"

"Owen, this is just hard for me. There are a few roads I could walk, but I don't like any of the choices. We agree that your dad is not ready to accept what you are, but we could try to tell him, or I go with your dad and leave you with White Eagle, or we send him on his own. No matter what I choose, someone will be hurt. It's painful for me. I can't stand to hurt people," she said with agony in her voice.

I was silent for a bit as I thought it all through. In my heart I knew she was right; there was no good solution here. I reached into my Miles memories but he was twenty when he became a *watcher*. He was in college so he could keep it from his parents and the rest of his family. They never knew.

"I guess we try to tell him about me. I feel strongly that he will blow a gasket, but we have to try, right? I just know he's going to think I'm lying even if I try to prove it to him and then he'll be mad at you for believing me. He'll say something like I have pulled the wool over your eyes. He's all science and no mystical. Still, I think we have to try. Do you know for sure when he comes home?"

"Today or tomorrow I think. He never even told me that part," she sighed.

"Maybe Sarah could take the little boys so we have one less thing to deal with?" I asked her.

"We can try, Owen. She knows we're having problems. She sprung her evidence on me but I didn't deny it. She doesn't know what you can do."

"I think she suspects, Mom. She's really smart and observant. She sprung the Dad situation on me also. I didn't deny it either. She does love us like family and would want what's best for us. I almost wish that White Eagle could be with us to help like he did with Marlo and Adrian but I know it would only make things worse."

"Well, good luck to all of us then," she said, not sounding too hopeful.

Dinner was subdued and not like it had been up until now. Everyone was quiet and thoughtful in anticipation of Dad's arrival. We arranged, as best we could, for Sarah to take the boys so we could talk. White Eagle and I cleaned the kitchen so that I could tell him the plan that Mom and I had concocted. His advice to me was to do what I thought was best, but I most certainly could live with him until I finished school. The thought of being without my mom and brothers made my heart squeeze. It was not the choice I wanted to make. My first choice was to have my dad understand and accept me.

I couldn't sleep that night. I was plagued by nightmares. I tried to tell my dad about me but he wouldn't listen. I was on my knees in the mud when Clive came after us. Dad was able to run but I had to pull myself through the mud, unable to rise. Clive lost interest in me and went after my brothers but they were being protected by White Eagle, Sarah and my mom, who were all wearing suits of armor and hefted big swords. Clive came back to harass me. He lunged at me and I tried to roll away. I woke up when I hit the floor tangled in my bedding. It was only 5:30 but I was done trying to sleep. I wandered downstairs in my boxers, thinking that I was alone.

I was surprised to find Mom and White Eagle visiting at the breakfast table. He looked like he was ready to bolt out the door the minute Sarah arrived and Mom was in another pair of her funky jammies with a sweatshirt on. They both looked up startled, when they heard my footstep. "Um, hi? You couldn't sleep either?"

White Eagle shook his head but Mom answered. "I gave up almost an hour ago. You know this will all go so much better if I am completely exhausted," she groaned sarcastically.

"Well, I guess I'll go get dressed for the day then," I said lamely, making for the stairs.

I came back when I was all ready for school and joined the happy gathering at the breakfast table. I even joined them in a cup of coffee. You know you're tired when you need coffee to start the day.

Miles had fond memories of coffee. I wasn't so hip to it. Maybe it was an acquired taste.

Time dragged until the bus came and then the whole rest of my day followed suit. Lucie looked terrible. Katie wondered what was wrong with me. I just said my folks weren't getting along. Marlo and Adrian watched my back when I was with them. Calvin left me alone. It was probably a good choice on his part. I was not my best self and undoubtedly would have made a bad choice given half the chance. Today I would have loved any excuse to wipe the floor with him. I called Mom before I left school and since there was no word on anything I decided to head to the pawnshop. White Eagle set me up with the heavy bag away from everyone so that I was not a danger to myself or others. I pounded out my frustration until there was nothing left. Then I just sat on the mat still in my fighting gloves.

"You know you're going to have a permanent wrinkle in your forehead, right?" Marlo asked softly.

"I'm probably working myself up over nothing. I just have a really bad, make that *epic*ally bad, feeling." He patted me on the back and went back to bookkeeping. Adrian didn't even try to talk to me. He just looked at me, shook his head and moved on.

I felt like I was going to puke by the time White Eagle said it was time to go. I got to ride in back with the window down since I had not showered yet. The guys didn't try to joke with me.

I checked in again with Mom before hitting the shower. I checked in with Mom after my shower. Sarah decided to take my brothers after dinner so that they could watch a movie at her house. She figured Mom and I could take care of ourselves if we had any visitors besides Dad. White Eagle made sure every trace of his stay in our living room was gone and then said to call if we needed anything. Mom and I cleaned the kitchen to within an inch of its life and then alternately sat and paced relentlessly in the living room while we waited for Dad's return.

An hour later, we were both nervous wrecks and exhausted when Dad finally pulled in. He walked in and looked around. "I see," he said as he dropped his suitcase on the floor.

"Can we talk to you," my mom asked calmly.

"What is there to say? I asked you to be packed and ready to go. I have a new job in Atlanta. It's not safe here anymore so why stay? I spoke with my father while I was gone. He agrees that this is *my* decision to make. You aren't earning anything so you don't get a say," he replied defiantly looking at my mom.

"Wow, that sounded like old Cuba. How about United States in the current year? Can we please talk?" she repeated with a slight edge to her voice.

"Fine. Talk."

"I like it here, the boys like it here and besides, my father is buried here. We know no one in Atlanta. The problem with the people we had trouble with is almost resolved." She paused for a deep breath. Dad looked like he wanted to interrupt but waited. "Owen has learned a new skill and his teacher cannot go to Atlanta."

"Then he will get a new teacher," he said, dismissing her other arguments.

"Dad? I don't have a skill. I have a gift. I can tell things about people by touching the objects they have touched. I help people," I said quietly in my most adult tone.

He threw his head back and laughed. "You're saying that you are a psychic so you don't have to move? That's funny." When he said it, it did not sound like he thought it was funny at all.

"I'm not a psychic. I see the echo left in an object. I can show you," I pleaded.

"You bought this? Did the little people tell you to believe it or was it your medicine woman grandmother or some spirit animal? Magic is nothing but undiscovered science," he stated firmly to my mom, glaring from one of us to the other.

"Dad, let me try," I said as I stood and approached him. He waved me off to move over to my mother, so I touched his suitcase. There were many images, none of them dark but all were a strange gray. I assumed he was neither good nor evil; he was simply a complete nonbeliever and completely neutral. He had spoken to my Cuban grandfather. He was old country, old rules, and old fashioned. He had never liked my mother because she was of mixed blood. I didn't know whether I should laugh or cry. Mom always thought my grandfather disliked her but she wasn't sure. The whole mixed race thing was killing me; what a hypocrite! His own wife was from Florida and was no pure blood Cuban. He did not believe in any kind of magic either. Grandpa wanted Dad to come to the east coast and start over. Grandpa had gotten Dad the new job too. I had no idea he had so much power and leverage.

I could only see Dad when he was in the hotel room. He seemed to really like the new job and truly believed that this was best for us. He was frustrated that Mom had not called him but he had not picked up the phone either. He was disappointed that she didn't seem to need him to make decisions at home.

Mom and Dad were talking quietly but their voices were tight. I walked up silently behind him and looked at him with my *other* sight. I just didn't see anything to read. Nothing he had on him wanted to talk to me. Even Adrian had done something he shouldn't have done. Dad seemed to follow every rule. He was a literal guy. So I pulled out what I had in my arsenal. "Dad, you talked to your father. He really doesn't like Mom because she isn't the same race he is. He also got you the job. He wants you home."

"What?" He flipped around to look at me like I had sprouted another head. "I'd accuse you of a wire tap except that isn't quite right. You hired a PI with a bad listening device? You had me followed, Lila?"

"No, Brad," she denied.

I cut in. "No, Dad I looked at the images from your suitcase. It was in the room when you talked to Grandpa. I can't hear what is said but I see things and I sense feelings or moods."

"Baloney, I refuse to believe that you see things. It was a lucky guess. I can't deal with this right now. If you want to stay here and think about what you are doing, fine, but I have a great new job where I'm appreciated and respected. I'll tell them that you will come when school is out. I leave tomorrow. Where are Lukey and Al?"

"They are with Mrs. Lando so that we can talk. I'd still like to talk," Mom tried again.

"I want to see my boys and I think it's clear that we agree to disagree at this point anyway. You think about what you're doing. Then you'll see I know what is best for this family and you will come to Atlanta."

"Brad, you're not listening. Owen can't leave because he needs to be trained and I don't want to leave. Your old job provided us with plenty. If it's the money, I can go back to work next year with Lucas in first grade," Mom said, her voice rising a little like she was repeating herself.

"Owen doesn't need training. He needs to get with reality and focus on school. Now call Mrs. Lando or shall I go down there myself?"

"Brad, please listen to me," Mom begged.

"Mom, I'll go get them," I said with resignation. She gave me brief eye contact but then turned her attention back to Dad. I could tell by his body language that he was done listening and I was surprised that she didn't see it. Maybe she didn't want to.

I walked slowly to Sarah's house. I noted that it was past time to cut her lawn again. Considering everything she was doing for us I needed to step it up a bit in the return department.

I knocked softly on the door and tried to work on my facial expression. I didn't figure that bleak was a good look for me. I needn't have bothered. Sarah answered the door alone. She took one look at me and pulled me into a hug. "I'm so sorry," she whispered. "I was afraid he wouldn't understand. He can't help it. It isn't in his nature. It's as if you are trying to convince him the sky isn't blue, it is red. He just can't see it." Again she was scaring me with her perceptiveness.

She released me and I scrubbed at my moist eyes. "I'm here to bring Alex and Lucas home. Dad wants to see them before he leaves again."

"Call me if you need anything. I am *always* here for you," she said, looking deep into my eyes.

"Okay boys! Guess what? Your dad is home. Owen is here for you," she raised her voice in a happy carefree tone that I recognized as a total fake.

"Can we come again? Do you have more cartoon movies?" They excitedly chattered at her, hugging her on their way past.

"Sure. We'll get together again real soon. 'Night boys." She kissed her hand and threw it out to us. She showed my brothers a smiling face but I saw it change to sadness as she shook her head, closing the door.

My brothers bounced and chattered all the way home. I tried not to ruin their good mood but it was one of the hardest things I had ever done. Mom and Dad were still working on their whispered argument as we walked in the front door.

Dad hugged my brothers. "Your mom isn't ready to go to Atlanta so we'll see you when school is out. I have to go back to work tomorrow but in the morning we'll have a special breakfast."

I couldn't fake it or stand it anymore. "I need to go do some homework," I said, edging out of the room.

"That should have been the first thing you did. I thought I said you were grounded," he said in a cold voice.

I did not even look at my mom. I looked him right in the eye and did the thing I hate most. I lied. "I have a big project due. I want to be sure it's perfect. Besides, I'm tired. I have lots of healing I'm doing. Look," I added raising my pant leg, "the brace is smaller."

"Well then, that's good. See you in the morning," he said loosening up some.

I hugged my brothers, looking at my mom as I did it. We communicated with our eyes. It was not going well for either of us. I walked out of the room wondering how my mom could stand it. I guessed I was being a coward for leaving her but I was afraid I would do or say something to make things worse.

I went over all my homework and made sure my planner was up to date. I worked slowly and meticulously so that if I was checked on I look appropriately busy. When I had nothing left I could possibly do, I re-cleaned my already clean room. I put all my remaining toys into a bin for Lucas and Alex. I even dusted. I didn't want to vacuum and draw attention to myself. I checked my phone and quickly returned all the texts I had received. Then I erased all my logs just in case. I was in bed reading when Dad finally knocked.

He smiled when he saw I was doing a legitimate activity. "I'm glad to see that you are finally taking school seriously. That will get you a scholarship to a good college. With focus and dedication you will get a good education and a good job. I don't want to hear any more talk about this other thing you think you can do. It's silliness. You need to grow up. I'm tough on you because I want you to be a man. Understand? I love you Buddy, I just want what's best for you."

"I love you Dad, but you don't understand me so how can you know what's best for me?" I asked calmly.

"I have already argued with your mother. I don't want to argue with you too. You think about what I've said. You'll know I'm right," he answered.

"I know you're trying to do what you *think* is right. I just wish you'd let me explain. I wish you'd listen to me. I'm not like you but I don't want to argue with you either."

"I don't believe in psychics, magic, spirits or ghosts. I believe in what's real. If you want that other stuff then read a fantasy book."

"I'm sorry you feel that way. Am I still grounded?" I asked.

"I suppose you can be off restriction. Your mom said that they have one man in custody and are closing in on the other one. I just don't want anything to happen to you. I thought I almost lost you once. It was awful. I never want to go through that again."

"Me either." Though something bad probably will happen to me again, I thought to myself.

"You sleep well and I'll see you at breakfast," he said like he had won me over to his side.

"You too Dad," I answered wearily.

I was relieved when he left. Even though it was earlier than I normally went to bed I rolled over and clicked off my light. Then I remembered my teeth and silently got back up to brush them. Mom and Dad were in their room still arguing it seemed. I finished in the bathroom as quietly as I could, not wanting to get dragged back into anything. For the first time in my life, I could hardly wait until my dad left. I knew that we hadn't resolved our issues but we needed a new strategy. My mom deserved a gold star for continuing a losing battle. I had lost this round. Dad did not understand or accept me but I would NOT be moving to Atlanta anytime soon. I would complete my training with White Eagle and finish high school right here in Oregon.

I woke up around two in the morning. Someone was in my room. I froze for a moment to listen and observe. I was ready to defend myself if necessary. The breathing was... familiar - the sniffling was not. I made out the shape slumped by my bed quietly crying. It was my mom. I slipped out of bed and put my arms around her. She continued to sob silently. I could feel the shaking in her body. For the first time in my life, she felt small and frail to me.

"Mom, what is it?" I softly whispered.

"I'm sorry I woke you. I just... I just came to listen to you breathe. I do that sometimes when things are bad. It reminds me why I'm here and that no matter what – you're one of the three best things I ever did. I love you."

"Let me guess, the other two good things are Alex and Lucas, right?"

She just nodded. Her shaking wasn't so bad now. She took a tissue from a box I hadn't noticed and blew her nose. "I'm sorry," she whispered again.

"Why are you sorry, Mom? It's not you. He won't listen. We need a new strategy. Somehow I have to prove to him what I can do. I have to protect people. It's what I'm meant to do. If I tried to stop, it would eat me alive and the guilt would kill me."

"I know, Honey, it's why I've been fighting so hard for you. I understand. I'm at a loss as to how to make *him* understand. I've tried everything I can think of."

"Then let it be," I replied.

Mom hugged me like she was afraid she would never see me again. "I really didn't mean to wake you. I just had to listen to you breathe," she repeated. "I love you so much. This situation just sucks."

"I love you too, Mom. Try to get some sleep," I advised as if our roles were reversed.

I fell back into an uneasy sleep. My dreams returned and I was again trying to protect and defend everyone I knew. Clive was after them and Dad was telling me to stop playing around and get serious as if he couldn't even see Clive menacing our family and my friends.

I woke up even more tired than when I went to bed. I did realize one thing. My dad had no friends anymore, just us and the people at his work. No wonder he couldn't relate. His world had shrunk down to just work and family. I wondered what had changed to make him listen to a man that he had rebelled against when he was younger. My mother used to be his whole world and now he wouldn't even listen to her. It was all about my grandfather.

I showered, dressed and slowly made my way downstairs to join the family. The smell of bacon and eggs was wafting up the stairwell. Dad was flipping French toast on the griddle. "Well, there you are. What took you so long?" Dad asked all cheerful and like nothing was wrong.

"Dad, I don't even catch the bus until ten. It's only seven," I answered tonelessly.

"Oh? Why so late?" he asked perplexed.

"The middle school has late start Wednesdays so that the teachers can have meetings and do training and stuff," I answered calmly.

"Oh? Since when?" he asked.

"The whole time I've been in middle school," I replied patiently. In response he just scowled.

Lucas and Alex were eating at the table. They were not their usual happy selves but they looked okay. My mom on the other hand looked like death warmed over. She looked like she had been up all night and maybe she had. She had a plate of uneaten food in front of her and a cup of coffee that she held in both hands. I went and stood next to her and put my hand on her shoulder. She reached up and patted it absently. I was afraid all the life was drained out of her.

Dad turned and slid a plate of food in my direction and looked at her like she disgusted him. It made me mad. I bit my tongue so hard I drew blood. I would not do this in front of my brothers. I sat and ate a few bites of food then I cut up and moved the rest of it around on my plate. Mom snuck her bacon to Alex and the egg to the dog.

Soon my brothers were ready to take off for school. Mom and Dad looked at each other, then Mom sighed, slipped on some shoes and walked them to school still in her jammies. She had never done that in all the years I had been in school. I could feel the heat rising in me. I thought my skin was about to shimmer with the rage building up inside me.

"Why do you treat her like that? You never used to," I tried to say calmly.

"What? How dare you. It isn't your business," he growled softly.

"Dad, it is. You're hurting her. Don't you see it?" I tried again.

"You will respect me!"

"Respect is earned. She has my respect. She earns it each and every day. She works hard to keep our house nice. She does most of the cooking and laundry, as well as all of the grocery shopping. I've seen her fix leaky faucets and toilets. She replaces every bulb that burns out. I have seen her stay up all night when one of us was sick. I have seen her cut out thirty-six felt teddy bears for the Kindergarten class. I have seen her teach Alex to cook and Lucas to read. What have *you* done lately except tell us what to do?" My voice almost broke on the sob that threatened to escape my aching chest and throat as my voice rose in volume from anger.

"Is that what you really think?" He genuinely sounded surprised.

"Dad, you're hardly ever here. You don't listen when we try to talk to you. What is going on with you?" I was nearly begging as the rage waned.

I could tell he wanted to be angry but he knew I was right and he hated it. The last batch of French toast was starting to smoke. With a yelp he turned around and flipped it off the pan and into the sink. He turned off the griddle as he sighed heavily and then he turned around to face me.

"My work keeps me away. My work is important and it provides what this family needs. This new job is more demanding but the money is fantastic. It could give us all the things we ever wanted." He made it sound more like an advertisement than true sentiment.

"Dad, no one ever said that we *ever* wanted more money. We would rather have you around. Maybe if you were here, you would see all the stuff Mom does. She works just as hard as you do, but in a different way. We would all give up some things to have you here. Besides even if we had more money what would we spend it on? You never take a vacation so we wouldn't use it for that."

"You just don't understand."

"I think I do. Your job makes you feel worthwhile and important. What you don't see is that you would still be those things without your job. You never used to listen to Grandfather and now you *only* listen to him. Maybe you need to remember how to listen to us too."

He was frowning at me so I threw up my hands and walked into the living room. I sat in my mom's chair to suck up some of her positive energy. I found a blanket and pillow stashed off to the side out of sight of my brothers. I picked them up and put them in my lap. I lifted the pillow, hugged it to my face and inhaled the scent of my mom's shampoo. The smell of it brought a flash of childhood memories. What would I do without her? I didn't want her and my brothers to go. Dad could leave and good riddance. Just then he came from the kitchen and looked at me in her chair with her bedding in my lap. "When did you get so old?"

"While you were gone," I answered sadly.

"Tell me again, what do you think you can do?" he sighed.

"Dad, I see things when I touch objects. I couldn't get any good readings off of you. Everything was kind of gray or neutral. When an object has been around something bad it has a dark energy that I can sense. The reason I was at Mrs. Lando's the night she was pushed down the stairs was because her handyman had left a hammer behind. I saw what he was thinking about doing. Remember the night you grounded me? I was letting a man know that something wasn't his fault. He thought he had killed a little girl and felt guilty, but he didn't do it. I showed him she was still alive. It was our anonymous tip that brought Adrian's Uncle Max safely home. I could see what Clive and Darren did to him. Mom knows what I can do because she's seen it. It's what I do, Dad. I fix the bad things to bring back balance. White Eagle helps me by teaching me how to handle my power."

"I just can't wrap my mind around it. It goes against everything I believe. Where did you get this power you think you have? Did White Eagle trick you or just tell you a bunch of Native American tales?"

"No, Dad. We think I got it from Mom but some people have it with no genetic link. They are just born that way."

"Well, wherever you got it, you can't do it anymore; if it's even real. We need to move to Atlanta. It is better for us."

"It is better for you."

"It's better for all of us, you just don't see it."

"Dad, it's better for me to stay here and finish my training with White Eagle. It would be dangerous to *not* complete it. Besides, I want to finish school here."

"A degree from a good college is all you need."

"I didn't say I wasn't going to college. I want to finish high school here."

"I get that you believe you have some special something. I just don't believe that you do. Atlanta is a good opportunity for all of us. I have to try and I want my family with me. My parents are getting older. They need me. I need to give back to them. I need to put you in touch with the rest of your heritage and Georgia is much closer to Florida."

"Really? Is that the prejudiced part where I make fun of the other parts of my heritage?"

"What are you talking about?"

"Yesterday you were making fun of Mom's side of the family by degrading her Irish and Native American roots. You have some Native American on your mom's side yet you put it down. Mom has always tried to honor all the parts of the heritage my brothers and I share. Why don't you?"

"It's not about that; our argument is about this thing you *think* you can do. This thing that you claim is keeping you from moving. I'll give you more time. We'll discuss it again in June. I need to go pack so that I can get to the airport," he said with a note of finality.

Mom opened the front door cautiously like she was expecting it to blow off the hinges at her touch. She watched my father's retreating form heading up the stairs and then turned her bloodshot gaze to me. I noticed how very green her irises were in contrast to the reddened whites. She took note of her bedding in my lap. "Well, the house is still standing. I guess that went okay," she said in hushed voice. "I need to get cleaned up to take your dad to the airport. We'll talk later." She picked up her blanket and pillow and headed upstairs.

I expected my dad to come back and clean the kitchen. Instead he took two suitcases, his laptop bag and a big box and headed straight to our SUV. It took him two trips but he didn't ask for my help and I didn't offer. He loaded up the back of the SUV and then hollered up at my mom. "You about ready yet? I can't miss my flight."

Mom came down looking nearly normal but there was a certain glint in her eye that told me that if he didn't start treating her better she'd give him a really big piece of her mind. Never mess with my mother. You have to push her quite a ways but once she is in a corner she fights back - hard.

Dad gave me an awkward hug. "My gosh, you're almost as tall as me," he said surprised.

"Have a good few weeks, Dad. We'll see you in June." AND finish this discussion about moving and special abilities, I finished angrily in my mind. I watched them pull out of the driveway. My dad never looked back but Mom met my gaze out the passenger side window. She was right, this situation sucked.

It wasn't even eight. I had two hours before school. I went upstairs to get some laundry from my room. I looked in through Mom and Dad's open bedroom door. His dirty stuff was dumped all over the floor and the bed was unmade. I felt angry all over again. What was he trying to prove? Why was he doing this to her? His father had a maid. He could act like a spoiled child if he wanted to. My mother did not deserve this and it sure wouldn't convince her to move.

I picked up his laundry and stripped their bed so that my mom wouldn't have to do it. Then I took both hampers downstairs and started the washer, cussing the whole time. Next I turned my attention to our kitchen. It never looked like this when he wasn't here. There was egg spilled on the counter, congealing. The burnt toast was still in the sink getting soggy because the faucet was left dripping. There was bacon grease everywhere, including the floor, where Beggar had missed it during her cleanup of all food items within her reach. The house was spotless when he had come home. I picked up the rest of my breakfast from the table and threw it across the room. I watched the plate hit the cupboard and shatter, sending egg, bacon and French toast bits flying everywhere. Beggar ran from under the table with her tail between her legs.

I stood staring at the wreckage, my anger draining away. I got out the garbage can and a roll of paper towels and started to clean. When the worst was up, I wiped down all the surfaces with cleaner. Then I went to the laundry room, put the clothes in the dryer that were done in the washer and started another load. I still had an hour, so I packed another, Marlo-approved, healthy lunch and put it with my backpack all ready by the front door.

I decided to go through some relaxation exercises before school so that I wouldn't unintentionally kill any innocents. My mom came home as I was finishing. She sniffed the air. "Hmmm, cleaning binge?"

"There was no way that I was leaving *his* mess for you to clean up after the way he treated you the last two days," I said with a snarl, feeling angry all over again.

"Owen, my guardian angel, his father brings out the worst in him sometimes. Don't let the same be said of you. Come here," she said, reaching for me. She hugged me tight. "Do you have everything you need for school? Got your lunch? Shall I make you one?" she asked, releasing me and heading to the kitchen where she stopped in the doorway. "You cleaned... all of it... Wow!"

"I'm all set Mom, I even packed my lunch," I said as I squeezed past her to head into the laundry room to switch loads. "I don't have time to fold anything right now but..." I turned to look at her. Her gaze was swinging from the kitchen to the laundry room and back again.

"You did your dad's laundry? What happened to the cupboard?" She sounded perplexed.

"Your door was open and I saw his mess all over your floor. It wasn't fair to you so I picked it up. The cupboard and I had a little misunderstanding. I broke a plate. I cleaned it up." I sounded staccato even to myself. Maybe I needed more relaxation.

"You had a misunder... Oh, I get it. You threw your plate against the cupboard and it shattered. You left a dent." I could tell she wasn't too mad because she started giggling. "Better the cupboard than your father's head, right?" Then she started laughing out loud until tears ran down her face. "Ahggg, so much stress. Now we have until June, then we get to try again. Oh boy! I can hardly wait." She seemed to be pulling herself together as she wiped her eyes. "Well, since you did such a great job, I think I'll have a nap until I need to get Lucas. Then *I will* finish the laundry. Thank you just doesn't seem to cover it."

She hugged me again and told me to have a good day at school. She reminded me to bring White Eagle to dinner. We were having meatloaf with mashed potatoes, his favorite. She also reminded me to lock the door as she headed upstairs. I watched her until she was out of sight. I fought the urge to go tuck her in.

I walked to the bus stop and for once I beat Marlo. I stood leaning against the street sign, my arms and ankles crossed as I stared at my feet. I looked up as Marlo approached.

"I take it the outcome was not what you had hoped for. Is he gone?"

"Mom took him to the airport this morning. We decided to tell him. He doesn't believe me. He thinks I'm trying to play a game so that I don't have to move. Now we have until June to change our minds. Ha! What we really have is until June to figure out a new strategy."

"I'm sorry, Owen, you don't deserve this. None of you do."

"Thanks Marlo."

Both of us were pretty quiet on the bus. Another day I just needed to end so that I could get on with the rest of my life.

I saw Katie waiting for me and felt something shift within me. Here was someone who liked me for me, moodiness and all. I was the happiest I had ever been to see her. She might be a bit over the top at times but she was always there and always positive. I gave her a big hug picking her up off the ground.

"Wow," she said, exuding pleasure. "I'm glad to see you too. What's up?"

Before I set her down I took a deep breath of her scent. Now that she had given up the perfume, she smelled nice - clean and fresh like rain on a meadow.

"Are you okay?" she asked in a worried tone.

Until that moment I didn't realize how much I was actually holding in. It felt like someone had gripped my throat from the inside.

I had to clear my throat before I could even speak. "Not really," I admitted, surprising myself.

"Tell me," she demanded. "I want to help you."

That was Katie. I took her hand and we walked to our lockers. I didn't say anything at first and she waited. I finally turned to her. "My folks aren't getting along. My dad blames me and doesn't understand me. He has gone back out of town and will be gone until June. If that wasn't bad enough by itself, I'm watching my friend turn into a shadow of her former self and they still haven't caught the guy who broke my leg."

I looked at her and she was staring at me openmouthed. She closed it with a snap. "I can't decide if I'm more surprised *that* you told me or by *what* you told me. We need to get to class but if I can help or you want to talk, let me know, okay?"

I nodded and walked her to her first class and then hustled to mine. I realized that I actually felt better. My day improved right through lunch. I held Katie's hand for most of it, just glad to have someone nearby that I could draft good vibes off of. I felt eyes on me near the end of lunch and looked up to find Lucie staring at me with a strange look on her face. She either looked a little better today or she was getting better with her makeup. The look she had given me was haunted though. She didn't meet my eye in choir or even walk with us to sixth period.

When I got to science she was at the far side of our lab table with her books stacked between us. Great. What did I do now? She wanted me to move on. I was trying but now she didn't want me to? Women can give a guy a headache. I went to push her books to the back of our lab table so we would have room to work and got an image off them. Calvin had not hit her but the image had that distinctive *yet* feel to it. He was unnecessarily rough. He'd left bruises when he had grabbed her arm. I wanted to choke him.

I reached over to take ahold of Lucie's arm. She was wearing long sleeves today. She cowered away from me a little but didn't resist when I pushed up her sleeve and saw the fingerprints. Still holding her arm I slowly looked from the bruises to her eyes.

"Owen, don't. It was an accident."

"Bull... loney." I changed what I was going to say when I saw we had drawn our teacher's attention. Lucie was covering the spot with her free hand and I released her arm. I turned to find the teacher approaching our table.

"Is there a problem here?"

"Nope," we spoke in unison. Our teacher gave us a strange look but let it go. We didn't cause trouble in her class so she was willing to give us a little latitude.

I surreptitiously touched her books again and I focused on Calvin and his energy. I sensed that he was a collector of popular girls. He didn't really care about them; he just wanted to 'own them'. I could feel the strong emotions coming in waves. There was love and hate – obsession and possession. It made me sick. Lucie stayed because her parents thought he was the right kind of boy for her, she had told me. I knew he had them fooled and they were so wrong.

Lucie and I did a terrible job on our lab and were the last to finish. Our teacher reminded us that if we wanted to talk about whatever was going on she would listen. We both told her it was fine.

Lucie walked with me to health. Calvin showed up in the hall and tried to walk on Lucie's other side. He and I scowled at each other all the way down the hall. Lucie finally halted saying, "STOP IT! Both of you just stop it." Then she marched on to class solo. I walked after her, ignoring Calvin.

Health was pretty much all reading and lecture so I didn't have to interact further with Lucie, who was ignoring me anyway. I was irritated with her for putting up with Calvin's garbage. I finally hissed at her at the end of class. "I care about you and I hate to see you treated badly!" Then I picked up my books and walked away from her for once.

I was so happy to go to the pawnshop that I think I could have run the whole way. I waited to tell Katie goodbye before I headed to the locker room to change for the run to the shop. Marlo followed me in but Adrian was already changed and waiting on a bench.

"What?" Marlo and I said together.

"Girl problems. I'm avoiding Jill. It's only a misunderstanding. I just want to get to the shop and forget about it for today.

"Oh-kay," Marlo said slowly. I guess I wasn't as good a friend as Marlo because I figured if he wanted to talk he would have. I was ready to leave it alone. I had enough problems of my own. I changed quickly but Marlo was sitting next to Adrian with his arm over his shoulder. I wanted to ask, *are we gonna run or what?* But I took the high road and sat down on the other side of Adrian. Marlo patted him on the back and started changing.

"Do you want to talk about it?" I asked, hoping the answer was no.

"Jill gets jealous when I talk to other girls. I know lots of girls and lots of them are my friends. I want to talk to who I want, when I want. I shouldn't need her okay to do it," Adrian answered in a frustrated tone.

"I understand your predicament. I wish I had some good advice. If I think of any I will share it with you and myself," I said with a smile.

"Yeah, same here. Ready Marlo? Let's run," Adrian said, sounding a little discouraged.

We picked up all of our stuff, headed out the back of the school and off to the pawnshop. When Marlo started lagging behind I took his backpack and the bag with his clothes in it. He looked both pleased and annoyed. As we neared the shop Adrian started running faster so I ran harder so that he would not beat me. We were neck and neck. We touched the building at almost the same time. I realized that Marlo was not with us so I ran back to where he was walking and got him to jog the rest of the way.

"You know, if you weren't such a great guy otherwise, I could really hate you for your athletic ability!" Marlo said in an out-of-breath but grouchy voice.

"Hey Buddy, remember that you are the brains of this outfit. You need to be in shape, but you don't have to be in the best shape physically. We're counting on you to be in top mental shape." I whacked him on the back as he tried to catch his breath.

Adrian was already in the back stretching so we joined him. White Eagle ran us through our Tai Chi and then set us up to box. He checked the brace on my leg, asked me about my pain levels and had me put on my padded shirt for sparring. Boxing was becoming one of my favorite things to do. Next we practiced some Karate and then cleaned up to go home. As we waited for our turn in the shower we worked in the shop at the various things we typically do. Max had stayed today to see us. We told him that as happy as we were to see him, next time he had to bring the dog!

Our meatloaf dinner was like a happy family reunion. Everyone was in a really good mood and seemed to truly enjoy each other. It stood in stark contrast to our recent time with my dad. A small part of me felt sorry for him but mostly I was still mad at him. I needed to work on forgiveness for me and for him. He couldn't help who he was but it really bugged me that he wouldn't even try to understand me.

Mom and I put my brothers to bed while Sarah and White Eagle chatted downstairs and cleaned the kitchen. White Eagle even offered to teach me how to fix the cupboard I had damaged. He figured it was a good weekend project to do before June. It felt good to be part of a team again. I remembered when I felt like my real family was a team.

My brothers were not as happy about Dad's return as they let on. They wanted to please him. They wanted him to be proud of them but they still did not want to go to Atlanta. They were worried about our Mom too. They had seen the change in her and had seen the way Dad had treated her. I personally felt that Lucas said it best. "I love my Daddy but if I have to pick between him and Owen, I take Owen." He said it with all the seriousness and ferocity of a grown person. It was one of those moments where you don't know if you should laugh or cry.

"We're hoping it doesn't come to that. We'll talk some more and try really hard to make everybody happy," Mom answered in a soft voice full of hope and comfort. "This time while Dad is gone we'll talk to him on the computer so you know how he is and so he knows what you are up to."

Mom and I hugged my brothers and then went to tell Sarah and White Eagle goodnight. White Eagle would be back on our couch until Clive was found or Dad was back. We have a decent couch but I really had to admire the guy. I offered him my room for the couch but he wouldn't take it. He also turned down the upstairs office and sometimes guest room. He preferred to be downstairs in case anyone broke in.

Mom and I went to bed early, each of us so tired and drained that we couldn't entertain anybody for even one more minute. Sarah hugged us and wished us goodnight. She promised that things would get better. I sure hoped she was right.

I fell asleep almost immediately. I don't remember any of my dreams. I woke up to sunlight streaming through my window, sending loving, gentle beams over my face. I closed my eyes for a moment and basked in it. I felt it calling to me, *get up, get on with your day. Be part of the goodness and light.* Too bad we were done with our poetry unit; I could have described the sun's song in the words of a poet. Then I looked at my clock and I think I had a mini heart attack. It was almost noon.

I levitated out of bed and ran to the bathroom and then raced to Mom's room. She was still sleeping. I left her in peace and sprinted in to my brother's room. They were gone, their room spotless and their beds made. I had to back out and recheck to be sure I was in the right place. I ran down the stairs as fast as my brace would let me and slammed into White Eagle, knocking myself flat on my back. See, Karma does exist. It was getting even for Miles helping me flip White Eagle over the back of the couch.

"Whoa there. Where's the fire?" White Eagle asked kindly, helping me to my feet. "Nice boxers," he added, to make up for my lipstick on the cheek comment not long ago, I was sure.

"First of all, it's almost noon. I overslept and so did Mom. Second, where are Alex and Lucas and did you see their room? It looks like the old Twilight Zone show. Third, I happen to like Scooby Doo!" I huffed, referencing my boxers.

"I can see you're well rested and about back to your old self. Well maybe yourself and a little Miles. Twilight Zone? What eighth grader today knows about that?"

I gave him a look and waited.

"Okay, relax. Sarah and I decided to turn off your alarms. You were both so beat. She helped the boys clean their room and took them to school. Max opened the shop so I could take the morning off or until after I get you to school. Your Mom added me to the 'safe to pick up her children' list. Sarah and I even filled out all the volunteer paperwork at school so we can cover field trips the rest of the year to keep your brothers safe. Everything is okay. You don't have to save the whole world by yourself. We're here to help."

From upstairs there was a squawk and thudding feet. I could tell by the pattern that my mom was making the same circuit I did except she skipped the bathroom. She was a little more circumspect about the stairs and didn't quite run into me.

I reached out to steady her shoulders. She was wearing another pair of eye-popping jammies but then who was I to say anything with my Scooby Doo boxers on? "Our guardian angels have been at work. The boys are at school. How can you sleep in florescent night wear?" Sorry, I couldn't help it.

"Eah, but... What?"

I figured her brain would catch up in about... three, two, one. I flipped out fingers one by one in sync with my mental countdown. Mom did not let me down.

"Wait – What? First of all I like my pjs loud. I think they are fun and happy. Are my guardian angels White Eagle and Sarah?"

White Eagle lost it and laughed so hard he had to bend over to catch his breath. "I like it here! You people are more entertaining than TV! And guilty! Sarah and I hatched a plan to get you two some much needed rest. Now Owen, how about you get ready for school before you miss any more and if I'm not mistaken that should be..."

"Mommy! Guess what?" Lucas squealed in delight as he rushed in the front door. "I got to show Mrs. Lando for show-and-tell. It was my turn and all I had was her. She makes a real good show-and-tell person. Everybody likes her!" he exclaimed, full of energy.

Sarah blushed and smiled.

"Mommy your jammies is *loud*. They make my eyes hurt. Owen, why are you in your Scooby shorts and home? Are you sick?" Lucas bubbled on.

"I'm better now, Buddy. I'm gonna go get ready for school. And Mommy's jammies *are* loud, not *is* loud."

"I know, I just forget when I have lots to say."

"Well," Sarah threw in, "who wants lunch?"

I sprinted for the shower and got dressed in record time. My *family*, all four of them, were at the table eating grilled cheese sandwiches and tomato soup. I slid into a chair and ate my share. Everyone seemed to be listening to Lucas and he was loving all the attention.

I hugged the ladies and Lucas goodbye and White Eagle and I hit the road. He let me know that he was in charge of physical therapy today, too. He wanted me to tell the guys that he would pick us all up and drop them at the shop and then we would head to therapy.

White Eagle checked me in at school saying I'd had an appointment as he charmed the socks off of our school secretary. I left him flirting and went to find my gang in the cafeteria. Marlo and Adrian waved but Katie leaped out of her seat to come hug me. Lucie did not look thrilled but Calvin smiled until he looked at Lucie and then the satisfied smirk slid away.

We had about ten minutes to hang out before choir and everyone else's fifth period class. Marlo brought me up to speed on Spanish, math and LA. Adrian filled me in on social studies. Both had taken class handouts for me so that I would not be behind. White Eagle had even texted them to let them know what was up and that I was okay. I gave them his message in return. They were both happy to get out of running.

Adrian and Jill seemed to have worked out their issue if only temporarily. I guess girls don't like to miss dances. I planned to watch and see. I wondered what things would be like when my now self caught up in age to my Miles memories. I knew how to be a child and a man but this in-between stuff was a challenge. I would love to follow the advice so many give, to just be myself, but I wasn't sure who exactly that was anymore.

Lucie looked like she could use a big hug and a good friend but what more could I do when she wouldn't listen to me or accept my help. How could I mess things up with her so badly all the time? I didn't seem to cause Marlo any trouble and the danger to Adrian's family was really Max's doing. Maybe Lucie would be safe enough if I dated her. I was really starting to like Katie but she would never be Lucie. It was so mixed up and unfair. Since Lucie was unavailable at the moment, I really should give Katie a chance, right?

I left Lucie alone for all of choir and didn't try to walk with her to class. I tried to be a calm and reassuring presence but I left her alone and only talked to her when our work required it. By the end of science Lucie had worked her way back to my side. We were once again knee to knee and hip to hip. She was back to sucking up my warmth and friendship. The situation was killing me. I tried to maintain my silent policy since she seemed to like me better when I didn't talk.

When the bell rang she pulled herself up and gathered her stuff without a word. Calvin and Katie both appeared in the hall. I chatted with Katie briefly but kept an eye on Lucie. She looked like thunder clouds were gathering in her face. Katie saw that she had lost my attention and turned to look. "Lucie's the friend you're worried about, right?"

"Yeah, Calvin bruised her arm the other day by squeezing too hard. It makes me mad. She won't listen to me though. For now I just watch and worry. I don't understand why guys treat chicks like that. I do *not* think it's okay."

I was watching Lucie so I didn't see Katie's face and I was a little surprised when she moved in to hug me tight. I was reminded again of how tiny and almost fragile she was. She tucked herself right under my chin. "It's too bad there aren't more guys like you out there, Owen. You know word is going around school about you; how you help people who are treated unfairly. You're like the school super hero. When you got that bully kicked out the next one in line was afraid to step up. No one wants to take you on, except Calvin. I think he dates Lucie just to make you mad. He is itching for a fight. He thinks he can win. After you got hurt the odds were in his favor but they are swinging back to you."

She had my full attention now. "What?" I said in a shocked voice. "People know that I have helped a couple of people? It was supposed to be a secret. I don't like the spotlight."

"You are so cute when you're humble," Katie laughed. "Come on, the bell's about to ring."

I walked into health expecting Lucie to be mad. Instead she was the most melancholy I had ever seen her. I sat down and reached for her sleeve to catch a glimpse of what I had missed. Lucie leaned right into me as if my intention had been to hug her. Her head fell to my shoulder as the bell rang; she left it there for a moment, then took a shuddering breath and straightened to pay attention.

267

Lucie had always dressed a little nicer than the rest of the kids at school. Today was no exception. She looked like a miniature businesswoman in her dark skirt and pink blouse. She had left her hair down but held back by a headband. She was even wearing low-heeled pumps. What school age chick does that? Lucie did and she looked good doing it.

I didn't get much from her blouse. Her dad had given her grief again this morning. No surprise there. It seemed to be chronic. Calvin had been dropped off at her house this morning and her dad had brought them both. He seemed to really like Calvin. Maybe he saw his younger self in Calvin. He sure didn't see anything but his shiny side; I could see the darkness below the surface. Lucie had tried to tell her dad about Calvin but he didn't believe it. She would be going to the dance because her dad thought it would be good for her to participate in teenage rituals, as best I could tell by what I saw. Lucie felt trapped. I wondered how I could save her. Obviously I needed a plan.

Katie met me in the lobby before she boarded the bus. She hugged me goodbye and said she was looking forward to tomorrow night. She was as happy and carefree as Lucie was blue and burdened. I watched her get into her father's fancy car with the look of a beaten dog. I would fix this for her. I didn't know how, but I would fix it!

White Eagle pulled up and Marlo and Adrian appeared. We all piled in and were off. We dropped the guys at the shop and headed to physical therapy. They x-rayed my ribs and leg and were pleased and amazed by my progress. 'Grandpa' White Eagle talked to them about running, karate, boxing, and the stretching he did with me. He showed them the practice shirt and I was released to full normal activity. I was to wear my brace and protective shirt for sparring. They ran me through my exercises and then I was to shower, change and hit the pool. White Eagle carefully watched my pool training and then watched me swim. He left for a bit but returned as I was getting out of the pool. He came back with another man dressed as a lifeguard. I would now have physical therapy once a week and advanced swimming lessons and lifesaving lessons once a week. White Eagle would cover the rest of my physical therapy. Yay?

FIFTEEN

Friday was shaping up to be a great day. I was so happy to be out of my brace that I actually felt like dancing. Except that I had to wear it to the dance. Just in case. Oh brother. Well, whatever, Mom and White Eagle were just trying to take care of me, right? Having caught my mom up on my progress last night, I found him and Mom along with Marlo planning my exercise and eating routines for the next month. I felt more like an experiment than a person in that moment. "You called Marlo in early to do this?" I asked appalled.

"No problem," Marlo answered happily. "White Eagle will give us a ride to school and rides home to get ready for the dance in exchange. Besides, you are my favorite project."

Great, I was right. I am an experiment. I ended up laughing and shaking my head. "Okay I give up. You're trying to build a *super* Owen? I'm game. What do I have to do?"

"We are going to keep track of the calories you burn and what you consume. We need a lean, mean, fighting machine. You need enough energy so we need to fuel you right. We are going to track, weigh and measure everything including you," Marlo said excitedly.

"Wow, that really sounds... great," I got out with just a hint of sarcasm. Make that a big glop of sarcasm.

"Come on, be a sport. We'll do most of the work," Mom said like she was a total convert. She grabbed me by the arm and dragged me back upstairs where she proceeded to weigh me, and measure my waist, hips, thigh, arm and neck. I asked her if I was being fitted for a suit. She glared at me. We hustled back downstairs where she gave the numbers to Marlo and proceeded to measure my height.

"He's five foot eleven inches," Mom said.

"Owen, you don't weigh enough. A hundred and thirty eight pounds is too skinny. We need to put at least fifteen pounds on you. Twenty five pounds of muscle would be better. You need more protein and more weightlifting. Your mom and I will manage your food. I will eat what you eat and so will your mom, except it will be adjusted proportionally for our heights and weights. White Eagle and I will manage your training. Questions?" Marlo asked seriously.

"Yeah, one, how did I get myself into this?" They all just looked at me and no one laughed. Oh well. I do try.

Marlo and I hopped in White Eagle's truck after our breakfast of egg whites with vegetables and whole wheat toast with kind of fake butter. I was even offered a cup of black coffee for a brain boost and a big glass of milk with something stirred into it. I've got to say Marlo is becoming quite the chef. I tried to help but he and Mom just pushed my hands away. I wondered if they didn't want me knowing what was in my food.

On the way to school Marlo brought up that he may have had a hit in Nevada on someone like me. "This stuff is so hard to track. No one wants to admit directly who they are, but I'm really suspicious of this kid who's a junior in high school in Fallon, Nevada. He seems to *help* a lot of people. It looks suspicious to me but other folks would just think he's in the right place at the right time. His mom is a civilian contractor for the Navy base there. He might be worth checking out. I could be wrong but I have the feeling he's exactly what we're looking for. Most of the sites who claim to help people don't match what you do when I get in there. You guys do seem to like your secrecy."

"I've been thinking of taking you boys camping. I want to teach you some survival skills. Let's go to Nevada on a long weekend. It would be about a twelve hour drive to Fallon. We'll camp and see if we can track down this kid. This is something done in person, not over the phone. I have to actually see this kid, to *look* at him; I can't do that over the phone. If he looks real, then we will reveal ourselves and see about meeting his mentor. Just remember Marlo, most guys like Owen work alone. You three are a rare exception. It's dangerous to have people know who you are. If we are the light and we seek balance, then to be balanced there must be a darker side. Those folks would want to get rid of people like Owen. It's how I lost Miles," White Eagle said.

"Hold on, I thought Miles died because he had revenge in his heart?" I questioned.

"That's true but not the whole truth. Who do you think killed his wife? It sure wasn't the good guys and it was not ordinary human evil. It's a small part of the reason I went underground. If I did not use my powers, I would be harder to find. I didn't know if they found out about me from Miles and… I had lost so many others. I was afraid they would find me too. Now I see that I have to help or I'm not doing what I was called to do," he ended on a serious note.

"I would like to remind you of what you once told me," I also said in a serious voice while looking him right in the eye. "Don't be hard on yourself; be proud of yourself and the good that you do."

"Thanks, Owen, I had a weak moment and I still feel guilty about it. Have a good day and I'll see you this afternoon."

Katie met us when we got out of the truck. She was doing the excited bouncing thing like she did the night of our movie date. She chatted happily all the way to her first period class. I left her at her door and headed to my own.

In LA, Marlo, Adrian and I finished our novel study and then made plans to work on our song over the weekend. I told them I had two lawns to mow in addition to our Saturday training. We would meet at the pawnshop at nine a.m. Adrian was back in his coming with his uncle routine now that Max was back at the shop almost full time. He was even making noises about practicing with us. I was hoping that Clive would be found soon and that Darren of the dreadlocks would confess and maybe the charges against Max would all be dropped.

Katie was so giddy in math that it was all Marlo and I could do to keep her on track so that we would not have homework. I reminded her a couple of times that I didn't have time for homework because I had to work this weekend. She would giggle and refocus only to lose it again.

I didn't see Lucie at lunch. On a hunch, I saved half of my sandwich. Marlo scowled at me. I promised him I would make up the calorie deficit later today. The girls chattered excitedly about the dance and I paid little attention. Adrian didn't look especially happy. Jill seemed like she was more interested in going to the dance than specifically going with him. I wondered if Marlo smelled the end coming as he looked furtively from one to the other all of lunch.

Katie and I walked to choir. Lucie had beaten us there and she wasn't looking like her usual self. Not even her self of late. She was dressed in somber tones and looked pale and gaunt. The dark circles were back under her eyes like she wasn't sleeping well. I wasn't surprised about the lack of sleep but the rest of her look had me worried.

She walked listlessly to science with us. We dropped Katie off at her class and continued on. "Lucie, you're scaring me. Did you even eat today?"

"I had half a grapefruit and a yogurt," she answered defiantly.

"Luce, what is with the weight loss? You looked better before. You looked healthy and fit. Now you look like a refugee and your clothes are loose on you."

"I'll be okay. Dad wanted me to lose some weight so that I could model. If I can't do gymnastics I need to do something. He says I have to pay for college somehow," she answered, resigned.

"I saved half my sandwich for you. I promise it's good for you. You can't starve yourself like this. It isn't healthy and it's bad for your organs. You could do some permanent damage."

"I know but..." For a moment I thought she would cry. "What would I do without you?" Lucie hugged me.

"What are you doing?" Calvin snarled.

I turned to face him, putting Lucie behind me. "I'm taking care of my friend, which is more than I can say for you," I answered calmly. I wanted this fight badly but not in the school hallway.

"You keep your grubby hands off her - she belongs to me!" Calvin shouted.

"Lucie belongs to Lucie and no one else. Now go to class Calvin," I said still calm. My calmness seemed to make him even madder. We were drawing the attention of kids in the hallway.

"Yes, Calvin, go to class or I will escort you to the principal's office." Our teacher must have heard us because she had stepped into the doorway by Lucie's shoulder. She was giving Calvin the best hairy eyeball I had ever seen her use. Calvin slunk off toward his class without another word out loud. I could see him grumbling under his breath the whole way. Our teacher put her arm around Lucie and asked her if she was okay, then she turned to me.

"Nicely done, Owen! Way to stay calm and try to defuse the situation. I'm proud of you," she said, leading us into class as the bell rang.

"Lucie didn't get lunch today. Can she eat the other half of my sandwich really quick, please? I know we aren't supposed to have food in here but, well, please?" If I was in her good graces I was going to use it!

"Ok, Lucie. Just this once," she said with a smile.

I don't even know if Lucie knew what she ate. The way she wolfed it down made me realize she really hadn't eaten in days. Now I wanted to have it out with her father *and* Calvin. I was a little mad at Lucie too for not standing up for herself. When she put her head on my shoulder I slipped my arm around her and let her suck up all the goodness I had to give. For the first time ever I did all the classwork in science. We were divided into partnerships for our big plant unit. We'd be doing some outside work sprouting a variety of seeds and then raising the plants and keeping notes. Lucie and I would be a team. Yes!

I walked her to health, expecting Calvin to show and was greatly relieved when he didn't. Lucie was still quiet and was right up next to me again. I was glad for myself, but I felt awful for her. I needed to fix this soon. I still wasn't sure just what to do. Maybe Marlo could find her a job. He seemed to be able to work all kinds of other computer magic, so why not ask him this? Ironically, we were on the nutrition unit. For the next three weeks we were to write down everything we ate. We were even given height and weight charts and suggested calories, carbohydrates, fats and protein guides. This part of my problem might be resolved anyway.

I walked Lucie to her locker. She didn't look like she was ready to face Calvin. "Are you still going to the dance tonight?"

"Yeah, my dad is driving us out to the hall where they're holding it. Calvin can be sweet sometimes but it bugs me when he says I belong to him. I did break up with him and then he worked really hard to get me back. Now he's getting along better with my father than I am. I don't know - I have to figure this out. Thanks for the sandwich and for being here for me. See you tonight?"

"Yeah, I'll be there." I watched her walk away, feeling grim.

Katie caught up to me in the hall. "Shall I meet you at the dance? It starts at seven."

"Sure, Katie, that would be great. Thanks. I'll see you there." I gave her a quick hug and sent her on her way.

I met up with the guys and we loaded up in White Eagle's truck. Adrian was pretty quiet. I had plenty on my mind but he just wasn't himself. "Girl problems?" I asked.

"Yeah, I like Jill but she's getting bossy. Melissa told Marlo that she complains about me all the time. I think we are past done, but we already had plans for the dance. I bet you five bucks she breaks up with me tonight," he said on a sigh.

"Maybe I should bet you five that if she doesn't, you do," I replied back, netting myself a half smile out of Adrian.

We went to the shop to do our usual gig. We cleaned, we moved and catalogued stock, worked out and goofed off a little. The best part was playing with Thor. Max finally had him at the shop. He was turning into an awesome dog with the right kind of loving attention. I'm sure the obedience classes that he attended helped too. Max was back to his old self which was a gift almost as good as the ones you get on Christmas.

White Eagle took Marlo and me home to eat and get ready. Adrian went with Max and Thor to do the same. We would all meet up outside the hall at seven.

Mom and Sarah had made an amazing chicken dish with vegetables. For healthy food it was darned good. Mom measured everything on my plate which was really weird. Marlo had fed me a protein shake at the shop to make up for the half a sandwich I missed at lunch. I was growing to hate those things but I would drink one every day for Lucie if it got her to eat.

Mom surprised me with a new black button-up shirt and dark blue jeans to replace the clothes the medics had destroyed from my mall misadventure. She'd been out with Sarah and Lucas. I wondered what had Lucas so excited at dinner. Keeping a secret is hard for someone in Kindergarten. He proudly brought out some wicked new shoes for me. They were black leather lace-ups with thick soles almost like a boot. They were both light weight and sturdy. "Wow!" was all I could get out.

"We all chipped in. You hadn't used your gift card to the skate shop so we got the jeans there. Then we found the shirt at the popular teen shop at the mall and the shoes at the outlet across the street. We had fun!" Mom said, beaming at me. Lucas and Sarah both looked proud of themselves.

"Thank you so much!"

"It's the least we can do for you. Look at all you do for other people and no one says thank you. We appreciate you, Owen," White Eagle said quietly.

"I... Thank you," I repeated, not knowing what else to say.

"Go get dressed. We need to get Marlo," White Eagle said, pushing me toward the stairs.

I was ready in ten minutes and we were out the door. Marlo was pacing while he waited for us. I think his mom was glad to be rid of him. His dad looked like he was working really hard at keeping back a laugh. Marlo was decked out in slacks, a nice shirt, a crazy tie and black Converse. It was a stunning combination. Somehow he made it all look good.

White Eagle drove us to the dance and asked us to call when we were done. Otherwise he would be waiting at ten when it ended. We were the first ones there. I was glad that Marlo and I had come together so that I wouldn't have to wait alone. The ladies showed up all together next. I could tell that something really was up with Jill. She didn't even want to wait for Adrian to go inside. Talk about a date wrecker. I didn't even qualify. Her stock went down two points for that move, in my mind.

I patiently told her that they could go in if they wanted but that I was waiting for Adrian. "As will I," Marlo added.

Katie looked torn but followed her buddies inside. We didn't have to wait long for Adrian. Max had him to us in less than five minutes. He took it really well when we told him the girls had gone on in. In fact he looked downright relieved.

The music was loud. The lights were low. I had no idea how we would find the girls. Fortunately they found us. Well, at least Mel and Katie did. Jill was already dancing. Adrian took that news better than I thought he would. If she was trying to make him jealous she was doing the opposite. Mel looked a little uncomfortable when she had to tell Adrian. She quickly escaped, dragging Marlo with her.

I was torn between staying with Adrian and asking Katie to dance. She kept looking longingly at the dance floor and then back at me with a pointed glance. My problem was solved for me in less than one song as another girl I didn't know asked Adrian to dance. I took Katie's hand and led her out onto the floor. The music was a fast contemporary tune that was frequently on the radio.

There were four fast songs and then they slowed it down. A popular romantic one came on and Katie stepped in close wrapping her arms around my neck. I put my hands on her waist and tried to hold her just away from me without being too obvious. I didn't want a repeat of the movie theater incident. She leaned in and rested her head on my upper chest, the top of her hair brushing along my jaw. I was kind of having fun and kind of wondering when the song would end. She loosened her hands and slid her right arm from my neck to my waist. Oh, boy. Here we go, I thought. I tried to push her just a bit away from me but she had other ideas and slid her hand down until it rested just below my belt, her thumb hooked over the edge. This time I had been smarter and had tucked my shirt in. "Katie," I said softly in her ear, "you're rushing me again."

She looked up at me with a mix of emotions on her face. She sighed, then moved her hand back to my lower back. She put her head back where it was. I took the remainder of the song to look around the dance floor. This being taller than most of the other kids was kind of awesome. I had a good view of the crowd - including Calvin the terrible who was holding Lucie awfully close.

Lucie looked like she was lost in the music because the expression of blissful happiness on her face while she listened to the music made her truly beautiful. She was wearing a dress with a swirly skirt that almost seemed to float with her movements. She had the look of a professional dancer or an angel. Her hair was swept up on one side in a sparkly clip. She was wearing makeup to cover her dark circles and had done some other stuff with makeup that made her look really good. She looked like the model everyone wanted her to be. As the song ended she seemed to realize where she was and who she was with. Her step back from Calvin looked almost startled. Then the creep tried to kiss her. She put both hands on his chest and shoved. He laughed at her but let her go.

I must have stopped moving because I was still holding Katie who was looking at me with questions in her eyes. "I like slow dancing but the beat is a little fast for it," she said, bringing me back to the present.

I asked her if she was ready to get a drink and thankfully she was. I for one needed a minute. Being at this dance with Calvin was probably a *really* bad idea. I found my boys out in the lobby. Sure enough Jill had broken up with Adrian. He seemed to be more relieved than sad but it looked like it was putting a monkey wrench in Marlo's evening. The ladies had gone off to the bathroom. Again.

Katie released my hand saying, "I'm going to go *check* on them." The way she said it made me think they were going to get a piece of her mind.

"Well?" I said to my boys.

"Now we have some fun," Adrian said with confidence.

Marlo looked like he was being pulled in two directions. Melissa came out of the bathroom and asked to talk to Marlo. He went but he didn't look happy. Adrian caught my attention. "I'm going to go dance. I'll see you later."

Now what? I looked around and spied a drinking fountain and decided I would go ahead and get a much needed drink. As I straightened I saw a flash of movement out the window. It was Lucie, and Calvin had a firm grip on her arm and was literally dragging her behind him. She was leaning back on her arm and skidding with her feet. That was it!

I quickly scanned for the nearest exit. Adults were standing at the front door but there was an unmanned side door. I tried to catch Marlo's eye but I wasn't sure if he saw me since he was deep in a heated conversation. I felt pressured to hurry before Lucie got into more trouble.

I slipped out the side door and paused to listen. I could hear Lucie faintly around the corner. "No! Calvin!"

I sprinted in her direction wishing I had my practice shirt on but knowing I would gladly re-crack my ribs for her. Calvin still had quite a grip on her arm. She would be bruised again. They were having some kind of argument. Lucie was madly trying to scrape him off of her with her free hand. He cursed when she made him bleed and went to backhand her but he was too slow. With a loud slap, his hand connected with my arm instead of her face. "Let her go, now!" I snarled in my most menacing tone.

"Stay out of this!" Calvin snarled back, releasing her to focus on me.

We stood one foot apart. Both of us had our hackles up like junk yard dogs. This was more than fighting over some bone or some bitch in heat. He was going to really hurt Lucie one of these times and I would *never* let that happen. I recognized the look in his eye. Lucie had taken so much verbal abuse off her dad for so long that she didn't even register the hateful things that Calvin said to her. He wasn't afraid to hit her anymore. I was sure he had thought about it before tonight. When his hand connected with my arm I *saw* that with each girlfriend he had been escalating, leaving broken hearted victims in his wake. All were degraded and verbally abused. He had switched schools because of an incident that his dad wanted to cover up. His dad hit him and his mom sometimes, so for him it was normal. Sick!

My hands fisted at my sides as my muscles strained. Give me a reason, my body language said. Calvin, the idiot, was more than willing to oblige.

"What are you Ryer, jealous? Want my girl do ya? Well she's mine 'till I say it's over." He grabbed Lucie and forced a kiss on her angry compressed lips then shoved her aside.

"I want you to leave her alone," I said through clenched teeth.

"Don't do this," Lucie pleaded desperately trying to place herself between us. It was a dangerous place for her. I tried to gently push her behind me but Calvin grabbed her arm again.

"Outta the way, Stupid. I'm gonna teach your honey here a lesson," he ground out, shoving her out of the way again. Lucie sprang right back, determined to save me, Calvin or both.

"Don't do this. It's fine Owen, I'll just go with him," Lucie pleaded, her voice choked.

"No you won't." *Are you nuts?* - went through my mind.

"Don't tell me what to do!" Now I was making *her* mad? Super.

"Yeah Owen, don't tell her what to do," Calvin mimicked with a sneer.

What an idiot, I thought again. What on earth did Lucie see in this guy? "It's real funny hearing you say that to me, considering you tell her what to do all the time. Do you feel like you're losing power over her if I tell her what to do?"

"What are you trying to do? Sound tough? I'm not afraid of you, you *wuss*. You don't even have a real trainer. I do. My dad can afford the best."

Was this guy mentally slow? "You should be afraid of me," I growled back with all the physical intimidation I could emit.

"Owen, NO!" Lucie stepped toward us again but Calvin was quicker and shoved her hard in the middle of her chest sending her flying, to land hard onto her backside. "Calvin!" she yelped from her spot on the ground and began to scramble to her feet.

"Don't touch her again!" I snarled, enraged. If he was smart, he would run. I felt a huge rush of adrenaline and knew I could kill him if he pushed me any further.

"You want me? Come get me tough guy!" he sang.

I knew better than to throw the first punch. I was more than ready to finish the fight though. I stepped in front of Lucie. "It's time for you to go home. Alone." Calvin tried to dodge around me but I blocked his way. Lucie made it to her feet but kept behind me when she realized that I was trying *not* to fight. I was ready to do whatever I had to do but I wouldn't start it.

Calvin lunged at me again and I easily sidestepped him. Lucie moved back behind me, always close, but not touching me. Calvin turned and tried again. I half hoped he would give up and half hoped that I could beat him senseless. He was so much slower than me that I could anticipate each move he made. I sidestepped him twice more and then he tried to put a shoulder into my gut. I braced and let him push me back a bit and used his own momentum to dump him on the ground, turning my body to the side so he slid past my hip. "Walk away, Calvin. You're done here."

"She belongs to me. You can't have her. I say when it's over," he said scrambling to his feet. Was this guy for real?

"Lucie belongs to Lucie and no one else. She's not your property. I've told you that before. Go home, Calvin."

"I won't," he said, shaking with rage.

I sighed. I had tried. "Lucie, it would be better if you walked away."

"No." Was she really still trying to protect me or him?

"Of course not," I huffed under my breath. I decided that the only way to end this stalemate was to let Calvin hit me so that I could hit him back. I just had to be sure he didn't get to Lucie. He went for a stomach punch but I was ready for it and barely felt it. I bent over like it hurt and quickly shouldered him in his stomach. As he collapsed over my back, I threw him on over and to the side away from Lucie. I seemed to have knocked the air out of him but he was otherwise fine.

"You're done here. Now go home," I said in a calm, quiet voice.

"I hate you, Ryer! I'll get you," he cried. Fine, better me than Lucie.

"Come on Lucie, I'll take you home." She looked a little stunned. She turned and walked several feet away and then turned back toward Calvin. Her gasp was my warning. Calvin was rushing me from behind. I turned and shifted my weight to deliver a round-house kick I had learned in karate from White Eagle. I placed it right in his mid-section, sending him back to the ground. There was a beat of silence where I stood ready and then Calvin rolled onto his side, coughed and threw up on the grass.

"Is he okay? Should we help him?" She was kidding right? Nope, I could tell by the look on her face she wasn't.

"He's embarrassed and angry. It would be better if we let him cool off. You really should break up with that guy. He treats you like garbage and you most certainly are not garbage."

Lucie took one last look at Calvin who was now on his hands and knees still vomiting on the grass. She turned, nodded and stalked away from Calvin. She had promised me nothing, but at least for tonight she was safe.

I walked her back to the dance. Before we stepped around the corner I stopped her to check her hair. She had a big grass stain across the back of her skirt. I brushed off as much as I could and tried to fix her hair. I tucked my shirt back in. Her arm was already bruising and her lip was swollen. I gently reached out to touch her lip.

"Lucie, why do you date Calvin? He isn't good to you," I pleaded in a soft voice.

"You made it clear you wanted to be my friend. You're not my mother or even my counselor," she wailed.

"I'm sorry, Luce. It's probably not my business..."

Angrily she interrupted, "You're right, it's not!"

"But I care about you. I hate to see you hurt. He better not hit you. The way he talks to you makes my skin crawl. The whole thing makes me sick. You're too good for him. Why do you let him talk to you like you're less than he is?"

"Yeah, right. If you cared about me, you would have asked me out yourself. You've had loads of chances. You gave up your rights – you don't want me - you just don't want to see me with anyone else. Besides, you hurt me plenty by *not* talking to me and by *not* letting me in. Sometimes I feel like I'm not even really your friend. You shut me out. Besides, you have Katie."

"What? Luce, it's not like that. To keep you safe you shouldn't be around me. Bad things happen around me. I don't want anything bad to happen to you... or to her. We aren't even officially dating. I've never asked her. I went to a movie with her and asked her here. That's it."

"Owen, you are so full of crap."

I could feel the angry heat rising in my body. I wasn't really mad at Lucie, but at the whole situation and at Calvin for taking advantage of her. "Lucie, I do like you *and* I want to be your friend. I would feel awful if something happened to you because of me."

"You make me crazy! You say you like me. I like you too. What's so dangerous? What's the problem? How can I think it's not me? You have me so confused. You send out more mixed messages than a... a... *Arg!* There aren't words. If you don't want me, stay away from me and leave me alone and stay out of my business. If you do want me around then stop pushing me away. You've got to stop dragging this on. Stop with the cutting me loose and reeling me back. Calvin's not perfect but I know where I stand with him. This brings me right back to...YOU MAKE ME CRAZY!"

I stood there wracking my brain for something, anything, to say. I had no idea she felt so strongly about me. Mostly Lucie pushed *me* away and I felt she was better off away from me no matter how much I wished things were different. "Lucie, my life is crazy right now. I have a lot going on. This is about me. You are... so... Look, I want you in my life. I don't want you to go away. I ... Oh Luce, don't cry."

Girls! Yeesh, I hate it when they cry. I couldn't even get my thoughts or words out straight. I wanted her to wait for me. Just a couple of years should do it. I wanted my gift and my life under control first. The only way I could think to keep her safe was to push her away. I wanted so badly in this moment to tell her who I was and why I was dangerous. I wanted to hold her but I had to let her go. I should push her away, break her heart a little bit now instead of crushing mine later. When it came to Lucie, I couldn't seem to resist pouring salt in my own wounds.

I stepped toward her and she swatted at me feebly as she sniffled. I gently placed my hands on her shoulders and she shoved ineffectually at my chest. Lucie, so full of light, citrus and springtime. I could smell her shampoo, see the flecks of color in her beautiful blue green eyes and see the curl and highlights in her blond hair. I could see the tears in her eyes along with the hurt and confusion. She stared at her hand on my chest and something in her seemed to break as her arm collapsed and she fell onto my chest, hugging me tightly. She held me for a long moment like an anchor in a storm. I was afraid to breathe. She held on as life went on around us, swirling by like eddies in a stream, her tears dampening my shirt. I slowly moved my hand up to her hair and smoothed it back. It was as soft as I had imagined. She hiccupped and stepped back - I felt the loss deeply.

She seemed to have regained some of herself. She looked once again like the old Lucie. "You hold me like you care too much but then you push me away. I don't get you, Owen. Maybe I'll still be here when you figure it out and maybe I won't. Calvin's not perfect but he won't hit me. You're wrong about him."

"Lucie, wait." I grasped her hand and pulled her back. I drew her close enough to kiss her forehead. She didn't resist like I expected she would. "I care about you too much to see you hurt," I mumbled into her hair. "Please - break up with Calvin before he really hurts you. He would have hit you tonight if I hadn't have intervened. If he ever hurt you, I would feel like I had to hurt him."

"No." I wasn't sure what she meant - no what? So I pushed harder.

I gentled my voice even further and begged. "Please," I said softly as I released her hand and touched her face, easing it up so she would be looking at me. "Promise me." I could sense her wavering. "Please," I whispered again as I moved in to touch my lips to hers. I whispered "please" once more, softly, against her lips. The warm salty taste of her tears blended with her sweet lip gloss. She stood perfectly still for a moment not fighting me, then she turned and bolted away. She was killing me by inches but I had to keep her safe. I knew she wanted me to go after her and tell her everything would be okay and I wanted to. There was a tightening in my chest like a fist squeezing my heart. I wanted to cry. I held myself tightly together so no one would know and slowly walked away from her. If only I could get my thoughts to move away from her like I was forcing my feet to do.

Calvin was no longer on the grass. I hoped he really had gone home. I tried the side door and miraculously it was unlocked. I peeked inside before I entered. The coast was clear. I pulled out my phone and texted Marlo and Adrian. Then I settled in to wait for their reply and watched the door for Calvin. I saw Lucie walk out of the women's bathroom. She seemed to sense my presence because she looked at me, her head held high, and then she walked out the front door. I watched until her father's familiar car pulled up and whisked her away. I wondered if she would be talking to me come Monday.

Marlo finally texted - he was about ready to go. Jill and Adrian were both acting like they had never dated and were making life difficult for Marlo and Mel. Katie was looking for me, Marlo told me. I found her searching around the perimeter.

"Hey," I said as I came up behind her.

"Where have you been?" she asked in a half worried, half irritated voice. Then her eyes narrowed in on my mouth. "Lucie," she said through tight lips.

I flicked my tongue over my lip. Shoot. Lip-gloss. Busted. "Katie, I'm sorry."

She held a hand up to stop my excuse or apology. I didn't even know what it was. She took a deep breath to calm herself. "Owen, I really like you and I thought we... well, you kept trying to tell me you wanted to be friends but I thought we were more than friends. I feel like you aren't even really giving me a chance," she said sadly.

Great, was I going to make another girl cry?

She placed one hand over her heart and then grasped the front of my shirt and pulled my face down to her level. "I wish you liked me as much as you like her. I will try to be your friend but I don't know if I can do it. I think I'll go home. I'm sick of Jill tonight anyway. Do one thing for me, would you?"

"What is it, Katie?" I asked, half scared and half relieved it had been this easy.

"Kiss me once like you mean it," she pleaded in a brave voice.

Could I mean it? I reached within myself and pulled up all the best parts of Katie. I thought about how she had been my friend the last several weeks, her laugh and her beautiful voice. Her face was still just inches from mine and she had a death grip on my shirt. I slowly and carefully moved toward her and she moved toward me to meet me in the middle. I knew I cared about her but not enough. The kiss ended up feeling like goodbye - at least for me. She was the second girl I had kissed tonight with tears in her eyes. I pulled back and she came in once more, to quickly touch her lips to mine this time.

"Good bye, Owen." She turned and walked away, leaving nothing but the wrinkles in the front of my shirt.

What a way I have with women. Marlo came up and touched my shoulder. "Can we go now? Please? Mel just did a courtesy break up as a show of solidarity with Jill. Can you believe it? Chicks are so weird. I want ice cream... and cake. I need some of Mom's cake."

I had to laugh. "Marlo, you said it! I think Adrian has done the damage tonight and ruined date night, *not* me. Let's take him

287

home and make plans for our weekend! Shall I be a good friend and help you eat dessert or talk you out of it?"

I called White Eagle while Marlo went in search of Adrian. We dragged him out reluctantly. He already had a new girlfriend prospect. Can you say rebound? White Eagle picked us up just after nine. "So boys, how was the dance?" he asked. The look on his face hinted that he knew there was a good story coming.

We filled him in. Everyone was worried about Lucie. We would all keep our eyes open. Adrian called home to see if he could come over for a while or even spend the night. His parents would let him stay so we only stopped at his house long enough to grab his stuff. Marlo got permission to stay too. His dad would deliver his stuff to my house.

My brothers were in bed when we got home so we had to be quiet. We practiced our promotion song in the garage and made plans for the rest of the weekend. As I sang, I could only think of Lucie and in my mind the song became hers – *Shape of My Heart* by the Backstreet Boys.

A little after ten, Sarah came out to the garage and frantically called us in to listen to the news. An unknown man was found dead. He had been weighted down and thrown in the river. He might not have been found yet if a fisherman had not snagged him on his line. We watched the clip carefully but the guy was pretty well covered. Was that a hint of a tattoo on his ravaged arm? Is it Clive we all wondered? Both White Eagle and Sarah whipped out their cell phones and started dialing their contacts.

The rest of us waited *not* so patiently. Was this the end of this terrible business, finally? They both closed their phones at about the same time. Both shook their heads. "No, it's not him or no news?" I asked, agitated.

"No news yet," White Eagle said, as Sarah spoke, "I don't know."

"The police have the body. They have already begun the autopsy. Owen, it's time to tell Sarah who you are. I have an idea about how

288

we can find out what we need to know." White Eagle spoke to me but was looking at Sarah.

"He *is* one isn't he?" Sarah asked before I could speak. She was looking at White Eagle, not me. Mom, Marlo and Adrian were swinging their heads back and forth between the two without saying a word. It would have been comical if the atmosphere wasn't so tense.

The others might be tongue-tied but I wasn't. "What do you mean, Sarah?"

She finally looked at me to answer. "You *know* evil. You can see it and you have to fix it, don't you?"

We all gaped at her, except for White Eagle, "How long have you known?"

"I have known this boy since he was little, about Alex's age. He's always been different. He's uncommonly aware of what's fair and just. He has always watched out for his brothers, the weak and defenseless. He started changing dramatically around his birthday last year. These special folks, these *balancers* seem to manifest around age fourteen at the youngest. Clearly Owen is one of light energy and I am betting great power. I have seen both in my career. The dark ones are really scary. It all makes sense now. All the trouble around here... I have no gift, but even I can almost feel the swirling energies, dark and light at war, trying to fight for balance and who is in the middle?... Owen. Let me guess, he must be a *reader* of some kind." She looked into the distance for a moment. "The hammer, you *read* the hammer. That's how you knew. Right place at the right time, my foot! That's how you knew to be at my house that night." Then she turned to White Eagle who was just smiling at her. "You need my help to either get the physical evidence or get him in to touch the physical evidence, don't you?" she finished.

White Eagle gifted her with the biggest smile ever. He looked at her like she was the smartest lady in the whole state. She reached over and gave me a big hug. "Well, I do so love it when I'm right!"

and she laughed one of the best laughs I have ever heard. Then everyone started talking at once.

White Eagle and Sarah had some work to do first but the tentative plan was to have me skip school to get snuck into the evidence locker. I wondered if I would spend the rest of my days in jail. I hoped they knew what they were doing. I couldn't decide if it was a good thing or a bad thing that my mom was totally into it. She acted like a kid on Christmas morning. The last time I saw her this excited was the last time she went with us. She really needed to get out more.

The guys and I went on up to bed and left the adults to their excited planning. It was already starting to sound like Mission Impossible. Grownups! Who knew they could act like such excited kids?

SIXTEEN

The next morning my house was bustling. Sarah was either still over or back over and she, White Eagle and Mom were cooking pancakes, bacon and eggs - make that whole wheat pancakes, turkey bacon and egg whites. I was wondering if I would ever see a cheeseburger and fries again or how about pizza or even ice cream? Beggar was curled up under the table hoping for dropped food. Ron, our cat, seemed to think that the bacon smelled great because he too was in attendance.

The guys and I pulled up chairs ready to dig in. We were informed of our schedule for the day. We would eat, go to the shop, work out, do whatever Max needed doing and then we would come mow our lawn, Sarah's and White Eagle's - one of us per lawn. Then we would meet up at Max's house. It had been released back to him. We would help out over there and then meet back here for a strategy meeting regarding Monday.

I was tired just thinking about it, but at least we would get to do most of it together. The guys and I headed upstairs to straighten my room and get ready for the day. I changed into work shorts and my worst running shoes. I stuffed my leg brace and three work shirts in my bag and then pulled a fourth over my head. My tees were really taking a beating. So many workouts and washings would leave nothing to pass down to Alex. I sent a text to Lucie but didn't figure I'd hear back from her.

We loaded up in White Eagle's truck and were off to the shop. White Eagle ran us through our circuit training again. It was murder but I could feel my body responding to it. After an hour he started working with us one on one and releasing the others to work with Max.

Now that Clive was done bringing in dirty goods, I found very little that came into the shop had anything to tell me. Nothing at school had spoken to me either. It left me wondering if my next big thing was lurking out there. I was ready but I felt apprehensive too. When it was my turn to work with White Eagle, I mentioned my thoughts to him. He shrugged them off. "Things may come in waves and then you will have a lull. It is what it is. Don't push it, things will come to you," he said in his mystical way.

I didn't often spar with him. He usually worked with me by coaching. Today was different. White Eagle held nothing back. I had no idea he could be so fierce. I found him scary. He even started grabbing things around the perimeter to try to hit me with or throw at me as a distraction. We must have been making a lot of noise because we were attracting a crowd. Thor, Max, Adrian and Marlo all watched from a safe distance on the sidelines. "Again, again," White Eagle shouted, "I am the enemy, try again!" I dodged the heavy bag he tried to push into me to knock me down. I leaped up with both feet and kicked it good, sending it into him and sending him flying backwards. I landed and ducked the bag swinging over my head. I rolled to the side and sprang to my feet. I lunged at the prone White Eagle and stopped a jab one inch from his throat. "Now that is what I am talking about," he gasped.

Everyone started applauding. I felt pretty good. Powerful. Whump! I was flat on my back with White Eagle over me. "And don't lose focus or turn your back on the enemy." The applause turned to cheers. "I think we're done for today," he gloated.

"Owen that was truly *a-maz-ing!*" Marlo chortled.

I put on a dry shirt and we were off to our next adventure, lawn mowing. "So Marlo, how many calories are we burning today, anyway? Do we get ice cream?"

"No Dude, we can have a bit of frozen yogurt or a soy bar!" What was wrong with him? He sounded almost gleeful! What had happened to my fluffy buddy who LOVED junk food???

"Please tell me we're not going to eat this way for the rest of our lives. Seriously, Mar, your dedication is above and beyond the call of duty. Obsessive much?"

Marlo laughed. "If you're really good, we can take a day off to have a special treat."

Oh boy. Soy bar, who was he kidding? So *not* yum. Well, to be fair I had never tried one. It just sounded so... healthy.

The lawn mowing was a success. We were all done in an hour and met up for healthy sandwiches. They weren't too bad really but I miss mayonnaise. We were off to Max's next including my brothers, my mom and Sarah. Poor Max, I don't think he knew what hit him. Adrian's dad and his sister showed up too and we had his place clean inside and out and his lawn mowed in no time. We were a machine. Sarah could direct an army I decided. I was feeling better about our break-in on Monday. With her in charge, how could we go wrong?

Adrian went home with his family. I think he was secretly glad because it gave him a chance to text the girl he met at the dance. Watching him text made me think to pull out my phone. I had missed a call... from Lucie. Crap. I quickly pulled up my voicemail.

"Hi Owen, it's Lucie. Thanks for thinking of me. I'm fine. My dad is mad at Calvin. I showed him my arm. My dad called his dad. I bet it wasn't a good conversation. Anyway, I'm done with Calvin and um, thanks for being there for me, again. I'll see you Monday. Bye." She sounded both sad and hopeful. Now what?

"Hey, Marlo?"

"Yeah, Buddy?"

"I'm hoping you can do me a favor. Lucie's dad really wants her to model but she is getting kinda thin. Do you think you could see what modeling gigs are out there and maybe help me work up a diet and exercise plan for her?"

"Yeah, I could do that. Do you know what she weighs and what she wants to weigh? Oh, and I need her height too."

"She's about five foot seven. I'll find out what she hopes to weigh and we'll guess where she's at now but I would bet around one hundred ten. She just looks too skinny," I said, worried.

"Don't worry, my friend, we can fix her right up." Marlo patted my arm and wandered off to see what more needed to be done. Apparently nothing else because everyone was packing up to go home. Max graciously declined our offer of dinner. He had been around his family, and people in general, plenty and was looking forward to some peace and quiet.

We dropped Marlo off at home to tend to his neglected and lonely parents. Our new family group was back together for dinner and planning at our house. I almost hoped it wasn't Clive in the river. If it was, Sarah and White Eagle would go back home and I would miss them more than I was missing my dad right now. That thought made me feel bad. I guessed the stress was just getting to him but I had to find a way to make him listen.

After dinner I offered to help Sarah clean the kitchen so I could talk to her. "So now that you know about me, do you have some advice on how to handle my dad? You said you knew of others like me. Are you still in contact?"

"Wow, you throw it all out there, don't you? Yes, I still have a contact in D.C. I'll see what I can do. About your father, I just don't know. Let me think on it. I have known many like him over the years. Usually you have to prove it to them."

"I tried, he wouldn't listen."

"Well then, he is probably one of the ones you have to beat over the head with it. Scan his stuff regularly and start looking for the *thing* that will convince him. Eventually something will show itself," she advised sagely.

"Are you going to train me now too?" I asked half hopefully.

"My dear boy, gosh no, I ended up working alongside some folks with gifts like yours. Mostly I covered their butts so that they wouldn't be discovered. I did more paperwork than field work. We used to have an amazing agent who worked for us. She was smart, beautiful and talented. She could *see* the darkness too. I truly enjoyed working with her and I learned a lot from her. I will always mourn her loss though. She was murdered by a man who is the opposite of you. He was drawn to her good energy and snuffed her out. We never caught him. I retired soon after. When I first met you, I wondered. Did White Eagle tell you that too? That he thought you might be a *Balancer* before he knew for sure?" she asked softly.

"Yes, I think he did say something like that. Why do you call me a *Balancer* and White Eagle calls me a *Spirit Watcher*?"

"It's our backgrounds I guess. I'm thinking of one who balances the good with the bad. He is referring to what you literally do, I think. You see the spirit of what has happened and you sense the mood or intention too, yes?"

"Yeah, that's pretty much it."

"Maybe we just don't know exactly what to call you. *Owen the Omnipotent* sounds a little ostentatious, don't you think?"

"Yeah, I guess it does." A huge smile spread over my face. Sarah Lando was quite the surprise. Maybe between us we could win my dad over.

Mom put my brothers to bed as Sarah, White Eagle and I started planning. White Eagle had been on the phone with his contact, who had risen to secretary to the chief. Awesome. He let us in on the fact that she continued to help him because of all the good he and Miles had done back in the day when she was a young file clerk. They had even helped her personally; hence, she would do almost anything for White Eagle in return. Monday I would be home 'sick'. Marlo and Adrian would pick up my assignments for me. White Eagle's contact, Evelyn, would check out the evidence box for the chief. This was done sometimes to check inventory logs. She would keep it safely locked up in a small conference room. Sarah and I would go to meet her for lunch. White Eagle would sneak in with us. Evelyn would take us with her to get her purse and leave me and White Eagle in the conference room while she and Sarah stepped out like old friends. When they returned we would leave. While they were gone I was to examine the evidence to confirm that the body was Clive. Fear, nerves and excitement caused my body to hum with anticipation.

Sunday was supposed to be a quiet day but I could neither settle down nor focus. I did the minimum on my homework. I texted my friends and even did a few chores. When I couldn't stand it anymore I went for a run. I ran until I couldn't run anymore and had to return home at a walk, my leg aching in complaint. I took a shower and looked at the clock again. The day was creeping by, yet I had missed lunch. I knew Marlo would be mad at me and I was a little hungry so I slapped together a sandwich. Dare I sneak in a little mayo? Yeah.

I tried to play with my brothers but my nervous energy quickly built back up. Alex and Lucas finally kicked me out, frustrated by my level of distraction. "Don't go away mad, just go away," Alex finally pleaded.

Finally I grabbed my gear and asked my mom if I could go to the pool to swim. She seemed excited to see me go. She offered me a ride but I opted to take my old neglected skateboard. I promised to call her when I arrived and when I was ready to leave. The swimming cleared my head like nothing else had. I would need that calm and focus tomorrow. When I had again exhausted myself, I climbed out of the pool and headed to rinse off the chlorine and change.

As I exited the locker room I almost collided with someone else. Jesus and I looked at each other in surprise. "Hey, I didn't know you were a swimmer," he exclaimed.

"Yeah, you?" I asked in return.

"My sister wants me to get my lifeguard certificate so that I can teach little kids to swim and be a lifeguard here. I need to start helping out at home ya know. My folks are coming back from Mexico soon. They may or may not be able to get their old jobs back. They've been gone for a long time taking care of my grandma and stuff," he said in a resigned voice.

"Good for you! I hope everything works out okay for you guys. My dad is gone right now too. He wants us to move to Atlanta for his new job but the rest of us don't want to go. It's kind of a mess." I clapped him on the shoulder as I passed. It was a relief to not capture any bad vibes off of my friend.

I called Mom on the way out the door. I threw my board and hopped on as my call connected. I let her know I was on my way. The ride home was nice. I had missed the hum of my wheels on the pavement.

The evening passed better than the rest of the day had. I hated to wish my life away but I felt a sense of urgency to get on with tomorrow. I went to bed early and had strange Clive dreams. It had been awhile. Tonight's dream had him soggy and coated in seaweed. Maybe I had been watching too much TV.

Sunlight washed over my face, waking me up. I was glad that my criminal career would hopefully end today. Please don't let me get caught. I really didn't want to go to jail. My life was plenty difficult without being sent to juvie. A scarier thought was what they would do to White Eagle, Sarah and Evelyn. I needed to be my best self today for sure. I needed to be on top of my game!

I got ready for my day, dressing in the nice clothes that had been purchased for me for the dance. I wandered into my mom's room and headed for the closet. I thought I would channel a little Marlo and add a tie. I stood in my parents' walk-in closet and tried to figure out what look I was going for. Royal blue would look good with the black shirt and dark blue over-dyed jeans. I had on black socks and the black shoes Mom had picked out. I found the ties and went to reach for the royal blue one I saw. I brushed another tie that Dad had not worn in awhile. I closed my eyes and focused - Christmas time from two Christmases ago. I could see Dad dressed in a suit and Mom wearing a black dress going to a holiday party for his work. They looked wonderful. It felt like they were happy. They were talking to someone important, my dad's boss maybe? I could see my grandfather coming across the room. My mother stiffened. He ignored her and spoke to my dad. I wished I knew what they were saying! My dad was shaking his head as he put an arm around my mom and turned away. My grandfather was staring daggers into the back of my mom's head. The scene shifted to show my parents in Dad's car. They were arguing.

"Owen?" I heard Mom call from the hall.

"I'm in your closet," I answered.

She wandered in and leaned against the doorjamb. "What are you up to?"

"I was looking for a tie for my 'lunch date' but I got distracted. Will you help me? It might hurt a little," I said, giving her a significant look.

"Okay, what do you need?"

"Several things. First, I'd like permission to scan your closet. Second, I need to look at some of your personal business. Third, I want your help to do it. It has to do with Dad and my grandfather."

"Wow, okay Owen. Yes, you can and I'll certainly help you," she said, though sounding somewhat surprised.

I closed my eyes again and *felt* the closet. A pair of shoes and a suit coat had something to tell me. "Mom, is White Eagle here?"

"Not yet."

"Then give me your hand, maybe we don't need him," I said, reaching for the tie as she clasped my hand. This was a shared memory so I hoped it would work. "Close your eyes and try to remember Dad's Christmas party two Christmases ago. I felt the weak electric current go up my arm as I looked at the images again. They were now amplified but they were also warped somewhat by my mom's perceptions. Mainly the change was in my grandfather who looked a little more sinister.

"Mom, talk to me and tell me what you see," I begged.

"We were having fun at the party. I liked your dad's boss. He was kind and generous as well as being very hard working. I saw your grandfather approach. We have never seen eye to eye. He doesn't like me and doesn't think I am good enough for your dad. It's a cultural thing. I always thought when he got to know me, he would get over it. He was trying to get your dad to transfer to the east coast. Your dad said no." She made no comment on the rest.

"Mom, what was the argument in the car about?" I asked softly.

"Your dad wanted me to consider moving back then too. My whole life is here. I didn't want to do it then and I still don't now." She dropped her head like she was ashamed.

"Mom, it's a decision that we have to make together. Don't feel bad about having an opinion about your own life. We have to weigh and measure all of it and not just go because Dad says so." Then I had another thought. "Did you just not want to go or did you have the feeling you shouldn't?"

"Well I... I didn't want to go but I did feel like I shouldn't go. It felt... wrong." She looked at me perplexed.

"Who would have found me if we had left? It would not have been White Eagle," I said, hoping she would see my logic.

"I wonder." she said, looking thoughtful.

I reached for the shoes, still holding her hand. I did not seem to get a boost from her here so I switched to the suit coat. Boom! The images were strong. I could see my mom in them and feel the anger, resentment and fear. Last summer we had visited both sets of grandparents. One night while we were in Florida we were left with the housekeeper and my grandparents had taken my parents to dinner. I remembered having mixed feelings about being left with the housekeeper. I was glad my grandfather was leaving but at the same time we had come to see them and it felt a little rude that they would leave us behind. We were always well behaved.

It seemed that Mom had some of those same feelings. Again my grandfather was pressuring my dad to transfer. Mom wasn't having it. They got into a huge argument and Mom walked out and paced outside so she wouldn't reach across the table and choke the old curmudgeon. He was acting like a spoiled child. From Mom's memory I saw that he had called us half-breeds and suggested that Dad just leave us all behind. My grandmother looked like she wanted to crawl under the table but tried to calm him down by placing her hand on his arm. He threw it off. Then he threatened to cut my dad out of his will. Mom's memory faded. I could still see my dad but it was a weaker image. He only stayed at the table to try to make some peace. I remember that mom had slept in the room with us that night.

Mom dropped my hand and the image went with it. "You know I only pretended to fall asleep in the room you shared with your brothers in Florida because I had to remind myself why I was there. I never wanted any of you to know the truth of that. I'm so sorry."

"Mom, this new job, it has to do with Grandpa, but how?"

"I don't know. Your dad won't tell me but there is something there," she said with new understanding.

I touched the shoes again. Dad was talking to his boss. His old job was being recategorized. There was a big bonus for the company if they hired a certain new person for the newly created position. It was to be a woman from Florida. Dad was offered the job in Atlanta. It was a 'can't miss' opportunity. I smelled a big rat but Dad couldn't or wouldn't believe that his father had manipulated him like that.

"Mom, he feels trapped. He isn't sure who's pulling the strings. Grandpa looks guilty but Dad doesn't want to accuse him. Do you think he would push us away on purpose to protect us?" I guessed I was thinking of Lucie and my own secrets.

"I don't know. I just don't know. I came to tell you breakfast is ready. I need to get your brothers to school. I agree, the royal blue is a good choice," she rattled as she turned and headed out.

"Wait, I didn't say that. How did you know what tie I was looking at?" I asked, confused.

"You must have said."

"Mom, I didn't. Did you see it when we were linked?"

"I... I don't know... maybe?"

"Well that stinks, I won't have any secrets soon. I'm a teenager. I don't want you knowing everything I think. That would be..." What - embarrassing, awkward, ugly, bad? There were not words! Who wants their mom in their head?

"Well you get to be a teenager and an adult. I could experience being a teenage male. Imagine what I could learn!" she giggled and hustled away.

I snatched the tie off its special hanger and had it tied before I even realized what I was doing. Thank you, Miles. I headed downstairs feeling a little out of sorts. I needed some calming before I left for my meeting with the evidence box.

I rounded the corner into the kitchen and all the conversation stopped. "Wow, Owen, you look like a grownup," Alex said in awe.

"Nice," Lucas added.

"Very nice," Sarah said, pleased. "You're all set for our date. Perfect!"

White Eagle smiled at me. "I hope all this spit and polish does the trick. Your couch is starting to hurt my back."

"I offered you my..."

"I know, I know. I went to the bakery and got treats!" he exclaimed, changing the subject. "Doughnuts!"

My brothers were so excited you'd have thought it was their birthday and Christmas combined. Apparently I wasn't the only one who missed junk food. Sarah made coffee and Mom poured milk. She had fixed real eggs today but I still got turkey bacon. I had a hard time choosing a doughnut. I figured I should only have one or face the wrath of Marlo, who had lost ten whole pounds and grown another inch. He was fluffy no more but I was pretty sure that he would begrudge me more than one doughnut.

Mom asked Sarah if she could take my brothers to school so that we could talk to White Eagle. She, of course, was happy to help. White Eagle looked at us curiously as we began to fill him in on our discoveries. He was downright astounded when I told him about Mom's tie comments. We all wondered how we could solve our troubles involving my dad.

Sarah came back as we were finishing so we filled her in. "I would love to have someone watch your grandfather but I don't know who to ask that wouldn't raise eyebrows. We need a private eye."

"We have one, but I can't miss that much school and I don't have any official ID. Miles' memories are good for all kinds of stuff," I said, pointing at my perfect Windsor knotted tie.

"I asked you at the beginning of the year what you wanted to do when you grew up. Now you're grown up. What do you want to do with your life after college now?" Mom asked with genuine curiosity.

"I still like animals but I'm being drawn in another direction. I see why Miles made the choices that he did. I think I'll have to start out with the military or law enforcement. I don't know. I'll have to carefully choose a job that keeps me out of the public eye and allows me some latitude to do what I need to do."

Having left them speechless I excused myself to go out on our deck and try some Tai Chi. White Eagle soon joined me. I focused and moved through our routine. I heard the door open again and pretty soon Mom and Sarah were on the deck with us following our motions. Beggar had come out with them but she made use of the yard, then cocked her head, looking at us in her doggy version of "Y'all are crazy humans!" I ran though the whole routine twice more. By the last time through we were moving like a single unit. I hoped we wouldn't end up on the internet because some curious neighbor found us interesting. I could see the title on You Tube now, 'Crazy Neighbors Move Like Synchronized Swimmers.'

I looked at my watch and nodded at Sarah and White Eagle. We all went inside. "I thought we should go over the plan again before it's time to leave. I have to tell you the waiting is hard for me. I wish we could just go now," I said to no one in particular.

"Waiting is often the hardest part," Sarah said sagely. "The trick is finding something to do while you wait, then the time goes by quickly. Why don't you go get lost in a good book? We'll let you know when it's time to go."

I went back up to my room. I looked at all the books on my book-shelf and then at the book I was supposed to be reading for LA. I flipped through the required reading. I could barely find my place let alone focus on reading it. I set it aside and ran my finger along the spines of the books on the shelf. I couldn't seem to relax enough to even pick one. I paced. I looked at my watch. I still had over an hour. I took my tie and shirt back off and changed into workout gear.

I did push-ups, crunches and some stretches. I still felt agitated so I went downstairs. Sarah and Mom looked like they were doing some meal prep in the kitchen. White Eagle was carving some-thing with a wicked looking knife. The little shavings were falling onto a piece of today's newspaper he had laid between his feet at the breakfast room table. He looked up at me with a half smile on his face and nodded. I ran. I calculated that I could run twenty minutes out, then turn around and come back. I would still have time for yet another shower and then we could leave.

It only took about ten minutes to calm me down. My Clive dreams had mostly vanished so maybe this whole thing was about done. It almost felt like a letdown. After everything that happened this was it? Or not, and if not, where was he and why had he done what he had done? No one was going to get the drop on me with a car again, that was for sure. The burst of anger gave me extra speed. It was time to turn around. I ran back, giving it all I had, to burn out the rest of my worries.

I was soaked with sweat, my sides heaving, as I returned home. Nothing in the kitchen appeared to have changed. I wiped the sweat out of my eyes and gave White Eagle a small wave as I headed back upstairs. I let the water pound over me and wash away the last of my anxiety. Breathe. You can do this.

I redressed in my work clothes of the day. I combed my hair and brushed my teeth for good measure. Then I hustled back downstairs, ready to go. White Eagle pointed at a chair and I sat. Sarah washed her hands and turned to look at me. "How was the book?"

I couldn't help it. I busted up laughing. White Eagle joined in. Mom and Sarah just looked at each other, not sure what to make of our outburst. When I caught my breath I let them in on the joke. "I couldn't settle down to read. I ran."

"Oh," was Sarah's only reply. She did look a little disappointed in me.

We set off for the police station. I was able to maintain my calm all the way there. We parked and walked in just like we knew what we were doing. Sarah showed her driver's license and asked for Evelyn. We were expected. Evelyn greeted us like long lost friends and led us right back so she could get her purse. She quickly stashed me and White Eagle in a little windowless conference room, told us we had thirty-seven minutes and then swept out of the room with Sarah.

The box was on the table waiting for us. Several strips of evidence tape were stuck to the table and already had her initials on them ready for us to reseal the packages. There was a neatly detailed log on the table showing that she had gone through and checked everything. We would seal it up and she would put it away as if no one but her had checked the contents. There were two sets of gloves. I had never tried to work with gloves on but I guessed that now was as good a time as any. The gloves themselves had nothing to say. White Eagle carefully pulled out the contents in order and pointed to where he wanted me to start.

He picked up the evidence log and looked at the top two sheets carefully. A huge smile split his face. He pulled off the top sheet and held up two fingers and then gave me a thumbs up. Ah, one for them and one for us. Then his grin got wider. She had also snuck in a copy of the preliminary autopsy report.

I touched a shirt of light blue chambray by reaching my hand into the unsealed bag. It was like trying to look through the glove. So I tried the trick I had used before. I kept the glove on but exposed part of my little finger. I touched the shirt with my knuckle. I had not braced myself for the images and went down on one knee. White Eagle came to my side concerned. I swallowed hard and waved him off.

"It's him," I said in a nearly silent whisper. "Let me get the rest of the story." I made my way through every piece of evidence. I touched each one with the side of my knuckle. As I set them aside, White Eagle carefully resealed and then restacked each evidence bag back in the box, just the way they looked when we started. In addition to the shirt was one boot, one sock, a pair of jeans, boxer briefs, two dimes, a penny and an illegible movie ticket stub.

When we were done I sat on the floor with my legs bent, my head between my knees and sucked air. White Eagle gave me my space. He took our gloves and put them in his pocket after putting the lid back on the box. When the door opened exactly thirty-seven minutes after we had entered, I still jumped. Evelyn looked at us, picked up the box and let us into the lobby. White Eagle handed her a business card and we were off.

Sarah rattled on about what a lovely lunch it had been and how we would all have to do it again and maybe next time I should skip dessert as it didn't agree with me. White Eagle and I feigned interest all the way to the car. No one said another word until we were on the road.

I sucked in a deep breath and took off the tie and unbuttoned the top buttons of my shirt. I shook myself like a dog emerging from the water. "That was bad. How do cops do this stuff? Um, Sarah you gotta pull over... now! Sorry!" I barely made it out the door of her sedan before I emptied my stomach on the grass by the side of the road. White Eagle was out of the car before I finished and handed me some tissues from Sarah's purse. They both looked at me in concern. I got back in the car and White Eagle followed suit.

"Guys, Mom can't hear this but I know that we need to get the information to Evelyn. It's Clive's body. He and Darren were having an argument. You know I can't hear what's said. They argued at Darren's house. They went off in the jeep. It was dark and I'm not sure where they went other than they headed to some bar on the highway and got plowed. Then instead of going home, Darren took a side road. He didn't really drink much; he faked it. They went down a heavily wooded road. Clive seemed confused. Darren reached in the backseat and hit him about four times with a tire iron. Then he drove to the river. He was somewhere higher up, almost like a cliff. He had driving gloves on. He pulled Clive out and knifed him through the diaphragm. Then he tied the two cement blocks he had in the back to Clive's feet and sent him over the edge. The water was deep and he sank quickly. There should be evidence in the jeep. Have them check the tire iron and the passenger seat. Oh and tell Evelyn they need to pull apart the door panel because some blood ran down the inside of the window. I wish I had touched the jeep the day we were at Darren's. I... I need to... White Eagle, we need to work out at the shop before I can go back to school. I need a break, but I do need to go to school and do something normal for the rest of the day. I can't keep seeing that stuff, knowing it's real and not from a horror film."

Sarah had a white-knuckled grip on the steering wheel. She changed directions and started to head for the shop without a word.

"I need my workout gear," I said from the back seat.

"Don't worry, I've got you covered," White Eagle said as he whipped out his cell and dialed my mom. "Hey Lila, we're fine. It was Clive. You and the boys are completely safe. We're running a quick errand to the shop and then we'll take Owen to school. How was Luke's day?... Super. So you'll get Alex when he's done and we'll see you for dinner, right?... Good. Thanks."

White Eagle had a way with words. That was easy but I was too sick to care. Max was surprised to see us. I don't even know what excuse White Eagle gave him as I hustled into the back. He quickly introduced Sarah, who then came to the back to watch. White Eagle pulled some clothes from a drawer and I went into the bathroom to change. He put on his special music and we went through our Tai Chi routine. At some point Sarah joined us because I noticed she was no longer on her stool. Then he had me put on my practice shirt and we did something new. He put practice weapons all around the perimeter of our mat.

"Remember how you took me out with the heavy bag? No rules today. Try not to kill me or I'll let Sarah at you." I looked at her and grinned. She wasn't having it. He continued, "No weapons except those on the mat and you may not leave the mat. Ready?" I nodded and off we went. Back and forth across the mat, kicking, hitting, blocking, dodging, and rolling. I tried several weapons. I was about to get the upper hand when I was smacked from behind with a practice sword. Sarah had taken another pair of White Eagle's sweats and was in on the action.

They were good. They both moved instinctively so that I could not watch them both at once. I kept avoiding hitting Sarah and I was getting pretty creative about it. I'd block her but I could not bring myself to hit her. She had a style of fighting that I was unfamiliar with. White Eagle finally backed me into a corner forcing me to go after Sarah. I tried to step around her but she wouldn't go for that so I had to knock her down. I swung low to sweep her legs out from under her. She went down but she caught ahold of my sweats as I tried to leap over her prone form causing a spectacular belly flop on my part. I hit the mat chin first and my head exploded with pain. Sarah had rolled to her feet to sit on me when she saw the blood. She collapsed next to me instead. "Medic!" she hollered at White Eagle.

"You gotta love head wounds; they bleed like a son of a gun. Guess this means I win! Now sit up so the *old* people can look at ya," she said with authority.

I sat up. I had a monster headache and my jaw ached. I tried to move it a bit. No bone or tooth damage but I had split my chin. "Well, what do you think, Sarah? Think a butterfly will do it or does pretty boy need stitches?"

"Can't you do it? He'll miss the whole day otherwise," Sarah almost whined.

"Well they like the doctors to do 'em but I 'spose I could do it. You ice him up and I'll find my kit."

They were joking, right? I tried to get up but Sarah was back with the ice. White Eagle appeared with his medic kit. It looked like he used it for camping and hunting. Sarah removed the ice and he injected me with a prefilled pen of some kind of drug from the 'caine family. The needle prick made my eyes water. He pulled out a slim curved needle and I felt the urge to vomit again.

"Come on kid, show some backbone. How'd you survive the mall incident? That was a whole lot worse than this," White Eagle said with a touch of disgust. He dug right in, literally. I wasn't even quite numb yet. I will give him this, he was quick and efficient. He swabbed me down with disinfectant and then smeared me with antibacterial goo. He cleaned his needle, put his kit back together and threw away the trash. "Go get ready for school. We're done here."

Yeah I guess! I thought sarcastically. I really *did* want to go to school now. Maybe Sarah had done it on purpose because Clive's death was no longer the main thing on my mind. I cleaned up and looked at myself in the mirror. My new scar, when it healed, would be about an inch long and run right across the bottom of my chin. People would only be able to see it if I looked up. Not that I cared. Well, much.

My jaw and head still hurt. Sarah was prepared for me. She had a granola bar of some kind and a glass of milk with three Ibuprofen tablets. Maybe she wasn't all bad after all. "Good thing you wore a black shirt. If you bleed it won't show much. Sorry I dumped you so hard."

"It's okay," I said, marveling at this whole new side of her. I about laughed out loud when I realized I used to think of her as a little old lady. HA! I thought she was tough when she smacked her bur-glar with the baseball bat. I'm not sure she needed me at all that night. I think I just helped her keep *her* cover.

Sarah walked me into school. She handed off a very credible look-ing doctor's note that she took from her purse. I wondered where she had gotten it. I probably didn't want to know. She apologized for my being late; as the secretary could see, I'd had a little acci-dent. Would she please excuse me from my morning classes and didn't choir start in a few minutes? WOW! I'm glad Sarah's on my team. I was given a late slip with no further questions asked. I gave Sarah a hug and headed for my locker.

I rushed to choir where Lucie and Katie along with most of the rest of the class just stared at me. What? Was I bleeding again? I handed my slip to the teacher and took my spot. I touched my chin to check for blood. Jesus leaned back and said out of the side of his mouth, "What happened to you? Fight?"

"I had an accident," I whispered.

He shook his head and smiled at me like he could hardly wait for the real story. I asked him if he wanted to sing at graduation with us and he turned me down. Choir passed quickly enough. My jaw was still hurting. Man, Sarah had cleaned my clock good! Who knew!

Lucie stopped me on the way out. Katie gave me a long sad look and then left without a word. Lucie laid a hand on my arm to get my attention. "What happened to you?" she asked, the worry plain in her voice.

"I tripped," I answered, mostly truthfully. What I didn't add, was that I had a little help.

Lucie gave me quite the look. I could tell that she didn't believe a word of it. She shook her head in a fashion much like Jesus had. "Please tell me Calvin wasn't involved," she begged.

"I can honestly say that I have not seen him since Friday night puking on the grass," I replied.

"Well, I have and he's ignoring me. It's kind of nice after Friday night. My dad really did call his dad and then my dad called the school and said he isn't to be anywhere near me. We'll see how it goes, but so far so good. Are you ready to get our lab stuff in science, partner?"

Well, this was going better than I thought it would. We walked side by side to science. Lucie was in a good mood and seemed to be her old self. I saw Calvin as we crossed the main hall but true to Lucie's word he stayed back. He settled for giving me dirty looks instead. It was tempting to rub in Lucie's proximity but I didn't want to make her mad and ruin a good thing.

We received huge packets in science. For the rest of the year we would be working on our plant labs and seed germination experiments. We spent the whole time going over the packet, due dates and expectations. Fun! Not! Lucie remained in a good mood all through class and we headed to health together.

Since Lucie was in such a good mood I risked telling her about what Marlo did for me when it came to diet, nutrition and exercise. Once Marlo had plugged in all the data we were supposed to journal about our habits, the reports he generated would be accepted by our teacher instead of the hand-written logs. I told her that Marlo would happily do one for her too. I'd been worried for nothing. She was pleased. I even snuck a peek at her written log; she had eaten a little lunch today. I bid her farewell when class ended and headed to the lobby as usual. No Katie. I was only a little disappointed and a whole lot relieved.

I met up with the guys so that they knew to get to the shop on their own. I had physical therapy today and I'd now be swimming on Thursdays. I would meet them at the shop after PT if it didn't take too long today. I also gave Marlo the good news about Lucie and I hoped they'd get together soon.

Mom was waiting in the parent pick-up loop. She was greatly relieved about Clive but still worried about Dad. What could I say? Me too. She seemed to really look at me for the first time. "What in the world happened to you?" she asked, as she pulled over to scrutinize me more carefully.

"Well... Looking at the evidence the police had was a little... intense so I asked if I could take a break and work out a little before I went back to school. I had a slight accident during practice," I replied hesitantly.

"A slight accident? Have you seen what you look like?" she asked somewhat appalled.

What was with people? You could barely see the stitches. I pulled down the visor and looked in the mirror. Ohhhhhh. I was bruising spectacularly along my chin and lower jaw. Nice! I had some swelling too. "I did a belly flop and landed chin first. It really was an accident," I said with a shrug.

"Did White Eagle do this to you?"

"Nope, Sarah did."

"What?" she squawked.

"Yep, it was Sarah. Ask her." My big smile made my face hurt but it was worth it. My mom was looking at me like a fish out of water.

She gave her head a shake, very carefully checked her mirrors and drove off without another word.

I had to tell my story again at physical therapy. Of course I left out the beginning of the story and just told the belly flop on the chin part. They probably thought I was the biggest klutz ever for tripping, but oh well. I did get some ice for my face out of it. On a happy note they only booked me for the next three Mondays and then it was a holiday and I was DONE! I would still be swimming but that was fine.

SEVENTEEN

May began with the expected Oregon rain. I was settling into a routine that I could live with. My classes were going fine. Practices at the shop were the best part of each day that I able to go. Katie barely spoke to me. She seemed a little sad but still worked with us in math. Lucie and I planned to work on our plant project at my house on Saturday evenings when I was done with work at the shop and swimming.

The first Saturday Lucie came over we organized all our plant stuff and found a place to keep it where it would get plenty of sunlight. It was my job to be sure it stayed moist during the week and to measure how much water I added. I also had to record the humidity in the room twice a day.

The next week followed the same pattern: Calvin glaring, Katie sad and quiet, Lucie being her old self, physical therapy on Monday, swimming on Thursday and Saturday. The best part, as always, was going to the pawnshop to work for Max, workout, spar and now sing. Max thought it was pretty darn funny and happily sold every karaoke machine he had in stock, so we must have sounded pretty good. We cut our dinners with Sarah and White Eagle back to twice this week. The only super exciting thing that happened was getting my stitches out before swim practice on Thursday.

That Saturday, as Lucie and I worked with all the data I had collected from the week prior and measured the only seeds that had sprouted, bean seeds, she mentioned that her birthday was coming and that she thought her parents had forgotten. It wasn't on any calendar that she could see and no one had said a word. She was a little sad and a little frustrated. I think a part of her even found it a little funny. Lucie's birthday would be on Monday and I knew that I would not forget.

After Lucie left, I asked my mom if I could go through her never-ending supply of cards. She, of course, said yes and happily got them out for me. I wasn't sure what I was looking for until I found it. The sentiment was simple and upbeat but the best part was the bird in flight on the front. As I held the card I remembered a batch of ceramics that had come in from an estate sale. In the stuff, which I had of course *looked* at - as that was part of my job, to scan each thing before Marlo entered it in the computer - I had seen a bird in flight. It was small and delicately depicted. The artist had a really good eye. It was a bird common to these parts, a Song Sparrow, its body brown and white- streaked with bright black eyes and an amazing voice. Perfect.

I called White Eagle to see if I could pick it up on Sunday. He would meet me there. Mom found a box that it would fit in so that I could safely get it to school and Lucie could safely take it home. She found me some sky blue tissue paper to pad the box with and a little gift bag to put the whole thing in.

I felt almost nervous on Monday. I wanted Lucie's birthday to be nice but I didn't want to embarrass her either. The little bird felt like it was weighing me down. I was trying to decide when the best time was to give it to her. I finally settled on the very end of health but it was all I could think about all day. I said nothing about her birthday and it seemed like no one else did either. Most kids our age are thrilled that it's their birthday but Lucie seemed blue. I figured it was because her parents forgot. I practically counted the minutes that day. I kept the bird in my locker until right before health. I wrapped it in an old sweatshirt I kept in my locker for emergencies and snuck the whole thing under my chair. When there was seven minutes left and most students were distracted by getting ready to clean up and go home, I pulled the bag out. Good thing it was small because I had a hard time keeping it out of her sight and below other people's radar. Fortunately no one thought it was weird that I was carrying a sweatshirt around.

"Hey Lucie?"

"Yeah?"

"It might have seemed like I forgot, but I didn't. Happy Birthday," I said quietly for her ears alone, as I pulled out the bag from under the sweatshirt.

"You remembered? A couple of my girlfriends wished me a happy birthday this morning but no one else remembered. I keep hoping my parents will remember but I hate to get my hopes up." She took the gift bag and held it in her lap to keep it off the radar of kids around us. She slowly pulled up the box and set the bag aside. Then she lifted the lid. The bird was nestled on its tissue paper bed. She carefully lifted it up by the wire attached between its upswept wings. "It's beautiful," she whispered and I thought she was going to cry.

No one seemed to notice us. We were the eye of the storm amid the crash and bang of chairs hitting desks, students talking, the slam of textbooks closing and being stacked, the ringing bell and the mad rush for the door. "Owen, it's wonderful. Thank you so much."

"It's a Song Sparrow. It made me think of you. It's delicate and has a beautiful song. I wanted you to remember that you can fly too. Don't let people, including your parents, drag you down. Happy Birthday, Lucie," I said as I smiled at her.

A tear escaped and she leaned over to hug me. I happened to look up and I saw Katie in the doorway. I'll never forget the desolation on Katie's face. I never wanted to hurt her but I had done it again. I didn't even know what I could say that would make it better. I had never promised her anything. I had given her some of my time and a piece of myself but I still felt awful. I should talk to her.

"I need to go. I'll see you tomorrow, okay? Call me later if your parents forget and you want to talk or whatever," I offered, as I got ready to go. I went to Katie's locker and she was still there packing her stuff and trying not to cry.

"Katie," I said softly as I knelt down next to where she bent into her locker.

"Go away, Owen. I don't want to talk to you right now."

"I know. I'm sorry I keep hurting you. I don't want to hurt you but I just seem to keep doing it. It's not fair but I can't help how I feel. I like you, but as a friend, I can't do more. Can we try to be friends? Please Katie?" I felt wretched for making her feel so bad.

"I would like to be your friend, I think. I just can't do it right now. Please give me some time and don't go out of your way to be so nice; it just makes it... harder or worse. I don't know, just go away please," she begged.

"Okay, Katie." I rose to my feet and walked to my locker to get my things to take home. My mom was out front for physical therapy. This would be my last session. I felt almost euphoric. I felt bad for Katie but things were going well with Lucie. I was also very much looking forward to our campout with White Eagle. All the parents seemed to be on board, even my reluctant father, though everyone wondered why we needed to go so far away. The guys and I kept mum except for my mum. Ha! Mom knew why we were going to Nevada. The rest thought we were looking at some mining history and geology.

It felt so good to be a free man, I felt like dancing in the parking lot. Mom was in a good mood too. "Ice cream?" she asked playfully.

"I can't, Marlo would smell it on me. How about some fat free frozen yogurt to share with the gang at the shop?" I offered in return.

"Deal, my virtuous boy!"

"Besides, we agreed to pig out on the Washington D.C. trip and then we'll come back and be good for football season. I can handle all this if I do it a piece at a time."

Mom drove to the closest grocery store and we got napkins, bowls, spoons and the yogurt in vanilla so we could put some fresh berries on top. Then we rushed to the pawnshop. We were shocked to find Sarah manning the counter.

"Wow, what are you doing here?" I asked in surprised.

"Max has a court date so I am doing a little volunteer work. It keeps the brain active you know," she said with a smile and a wink.

"Besides, White Eagle is here, right?" I winked back. "Are my brothers here?"

She just smiled. We invited her into the back to celebrate my graduation from PT! Marlo approved of my dessert choice. The mood was positive and upbeat. Lucas was having the best day ever. The pawnshop was his new favorite hangout. White Eagle and Adrian were teaching my brothers karate. They were all having way too much fun.

We were hoping that good things would come to Max as well. Evelyn had called White Eagle earlier to let him know that the evidence against Darren was stacking up and he was starting to sing like a bird. I hoped that his confession would help Max too.

Max walked into the shop just after closing. "Why's the sign still on open? Can't I trust you people?" he asked, faking exasperation.

"Nope," several of us said at once, mixed in with, "How'd it go?"

"Darren admitted that he and Clive blackmailed me. I was not the only one either. They let me go because I came forward. They're after some other poor schmuck and of course our boy Darren. They have him on assault, kidnapping, dog abuse, drugs, blackmail and... drum roll please... murder! He proudly admitted he murdered Clive and he admitted to a bunch of other stuff too. He said Clive deserved it because he made him mad. Clive had been the leader but Darren wanted a bigger cut. His habit was expensive. It was so weird. We were there about me, but he just went crazy and let out all the other stuff. They couldn't shut him up. It was the darnedest thing, almost like he was possessed or something. Oh shoot, wait, I forgot the best part... he admitted to tax evasion,"

Max burst out. He then started laughing so hard I thought he would roll on the floor.

We offered Max the last bit of melted fat free frozen yogurt. The look he gave us made us all laugh harder. Max took Adrian home and the rest of us split up between the remaining cars. Lucas went with Mom, Alex went with Sarah and Marlo and I went with White Eagle. We dropped off Marlo and the rest of us had veggie pizza with light cheese on a whole wheat crust. Unbelievable. Just look at what my life had become. First thing on my DC food list? You got it. Pizza – real pizza. Number two on my list was a cheeseburger, fries and a milk shake. The rest I would have to figure out as I went.

Lucie called while we were eating. Her folks had forgotten. She had lost the battle and was feeling really blue. I asked if they'd let her come over. She doubted it since it was a school night. I suggested a 'plant lab' emergency. She giggled and went to ask.

"Um, Mom?... It's Owen. There's a problem with our plant lab. Can I please go over for a little while to help him fix it?"

"I don't have time to take you and it's a school night." I could hear her answer sharply in the background.

"Tell her we'll get you," I urged. Lucie seemed to be able to hear me.

"Mom, Owen's mom had already offered to pick me up," Lucie said in a calm soothing voice.

"Fine, whatever. Be home by 9:30." She sounded like she could care less as long as Lucie was out of her hair. Lucky me!!!

"We'll be there in about ten minutes."

I had stepped away from the table to answer the phone but not far enough. I came back in to find it silent and everyone looking at me with a mixture of humor and teasing on their faces. For Lucie, I would take it.

"Would someone please take me to pick up Lucie?"

318

"I dunno, Bucko, what will you do for us in exchange?" Mom asked as her eyes danced.

"Owen has a girllllll friend," Lucas sang, gleefully.

"Mom, it's her birthday and they forgot," my voice ground out, showing my anger. I was mad at her parents, not my family, but I probably sounded grumpy to them.

I was met with a chorus of "No!" and "What?" all jumbled together in outrage. No one thought her parents were the good guys tonight. Mom left her pizza half eaten and grabbed her keys. Sarah said she'd bake an angel food cake and White Eagle offered to clean the kitchen. My brothers wanted to decorate. "Why not!" was Mom's reply and we were off. I admire and appreciate my family of problem solvers and general do-gooders.

I had never been to Lucie's but she texted her address. She lived in the older part of town. Her house was bigger than ours by quite a bit and they had maybe three times the property. Our SUV, although clean, was five years old and looked under-classed next to the newer BMW and Mercedes. I would take my life any day over Lucie's!

Lucie was out the door before I even got out of the car, let alone before I could walk up to her door. She ran for our car like she was afraid they would change their minds and threw herself in the backseat.

"Happy Birthday, Lucie," Mom said as she pulled out of their driveway.

"Thanks, Mrs. Ryer," Lucie answered quietly. She almost seemed to shrink in on herself back there. I reached back and took hold of her hand.

"Do you want to talk about it?" I asked.

"Nope. I want to forget about it," she said, defiantly.

My mom tried to break the ice. "So you and Owen have science, health and choir together, right?"

"Yes."

"Did Marlo show you his amazing health program? He even has me on board. I've lost five pounds so far. I think Owen has put five pounds on. Maybe he found the ones I lost. Of course I lost fat and he gained muscle. It almost doesn't seem fair." That got a half smile out of Lucie so I gave Mom a slight nod. "Are you singing for promotion?"

"Yes, but I don't get much practice time," she answered sadly.

"That's too bad. What are you singing?"

"*Keep Holding On.*"

"Oh my gosh, I think we have that on karaoke. The boys have been practicing their song on it. They're sounding pretty darn good too. Maybe we'll sing and be silly tonight," Mom said joyfully. It was funny how, when she talked like that, she could make anything sound like fun. I turned back and looked at Lucie who now had a complete smile and was shaking her head at Mom's enthusiasm.

The trip home was faster than the trip to Lucie's house. She let me hold her hand when we walked up the front walk. My brothers banged open the front door before we even hit the porch. They were quickly followed by White Eagle and Sarah.

"My goofy family," I said waving my arm at them in indication, "White Eagle, my coach and mentor; Sarah, our neighbor and part time nanny; Alex and Lucas, my brothers."

"Happy Birthday to you, Happy Birthday to you..." they all began to croon. Mom quickly joined in.

Lucie had a look on her face that let me know she was shocked, pleased and embarrassed all rolled into one. "Thank you," she whispered when they were done.

Lucas came and dragged her inside so he could show her the poster he'd made for her. We trooped into the living room where my brothers had set up a board game we could all play. The timer went off before we had even finished one round and Sarah took the cake out of the oven. She and Mom brought in slices for us as we continued our game. They even put a candle in Lucie's piece. I was afraid she was going to cry but the tears didn't leak out past her eyes and she kept on smiling.

I guess I should have been jealous, but Alex and Lucas were so cute I just couldn't be mad at them when they both hogged Lucie all evening. They sat on either side of her. She didn't look like she needed to be rescued. She seemed to enjoy the attention. Mom brought the karaoke machine in from the garage and found both of our songs. Lucie didn't want to sing alone but she sang with the rest of us. As we all finished one piece I laughed and said, "Look at us, we're the Partridge Family."

Mom, White Eagle and Sarah laughed but my brothers and Lucie looked at me like I was nuts. Geez, did I really just say that? Oops. Shut up, Miles. "I, ah, saw a re-run. It's a show from the '70s where a mom and her kids form a band." Mom and White Eagle just looked at each other.

Soon it was time for my brothers to go to bed. They didn't want to go. Lucie had a fan club. White Eagle walked Sarah home so we had a few minutes alone to talk. Lucie finally told me that both her parents were wrapped up in work and probably didn't even know what day it was. She was just wishing they could be a normal family and not be so absorbed in themselves and success. We sat side by side on our couch, her head on my shoulder. It was nice. I knew she'd had a good time but she almost seemed sad about it. It must break her heart a little that my family had paid more attention to her than her own had. Maybe true success is having just enough to pay your bills and be comfortable so that you can spend time with your family.

When White Eagle returned we took Lucie home. She got out of his truck reluctantly. "Happy Birthday," I said softly one last time.

She gave me a long speculative look and got out. I started to get out to walk her up to the porch, but she shook her head, squared her shoulders and headed for the door on her own. We waited until she was inside before we left.

"That girl's parents make me mad," White Eagle huffed.

"You and me both, but what can I do about it except clean up after them. At least she saw what a family is supposed to be like."

"There is that."

"There you go," I replied.

Tuesday Calvin seemed to have a new girlfriend. It was a girl I didn't know but I still watched. There was no way I was going to let him tromp on any girl. It wasn't right. He seemed to be starting out okay. He continued to talk to lots of chicks. They seemed to like his attention. What they saw in him I couldn't say. I thought he was lower than slug slime. Katie had gone back to her old group of buddies in math. I missed her, but I gave her space. Lucie was quiet and a little distant so I gave her space as well. I tried to be a quiet steady presence. Neither one of us brought up her birthday.

The guys and I had agreed to meet in the locker room to change and run to the shop. Personally I thought it was great to not be hampered by women but Adrian was thinking he really wanted another girlfriend. It was his life, so what could I say?

We headed out the back of the school and took the shortcut to the shop. The big hill still killed Marlo but he was getting better all the time. I took his backpack and duffle from him again today. "Maybe you should think about playing football with us this fall," I suggested.

Marlo looked at me in disgust. "Yeah, right. No thanks, but I will consider trying out for soccer. Won't my parents be surprised!" he wheezed. "Hey, in my honor, my mom has started a new healthy gourmet line to her home catering business. She wanted to put some of my research to good use."

"You two!" Adrian puffed at us. "We could be talking about that hot girl in my math class. She's fine!"

"Anyway," I said, "good for you Marlo, and have you had any luck finding any more *watchers*?"

"Nah, it's tricky but I have found the best way is to track 'hero' articles – except, there aren't even many of those. As we all know, you guys like to stay well hidden. I won't give up though. Most of the websites out there seem to be fakes. I'm doing what I can. I have to cover my tracks though because I don't want the wrong kind of people doing a reverse lookup and finding us." He had a very valid point. I hadn't considered all the intricacies to his work.

White Eagle was ready for us. He had us stretch and cool down. Then he sent us off to do all the little things we did around the shop. He'd even begun to teach us all kinds of minor repairs that could be done to the small appliances and equipment that came in to a shop like this. Marlo mostly did computer work but now and then he did some computer repair. White Eagle wanted us all to be self-sufficient. If nothing else he wanted all three of us to know if something could be repaired or if it was a lost cause. If it could be fixed, could we do it or did it need to be sent out? I seemed to have the best mechanical skills from all the car work I did with my dad. Adrian seemed to have quite the aptitude for all things electrical but he was gaining on me fast when it came to the mechanical stuff.

Today's special lesson with White Eagle was compass and map reading. We also worked with GPS units. Of course Marlo was really good with the GPS! White Eagle was surprised that I was as good as I was at orienteering. Miles, I reminded him. "Ah, of course," was his reply.

"White Eagle, why are we doing this stuff? I thought the real reason we were going to Nevada was to find that kid that might be like Owen," Adrian complained. He was not picking up the GPS or the compass skills very well.

323

"My dear young man, no skill learned is ever wasted. You never know when you may need it!" White Eagle replied with firmness.

"Yeah, but I'd rather be boxing," Adrian whined. Yeah, I thought, wouldn't we all? But I could see White Eagle's point.

On Wednesday we practiced packing our gear and going over what we would need for camping. Any supplies that we didn't already own, we were able to collect from the shop. Max was perfectly willing to give us stuff in exchange for all our hard work. He was also happy to provide us with a safe place to hang out and train. He didn't know what we were really doing but he appreciated what he knew of our contribution to the whole Clive and Darren ordeal. All three of us had earned most of our DC trip money by working there. Thanks to White Eagle it had been a win-win situation for everyone.

I was proud of Marlo. He only staggered a bit under the pack. In the old days he would have fallen over under its weight I'm sure. Adrian looked a little unsure of himself, but tried to put up a brave front. I was ready for this adventure. Bring it on! We would be dry camping which had the guys a little nervous.

"If my pack is already heavy and we don't even have our food or water packed yet, how are we going to be able to even walk?" Marlo asked in a worried voice. "You know this is a ten hour drive if we don't stop, right? This will be the longest I have ever been in a car."

"Bring your laptop and your car charger," I advised. "Maybe White Eagle will even let us watch a movie on your computer and we could listen to that last book we need to read for LA on your laptop!" I added, patting myself on the back for my own burst of genius.

"Don't start panicking. We'll keep some stuff stored in the truck. We need to put my canopy on today. I'll sleep in the truck and you guys will sleep in the tent. We'll keep our food and water in the truck. We shouldn't have to pack very much in to the campsite. We'll be in a state park by the Carson River," White Eagle responded.

We stacked our gear and went out back to wash and dry the truck. We cleaned out the inside and then rode over to White Eagle's to put the canopy on. Adrian and I lifted the front of the canopy, Marlo directed and White Eagle backed up under the edge. White Eagle assigned Marlo and me on one side. He and Adrian took the other. Then with everyone on a corner we lifted it up and on and bolted it down.

Thursday went much as Wednesday did at school. Calvin and I continued our stare-down. Lucie was a little distant and Katie ignored my existence. Marlo, Adrian and I could only think of our camping trip. We would pack tonight and leave first thing tomorrow morning.

After school, I swam, practiced diving and worked on my water rescue skills. Working one-on-one with the coach that White Eagle set me up with moved me along quickly. I would be able to take my lifesaving test soon. Then I would just need to keep my skills up. After swimming we met the guys at the shop and did our meal planning and grocery shopping. Mom let us store our cold goods in the extra refrigerator we have in our garage. We put all the nonperishables and our gear in the back of the truck. White Eagle prepared to take Adrian home, reminding us he would pick us up at seven in the morning. "Ugh, so early?" Adrian whined.

"Maybe White Eagle will let you nap in the truck," Marlo laughed.

We waved them off and I walked Marlo home. All we could think about was the upcoming trip. Marlo worried about all kinds of potential problems. I tried to convince him to go with the flow and that everything would be fine. I left him at his driveway and jogged home, sprinting the last bit. It was fun, almost as good as flying on my board.

EIGHTEEN

My alarm screamed at me at six. My room was lit with the shiny newness of the day, really clear and almost bluish. I got myself ready, put my room in order and picked up my school backpack with the items in it I needed to work on while we were gone. Fortunately there wasn't much. Most teachers were wrapping up the year. When I got back we had to face the last unit in health... Sex Ed. Yikes. The biology behind it didn't bother me; it was the sitting next to Lucie while I listened that bothered me. I would try to take my own advice and go with the flow like I had told Marlo.

I tried to be quiet but Mom was up and in the kitchen when I came in. "I thought I'd make you a good breakfast for the road. I'm so excited for you all and I think that there's lots of practical experience you'll be able to gain out there. Just be careful. We don't know anything about this young man you're looking for. I know you can handle yourself but I still worry. Don't give me that look, I can't help it. It's a mother thing!"

"I love you too, Mom," I said with a smile to soften the disgusted look I had given her, complete with eye roll. I could smell the pancakes so I took the flipper from her hand and turned them before they were overdone.

"Oh, thanks," she mumbled. She took eggs from the carton and started cracking them onto the grill. Then she put on some turkey bacon.

"Mom, do you miss the stuff we used to eat?"

"Some, but I feel better and have more energy. We'll still have a treat once in awhile but we can't eat treats every day. Your brothers haven't complained much. I'm proud of them. Your dad will be in for a real shocker when he... if he... I hope we can fix things. I'd like for us to make decisions with clear heads and not have your grandfather meddling, if that's what he's doing. Your dad mostly talks to your brothers on the computer. He asks about you. Maybe you could talk to him?"

"I talked to him when I asked if I could go on the camping trip, like you wanted me to. He's watching my grades on the computer. He knew how I was doing, down to the percentile. I'll try to repair our relationship but I don't feel like he is trying, so I sure don't give it my best. This time apart has been good for me at least; I don't feel so angry anymore. If Marlo's computer is up to the task I'll try to contact him from the road." She was probably right; I did need to try harder but I just didn't feel like it.

Mom dished up our breakfasts and we sat down to eat. I offered to clean up but she still wanted to cook for my brothers so I was off the hook and Alex would be on it. Yes! I could always do the cat box before I left if I had extra time, she offered. What a deal. Thanks, Mom. For her I would do it but even as much as I liked animals, I was about done with them. When I had my own place, some day, I thought I would go petless.

I cleaned up my plate at least. I rinsed it and put it in the dishwasher, then settled in to wait. White Eagle was only five minutes behind the schedule he had hoped to keep. We loaded up and I hugged my Mom goodbye.

By the interstate, Adrian was sound asleep in the back. It seemed like a great opportunity to pick on him a little bit - something we didn't dare do when he was awake. "So while the womanizer is out cold... What's up with you and Lucie?" Marlo asked curiously.

"I had her over on her birthday. She was so sad. Her parents either forgot or didn't care that it was her birthday. I was afraid that she'd be mad at me after the dance but she wasn't. I want her safe. I'd hate it if she ended up involved in a Clive-type incident, but I really like her. I'd do all I could to keep her from the ugliness we find ourselves in sometimes. I just wish she was my girlfriend but I'm afraid to ask her. Now she's playing the distance game again. I got that when she was dating Calvin, but why now? We get close and then one of us pulls away."

"I think that you've liked each other for so long that you're both just scared. I bet that you're both afraid that it will be hard to still be friends if it doesn't work out and neither one of you wants to lose that," Marlo said sagely.

"How come you're so smart, Marlo?"

"I am a student of the human condition," he laughed. "Just kidding. I watch people. I watch you and I have watched her. I think she's crazy about you but you're one of her best friends. Now me, I can be your best friend. No problem and no conflict. It's nice to be a guy. I kinda got my last woman because of you. Of course we know how that worked out."

"Hey Buddy, I know there will be plenty of others. Right, White Eagle?" I added, trying to draw him into the conversation.

"I was enjoying just listening. How did I get dragged into this? If I would've done things better I would have been married by now. Clearly I am not the one to ask for advice," he said, sounding somewhat embarrassed.

"You haven't been married?" Marlo asked.

"I was almost married once."

"What happened?" Marlo asked. I was glad because I had been curious for quite awhile myself.

"She died. She was a *watcher*, like Owen, but not nearly as talented. Her gift was her ability to know truth from lies. She was so beautiful. I told you I lost many young ones in the beginning. She didn't know what she was until she was twenty-three. I didn't have the heart to get that close to someone again. I didn't want to live through the loss. Then I had to lose my best friend, Miles. I hope I'm wiser now. I have to keep you all out of trouble. It's why I'm driven to teach you so many skills. I just hope I can teach them to you fast enough and at a high enough level that you all can take care of yourselves and each other," White Eagle said and then grew silent. Marlo and I looked at each other and then remained silent for a bit ourselves.

We stopped in Medford for lunch. Adrian had slept most of the way and woke up in a decent mood. We ended up not playing a prank on him because we knew he would get even. White Eagle took us to a truck stop he liked so he could gas up and get us some chow. The food wasn't too bad. He wanted to be sure we ate plenty because the next stop was Reno. He bought us some snacks to tide us over. Marlo plotted our course on his laptop using the GPS. White Eagle just laughed at him, saying he knew the way but Marlo claimed it was good practice for him. He was able to get an adapter to plug the laptop in to the cigarette lighter of the truck so with Adrian awake, White Eagle let us watch a movie while he drove.

When the movie ended, Marlo surprised me with a copy of our language arts book he had been able to download. He had taken me seriously when I had suggested it! We listened to the book all the way to Reno. We were even able to discuss it and fill out our logs for class. Homework managed the easy way! Yes!

So that we would have something to tell the folks when we returned, White Eagle drove us down the main drag so we could take in the sights. There were so many neon signs and flashing lights! I would have loved to have seen the insides of some of the casinos but we wanted to be set up before dark and do a little exploring.

We drove on to Carson City listening to the next segment of our book, courtesy of Marlo. He seemed to be having the best time ever. "I love this guy stuff," he said with a big smile. "Maybe I'll even like camping. Who knows? By the way, I have sworn off women for now. All they do is cause you problems and want all your time."

"Yes, but some of them are so fine. Take Jenn, she is *hot*! I could just watch her all day. Holding her is better yet and she can kiss. Wow!" Adrian enthused.

"Stop," Marlo grumbled. "I don't think I want to hear this. I have PG-13 ears. How do you get all these women anyway? Where do they come from? How do they find you? I don't get it!"

"What are you saying? I'm not a likeable guy?" Adrian complained.

"I am not saying that. It just seems like you go through girlfriends like tissues. You are kind of a *love 'em and leave 'em* type of guy, yet they don't seem to go away mad too often," Marlo marveled.

"Yeah, that's 'cause time spent with me is a learning opportunity," Adrian bragged.

"Wow, really?" I asked, emphasizing the *really* like I was asking him if he was truly serious. "Your ego is growing. I can see it happening."

"This from the guy who had a hot girl at the movie theater and missed a chance to make out," Adrian griped.

"I had only known her a couple of days and... BOOM!... I'm gonna make out with her? Are you serious? I didn't even know if I liked her like that yet."

"It was a missed opportunity," Adrian answered, like I was the one who was crazy.

"I couldn't hurt her like that. It wasn't right."

"You didn't even give her a chance. She's a nice girl and a good kisser. Geez!"

"Hold on. What?"

"Geez, all you see is Lucie. I dated Katie in September and you didn't even notice. Dork."

Well, great. Now I was really glad that things didn't go too far with Katie. It would have been too weird. "I'm glad you are a guy friend, Adrian. I think women need a warning sign when it comes to you. Aren't you afraid you'll hurt them?"

"It's mutual. I never make them do anything; I only take what's offered. What do you think I am?"

"I'm thinking you are a little over the top. My mom would say that you should be careful of how much of yourself you give away. You can move forward in a relationship but it's difficult to move backward, so make good choices. Most importantly, think before you act."

"Adrian, I'm glad the girls like you but it is a little disturbing how you charge from one to the next without even a break or time to get over one before the next. You are in a constant state of rebound," Marlo added.

"You're ganging up on me now?"

"Just think about it before you or someone else gets their heart broken," I said, hoping I was getting through. Adrian and Katie? Wow. Well, now I knew why she was so aggressive; she had learned from the best.

I could tell that White Eagle was working up to something or maybe he had indigestion. "You know, Adrian, you should probably listen to your comrades."

"And I thought you weren't going to give advice," Adrian huffed, crossing his arms over his chest and turning to look out the window. He rode the rest of the way in silence.

"Adrian, I'm sorry if I hurt your feelings. I worry about you, bro. I thought you should know," I said as we pulled into the campground.

"I guess," he huffed back and then brightened. "Hey, this place is kinda cool, ya know."

Leave it to Adrian to turn his attitude on a dime. He was right about this place though; it was kinda beautiful in its own way. I had been watching the Douglas fir and green of the Willamette Valley turn into rolling hills and stubbier trees. Now we were in the desert. We found our campsite and put up our tent. We prepped our fire ring and organized our supplies. White Eagle made sure we had flashlights before we headed down to scope out the river.

It was the in-between time where day is off to bed and the night is new and fresh. The sky was an amazing shade of red that lit the rocks and water with a pinkish glow. The air held a crispness that was a surprise to me. I could feel the heat leaving the day, as if the reddened sky was absorbing it right out of our surroundings. I was beginning to wonder if the river and rocks were going to stay stained pink.

All of a sudden everything changed. The sky turned purple black and the stars began to wink on. I wished I'd brought my sweatshirt. The stars grew brighter and more numerous than I had ever seen at home. It was as if I could see every detail of every constellation all at once. It was almost more than my mind could absorb. I leaned so far back to look at this natural phenomenon that I almost fell over. I heard White Eagle's low chuckle and realized that none of us were talking; we were all absorbing.

My gaze dropped back to the water. I was amazed that it could be so shiny in the dark. The moon had risen and appeared to dip and dance upon the surface. The sounds of the night creatures joined in with the music of the river to swell around us as nature's song commenced. I was glad to share this with my friends but I wished that I could have shared it with Lucie. Always Lucie.

We sat around the campfire strategizing our moves for the next day. Marlo had hacked into the school database and had our boy's home address and class schedule. Not that we would be around to catch him at school. Next Marlo pulled up a satellite view of Mitchell's neighborhood. Right across the street from his house was a park. How lucky can you get? We could hang in the park and watch the house and hope for a hit.

The guys and I dressed in sweats and crawled into our sleeping bags. We had a five man tent but it still felt crowded. White Eagle had set up an air mattress in the bed of his truck for himself. The night sounds were strange. Our *tenting it* was both exciting and left me wishing I was home in my own bed.

Something woke me. I wasn't sure what. I listened for a moment and heard nothing but the soft swish of the river and my tent-mates' sleep breathing. I opened my eyes and discovered that the first blush of dawn was caressing the tent, turning it a softly glowing blue. As quietly as I could, I slipped off my sweats and got dressed for the day in jeans, heavy socks and a t-shirt, topped by a flannel shirt. I grabbed my camera from my pack, laced up my boots and slipped out of the tent. Perhaps it had been the lack of sound that had woken me. White Eagle still seemed to be asleep. I went and relieved myself and then got the fire going again. I placed some water on to boil and checked out the menu for the day. I decided it was too soon to start cooking so I wandered down to the river again.

I loved the beauty of the northwest but there was a certain beauty to the desert too. I had never seen so many shades of beige. I watched the glints of light sparkle on the water and snapped a few pictures. The sun turned up the volume on the color of the sky. A few clouds caught bits of color in another in-between time and then it was day.

I strolled back to camp to find White Eagle up and poking the fire. "Did you find what you were looking for?"

"I guess you can only find something if you are looking. I think I was just absorbing. I wasn't trying to think about anything," I answered, wondering if this was another of his tests.

"Tell me, is your inner well of peace full?"

"Yeah, I guess it is. I don't know what to do about Lucie or my dad but I think that I'm okay with not fixing everything. Sometimes it's okay to just be, right?"

"Yes, Owen, sometimes we can just *be*. We all need to refill our well of inner peace so that we can deal with what is to come. We don't always have to rush into the next adventure. We need to appreciate the calm. You are like me, nature refills your batteries. For others it is something else. I think that for your father it is his work and for your mom it is raising you boys. I'm glad that you're learning what you need to be complete. Someday you may be in a situation where there seems to be no peace and you'll know how to find it in a place where it seems it could not exist."

We sat together, watching the flames dance in the fire pit. A rustling in the tent let us know that it was time to start breakfast and get on with the day. Marlo stepped out first with his glasses askew and his hair severely rumpled. He stumbled out and sat with us for a while in silent camaraderie. Adrian was a couple of minutes behind him. Unlike Marlo, he came out of the tent looking spiffy and ready to start the day. "What's cooking? I'm starving," he said enthusiastically.

After cleaning up, packing some snacks and securing our campsite, we hit the road for the trip to Fallon. We went prepared to spend the day at the park just in case. We made it more quickly than I had anticipated. Mitchell's house looked quiet. The car in the driveway was the one that Mitchell had a parking permit for, according to his school record. We pulled out a football and proceeded to toss it around while we watched the house.

At ten-thirty a kid matching Mitchell's description got in the car and drove off. We jumped in the truck and were off in casual pursuit. He headed back to the main drag and into Fallon proper. He pulled into a restaurant parking lot, got out of his car and headed inside. We pulled into a shop's parking lot across the street to watch. Marlo flipped open his laptop and White Eagle pulled out an old map and we pretended to look for tourist attractions around Nevada. We all took turns staring at the restaurant and watching Mitchell's car.

White Eagle asked me to hop out and check what time the restaurant opened and to touch Mitchell's 1987 Volvo. He doubted that it had an alarm system and it might tell me something. I waited for traffic and casually crossed the street. As I neared the Volvo I bent to tie my shoe and touched the car. It was on its third owner.

I focused on Mitchell. Well, yipee, he was a good driver and had been in no accidents. No wait, there was something here. I closed my eyes as I hunkered down by the front passenger tire.

"Hey, kid, what are you doin'?" an angry voice hollered.

I looked up to see a man in his middle years, scowl firmly in place, coming my way. "I'm sorry sir. I bent to tie my shoe and felt a little dizzy. I'm sorry I touched your car. I thought I was going to fall over. I just touched it. I didn't hurt it, I swear. You can look for yourself," I replied quietly. With my body language I told the man that I was young, vulnerable, and innocent, not a threat and possibly a little ill. I also hunched up, kept my knees bent and rounded my shoulders to appear smaller as I stood before him.

"Oh? I'm sorry. How are you now?" he asked, much calmer.

"Better, thank you sir. I apologize for touching your car. I better get going. My aunt will wonder what's keeping me."

I turned and walked two blocks east, crossed the street, removed my flannel shirt and headed back to the truck.

"Well, that was exciting," I said as I climbed in the truck.

Three pairs of eyes just looked at me. Marlo broke the silence first. "How did you do that? Even from here you looked small and scared."

"I bent my knees, hunched my back, kept my eyes down, and rounded my shoulders. Then I just kept apologizing for touching *his* car. He bought it. I got a hit too." Three pairs of eyes were now looking at me intently. "I really think Mitchell's our guy. I think he's just like me. I don't know if he knows who he is though and if that's true, I'm very scared for him. He needs a trainer, coach, mentor - whatever! I think he gets bursts of insight or something. He seems to avoid accidents with that car. He has done things that seem counterintuitive that get him *out* of trouble. We've got to learn more." Still all eyes were on me. "By the way, the restaurant opens at eleven." More dead silence and then all heck broke loose and everyone started talking at once.

When they calmed down we decided to go into the restaurant and order lunch and scope out our surroundings. Marlo would bring the laptop and White Eagle the old Nevada map and we'd pretend to strategize again. I ditched my flannel shirt, rearranged my hair and swapped my sneakers for my boots to maximize my height.

"How did you do that?" Adrian asked, sounding a little confused. "You even look a little different to me."

"White Eagle and I spent some time studying Miles, the former owner of my watch. He was a PI so he had lots of tricks to fool the eye. I think the guy in the lot was the manager. If I'm right, he'll be in the restaurant so I need to look like a different person. I plan to stand tall and exude confidence. I'll now also be part of a group so I hope he won't recognize me.

We drove over to the restaurant and walked inside. I brought up the rear just in case. Remembering what my mom had said about us all starting to look alike, the three of us did what we could to look related. Marlo would shrink himself and be the youngest. Adrian could be himself and I would do the tall, confident oldest brother thing. White Eagle asked the hostess for a large table so he and his boys could do some sightseeing planning. I asked Adrian and Marlo to choose some brochures from the entryway that they thought they would like.

She seated us at a six top table, restaurant speak for a table for six. I spied the guy from the lot and he did appear to be a manager. His gaze flicked right over me. I sat with my back to him so that I would draw less attention to myself. I'd have to count on the others to watch for him. It wasn't long before Marlo spotted Mitchell wiping down a table on the far side of the restaurant. He then proceeded to set it up for the lunch crowd. Next he went in the back and returned with water for all of us.

"Hi," I ventured. "So what would you recommend we see around here?"

"Um, there's a petroglyphs site off Hwy 95... and... there's some hiking you could do. Most folks go to Carson City or Reno. Good luck," he added shyly and headed off. White Eagle was staring at him intently.

When his attention came back to us, I asked, "Well?"

"Yep, he definitely has some kind of gift. It's a weaker one, but he has it."

A waitress came by to take our orders. We held with the dad and the kids on vacation illusion. We pretended to plot what we'd do the next couple of days and all the while watched Mitchell. At one point Adrian sucked in a breath. We all turned to look as a man across the way knocked his glass off the table. Mitchell appeared out of nowhere and caught the glass before it hit the ground. He looked around to see if anyone was watching. We all quickly averted our gazes.

The waitress brought our burgers and fries. Marlo suggested a hike later to burn off all the fat, carbs and sugar. While he was going on about nutrition I turned and looked toward the kitchen in time to see flames shoot up from the grill. There was Mitchell again. The cook's sleeve had caught fire and Mitchell was there ready to wrap a towel over his arm to snuff the flames. Again he looked around. This time he caught me watching.

As we were finishing our meal Mitchell came by to refill our water and sodas. I reached out and touched his arm. "We need to talk to you," I said softly.

"Look, I don't know you and I have to work. I don't want to lose my job," he answered firmly.

White Eagle gave it a try next. "Mitchell, we know who and what you are. We're here to help you."

"Wha... who... what if you're... No, I see that you're here thinking you can help. You can't. I don't need your help. Leave me alone."

"Mitchell, please," I begged.

"Fine, I get off at four."

Thanks to Miles, I have learned that if you look carefully right in someone's eyes the first few seconds they look at you - you can see the truth shining for just a moment before it's hidden away. Mitchell's eyes told me in a flash that he was *not* telling me the truth.

"Is there a problem?" Damn, I was so busy watching Mitchell, that I had missed the arrival of the manager. I quickly averted my gaze and sat very tall, forcing my shoulders back. Mitchell fled while the manager was there to distract us.

"Nope, no problem. I just thought the young man could suggest some things for me and my boys to see while we're in the area. I was hoping that someone close to their age would know what was fun to do around here," White Eagle smoothly put in.

"Oh well, fine then." He gave me a long look. "Do I know you?" Crap.

I deepened my voice. "No sir, we're new here," I said without looking at him.

Marlo went for a squeaky younger brother voice to draw his attention from me. "We're camping. We haven't been to the desert before."

"I see, well enjoy your visit," the manager said, turning to leave.

"Mitchell's lying. I need to see a copy of the shift schedule." I nodded at the guys and headed for the bathroom. I peeked back and saw that the manager had gone into his office and our waitress was presenting our bill to White Eagle. The rest of the staff appeared to be occupied. I headed for the kitchen. I tried to stay out of sight as anyone here would immediately know that I didn't belong. One cook had his back to me and the other was at a storage closet looking for a new chef's coat. There was a clipboard hanging right by the door to the kitchen. I snagged it and ducked around the corner of a workstation. I memorized Mitchell's schedule for today and tomorrow.

I peered around the corner and everyone still seemed to be busy. I hung the clipboard back up and slipped out of the kitchen. I walked toward our table but the guys were ready and met me at the cash register instead. We paid and left.

None of us spoke on the way to the truck. "He was lying. He gets off at two. Should we jump him here or follow him?" I asked, looking at White Eagle.

"That manager guy seems a little suspicious of us. Maybe we should follow him?" Adrian suggested.

"I think that might be best. Any other ideas?" White Eagle asked.

"Nope, so we have two hours to burn. Who brought their homework?" Marlo added.

We loaded up and drove around the block, parking in the lot next door so that we were ready to pursue.

"I see that we need to invest in some technology. We could use a magnetized tracker to put on cars and maybe a smaller unit to hide on people. I also need to start looking for headsets. I just don't know what we are going to get ourselves into," Marlo groused some time later. "I have to go to the bathroom but it's almost two. What if he gets off early?"

"Run to the gas station. We'll just have to find him again or come back and get you," I said, hoping I sounded practical.

"I'll go with you Bud, and then none of us are alone. If you have to leave us, come back when you can. We'll find something to do in town for a bit," Adrian decided.

They hopped out and walked to the gas station. White Eagle and I watched the restaurant and Mitchell's car. By two Marlo and Adrian were back but Mitchell was still MIA. At two-ten he came out, looked both ways and headed for his car. He got in, buckled up and headed back toward home. He didn't turn off to go to his housing development though. At the edge of town he pulled over and waited.

White Eagle pulled in behind him and I got out. I walked up to the passenger side cautiously. I held my hands loosely at my sides ready for anything. Mitchell rolled down the passenger window and sighed.

"What's up with you people?" he asked in exasperation.

"We just need to talk to you. Please listen to us."

"I give up, what do you want?"

"We need to go somewhere and talk about your ability. I know what you did at the restaurant. You do it all the time. Your good deeds have made the paper. There are bad people out there who will hurt you or even kill you if they find you. We want to help you."

"Fine," he said resigned. "Get in and I'll take you to Emiline."

I waved to the guys and climbed into the Volvo. "Who is Emiline?" I asked. I was pretty sure I already knew.

"She's my mentor," he groaned, "and she is going to be grumpy."

Well we would just have to wait and see. We continued on out of town and finally onto a ranch. A creek ran across the back of the property and a small cabin sat huddled in the trees. We were so far from the road that only the buzz of insects could be heard once the vehicles were shut off.

A tiny white-haired woman appeared on the edge of the porch leaning on a cane. I was surprised to find her dressed in well worn jeans, sneakers and a western shirt. "Well, well, well, what have we here, Mitchell?" Her voice was raspy from age, smoking or both.

"Ma'am," White Eagle said, seizing control of the situation.

She whipped a revolver from behind her back and pointed it at my head with a surprisingly steady arm. Marlo and Adrian dove for cover behind the truck. I froze where I was. Most of my attention was on her, the rest was taking everything else in. White Eagle also froze.

"They found me at the restaurant. If they found me, others could too, right?" Mitchell said, sounding scared.

"I warned you to keep a low profile!" she barked at him.

"I couldn't help it. I have to help them," he whined.

"Emiline, I too have a gift. We are looking for others like me."

"You will call me Miss Clairmont, young man!"

"Yes, Miss Clairmont. May we please come in and talk with you?" I asked in a gentle, soothing voice.

"I see that you do have talent. Those other two with you do not. The old man is your mentor isn't he?"

"Yes, ma'am."

A breeze kicked up and fluttered the leaves of the olive tree near the porch. The two sides of the leaves showed in the breeze, silver white on one side and green on the other. The silvered trunk and heavy branches groaned with the movement. In that moment Emiline seemed to falter. Mitchell must have seen it because he was moving before she began to crumple. I was at her other side helping to catch her before she hit the boards of the porch.

A tingling travelled up my arm and settled in my heart. "You are a good guy and a powerful one," she whispered as she closed her eyes. I immediately reached to feel the pulse in her neck. It was weak and light like the flutter of a baby bird's wings.

"Give her a minute. She'll be okay. She has angina." Mitchell pulled at a chain around her neck and came up with a vial. He unscrewed it, poured out some tiny pills into his hand and slipped one under her tongue. I held her shoulders and supported her head in my lap. White Eagle crept forward. I gently removed the revolver from her limp fingers, made sure the safety was on and handed it butt first to White Eagle.

"Not even loaded," White Eagle commented, checking the gun.

Emiline tried to open her eyes. She reached for Mitchell's hand. "You can trust this young man, Mitchell. I've seen his heart. He is pure *light*."

"Let's get her inside," Mitchell said making to lift her.

"I've got her," I said, "you take her cane." I kept one arm under her neck and shoulders, moved to her side and put my other arm under her knees. I rose up slowly from my squatting position, careful to keep my back properly aligned. She was lighter than I had thought but semi-unconscious weight is always heavier than when the person helps you.

Marlo peeked up from behind the truck as I was lifting Emiline and spoke to Adrian before scuttling forward. Mitchell held the door and we all entered. The place was nicer inside than it was outside. She had a small sitting area with an eat-in kitchen. An arched doorway indicated that there was some kind of side hall. Judging by the outside dimensions I would guess that there was one large or two small rooms through the arch.

"Do you want her in her room or on the couch?" I asked.

"Just put me in my chair and give me a minute," Emiline mumbled. "And tea," she added. I noticed that her tone was getting crusty again. I figured that she must be feeling better. I eased her into her chair and Marlo joined Mitchell in the kitchen. I could hear cupboards and pots softly banging around. I could also hear Marlo and Mitchell mumbling. Marlo called for Adrian and sent him on a mission out to the truck. He came back with a variety of snacks and headed for the kitchen, giving me a dirty look on the way past.

I stayed by Emiline and watched her come around. She rolled her head on her neck some and looked over at me. White Eagle had settled in on the couch across from her, where he watched her closely and waited.

"I had been retired for almost twenty-five years when I found this boy," Emiline began, her voice barely above a whisper. "He was looking for work and I needed help around here. I knew what he was the moment I saw him and I wondered, why now? Something has put things out of balance. Evil is growing so goodness is calling these young people. I wish that *goodness* realized that I am getting too old to train them."

"You still have enough left in you to see this young man through, otherwise he would not have come to you," White Eagle said, in that way of his that made you feel like you were receiving some great wisdom.

Emiline pushed herself a little more upright. "So, how did you find us and where are you from?" she breathed out on a sigh.

"We are from southeast of Portland, Oregon. We found you because one of the boys I work with found your boy on the internet. The young man who is so good with computers may not have the kind of talent that you are used to but he still is one of great ability."

"Hmmm, well, I just can't keep up like I used to but I do all I can. Mitchell works for me part time and I train him to the best of my ability. I mostly work with his gift. I have enrolled him in activities that we can find locally and cheaply. Maybe he could work with you some. His family is to be transferred soon and he will stay with me to finish his senior year. Then he will be off to college. I will miss him terribly but he needs more than I can offer."

Marlo and Mitchell came back into the room with trays of tea and snacks. "That's my good boy," Emiline enthused at Mitchell with a fond smile. Adrian leaned against the doorjamb, still grouchy.

"What?" I asked, looking at him.

"I find I'm again asking myself why I'm here. I feel useless and it bugs me. You get guns waved in your face and I hid. I guess I'm mad at myself."

"Adrian, you do contribute. I'm glad you're here and I'm glad that you were smart enough to get behind something solid. You and Marlo would have needed to rescue me if she had taken me out. I do need you," I said as I looked him in the eye.

"Don't be jealous, young man; the road these two walk is not easy," Emiline added.

Adrian shook his head and continued to sulk.

"You may have little or no gift but that doesn't mean that you do not have a role to play. There is goodness and caring in you. This work is not always about the talent or gift; it is who you are inside that matters. I'm not some fairy godmother that goes around bestowing talents; they are in you or they aren't. We must deal with the cards we are dealt. This is important! Remember it. Make the most of who *you* are. Don't waste energy wishing you were *him*," she said, pointing at me. "It's not what you have. How important is that in the overall scheme of life? It's what you *do* with what you have – now, *that* matters. The whole problem with you young people is you don't know what matters and what doesn't. Learn what matters and *choose* it."

Her speech seemed to have exhausted her. Emiline took a cup of tea and sipped it and sat for a bit without speaking. Adrian straightened his shoulders and moved over to sit by White Eagle on the couch.

"Let me touch you," Emiline said and pointed to White Eagle.

White Eagle stood and moved slowly toward her. He held out his hand to her. I could sense the energy in the room the moment their fingers met. They both remained frozen for a moment, their eyes a little wide. I did not look away from them but I could tell that the others were all looking at each other. I knew that the two mentors, White Eagle and Emiline, were evaluating each other. They may have been sharing a memory or powers. Who knew?

"Help him," she begged of White Eagle. "I need a nap," she said to the room at large. "Mitchell?"

"Yes, Ma'am," he answered as he picked up her cane and then escorted her to her room.

White Eagle asked Marlo and Adrian to clean up the kitchen and then to meet us outside for some sparring. He then led me outside and to the truck and began gathering some supplies including my practice shirt and gloves. I didn't even realize that they were in the truck.

"She doesn't have long. Miss Clairmont is eighty-nine. She has enough left in her to give Mitchell the basics. I'll need to help all I can and so will you. First, let's see if he can defend himself but don't hurt him. By the way, she doesn't know of any other *watchers*. Like me, she has been out of the game for too long. We'll stay in touch. For now I need you to show me what he's got so I know what I have to work with."

I reached for my practice shirt. "No, give it to him. You can take it."

Mitchell came out front looking a little worried. White Eagle called him over and suited him up in gloves, a helmet and my practice shirt. To me he gave only gloves. White Eagle had me take off my shirt and change back to my sneakers. "You may kick at him but do not connect." Hearing that and looking at me, Mitchell looked a little terrified.

I rolled my neck and stretched while White Eagle gave him instructions. Mitchell kept looking at me. He was a little taller than me but I think I had a good ten to fifteen pounds of muscle on him. As he listened to White Eagle his eyes grew wider. White Eagle marked out an area with his boot.

"Stay within the marked area. Begin."

I spent the first several minutes chasing him around the ring. Finally I just held still and waited for him to come to me. When he did, I could tell that he had some training but he was slow and I could easily evade him. It seemed to be a lack of practice rather than a lack of skill problem. He appeared to be more worried about doing it *right* than just getting in there and fighting with me.

Lightening quick, I feinted one way and then surprised him with a leg sweep sending him onto his back. I didn't pursue him and he rolled out of my way. "Don't just roll, jump to your feet. Show him, Owen." White Eagle advised from the sidelines.

I dove to the ground and sprang back up a few times in different ways. Mitchell watched with his mouth hanging open. "Try it," I encouraged.

It only took four tries and he was looking better as he jumped to his feet. He began to watch me more closely and started to mimic some of my moves. This was something I could learn from him. I needed to watch my adversaries more carefully and learn from them. Marlo and Adrian came out and leaned on the truck to watch. After several more minutes of sparring, White Eagle called Mitchell in and set Adrian on me while he talked to the other two. In a bit Marlo was in the ring as well, while Mitchell watched.

Adrian was tough enough on his own but tag teamed with Marlo was becoming difficult for me. They were starting to get in some good hits by the time White Eagle called them off. Emiline, I discovered, had made her way out to the porch to sit in a rocker.

"Well, well, well," she said as White Eagle called it quits. "What a show you do put on. I've not seen this many half dressed men in... well, ever. What a treat at my age." And then she cackled, clearly enjoying herself. "Come in and get cleaned up and we shall visit."

We all helped Mitchell with his chores and then took turns in the shower. Marlo got to shower first because he would be helping Miss Clairmont with dinner. Adrian said that he would help too. So he took the next shower. I'm more of a manual labor type of guy so Mitchell and I did the heavy lifting while White Eagle looked into some plumbing and electrical issues. I could hear Marlo and Adrian joking with Emiline through the open window.

"She loves you a lot you know," I said to Mitchell as we pruned up an overgrown tree out back.

"How do you know?"

"I can tell by her body language. I can kind of sense how she feels. My gift is mainly seeing images from objects. The dark ones call to me. The light ones are harder to read; they are peaceful, almost sleepy by comparison."

"I get little bursts of insight," Mitchell responded. "When something bad is about to happen, I get a small warning. I feel a pull in my belly. If I pay attention, I get a flash of an image and know that something bad will happen near me. I live in fear of ever being near a natural disaster. I think it would be totally overwhelming."

"White Eagle believes that we are, for the most part, only given what we can handle."

"I hope so. Hey, what does he help you with besides fighting?"

"Ah, he does teach boxing, karate, street fighting, some weapons and he teaches us how to hold our bodies. For him, body language and tone of voice are an art. He also helps me to control my gift and to focus it."

"Emiline teaches me how to control and focus my gift too. She's taught me many useful things but she has to farm me out for fighting skills. You look like you really could fight if you had to."

"I have and I do not recommend it. White Eagle also teaches us to use our heads and negotiation skills. He'd like us to *not* have to fight but he wants us to be able to defend ourselves if we need to."

"He told me he's afraid that I'll need to defend myself because people are learning about me. He thinks that *dark stalkers* will find me. Beware 'the dark side," he add, in a deep voice, using air quotes and making me laugh.

"Look, Mitchell, he does worry. Generally we don't want people to know about us but sometimes we have to let them know so that we can do our job. When you feel the pull and see an image you just have to fix it, right?" He nodded. "The same is true for me. I can't *not* fix things that I know are wrong. They're out of balance and the inequity almost... hurts."

"Yeah, I see what you mean. So how did you end up with teammates?"

"I guess that I'm somewhat of an anomaly. Most of us are loners or at least work alone. I've been friends with Marlo since

Kindergarten and with Adrian since about fifth grade. We spend so much time together that there's no way they wouldn't find out. Besides, Adrian is a great wingman and has really good charisma. He can charm anyone. Marlo is a computer genius. He's the reason we found you. So tell me, how did you find out what you are?"

"Emiline posted a request on the community board at church that she needed help with her property. I was looking for work and not many people will hire someone under eighteen. Somehow I think she already had her suspicions about me. When I showed up to interview, she took my hand and I got that electric shock up my arm and into my heart like you did today. I guess it doesn't work on *normal* people. She took me to my knees. All of a sudden the weird things that I felt and saw in spurts suddenly made sense. She explained it all to me and then we worked on the control thing. I think our gifts are always there and that they grow over time until, boom, they're too much and we find our mentor."

"There is truth in what you say."

"You know, it's funny. I didn't realize I was different until my freshman year. We moved here the end of that year. We weren't supposed to be stationed here at all, but all of a sudden this amazing job came open for my dad and they could take my mom as a civilian contractor. Emiline found me shortly afterward. I didn't know anyone here so a job seemed like a good idea at the time. She even let me work off the Volvo. She's kind of like a grandma I guess. I'm glad to have the time with her but my dad is about due to change duty stations again. They're going to let me stay with Emiline and finish my senior year. Then it's college anyway. I'll miss her and them."

"If you aren't ready to be on your own, maybe you would consider going to school in Oregon. There are lots of college options near where we are and I know that White Eagle would help you if he could."

"Really? That's generous of you. I understand that most mentors only work with one person at a time but then I can see that you guys are different."

"I could be mistaken but I think the time for us all to work together is coming. White Eagle was out of the game until he found me and then Emiline indicated that was true for her also. I'm afraid something big is coming."

Mitchell sent me in to take the next shower while he put away the tools and equipment we'd used. As soon as I was done, I checked on him but he was just finishing. White Eagle was almost done as well so I went to help in the kitchen.

Once again, Adrian's charm had done the trick. Marlo had won Emiline over with his cooking skills but Adrian just seemed to have a way with women. I think they were wrong about him. How could that not be a gift? He had Emiline giggling like a girl. She had good color in her cheeks now too.

The conversation around her table at dinner was happy and relaxed. I don't think any of us missed cooking over a campfire and Emiline Clairmont acted like our company was an unexpected gift. Mitchell was just happy to know that he was no longer alone. We headed out after cleaning the kitchen. We agreed to meet back at Emiline's on Sunday to do some more practicing with Mitchell.

When we got back to camp we did some survival training with White Eagle. We worked with our GPS units and did more compass work. We also practiced finding our way without a compass. White Eagle wanted us to try all these skills again in the deep woods where it was easier to get lost. We built shelters and purified water. He also taught us how to build a snare. I suggested that finding your way within a city would also be useful. Initially White Eagle frowned but then he agreed that it would be a useful skill. Right now we were only experts at surviving in the suburbs.

Sunday at Emiline's was fun and educational. It turned out that she had been on the rodeo circuit and had been a lasso tossing, horse riding, and knife throwing champ. She'd also been a trick rider in shows because of her exceptional skills of shooting and throwing knives from horseback. She didn't keep horses anymore but we practiced shooting and throwing. We hadn't gotten to do this with White Eagle so it was really fun to pick up new skills. Marlo didn't like the rifles much but he was decent with them. It surprised none of us that with his cooking skills he was a crack shot with the throwing knives! Adrian was really good with the rifle and when Emiline brought out one with a scope he was downright dangerous! Mitchell had learned these skills from her and was a really super tutor and assistant.

White Eagle worked with all of us on handguns. We only had limited knowledge of them from our time at the shop. We'd cleaned them and knew makes and models but we hadn't been to a range. Emiline had helped Mitchell build a range for shooting and throwing practice. The shooting was something she could still do and enjoyed. Her arthritis made the knife throwing painful but she still nailed quite a few rounds.

We left them after lunch with promises to stay in touch and headed for Carson City to be tourists for a little bit as part of our cover. We took the tour and walked around, ending at an old west style bar to drink sarsaparilla.

Back at our campsite we organized as much as we could for an early morning start. For dinner we cleaned out all the miscellaneous stuff we had left over that wasn't for breakfast and found a way to divide it up into suitable dinner fodder. We sat around the campfire and relaxed and looked at the stars. White Eagle talked about finding our way in the dark should we ever have to do so. We even practiced starting a fire without a lighter or matches.

I admired the night-darkened sky with its pin pricks of light and the bright moon. I felt like we had accomplished our mission and I was feeling pretty good. My ego swelled with the thought that I was already better at my job than Mitchell was. I knew that most of that credit went to White Eagle. I realized that this was the best I had felt in a long time. I tried to keep my dad and Lucie out of my head but the more I tried not to think of them the closer to the surface they would float. It was moments like this that I was ready for Lucie to be my girlfriend and to heck with the consequences. I kept asking myself how to make someone listen that didn't want to. That applied to both my dad and Lucie. I leaned back with my hands behind my head, my feet crossed at the ankles and pondered all the great mysteries in my life.

White Eagle finally kicked my boot, probably thinking that I had gone to sleep. "I thought you were out but now I see that you are just deep in thought. Marlo and Adrian hit the hay and you didn't even notice. What's got you so absorbed that you don't even know what's going on around you?"

"Lucie and my dad. I don't know what to do about either one of them."

"What's the rush? Maybe just let it be and see if it doesn't work itself out."

Could it really be that simple? I guess for now he was right. It was all I could do. "I'll see you in the morning then. Thanks for bringing the three of us out here. I think that every one of us got a lot out of this trip."

"You are most welcome. I think that this was a worthwhile adventure. You have about two and a half weeks left of school. Let's continue the way we have been; then this summer let's get together every weekday and leave your weekends open. I think we will add the shooting range - I don't want you using guns but if an emergency arises it would be good for you to be familiar with them."

"Is that like the swimming and lifesaving? You want me prepared for anything, don't you?"

"I do."

Well if that wasn't a scary thought, I didn't know what was.

When the first fingers of dawn reached out to caress the top of the tent, I again woke up. Having our trip end brought a sense of melancholy and happiness. My dad would be back soon to pressure us again to move but time at home meant time with Lucie. My time with her was also coming to an end. I still had the D.C. trip but I could almost see the last few grains preparing to leave the hour-glass of our eighth grade year.

I restarted our fire and put water on to boil much as I had the first morning. Then I once again went to stand by the river and soak up as much happiness and beauty as this place had to offer. I thought of endings and beginnings as the sun crept up the sky in this in-between time of night and day. White Eagle found me at the river watching it flow by. He put his arm around my shoulder and squeezed.

"It isn't your job to fix everything or even think about it so much. Relax and go with the flow. Don't hold the weight of the world on your shoulders. I know you have to be a grown up a lot of the time but please don't forget how to be a kid," White Eagle said softly.

"Okay," I whispered, not wanting to break the moment.

Breaking camp and heading home was... anticlimactic. We finished our homework in the truck and watched another movie on Marlo's computer. We dropped the guys off and then White Eagle got rid of me quickly enough so that he could go see Sarah. He said we could clean up the rest of the gear at the shop after school on Tuesday. I brought my personal gear in to the house. I hugged my mom and brothers and told them about the trip. After they went to bed I told Mom the rest of our adventures.

"If White Eagle can't put Mitchell up at his house maybe we could have him here with us," Mom offered.

"Mom, Dad still wants us to move. How would you offer someone a place to stay when you may not even be here?"

"Owen, I know that we can't go. I won't go. I could leave you with Sarah and White Eagle but I won't do that. What you do is dangerous. I don't want to miss a thing. I would never forgive myself if something happened to you and I... if I wasn't here... I thought about a lot of things while you were gone. I'm staying here with you boys. Your dad can stay here if he wants. If he won't, that's his choice. He has to choose to believe in us and trust us or not. He had a good job here. I can go back to work. I chose you. Do you understand? My heart tells me that I have to choose you. I have to listen to my heart," Mom said, her voice cracking.

I put my arms around her and held her. Something had broken in her while I was gone. "Mom, what happened while I was gone?"

"Your dad is coming home for your graduation and to see you off to Washington D.C. He's convinced he's coming home to help us pack. I'm not looking forward to another big argument. He simply can't fathom us not agreeing to go. If this job really wasn't a choice, then maybe things would be different, but that isn't the case. He has basically chosen your grandfather over us. His father cut him off and out of his life when he married me. Now he sees his way back but your grandfather doesn't really want us around. He's just getting older and has decided that he can't live without his son. Well I'm not choosing to live without mine!"

"I wish we had a way of knowing what Grandfather is really up to."

"Me too. Hang in there and I'll try as well. They say it's darkest before the dawn. Never give up hope." With that she went off to her room for some sleep.

NINETEEN

The guys fit right back into school like nothing had changed. I felt like I was someone else living my life. It was like I didn't quite fit anymore. I watched other students walk by and realized that I really didn't belong here anymore. I was both old and young. I felt like an observer instead of a participant. With a sense of relief and sadness, it was all coming to a close. I tried to do what White Eagle said and go with the flow but I was like a boulder in the stream, stuck and unmoving as the rest of the world flowed by.

I perked up a little in choir. Lucie gave me eye contact and actually smiled. She walked with me to science. "So how was the campout?"

"It was good. The desert was more beautiful than I expected. We learned some new stuff. White Eagle is all about a teachable moment," I said smiling.

"You seem sad today. What's going on?"

"I'm still having trouble with my dad and I'm worried that we may yet have to move."

"No! You can't move. You're my only real... I mean, you're my best friend," Lucie gasped, distraught. "Please don't go."

I put an arm around her shoulders. Lucie and my mom seemed as if they were in similar places mentally with the whole moving idea. It was nice to know Lucie cared so much. I guess best friend was the best place she could be for now. A big part of me wanted more but I was glad that she had moved me up to that status.

We walked on in to science, my arm still around her. Lucie put her stool right next to mine. I don't know who was sucking up whose goodness and light today. Our teacher checked the progress of everyone's labs as we worked on another plant activity. We had two weeks before they were due.

"Lucie, tell me about your weekend."

"I didn't really get one. I didn't tell you before but I got hired by a local cheerleading supply company to model. The shoot took all day Friday and was tiring. The staff was nice but some of the other girls... not so much. It's very competitive. There was a separate shoot on Saturday and Sunday for our local department store's fall line. Some of the same people were there. Some of those girls..." Lucie shuddered. "They're just downright mean the way they cut each other down. It's worse than gymnastics. In a way it was funny though. I'm not quite tall enough to model and I'm too tall for gymnastics. I can't win."

"My mom would tell you that you only need to be the best Lucie you can be and that the other stuff doesn't matter."

"I wish I had your mom. My dad is worse actually than my mom but they both want me to lose weight, yet grow taller so I can do runway work. I don't want that. I'm saving almost everything for college and I figure I'll have enough when it's time to go if I keep working. They make too much for me to get any financial aid but they won't help me. I have to go, but they think it builds character if I pay for it on my own. I'll never make them famous which makes them sad. Sometimes I feel like I'll never make them proud either."

"Lucie, I'm so sorry for your pain. I wish there was more I could do."

"You know what? We've had our ups and downs but one thing is for sure... You're always there for me even when I don't think I want you there. Like when you helped me with Calvin... He was what my parents thought they wanted. Did you know that he is on his third girlfriend since me? I'm not sure that he cares about any of them. I took a page from your book and really started watching him. He treats none of them with respect. He seems to be a bad boy and appealing until you really get to know him. He always picks the pretty ones or the popular ones. Girls want to date him because they think he's popular. He still hates you, by the way."

"I'm not worried about Calvin."

"Just watch your back, okay?"

Our teacher wandered over. "You know, I would give you a bad time about talking except for two things... You have the two highest scores in this class and you're farther on your plant lab work than anyone else. At least try to pretend you're on task, to set a good example, okay?" she said with a smile.

"We'll do our best," I replied, smiling back. To Lucie I added, "My mom did our plant measurements while we were both gone and recorded them on the clipboard. Alex helped her. We might want to start compiling the bulk of our data this weekend and then we can put the finishing touches on it next weekend. What do you say?"

"Sounds good."

"Do you have to work this weekend?"

"I haven't booked any jobs until after our D.C. trip," she replied with a smile. Then she sobered. "Then it's only two years until I can drive and get a normal job though I know I'll have to buy my own car. I'm sure of it. They gave one to my brother so he could drive himself to practices. Since I'm no longer a star athlete, no car for me. It's just a guess though."

"You and I just need to hang on and see what comes, right? White Eagle would tell us to go with the flow."

Our conversation continued easy and smooth for the rest of the day. It was the best part of Lucie and the thing I would miss most if she ever left my life. It was one of the things that scared me about her being my girlfriend. If we broke up, would she ever talk to me again? Katie and I hadn't actually been boyfriend and girlfriend and she still ignored me. It would be horrible if someone like Clive came along and did something to Lucie like he'd done to Max and me. Friends, we had to stay friends.

At the shop we cleaned all of the camping gear and White Eagle's truck. Marlo quizzed me on my lifesaving and water rescue information in preparation for my test. Then White Eagle started us on an online gun safety course.

The rest of the week and all of the next fell into a routine pattern: school, time at the shop, finishing up end of the year stuff for school and schedule planning for next year at the high school. Lucie continued to act the same. It was such a relief to be on the same page for once. It felt like we'd spent so much of the year at odds with each other.

Lucie had come over almost every Saturday since the beginning of May for us to work on our science project. We had raw seed and plant data we'd collected that needed to be put into organized reports, charts, graphs and tables to show our work. The time spent with her was a mix of joy, comfortable companionship and awkwardness all rolled into one. It passed much too quickly and dang if it wasn't hard to concentrate on schoolwork. All I wanted to do was talk to her and forget the school stuff. I could not believe that this would be our last Saturday together. We really had become best friends. I was sad that our time together was at an end. I knew that it would be challenging for us to see each other over the summer and I had no idea what classes we'd have together next year.

Lucie arrived a few minutes early. She had ridden her bike. My mom picked her up or took her home on occasion and her parents or her brother drove her to my house some but mostly her parents complained about the inconvenience of having to shuttle her around so we just avoided it. We were both glad that we had done the experiments at my house. Since my mom was a teacher she didn't mind at all and saw the necessity of a place to work in peace.

"Owen, you have changed so much this year. Do you even realize it? We could have done our plant growth experiments on you," Lucie stated out of the blue.

"What?" I gasped, flabbergasted.

"You're even taller. I can almost see you grow. All the boy round-ness has left your face. You're not as skinny as you were and, geez, do you shave now? I remember you from sixth grade. You're not that boy anymore; it seems like so long ago. I'm glad you really talk to me now. I thought you didn't like me for the longest time. Now our friendship is pretty comfortable. I think you know me better than anybody. I've spent so much of this year confused about how I feel and how you feel. I wish I hadn't wasted that time."

"I dunno Luce. I feel different now. I guess it's a lot of things and yeah, I have to shave a couple of days a week. It's kinda weird. Some days I feel like an adult and some days I just want to be a kid. As for how I feel about you... I've always admired you. I've found you to be smart, funny, outgoing and... beautiful."

"You know you're the only person who calls me Luce? I like it when you say it. I think I would have punched out anyone else," she said in true Lucie fashion. "I like it that you think I'm smart and funny and stuff. I haven't always felt so smart this year. You've been a really good friend and lab partner. You know, you're pretty much those things you said about me except for the outgoing of course. It took you forever to open up to me, but you always seem to be there when I need you. What would I do without you?"

I could feel a big dopey grin spreading across my face and she smiled in return. Things were like that with Lucie, serious and fun. Who knew? I'd never spent this much time with any other girl. Unless you wanted to count Adrian's younger sister and I didn't. My smile slipped off my face as I began to worry about Lucie get-ting close and learning too much of my secret. Worse, I didn't want her in any danger because of what I do. She seemed to find enough of her own.

"Why do you do that?" Lucie asked bewildered.

"What do you mean?"

"I don't know? Everything is going well and you're happy. I can feel it. Then this cloud passes over your face and I lose you. What's going on? What are you thinking?" she queried.

Now what? Push her away like I knew I should or be selfish and keep her around? "Luce, I'm... I'm not good for you. I shouldn't even be your friend. We should finish this lab and you should walk away and not look back," I said with remorse I knew she could hear.

"Owen, No! We're a good team. We're good lab partners and good friends. You really are my best friend. I look forward to seeing you each day. I want you around! You're the one person I know I can count on even when I... well, I push you away sometimes."

"I just think it's better for *you* if you aren't around me."

I could see her almost begin to quiver with anger and shame. She started grabbing up her books, her cheeks pink. Her frustrated, hurt eyes met mine and I felt my heart begin to break. She must have seen the raw emotion on my face because the books slipped from her numb fingers and back onto the kitchen table. I could feel tears begin to burn at the back of my eyes, but I couldn't seem to pull it together. She looked as bad as I felt.

"Why do you do that? Please don't leave me, Owen. Why do we hurt each other like this? We both do it. I hate it when you aren't around yet I push you away. You get close to me like at the dance and then you give me the cold shoulder. Why is that?"

"Oh Luce, they say there's a fine line between love and hate. In my case maybe it's love and worry. They are passionate emotions that all bubble just under the surface for me..."

"You hate me? You can't, what are you saying?" Shock and something like fear crossed her face as she interrupted.

"Of course you would pick out *that* word from what I said. No, I don't hate you. I like you too much but I don't want you to get hurt. I'm afraid you'll get hurt because of me so I push you away. Maybe I'm my own worst enemy. I don't know. You make me all confused too. When I'm with you my feelings are all mixed up. I want you to be safe. I'm not sure that I'm safe for you but I want you for myself. I want to be more than your friend, but I'm afraid we'll lose our friendship or I'll lose you if..." I choked out, my throat feeling tight.

Then she did something completely unexpected. She closed the space between us and wrapped her arms tight around my waist. My arms automatically wrapped around her. I could barely breathe. Her soft hair brushed along my cheek as she placed her head against my neck. She smelled amazing, like oranges and some exotic flower. I didn't want the moment to ever end. I'd been hugged by my parents and other family members. I'd been hugged by friends, both guys and girls, and of course by Katie. None of them ever felt anything like this. She pulled back a little and reached up to touch my face. I held my breath as her face came close to mine and she rose up on her tiptoes. Her lips were within a couple of centimeters of mine. I gulped and wondered if I should kiss her or not. She usually ran away if I tried. Fortunately she made the decision for me. Her lips touched mine, light as butterfly wings, and for an instant, time stood still. She kept one hand on my jaw and slid her other arm around my neck to pull herself up closer. She parted her lips a bit and she flicked her tongue along the edge of my lower lip. My chest felt light and achy, like all my molecules had suddenly moved apart. I slipped one arm up her back to her head and the other down to her waist. I parted my lips at the same time. I didn't want her to stop but she stepped back. This was different, amazing, wonderful and scary as hell. I had kissed her once but she had run away. Things would never, ever be the same with Lucie Ness. I'd had another taste of what I shouldn't, couldn't have.

"I like you too, Owen. I'll see you tomorrow. I gotta go now. Bye."

I stood there speechless as she grabbed her books, slipped out the front door and was gone. Heaven help me. What do I do now? Was she my girlfriend? Did I want that? Of course I did but I shouldn't put her in danger like that. I didn't want to hurt her, yet the thought of her with anyone else made an ugly green monster within me raise its head and sniff the air. Lucie may be a bigger problem than my growing abilities. She was a distraction spelled with a capital D. Maybe I just needed to get her out of my system.

Lucie was back on Sunday so that we could type up our lab to turn in on Monday. We'd each finished up our part so that it was ready to go. What I was not expecting was to have her show up a whole hour early. I was still in the yard, shirtless, cutting the grass with my ear buds in, listening to music. I was good and sweaty as well as dirty and I was sure I smelled *great*. Lucie hopped off her bike and just stared. I wondered if my fly was unzipped. I did a quick check as I shut off the mower and pulled out my ear buds.

"Hey Luce, you're early. I'm almost done here and then I'll take a shower. Or did I get the time wrong?"

I approached her. She had not moved from the driveway where she stood motionless, holding her bike. She continued to stare. "Luce?"

"Huh?"

"Did I get the time wrong or are you early?"

"I had to get out of the house. I'm sorry I interrupted your work. I'll... um... wait."

"You can put your bike by the garage and then wait inside or out here, if you want." She was still staring at my torso like she was in a daze. It was making me feel self-conscious and something else. I knew I was in pretty good shape but it was nice to be... what? Appreciated? Noticed? Admired?

I walked back to the mower and had to pull it three times to start it. She had me pretty distracted. Lucie had moved her bike to the garage but was still watching me. I tried to ignore her as I finished. When I was done I started rolling the mower to the garage. Having her watch me sent strange bursts of electricity through me. Lucie popped up off the front steps and followed me. "You never did tell me if you were early or if I was confused," I repeated.

"I was early. I had to get out of the house and I wanted to see you," she almost stammered, then seemed to catch herself. "I didn't mean *see* you, see you... I meant be here sooner to... You know, you could model. Look at you."

"I don't want my face out there. I've got plenty going on for work. Besides it would cut into my time with White Eagle and the guys. How is the modeling thing going for you?" Geez, what was wrong with me. She had short-circuited my brain and of course I couldn't have my face out there. It totally went against low profile. My face wasn't even on any social site on the computer. Mom had never put many family pictures up and now all our accounts were locked up pretty tight.

"I just get small stuff. I've netted around five hundred after expenses, nothing big. At least my parents can brag that I've been in a couple of catalogs. I mainly get sports stuff. I'm not thin enough for fashion. They want me to lose at least five more pounds and I think it's stupid."

"Luce, you don't dare get any thinner. I worry about you as it is. At least you look healthy again. I'm not seeing the dark circles and you don't seem so tired."

"I'm trying to follow Marlo's advice. When I do, I feel better. My mom still has the housekeeper weigh everything I put in my mouth. No sugar, low fat, low carb and low calorie. Ugh. It's so disturbing. I also found that being hungry all the time was making me grouchy. The housekeeper sneaks me food when my parents aren't looking. Bottom line, I ignore my mom, who isn't a nutritionist, and do my own research with Marlo."

I walked her into the house. "Make yourself at home and I'll go shower and be right back." She actually blushed. What was with her? She'd never acted like this before. It had to be the kiss yesterday. That was way past friend, but she'd started it.

I tried to hurry but I dressed carefully anyway. Then I actually tried to style my hair. I put on cargo shorts and my old Metallica t-shirt. I liked the color and it fit well and was soft. I figured she'd like it. I jogged down the stairs to find Lucie talking to Alex. They had out one of our old family albums. They were laughing and smiling together as they poured over the pictures. Lucie flipped back to my eight-year-old self holding a brand new baby Lucas as Alex peered over my shoulder, grinning like he'd just gotten the best gift ever.

"Hmmm, I can't decide whether I like this picture or this one better," she said as she flipped to one further back of my three-year-old self in the bathtub. Thank goodness for the bubbles. "Or maybe this one!" She flipped closer to the end and pointed to a picture taken of Adrian, Marlo and me last summer, all in our swim trunks at a pool. None of us were looking at the camera and we were all laughing and goofing around. You could tell we were all having a great time. "You've all changed." She looked up and I could see something in her eyes. "What are you three doing?" she asked, and then looked at Alex like she had let slip something she shouldn't.

I looked at Alex and indicated with my head that he should *beat feet* out of the room. He gave me his signature impish grin and took off.

"You tell me it's dangerous to be around you. You tell me that it isn't safe to be your friend. What's going on? What are you involved in?" she asked, concerned.

"Let's just say that I'm accident prone," I replied, looking for a safe yet satisfactory answer.

"Of that, there is no doubt, but we both know it's more than that!" Lucie said, exasperated, as she stood and walked toward me. She brushed the hair off my forehead and looked again at the slim white line where the evidence of my adventures with Clive remained. Then she pushed up my chin and looked at the scar Sarah had given me. She put a hand on my ribs as if she was remembering the hurt and pain I'd suffered. "Tell me," she begged.

I stood in indecision. I wanted to tell her. Would she laugh? Would she believe me? Could she handle it? Was it safe for her to know? She watched my face as all the emotions I was feeling travelled freely across my face: Hope – fear – worry – love - resignation. "I… can't tell you. I'm sorry." I dropped my head with regret. Lucie's hand slipped from my side.

"Well let's finish our report then. At least we have that." I could hear the sadness in her voice. I wanted to scream. I wanted her to know how helpless I felt. A part of me wished we could run away from it all, yet I knew I couldn't do that. I dragged my feet on the way over to our family computer and sat down next to Lucie. She put in her flash drive and we began to compile everything we would need for our report. We remained completely work oriented and spoke of nothing else until the last page came off the printer.

"I'll keep the flash drive as back up. You take the hard copy and turn it in. I'll see you tomorrow. When you get everything figured out, you let me know. Maybe we're just destined to be friends. I hoped it was... more. I tried at least." She hugged me and left. She looked back at me at the door. I knew she wanted me to say something. My lips remained locked, my heart in my eyes. I felt a headache coming on as the front door clicked shut.

Science on Monday wasn't any better. Lucie was coolly professional. She was even dressed the part. She looked more like she was ready for the office than for the classroom. Her frosty exterior did help in health though. I still sat right next to her and strongly felt her pull and presence but it was easier to pay attention with her ignoring me.

Tuesday and Wednesday went much the same way. My heart fractured a little more each day but I still couldn't bring myself to talk to Lucie about the real me. Marlo, Adrian and I spent much of our free time practicing for our singing debut. I thought we were sounding pretty good. Unfortunately our song made me think of Lucie.

Eighth grade promotion day started sunny and bright. We had practiced plenty and I knew we were ready to sing. Today was not a normal day as we would practice our ceremony and sign yearbooks and hang out. I had hot tea with lemon and warmed up my voice for singing.

We spent all morning practicing lining up and rehearsing. I was mentally in a place where I just wanted it all to be over. Most of the kids were bubbly and oblivious. I was looking at the end of eighth grade with a mix of melancholy and relief. Suddenly I truly knew what they meant when they called something bittersweet. It had been quite a year. Our experiences had brought me Lucie and taken her away many times. All of us had grown and changed. I wasn't sure what next year would bring. For now I had White Eagle and my boys, my brothers, my mom and Sarah - all of whom would be here today. No one knew if my dad would make it or not.

Lucie sounded amazing on her song, "Keep Holding" On by Avril Lavigne, but maybe I was just biased toward her. When it was our turn to sing all I could think of was her. I looked right at her as I sang "Shape of My Heart" by the Backstreet Boys. I tried to tell her all the things I couldn't say otherwise through the words of the song. Marlo and Adrian were doing a perfect job of backing me up. Our voices blended perfectly in testament to all our hours of practice. Halfway through the song I finally dragged my eyes away from her and looked at other parts of the audience. I brought my eyes back to her and her face looked… stricken. To concentrate, I looked away. Adrian sang his solo bit and I dropped to the background. Then Marlo stepped up for his turn to solo. We were sounding *good*. I could see feet tapping in the audience; we had them eating out of our hands. The yelling and screaming when the song ended was deafening. We bowed three times. I looked up to where I knew Lucie would be and her seat was empty. I felt another crack fissure across my heart.

I tried to be happy and celebratory for my family. My family, with White Eagle and Sarah, Marlo and his parents and grandparents and Adrian, his family and Max all decided to go get pizza and visit. I felt a change in the atmosphere outside the school. I turned and saw my dad walking toward us. "Congratulations, Owen," he said. It was almost as if a stranger was offering up the sentiment. A tenseness settled over our small gathering like a heavy layer of fog in winter.

"Thanks, Dad," I replied stiffly. "We're going to pizza. Would you like to join us?" Geez, did that sound as awkward as it felt?

"That would be nice. Thank you," he returned in the same stiff manner. Lucas and Alex looked from one to the other of us. I realized that everyone was looking at us. I met White Eagle's gaze and remembered what he had said on our campout about finding peace when the well was empty. I was aching. I had allowed Lucie to empty my well today. I couldn't even find her to tell her... What? Goodbye? Good Luck? Don't leave me? I love you? Congratulations?... Instead I took a breath and looked at Alex and Lucas. "What do you say guys? Shall we go get some pizza?"

I would draw some happiness from my brothers, friends and the people who loved me and put it in my empty emotional well. Then I would have to find the strength to deal with my dad.

TWENTY

Life went on almost normally for the whole first week of summer vacation. Well, normal for me anyway. I ran three days of the week, worked out with the boys another three days and met with White Eagle once to work on my mental gift. I was also still working on my swimming skills. I would complete my lifesaving class on Saturday. I was looking forward to our D.C. trip in about a week. For the week that we were gone we would be off our special diets and we would skip our workouts. What a relief because I needed to get some junk food back in my system!

It would also get me away from my dad while he and my mom tried to work things out. We had an uneasy peace, he and I. We didn't talk about my gift or my time with White Eagle. He tried to fit in like he had never left but we all knew things would never be the same. My grandfather was a taboo subject. A part of me wanted to go see the man for myself and figure out what was going on. I suppose it wasn't my mystery to solve. Although it was well hidden from my brothers, I knew that Dad was sleeping in the office upstairs. I didn't know if this was a visit or if he was back to stay. I for one was still waiting for the big explosion regarding our stance on moving.

The morning of the trip arrived, bright and cool. Forty-three of us from two middle schools met up at the airport with our chaperones. Adrian, Marlo and I would be sharing a room with another boy from our school named Mark. I didn't know him well but he seemed like an all right guy. His friends weren't on the trip but his girlfriend was. I doubted we would see him much except at bedtime. My eyes as usual were drawn to Lucie across the crowd. She was chatting with her parents and her friends. I had never really been able to observe her parents much before. They seemed serious and almost uptight. I knew that Lucie had an older brother who was going to be a senior this next year. I knew that Lucie's white-collar parents wanted him to get some amazing sports scholarship and go to an Ivy League school. I felt bad for the guy. What a lot of pressure - perfect athlete and perfect grades. What a lot of worthless pressure. Well that was my opinion anyway. I thought it was enough to be your best self at every opportunity and speaking of opportunities... "Excuse me a minute," I mumbled to my buddies as I worked my way through the crowd to Lucie. "Mrs. Ness, Mr. Ness," I said with a nod when I reached Lucie's side. I looked at Lucie and offered to take her bag up to be checked in.

"That's okay. I'm fine. Mom, Dad, you remember my friend Owen. We did the science project together."

"Yes, of course," her mother said stiffly as she looked me up and down. Her look seemed to say that I wasn't good enough for her daughter but I refused to break eye contact.

I only did when her father spoke, "So you are Owen. How do you do, Son?" I smiled politely and shook the man's outstretched hand. I hate being called 'son' by condescending adults. He squeezed a little harder than one should in polite social situations but two could play at that game. I figured he didn't like the power game I had just played with his uptight attorney wife. I looked him right in the eye. I was glad for all the things my parents, teachers and White Eagle had taught me. I conveyed, with every ounce of my being, that I was worthy, brave, intelligent and not to be underestimated. It was a tricky game to play, but he dropped his hand and gaze first. Good, round one goes to me. I was pretty sure that the reason Lucie pushed me away sometimes had to do with her folks.

"Well let me know if you change your mind about the help. Maybe on the way home after you get some souvenirs," I smiled and headed back to my boys.

Ever observant, Marlo asked, "What was that all about?"

My laugh came out a little sharp as I answered, "A little power struggle with Lucie's parents. I wanted to say 'hi' and properly introduce myself. I don't think they like me much, but then maybe they don't like anyone who likes their daughter. Maybe they think I'm another Calvin. Remember how they thought he was so great in the beginning?"

"Geez you're brave. You never would have done that a year ago. Come on, let's go get checked in." Marlo was right, I had changed - I was now a 34-year-old man in an almost 15-year-old body. What a combination!

I had pretty much pushed Lucie out of my mind as we hugged our parents goodbye, passed through security and found our seats on the plane. The three of us sat together in a row of three seats. I couldn't see Lucie but I could feel her eyes burning holes in the back of my head. She had barely spoken to me since the fiasco at my house on the Sunday we finished our plant lab. I was pretty successful at focusing on Marlo and Adrian for the flight. We were all feeling almost giddy as we made our final descent into the Dulles International Airport.

Lucie watched me every moment that she thought I wasn't looking. Otherwise she tried to remain coolly aloof. I wanted desperately to get back to the friendship and camaraderie we had shared at the end of our plant lab. Then she had tried to be my girlfriend but she couldn't stand that I had a secret. She wouldn't get close to me until she had completely emptied my closet of secrets. No more skeletons, but I couldn't tell her. I wanted to but I just couldn't. It was as if my secret was locked away. Nothing would come out when I tried to tell her.

Our days were very full of touring. We were busy from sunup to sundown and then some. The guys and I hung together, laughed, took pictures and ate junk food. Lucie and I constantly watched each other. Adrian said little because he was watching a girl himself. Marlo watched me with a worried look on his face. It was like travelling with my mother.

"You two are killing me. Why don't you just kiss and make up? Watching you pine for each other is almost more nauseating than having you together. Geez!" Marlo finally burst out the third day of our trip.

"She wants to know about me. She suspects things. I can neither confirm nor deny anything. I've tried to tell her who I am and I just can't. I guess I'm more afraid of having something bad happen to her than I am of losing her."

"I'm insulted. Did you never once worry about my safety?" Marlo asked, in a sarcastic tone, and then added, "You've put me in some amazing positions. Let's see, I have spied on and been pursued by drug dealers and murderers AND I've had a gun waved in my face. She's tougher than you think. If I can live with you, she can. You've let her get you so distracted that you haven't even noticed the biker dude dressed in black. I've seen him at least twice that I know of. He skulks around the edges of places we visit. I'd think that he had an itinerary but then, how hard can it be to follow a tour bus. It could be a coincidence but it doesn't feel like it. He doesn't really look at the sightseeing stuff. He looks at us. Here, look," Marlo said, pulling out his digital camera and setting it for viewing pictures. "I caught his image at the Washington Monument and at the Lincoln Memorial."

"Damn, Marlo, I really am slacking!" I said as I looked at the two pictures of the same guy. "Is he here now?" I asked, concerned.

"I don't see him at the moment. Have you tried to *feel* the area like you do sometimes?"

"I guess I have pretty much shut everything down for the trip. I just wanted to be a kid and have a good time." I sighed, frustrated with myself.

Our group was called next into the White House for our tour. I looked for Adrian who of course was in the middle of a group of girls from the other middle school. He was clearly too busy to help us. This would be up to me and my faithful sidekick, Marlo. I took ahold of Marlo's elbow and closed my eyes for a moment. I ignored the drone of the tour guide. When it was time to move to the next section I let Marlo lead me like a guide dog. I was bombarded by tons of information begging for my attention. Every human emotion and thousands of objects wanted my attention. I shut it back off. It was too much to even sift through.

"I can't do this, Marlo. There is too much here. I can't sift through it all. I would be here for hours. We'll have to just keep our eyes open for now." I looked automatically for Lucie and saw her watching me with concern. After some clear indecision on her part she made her way over to us.

"Are you okay? You don't look so good," she said, sounding worried.

"I have a headache. I'll be okay. Thanks, Lucie," I said, relieved that she cared enough to ask, yet angry with myself for letting her catch me at work.

"I have some stuff with me if you need it," she offered.

"Thanks, Luce. I'll have a caffeinated soda pop when we're done here and I'll let you know if I need anything else, okay?"

"Sure," she answered as she gave me one last hard look and moved back over by her girlfriends.

Marlo patted me on the back and our tour moved on. Marlo and I stayed on high alert. There was no sign of the guy on our tour. They let us out a different door than we came in. As we exited I felt a strange creeping sensation travel over my skin. It raised goose bumps on my arms and the hair on the back of my neck stood up. Marlo gave me a startled glance as I stumbled. I felt like I'd passed through a sick energy field. I looked around and spotted our guy. He was staring intently at our group from behind the fence. No one else seemed to notice. I looked back at the rest of our group as they exited the building. Lucie shuddered as she left the building but that could have been anything.

Marlo and I took turns watching him as we moved forward to load up on our bus for our next destination. Adrian smiled and waved at us, happy as a clam, in the middle of his group of women. We decided to let him have his fun. He was easier to get along with that way.

371

"What happened to you as we left the building?" Marlo asked in concern.

"I'm pretty sure we were just scanned by our boy. It's the kind of feeling that I think you would get if you discovered something dangerous crawling on you, like a black widow spider or something."

"Tomorrow we go to the Smithsonian and then we're on our way to New York. I wouldn't think he'd follow us there."

"I sure hope not. I don't know who or what he is. I don't think I'm ready for the big bad something that I know is coming for me eventually."

Two more days of high alert and we should be okay. Marlo and I could do that. We would bring in Adrian if we had to. It was a relief to go back to our hotel. We had a little extra time tonight and anyone who wanted to could go swimming. Marlo and I knew we had to go to keep an eye on everyone. Suddenly I felt more like a chaperone than a student on the trip.

Going to the pool turned out to be a big mistake. I couldn't take my eyes off Lucie. No bikinis were allowed on the trip but her suit showed off plenty of her slender, athletic form. Her suit was the same color as her eyes and really set them off. She was having fun with her friends and did a good job of ignoring me. I wished that I could do the same. The way the light caught the droplets of water on her skin made it glitter like diamonds. I watched her giggle and laugh as she went with her friends to line up at the diving board. She held her arms crossed over her ribs like she was cold. I could tell she was as she shivered. I watched the water run off of her in rivulets. I was most fascinated by the drop of water that ran from her collarbone and disappeared into the front center of her suit right between her...

"Stop it!" Marlo elbowed me hard in the ribs.

"What?" I asked startled, looking at him.

"What is wrong with you? Your eyes are burning. It's embarrassing. I think you were drooling. Get ahold of yourself! Other people are starting to notice," he said, exasperation clear in his tone.

I looked back at Lucie. It was her turn to dive. She was just as graceful and beautiful as I imagined. She swam almost the whole length of the pool before she broke the surface, coming up nose first so that her hair was skimmed back by the water. She looked like a water nymph.

"Oh, for heaven's sake. You are unfit to live with. Go talk to her. I'll take over the watch. Go. I can't stand it!" Marlo said, shoving at me.

I walked to the edge of the pool in a daze. Lucie stood in the water and leaned an elbow on the edge while watching her friend dive. I wished I was as smooth as Adrian. I wished I was as charming.

"Hey, Luce." Oh give me a break. Was that all I could think of?

"What's up, Owen?" she asked, tilting her head to the side.

"I just wanted to tell you that..." My throat locked up again. I swallowed hard and tried another track. "You look... amazing." She suddenly looked self-conscious.

"I modeled this suit and as part of my payment they let me keep it," she said shyly.

Lucie shivered so I reached down an arm and hauled her out of the pool. I snatched a towel off the nearby stack of hotel towels and wrapped it around her shoulders, keeping ahold of the ends. I was completely unaware of everything and everyone around us.

"Lucie, I miss you. I miss my friend and..."

"Owen, until you can tell me what is going on with you... I just... I just can't. You're keeping things from me and it hurts. Why can't you just be honest with me?" she pleaded.

"I..." a drop of water travelled down the side of her face and held me transfixed. I watched as it moved down to the corner of her mouth and her tongue flicked out to capture it. I was completely lost. I moved my mouth toward hers. Just as our lips touched I was shoved hard from the side sending me into the pool.

I stood shaking the water off of me. I looked at Lucie. She was trying not to laugh but there was regret in her eyes too. My third roommate, Mark, stood next to her laughing his head off. "No public displays of affection, my man! Get a room. Oh wait, you can't, you're underage!" He laughed so hard he bent at the waist and held his sides like they might burst at the seams.

Mark had barely talked to me the whole trip and he picked *now*? I stayed in the water for a bit to cool off. I swam laps like a man possessed. Lucie went back to her friends, the moment completely lost. Mark would pay. I would find a way to ruin a moment with his girlfriend. Yep, revenge would be sweet. At least the plotting of it would be sweet.

Marlo and I stayed at the pool until the last of the kids were heading up to their rooms. Adrian was still laughing about my pool plunge. What a guy. Someone should throw him in a pool next time he tried to kiss a girl.

Mark was lucky that I was too tired to get even with him tonight. I fell into bed and was asleep before bed check by the chaperones.

When the alarm squawked the next morning, I had to drag myself out of bed. I was having a great dream about Lucie and I did not want it to end. Lucie came and sat next to me at breakfast. It was the first time the whole trip. She was happy that no one was paying attention to what she ate for once. I found that we both still pretty much stuck to what we knew we should eat because it was so ingrained and we didn't want a bunch of extra work when we got back. Lucie had some winter sports gear that she would be modeling for in August.

Too quickly, breakfast was over and we had to load up for the Smithsonian. I asked Lucie if she wanted to walk around with me but she had plans with her friends. At least she seemed a little sad about it.

The Museum of Natural History was amazing. I love this stuff! The only downer was that feeling that we were being observed. Marlo, Adrian and I decided to head to the left, away from the general flow and natural tendency to go right. There was no way to keep the whole group together so I would just worry about us and Lucie. We walked into the Hall of Mammals and I felt the sinister vibration in the room. Lucie and her chick pals had followed us in. I scanned the rest of the room as if I were looking at the displays. There in the shadows near the door was a dark haired man. He was dressed in black including black boots and dark glasses. His hair was slicked back into a ponytail. I couldn't tell who he was watching. I closed my eyes for a moment and just felt the room. Waves of darkness seemed to roll off him like heavy perfume off a perfume counter at a department store. The hair on the back of my neck stood up again. Not only could I see that it was the same guy, I could sense it. He had scanned me at the White House. I knew his *touch*. He raised his head and looked like he was sniffing the air. I quickly shut off my powers. He could sense me too.

"What?" Marlo whispered, concerned.

"Bad guy at two o'clock. He's all in black. It's the guy you noticed earlier in the trip. When you mark him, nod." I waited for both Adrian and Marlo to glance his way and then give me a nod. "We gotta get our classmates out of here and away from him. Move to the next exhibit, then tell me who all is in the room that we need to protect."

We eased over to the next one. Adrian looked over my shoulder. "Dude seems to be watching Lucie and her girlfriends," he whispered out of the side of his mouth. There are a couple of kids from the other school in here but he's ignoring them. You saw this guy before and didn't tell me?"

"How many of our girls, Marlo? Is it three of them?"

"Yes, Lucie and two others."

"Adrian, I'm sorry, at first we thought it was nothing. I need you now though. Do you think you can charm the girls away? Here's a twenty. Offer to buy them a soda or coffee or something?"

"Of course. Cake!" he replied confidently and wandered off.

"Mar, help me watch. We'll either follow him or follow Adrian depending on what happens."

Marlo and I watched as Adrian poured on the charm. The little redhead with Lucie seemed to think Adrian was pretty darned amazing. The tall, skinny brunette was lapping it up too. Lucie didn't look like she was having any. Marlo and I could see lots of hand gesturing going on. The guy in the shadows just watched, his whole focus on the girls and now Adrian too. At the moment his attention was on that scene and not us on the far side of the next exhibit.

"I wish I knew what the guy was after. I just sense bad and not bad what. Ugh! I could use Mitchell right now," I rasped in frustration. I kept watching and the girls seemed undecided.

"Adrian looks like he's having a little trouble. Do you think you can track that guy on your own and I'll go pour on some Marlo charm? I'll stay alert, I promise," Marlo said, sounding more confident than I had ever heard him.

"Give 'em heck, Mar. I need to know what this guy wants."

Marlo ambled over and joined the conversation like he had just discovered that they were in the same hall he was. After more gesturing they took off. But wait. Lucie, NO! Lucie was staying behind. My friends exited with the other two girls and the dark biker man or 'Shades', as I would now think of him, was staying in the hall. Crap, he was after Lucie. Maybe I could draw him out since it seemed like he could sense me. I moved to the next exhibit and watched him in my peripheral vision. Shades didn't move. He still watched and waited. I turned on my power and tried to read him. He shivered a little but kept his eyes on Lucie. Double damn!

I moved again, trying to draw him away, but now I was farther from Lucie than he was and that made me nervous. He took two steps toward Lucie. I felt a moment of panic. Two people came into the Mammals hall and bumped into Shades, not seeing him as he moved toward Lucie. He turned, distracted and angry. I ran at Lucie and spun her behind an exhibit.

"Wha..." Lucie started to shout at me but I quickly placed a hand over her mouth.

"Shhhh. I won't hurt you. A guy is watching you. Be still. Please!" I frantically whispered.

I peeked around the edge of the exhibit. Shades was looking all over the room. The couple that bumped into him was still trying to apologize. He growled at them and hurried into the Human Origins room.

I gently peeled my hand from Lucie's mouth. "Come on, we need to get out of here."

"What is wrong with you? Geez, relax. It was probably nothing. Why would someone be looking at or following me anyway?" Lucie huffed.

She had to be joking. Did she really have no idea how appealing she was?

"I want to see the museum. You've been acting weird the whole trip. I'm trying to be your friend like you asked. You make things so difficult." She sounded frustrated. "You know when you grabbed me, I thought... Never mind. If you want to walk around and look at stuff fine, otherwise bugger off. I'm meeting the girls in forty-five minutes."

"Lucie, I really think..."

"I really don't care what you think that guy was doing. Stop being so overprotective and paranoid," she snapped.

She gave me an exasperated look. "I guess we could walk around a bit," I said resigned. The guy was bad but maybe we could avoid him. Something told me that he was big trouble but Lucie was my main priority and if I couldn't get her to leave, I would have to rely on the crowds and my own skills to keep her safe.

Lucie led me into the Human Origins Hall. I kept my senses on full alert but Shades was nowhere in sight. I let Lucie talk and I made interested noises. I couldn't even enjoy her company with all the worry weighing me down like a heavy wool blanket. We rounded the corner and entered Ocean Hall. I could feel the guy again but it was faint. We cut diagonally through and headed for the Ancient Seas area. As we passed the stairs coming down I felt a blast of evil touch my back. I flipped Lucie around and tucked her behind me and the nearest exhibit and peeked back around the corner. Shades was coming down the escalator and looked like he had seen us.

I pulled Lucie through the Fossil Lab and into Ice Age. She was not happy with me, but I let her peek back to see Shades wandering around. When he didn't see us he walked in to Dinosaurs and I pulled Lucie the opposite way toward African Voices.

"Our friends are in the Fossil Cafe. Why don't we go there or let's find security or something," Lucie said, nervously. At least now she believed me.

"Come with me, I'll keep you safe. I promise."

I held Lucie's hand as we made our way through the exhibits. I hoped he wouldn't look back at us or that we were rushing to meet him by mistake instead of running away. It felt like he was behind us. Lucie jumped at the darker parts of the exhibit. She kept looking over her shoulder and stayed close to me.

"Owen, he sees us," Lucie squeaked, as she looked over her shoulder yet again.

I hustled her out of African Voices and turned a sharp right. I jogged up the stairs behind Lucie. I was glad to see that she was now aware and not resisting me anymore. I scanned around and noted the cameras, people and did a quick check of the map of the floor on the nearby wall, White Eagle's training taking over.

I took Lucie through a gallery and past the elevators. I was headed for the area set for renovations. I looked for a way in but it seemed to be sealed from the public. I kept encouraging Lucie to keep moving. Then I saw an employee door. It hadn't closed all the way and I looked both ways before darting inside. I pushed Lucie behind a sheet of canvas hung near the door. I gave her the universal sign for silence and put all my attention into listening.

Lucie was practically vibrating behind me. She finally put a hand on my lower back. I turned my head to look at her and she was breathing heavily through her nose with her eyes closed, clearly trying to calm herself. Shades opened the door and looked in, causing me to step deeper into the shadows and press my back against Lucie's hand, pressing her into the wall like filling in a sandwich. Her whole body was pressed against me, her head resting on my back. She slid her arms around my waist. I could feel her shaking.

"Excuse me, sir," someone said from the other side of the door. Shades retreated and the door shut. I reached behind me and gave Lucie a quick backwards hug and then I pulled her further into the section hoping for a back way out. We were in an area that was almost like a hall with many small sections going off of it. I was trying to decide which way to go when I heard the door at the other end open again. I listened for a moment. Friend or foe? I felt the darkness snaking toward us. We were out of time and options. I tucked Lucie into the nearest room and silently shut the door. I was so worried for Lucie that my hands were shaking a little, I noticed with dismay. I took a deep breath through my nose. I quickly scanned the room for an exit and weapons.

"Owen, we're trapped," Lucie breathed, alarm clear in her whispered voice and eyes. She started backing up toward the corner of the room while frantically looking for somewhere to hide.

Please let me be wrong. Let it be a guard and let him kick us out for making out in a restricted area, I thought frantically. I listened intently. I could almost hear his footsteps and I certainly could *feel* him coming for us. I tried to hold very still as my heart tried desperately to beat its way out of my rib cage. Lucie was making soft desperate sounds behind me that sounded almost like whimpering.

The knob began to slowly turn. I prepared myself to fight. Once he opened that door, I had no idea what I was going to do with him or how I would protect Lucie. All I could do was be ready for anything, as ridiculous as that sounded. Don't worry about one impossible task until you've completed the first, I tried to advise myself but it was no use. My whole body was shaking.

I could taste the fear and hatred in the air the second the door inched opened. It was almost as if evil had surged in when the door cracked open. I felt icy cold fingers crawl up my spine and down my limbs. Every hair follicle on my body stood at attention. I wondered briefly what Lucie was feeling - praying that she wasn't as sensitive to this stuff as I was. I heard her breathy, frightened squeak behind me. Damn, she did feel it. Maybe she would just faint and miss the whole darn thing. Shades smiled a chilling smile as he pulled off his dark glasses. Another tremor ran down my tingling spine as I looked into his completely black eyes. There was something horrifying about his gaze. His eyes were like black holes that showed he had no heart and no soul. I tried to gain the upper hand. I looked him right in the eye and subtly shifted my stance ready for attack and to defend Lucie. "You can't have her," I said, with all the authority I could muster. I was alarmed to hear my voice come out pathetically weak, not at all impressive or tough as I had hoped.

His chilling smile widened but never reached his eyes. "I can have whatever I want," he said with a lazy sneer.

"You'll have to go through me," I said with as much courage as I could gather around myself. Something in my stance or tone must have gotten to him a little because the smile slid off his lips. He stiffened and the color drained from his face. He feinted to the right, then came at me on the left. I blocked his first and second assaults but I couldn't get a hit in. This was easier than the fight at the mall. I had learned more since then but this was difficult in its own way. At least it was one on one and not three and a car on one. I had to keep track of Lucie and the attacker. My attention was only divided two ways instead of three but I didn't care if I hurt those guys at the mall. I would die before I let anything happen to Lucie. For now, to protect her, I had to keep this guy away from her. I had to stay alert, focused, on my feet and stay between Lucie and evil.

He came in for a third time and slipped past my guard, punching me hard in the gut, forcing my air out in a whoosh. Lucie made a desperate sound behind me. She was shaking so hard I could feel the quiver in the air. I got a good kidney punch in on him and heard him grunt in reply.

"You thought this would be easy?" I asked to irritate him and keep his attention on me as I stomped down on his instep with the heel of my boot and landed an elbow to his jaw. This guy was tough. He could take a hit. What should have knocked him back barely had him taking a step.

I didn't have time to think or plan; I could only react. I was getting in some good hits, but it was rapidly becoming apparent that this man had studied fighting a lot longer than I had. Why hadn't I kept our group together? Adrian and I could have taken him as a team of two. I needed a weapon. I needed him *not* to get a weapon. I had to take him down. What had I done? How had I allowed us to get trapped like this? Stop it! Fight! I told myself.

He tried to get past me, like I was too much trouble to bother with. I dropped low and put my shoulder into his gut to push him back. Lucie squeaked and moved to my left. Good, she sensed that was the way to go. We were locked desperately together. My muscles strained; I couldn't let him turn me and get my arms behind me. Instead he sent two quick knees to my gut while pulling my shoulders down to his knee. I fell to one knee with a groan, turning to protect my head.

"No!" Lucie screamed. The sound rose up out of her like it was ripped from her very toes, then up and out of her throat. I could hear her scrambling behind me but I wasn't done yet.

His attention switched to her. If he thought she would go meekly and cower, he was wrong. She came at him with a screech and kneed him in the groin, taking him by surprise, as he tried to grab her upper arms. She followed that move with an attempt at an eye gouge and an instep stomp. Apparently she had taken some self-defense. She didn't know how to anticipate his moves so she wasn't ready for the slap across the face and didn't even try to block it. Her head snapped to the side as her body spun and she dropped to the ground in a heap. He laughed a sickening sound. The laugh about undid me. I recovered the breath that had left my lungs in a whoosh, leaped to my feet and came at him with new intensity. I tried a spinning back kick that connected with his head, which he had thoughtfully bent lower to get a grip on Lucie's collapsed form. I knocked him to the side but failed to move in for a knockout like I should have. He growled and was back on his feet, coming at me with death in his already black eyes. He roared in rage, hitting me full in the chest with his shoulder and sending me flying into a desk on the far wall.

Pain spasmed through my back and ribs as I hit the surface of the desk; his hands went for my neck in the instant that I had frozen from the impact. I could feel him cutting off my air. Lucie lay motionless. Black dots were beginning to dance in front of my eyes as I fought for leverage and consciousness. I scratched at his fingers with one hand and felt around the desk for a weapon with the other. A pencil was just out of reach. I lunged for it, cutting off more of my air in the process. "Please," my voice echoed inside my mind. I wasn't going to make it. I bucked my body and tried to kick. I had no leverage. I scrambled harder for the pencil and felt the muscles and tendons in my arm and shoulder scream in protest.

My middle finger snagged the pencil. I pulled it into my fist, then tried to turn it in my hand. My vision was down to a small dot of light and my lungs were begging for air. With what felt like the last of my strength, I plunged the pencil into the side of his neck. He screamed, releasing me. His eyes bulged as he clawed at the pencil, trying to pull it free. I rolled from the desk and landed on my hands and knees, sucking air. I forced myself up and dredged up enough strength to kick him right in the sternum as he struggled with the pencil. He fell to his knees. I kicked him in the head and he flopped over backwards next to Lucie, who was just coming around. She let out a strange, strangled gurgle and crab walked quickly away from his staring eyes as he gurgled. Her chest was heaving and I could see panic and shock settling in.

"Lucie! We've got to go!" She swung her head around at the sound of my voice and wild crazed eyes slammed into mine.

"N,n,n, no." She was losing it.

"Lucie, if they catch us here they will send us home and ask questions later, or worse, they will fly your parents out here." That got her attention. She seemed to regain some focus but appeared too weak to stand. I approached her slowly with my palms out in the generic symbol meaning 'no harm'. I gently put an arm around her and lifted her to her feet. Together we limped to the door. I looked both ways and moved into the hall. I was pretty sure I had seen a staff bathroom on our mad dash down the hall. Sure enough, there it was on the left. I cracked the door and hearing nothing inside moved her in. I quickly locked the door and sat her down on the closed toilet lid. She continued to shake. I ran some cold water on a couple of paper towels and held them to her pink cheek. I knelt in front of her and began to mumble soft words to her. It was all nonsense but I was trying to calm her down. I reached out and stroked her hair and tried to make eye contact.

"Lucie, it's going to be okay. We need to get out of here. To do that I need you to look calm," I soothed.

She took a shuddering breath, rolled her eyes and looked at me and said in a slightly hysterical voice, "So, this kind of stuff happen to ya' often?"

Yep, there was my Lucie. She was coming back. I smiled at her. "Not every day. I'm so sorry. You're not afraid, are you? Of me, I mean? I hoped you would never have to see me do something like that."

"I..." She blew out a breath, her lips forming a perfect O. She took another deep breath, closed her eyes and started again. "I was afraid *for* you, not *of* you! I didn't know you could fight like that. You looked like someone out of an action movie," she breathed, amazement clear in her tone.

"I've been learning some stuff from White Eagle at the pawnshop," I said proudly.

"Who was that man and why did he attack you like that? So many questions are going through my mind I don't even know what to ask first. Are you okay?"

I couldn't help it. The biggest, stupidest smile ever lit up my whole face. Maybe even my whole body. It must have been the adrenaline because I picked her up and swung her around in a huge hug. "I'm fine. It happens sometimes. It's what I've been trying to keep you away from. Maybe it's better if you know so you can make an informed decision about being around me. I'm really *not* safe. At least now you understand a little better. I don't push you away for any reason other than to keep you safe."

"Stuff like this happens to you all the time? I was kidding earlier. My Sweet Aunt May, Owen, why? How? What? Can't you stop?"

She was looking a little freaked out again. Nope. Make that a lot freaked out. "Put me down please." I complied with regret. "Walk me back to the hotel please. I need to... think. I will always admire what you did. You are amazing, cool and kinda scary. Don't ever let me get on your bad side."

"Ah Luce, I would never hurt you!" I felt desperate to make her understand but yet I could tell she wasn't ready to hear it. I felt I had to try. "Lucie I'm worried about you. Please talk to me. I know you haven't had time to make up your mind about me yet, but please let me help you try to understand. I'd do anything for you. I'd never, ever hurt you. I kept things back from you. I kept my secret from you. I have to do what I do. It isn't a choice," my voice came out wretchedly, showing my fear, frustration and exasperation.

"I need some time," Lucie said, sadly.

"When you're ready to hear it, I'll tell you more. Please don't be afraid."

Lucie pressed her lips together and shook her head. She dropped her gaze to her feet and clasped her hands in front of her. I stepped toward her to hug her. She didn't unclasp her hands but at least she let me hug her right over her clasped arms.

"Let's get cleaned up and get out of here before he comes around or someone finds us or him."

"Okay," she whispered.

We finished cleaning up in the bathroom and then I wiped everything down. I listened at the door and then I took a peek. The coast was clear so we walked carefully back down the hall. I stopped frequently to listen; then we would move on. I kept looking for alternate routes just in case. Lucie let me hold her hand and I stayed on high alert.

We got to the door we'd entered to get into this area in the first place but had to wait for a guard to be distracted by tourists before we could reenter the exhibit hall. I avoided as many people and cameras as I could on the way out of the building. No one seemed to be the wiser. No alarm had yet been raised. We were both alive and safe. I looked carefully at all the people we passed in each area and avoided as many as I could. Who was watching us? Who looked suspicious? These people I avoided even if I had to take a longer route. Our friends had left the snack bar so I headed outside.

Lucie held my hand but said little on the way back to the hotel. We decided our story was that she tripped and fell, hitting her cheek against a wall. I bought her an ice-cold soda from a vendor on the way back for her to hold to her face. I was hoping that the cold would limit the swelling and redness. We kept walking, trying to pretend it was a normal day.

"Should we call the police?" she worried.

"If we do they will call your parents," I replied.

"Is he... d... dead?"

"I don't think so but it will take him awhile to come around. I doubt he'll want to admit he got beaten up by two kids." She nodded, but said nothing further. I stayed alert but no one seemed interested in us. Tomorrow we would leave for New York and then two days later we were headed home.

When we got to the hotel I checked us in with a chaperone, saying that Lucie had a headache and wanted to come back early. Lucie waved weakly from a few feet away, keeping her cheek averted. We took the elevator and I walked her to her door. She fumbled with the keycard so I gently took it from her limp fingers and opened the door for her. "You okay?" I asked more than a little worried.

"Yeah, I'll be alright. I've had worse injuries in gymnastics. I just need to be alone. I'll see you at dinner."

"Ok, but if you need me I'll be here. If you want to talk, I'm here for you too. You know that, right?"

"Yeah, Owen, I know."

The door closed with a soft snick. I wondered what would happen now. I pulled out my phone as I headed to our room to check in with Marlo and Adrian. "Hey Aid, where are you guys?"

"We're still at the Smithsonian. Where'd you guys go?"

"We're back at the hotel. Lucie wanted to come back. We... well, I look forward to seeing you guys. When will you be back here?" Sensing a good story they decided to hotfoot it back to the hotel. We agreed to meet in the lobby to talk. Maybe I was getting paranoid but I was afraid to talk in our room. We only stayed in the lobby for a few moments before we decided there were too many people around. We strolled around the grounds and out toward the pool instead as I told them our story.

"Man, why do I miss all the good stuff?" Adrian asked sadly.

I squinted at Adrian, shaking my head. "Are you nuts?"

"Um, Owen, did you ah, know that your neck is um kinda..." Marlo breathed in deep through his nose and tried again. "You're all bruised. I see fingerprints."

"Crud." I exclaimed. "Guess I'll need a collared shirt the rest of this trip. Maybe Lucie has some make-up too." I tried to call her cell but she ignored my call. Marlo tried to call her and of course she answered him. She grudgingly agreed to meet me before dinner to fix my neck.

We went to our room to get ready. I decided a shower was in order but as I stripped down I caught a glimpse of myself in the mirror. Oh hell, I was screwed. My neck was technicolor, my fists were swollen and slightly bloodied. I had bruises all over my ribs, back, on my forearms and above my right knee. It was quite a look and went well with the scars from my stitches. No wonder my mom worried. I looked like the loser from an Ultimate Boxing fight. Great. Just great. At least my face was undamaged. I showered quickly and threw a towel around my hips to go re-evaluate my wardrobe. The guys sucked in a breath and looked at each other, then back at me as I came into the room. "Yeah, I know. I look like crap. Now do you think you missed all the fun, Aid?"

"Ah, nope," he said, popping the 'p' in nope.

Between us we came up with an outfit that covered as much as possible. I put on cargo pants and a long sleeved button up shirt. I turned the cuffs just once to keep my bruises out of sight. We had about ten minutes before dinner. Lucie would have to hurry to make me presentable. She knocked on the door as I was buttoning my shirt. Her eyes took in my neck and widened a bit, showing her shock.

She looked a little rough herself. Her cheek was still a little off color and her eyes looked haunted. Lucie evaluated my neck and sucked in some air when she saw the condition of it close. "You're going to have to take your shirt back off or I'll get makeup on it," she said in a businesslike tone. She sucked in more air through her teeth as she took in the rest of my bruising. She pressed her lips together tight and I thought she might cry. She straightened her shoulders and got a grip on herself.

She said little to the guys as she went to work covering the bruising on the front and sides of my neck. She had brought both liquid foundation and a powder. She dabbed on the liquid stuff and carefully rubbed it in. Her cool fingers felt great. I could have sat there all night but we had an audience and she seemed anxious to leave. She lightly dusted me with powder then handed the make up to Marlo.

"It's the best we can do I'm afraid. Try to keep a low profile. I'll see you at dinner," she said in the same businesslike tone she had used earlier. She had sent the other girls on ahead, thank goodness; the less folks around to ask questions, the better. When she was done with me, Marlo stuck his head out the door to be sure there were no chaperones around since she wasn't supposed to be in our room. With the coast clear, we headed to dinner. Her friends had saved her a seat and she quickly slipped in beside them. The guys and I sat as far from the chaperones as we could manage. We went right back to our room after dinner and basically hid out. Mark didn't show up until almost bedtime. I stayed on the far side of the room and pretended to be absorbed in the TV. I slipped into the bathroom for room check but let them know I was there through the bathroom door so they couldn't get a close look at my destruction.

As we crawled into bed all I could think was get me outta here! New York could not come soon enough. The next morning was the same routine. Stay as far away from the chaperones as possible. Lucie had left the makeup behind so I did my best to cover my own neck. I missed her doing it. We melted into the middle of the crowd. Marlo checked us off on the clipboard and Adrian and I handled the luggage. We spoke to as few people as possible and hid behind kids who were oblivious to us. I made sure to take a window seat on the bus and Adrian quickly sat beside me. Somehow Marlo managed to peel Lucie away from her buddies and sat next to her. Man did I want to be a fly on the wall.

The trip to New York was both too long and too short. The four hours passed. I napped some and dreamed of Lucie. Forgive and accept me, I kept repeating in my mind. Adrian snoozed and visited with me. He had his eye on the curly red haired girl from the Smithsonian with the nice smile. Watching her seemed to keep him pretty busy. I smiled to myself. All in good time; knowing Adrian, he would be talking to her by the end of the day. Besides, with the way things were with Lucie, who was I to give advice.

We finally made it to New York. We checked into our hotel and got right back on the bus for touring and our Broadway show. Lucie stayed far away from me. As sad as it made me, I gave her space. Every chance I got, I grilled Marlo about their conversation on the trip from D.C. and what he had discussed with Lucie. I was disappointed to find that she had said little to Marlo and had basically told him that she needed time to process everything. She had to wrap her mind around it. *Grrrr*. Marlo had tried but she wasn't ready.

I couldn't tell you what Broadway show we saw. I watched Lucie the whole time. She seemed to have a good time but looked a little withdrawn. She glanced over her shoulder a few times. I didn't even try to hide the fact that I was watching her. Who knows if it made her feel better or worse. She ignored me the rest of the trip but I watched her with an aching tenderness, wondering what it was exactly that connected us so strongly. It seemed that we knew about all the worst and hurting parts of each other. I longed to have her know about the best parts of me; those parts I had to keep hidden. I wanted to protect and shelter her. I hated having her ignore me and push me away. I knew that when it came to her, I was lost. There would never be another Lucie. I knew that part of her loved me too, she had just packed it tightly away. I stayed away from the chaperones and kept my mottled skin covered. I did find a way to stand next to her in our group picture taken in Times Square. I knew that I would look at it often.

I was relieved to get on the plane for home. The three of us sat together again. I slept most of the way home and dreamed of Lucie. Marlo woke me just before our descent into the Portland Airport. I made a quick trip to the lavatory to relieve myself, splash some water on my face and make sure my neck was covered.

Many parents were in the waiting area with welcome home signs. My brothers had made one for me too. It made me smile. They were pretty great when they weren't being annoying. My mom took one look at my face and wrapped me in a big comfy hug. My dad thumped me on the back, making me wince a bit. Alex grabbed me around the waist and Lucas grabbed me around my thigh. I noticed that other students were being mugged similarly by their families. Lucie was receiving stiff hugs and air kisses from her mom. What a gal, her mom. She could take some lessons from my mom who was hugging Marlo and Adrian almost as enthusiastically as she had hugged me. Marlo's mom put her arm around me and said she wanted to hear all about the trip. Fortunately the tide of people was sweeping us to baggage claim and I didn't have to answer.

On the ride home I entertained my brothers with the acceptable tales from the trip. My mom kept watching me as my dad drove home. She was keeping it together for Dad and my brothers but I could see the questions in her eyes. After we turned in the driveway and unloaded the SUV, she pulled me in for another hug. "Let me get them to bed and we'll talk." I nodded.

Dad settled in to watch some TV. He wouldn't want to know about my exploits. With him, the less said the better. I lugged my suitcase upstairs and began making piles of dirty clothes, souvenirs and other stuff. I gathered the goodies I had collected for my brothers and took them into their room. I had picked out a t-shirt for each of them, an Uncle Sam bear for Lucas and a book on the monuments for Alex. Both hugged me again and told me good night. My mom hugged them each once more and then waited for me at the door. She followed me into my room and sat with her legs crossed like a pretzel on my bed. "Tell me," she said, patting the bed next to her.

So I did. I left nothing out. I let the pain and grief over Lucie spill out to her sympathetic ear. I told her that with Lucie, I guessed I'd rather hurt than feel nothing at all. I thought it kept me human. I sensed her pride in me for getting us out of a bad situation and for being so grown up with my attitude. "I really don't know if I killed that guy or not. It was him or us, but what if the police come looking for us? I know I really scared Lucie too. I don't know if she will ever talk to me again."

"You need someone like a 'cleaner' or something. I wonder if we can find out without raising any suspicions. Maybe we should call Earl."

"What? Who?" I stammered.

"I've been working with Mr. Earl White Eagle and a 'cleaner' is someone who comes in after assassins and stuff to make sure the scene of the crime is clean and the good guys don't get caught in the legal system. At least that's the best explanation I can give you."

"You have been meeting with White Eagle? Wow, Mom! Does Dad know?"

"I want to help you, Owen. I need training. I worry about this house and your brothers. I also worry about you. My gift is nothing compared to yours, but I can still work on it some and make the most of it. He's teaching me self-defense too. Your dad is fine with me being physically fit. He still isn't completely on board with the other stuff. I guess you could say he is willing to let us try. Mostly he is burying his head in the sand. If he ignores it he hopes it will go away. He's going to work from here for a couple of months. He'll have to fly to Atlanta about one week out of every three or so," she said, her mixed feelings clear.

I really looked at her. She was thinner, calmer and a little different; maybe it was that she was a little less fireball and a little more controlled burn. She definitely had the mark of White Eagle on her. "I just wish you'd have called sooner. We might have been able so save you some heartache and pain."

"I felt paranoid, like someone was listening or something," I replied, wishing I would've done as she asked. "Earl," I said and smiled. "Yeah, let's call him. I should have done that from D.C." I picked up my cell and dialed. He answered on the first ring like he expected me.

"So, had a little trouble in D.C. did ya?" Gotta love caller I.D.

"News travels fast. How much trouble am I in?" My mom stayed close and watched me closer as if she could read the other end of the conversation from my body language alone. For all I knew, she could do that now.

"For now you're fine. Sarah helped me remake an old connection before you left. I didn't want to interfere with your trip so I didn't tell you. My friend and his *watcher* kept an eye on you from a distance. My former connection is still active in Virginia where he knew Sarah. He and his *watcher* cleaned up your little… accident. He still works with the FBI and has loads of contacts.

The guy who found you in D.C. is a *watcher stalker* for lack of a better term. They have been trying to catch him for months. He kept slipping through their fingers. You just saved their bacon by getting him before he took out any more of their young talents. They got to him before he was discovered by anyone else. You didn't kill him Owen, but he'll never bother anyone again. It's off your hands and he's in custody.

I can't figure out why he found you though; you're strong enough now that he shouldn't have been interested in you. He feeds off of the undiscovered and untrained. I don't get it. Come by the shop soon. Let's get you back in training. Life is gonna just keep getting more dangerous, I think."

"Yeah, soon. Thanks, White Eagle. Bye." My mom and I just looked at each other as I hit end on my phone.